VIBRATIONS
IN THE FIELD

DANIEL BURKE

Black Rose Writing | Texas

ISBN: 978-1-68513-185-2
PUBLISHED BY BLACK ROSE WRITING
www.blackrosewriting.com

Printed in the United States of America
Suggested Retail Price (SRP) $23.95

Vibrations in the Field is printed in Minion Pro

*As a planet-friendly publisher, Black Rose Writing does its best to eliminate unnecessary waste to reduce paper usage and energy costs, while never compromising the reading experience. As a result, the final word count vs. page count may not meet common expectations.

To Janice and Bob Thomas, my parents,
who always believed in me and cared so
deeply for our own Sweet Jane.

VIBRATIONS
IN THE FIELD

PROLOGUE

Tom Reynolds

The sun peeked above the grove of cypress trees that bordered the third hole of the exclusive golf course on the outskirts of Naples, Florida. An early morning tee time on Saturday in May was something reserved for the club's most select members. Meaning, those willing to pay an extra $8,000 annual prime access fee on top of the $22,000 annual golf dues, $5,000 annual social club dues, and of course, the $265,000 initiation fee.

The foursome of older white men, all dressed in plaid and striped golf pants and pastel-colored golf shirts, assembled at the tee. All of them were retired from long and lucrative careers. They were a former CEO for a car rental company, an ex-lawyer from a high-powered New York firm, and two medical doctors. One of the doctors had been a cardiologist in Boston and the other, Tom Reynolds, had, until a few months ago, been Head of Psychiatry at Bryce Mental Health in Tuscaloosa, Alabama.

Tom didn't pay for the prime access rider on his membership. Truth was, he was still reeling from the initiation and wasn't sure he could afford the exorbitant annual club fees, let alone an additional eight grand. His retirement portfolio might make him seem rich compared to most Alabamians, but he knew it was nothing compared to his high-rolling golf partners. Lucky for him, they were less interested in his financial standing than his five handicap and what that meant for their prospects of winning the club's fall tournament.

Each of the men took their turns driving. The CEO sent his ball midway down the fairway. Not bad, but not in range for par. The lawyer drove a beautiful shot, setting him up well to reach the green with a five iron. The cardiologist dribbled one off the tee. They all agreed to look the other way as he reset and hooked his ball into the tall grass just shy of the adjoining hole.

Tom placed his ball on the pin and set his stance. About to launch into his swing, a muffled ringtone broke his concentration. He stepped away, shrugged at the other men, and dug his phone out of his pocket. The number wasn't in his contacts, but the area code and exchange were known to him. Only one person would call him on a Saturday morning from a number like that.

"Sorry, fellas. I have to take this one."

"Wife?" the lawyer asked.

"Patient. I think," Tom said.

"You're retired," the men responded together.

Tom waved at them and stepped back to the cart path. "Hello. This is Tom Reynolds."

"It's me, Tom," said a familiar female voice.

"Where are you?"

"At the school."

"You're still in Atlanta?"

"Yes."

Tom glanced over at the men who stared at him. Soon, the foursome behind them would push to play through.

"I thought you were going back to Brookhaven."

"I can't right now. I need more pills."

"I told you the last time—I can't do that anymore."

"Please, just send them to the same place you did before."

"No."

"What am I going to do? They will come back if I don't have the pills."

"Can you get to Grady?"

"I'm not going to the hospital."

"Then you won't get any pills."

"Don't be like that, Tom. You know I need them."

"You need to be examined. I can't just keep FedExing you pills. I have to explain where those go. It's not like I am sending you aspirin."

"You've done it before."

"And I told you then that was the one and only time. You need to go to the hospital."

The cardiologist separated from the others and walked toward him. As another MD, the other two must have convinced him he was the best to intervene and get the game rolling again. Tom cupped the phone in his hands and said, "Just one more minute."

The cardiologist turned back to the others, and Tom resumed the conversation. "You need your blood levels checked. I'll call someone I know at Grady. She's in emergency psychiatrics. She will take care of you."

"They will keep me."

"Maybe for a couple of days. It will be okay."

"I don't want to go."

"Go. Go to the ER—you can use my name. Tell them what's going on. Show them your meds."

He hung up and returned to the waiting men.

"Everything okay?" asked the cardiologist.

"Just fine," he said and added, "you know how it is." Then he straddled the tee and drove his ball into a stand of tall palms.

CHAPTER ONE

Joe

Thump, thump, thump. The windshield wipers swung back and forth. Even on their highest setting they could not push the water off the glass fast enough to keep up with the deluge. The view between their frantic beats was a pulsating blur of red taillights.

Like an army staged on the border separating Alabama from Georgia, the storm had assembled to the southwest. He'd spotted the ominous columns of building thunderheads as he'd pulled into the parking deck of Grady Memorial Hospital that afternoon, and with curious expectation, he'd tracked their advance from the windows in the rooms of the patients he'd visited.

By the time the thunderheads had reached the city, their ranks had tightened to form one dark gray, impenetrable mass swallowing the late afternoon sun. The storm hit just in time for the end of day commuter exodus, turning the early evening into night and dropping millions of gallons of water on the lines of cars as they crept along the city streets on their way out to the suburbs.

Lightning lit up the sky, and for what seemed like several terrifying seconds, a jagged white and blue line joined cloud and ground no more than a few hundred yards from his idling car. Crossing himself, he blinked away the image the bolt had seared into his retinas, and to his amazement, noticed a person standing out in the storm beneath the streetlight at the top of the I-85 Expressway entrance ramp.

It was a small person, maybe even a child, wearing a hooded sweatshirt with the hood pulled tightly over their head and a bulging red backpack slung over their shoulder. The wind and rain lashed at the bowed form as car after car rolled up to them and moved on without offering a ride.

The improbable figure had the thumb of their right hand stuck out toward the passing traffic. The last time he'd seen someone hitchhiking had been on a dusty village road half a world away. Had to be crazy to do it in this weather, which might explain why no one stopped. The defiant hitchhiker seemed indifferent to the storm that raged around them and did not react to the explosive thunderclap that followed the nearby lightning strike.

He inched his car forward until the hitchhiker stood next to his passenger door. The drawn hood and driving rain had made it difficult to tell before, but now he was certain it was a woman's face staring trancelike in at him. He leaned over and pushed open the door, fighting against the storm to keep it open.

"Get in before you are struck by lightning," he said.

She did not move. He thought she might be reluctant to accept a ride from a man and pointed to his clerical collar to put her at ease.

An impatient driver behind him leaned on their horn, and the noise jolted the hitchhiker out of her trance. She tossed her backpack onto the rear floorboard and fell into the passenger seat as she pulled the door closed behind her. Another horn blast prompted him to get moving again before she finished buckling in.

She pushed the rain-soaked hood off her head, exposing long, dripping, black hair that lay slick against her pale, white face and neck. Her drenched sweatshirt was faded yellow with blue and white lettering spelling Georgia Tech across her chest. It was too heavy for the ninety-plus degree heat, and it clung to her body, calling attention to the extra pounds she carried on her compact frame.

He waited for her to say something, but she didn't. She just sat there, allowing the traffic noises and pounding rain to fill the void. Her facial expression was flat, and her light-colored eyes were fixed on some unknown point in the blur between the wipers. Water trickled from her hair and ran down her cheeks like tears. She raised her hand to wipe it away, revealing a hospital bracelet wrapped around her right wrist.

"Are you okay?" he asked.

"I'm fine, just a little wet." After a moment, she added, "Thank you so much for picking me up."

Her voice had just the slightest hint of a southern accent, not something usual for most Atlantans. The sound of it reminded him of evenings on a porch swing in a small Georgia town just outside of Columbus, and a girl he'd known a lifetime ago when he had a much different calling. Pleasant memories of that time were few, and he thanked God for them when they came.

"It looks like you were in the hospital. Were you in Grady?"

She seemed puzzled. "No. Why do you ask?"

"I noticed your bracelet."

She glanced at her wrist and then pulled the bracelet off with her teeth. She crumpled it up in her left hand. "Nope. No hospital," she said as if it was never there.

Her attempt to hide the bracelet was amusing and curious. He wondered if she was concerned about how he'd react if he thought she was sick. That wasn't an unreasonable fear after all the world had been through. Maybe she was ashamed of something related to the stay, or maybe it was just none of his business. He'd go with that. It was none of his business.

"My name is Joe Carroll. What's yours?" he asked as he guided the car into an open slot in the oozing six lanes of evening rush hour traffic.

"You can call me Sweet Jane," she said. Then, in an almost imperceptible voice, she sang "Sweet, sweet, Jane," in a way that seemed familiar, like a verse from an old song.

"Where are you heading, Jane?"

"Sweet Jane," she corrected.

"Right. Sweet Jane, where are you heading?"

"Home."

"Where's home?"

"Auburn."

"Like the school in Alabama?"

"Same one."

"Go War Eagles," he said.

"Go War Eagles." She brightened and seemed to wake from her trancelike state. She studied him, perhaps seeing his collar for the first time, and asked, "Are you a priest?"

"Not quite," he said.

"Then why are you dressed like one?"

"I guess you could say I am a priest in training."

She took a moment and seemed to consider his words. "I've never heard of a priest in training. Don't you guys just go to priest school?"

"That's true, but afterward we spend time as deacons until we are ready to be priests. That's what I am." He pointed to his collar again. "I wear this when I visit the sick at the hospital. It provides comfort to some and keeps the staff from asking why I am there."

"You look kind of old to be just out of priest school."

He grinned. "Yes. I guess I am. I got a late start."

Thunder shook the car, interrupting her questioning. After it passed, she asked, "Have you always wanted to be a priest?"

"Ever since I was a boy." His answer was truthful, but not complete.

"Why?"

"To serve God," he said without hesitation.

"Why did you wait so long?"

"I had planned to go to seminary straight from college, but the path turned out to be less direct."

"What happened?"

He shrugged. "I had a few detours."

"Detours, huh?" She gazed out the window for a moment, then turned back to him. "I've had a few of those myself," she said. "Should I call you Father?"

"No. You should call me Joe."

"What did you do before you became an almost-priest, not-Father Joe?"

He smiled at her wit. After standing for God-only-knew-how-long in that weather, it was good she still had a sense of humor. He wasn't so sure he would. "Lots of things. I went to college. I worked odd jobs, and I even built houses for a while." He left out much as he always did when faced with this question.

"So, you were just a normal guy?"

"I guess you could say that." He'd been anything but normal, but like the hidden tattoos that covered his upper arms and chest, there were parts of his past he was no longer comfortable exposing. He allowed himself an occasional lie of omission to avoid a series of more awkward and painful questions. Experience had taught him it was worth the trade, and besides, it gave his confessor something to listen to.

"Did you have sex?"

He laughed at her directness, but he was not shocked. She was not the first to ask this question. In fact, he got it often. People assumed priests were born priests and were always curious when they learned they were not.

"Don't you think that question is a bit personal?"

She shrugged. "There is no such thing as privacy anymore. There are people out there who know everything. Or almost everything."

"Well, God knows to be sure, and I think I will keep that information between Him and me for now," he said, still smiling.

She spread her arms. "Why would your sex life matter to God?"

He looked at her out of the corner of his eye, wondering about this strange person he'd invited into his car. "Because He knows everything about his children, and He has a plan for us all."

"That's silly," she said and wrung her sweatshirt out on his floor mat.

"Even the very hairs of your head are all known to Him."

"Is that from the Bible?"

"Yes. The Gospel of Luke. One of my favorites."

"Do you have to memorize the whole Bible to be an almost-priest?"

"No, but we do study it a lot."

"You really believe he has a plan for all of us?"

"I do."

She frowned. "Well, his plan for me sucks."

"Why do you say that?"

"I have lots of problems."

"That's okay. God has lots of solutions."

"I don't believe in God," she scoffed. Then she gave her sweatshirt a final twist before turning in her seat to face him. "To quote *The New York Times*: God is dead."

"I think they might have borrowed the phrase from an old German philosopher." In his best German accent, he said, "Gott ist tot."

"Whatever. I mean, really. Don't you think humans have outgrown God?"

He'd had this conversation a thousand times before he'd set one foot in Seton Hall seminary. He'd debated it on bus rides, during quiet moments in tents during missionary trips, in college dorms wafting with the funky scent of marijuana, on bar stools, and while hunkered down behind sandbags in distant places he no longer wished to think about.

"There's that old German again. No, I don't. I guess you think we have it all figured out?"

"Maybe not all of it, but we are getting close." She reached her arm behind the seat and searched for her backpack but came up empty. "You don't have a cigarette, do you?"

"No, and if I had, I wouldn't let you smoke it in the car."

She frowned. "That figures. So, you really think people still need God?"

"Yes. Of course." he said, unable to conceal the incredulous tone in his voice.

"I'm sorry not-Father Joe, but I don't think people believe in Him anymore, at least not the educated ones. Why should they? Just look at the mess the world's in."

"There is still much goodness and love in the world, child."

She furrowed her brow and scowled at him. "Who are you calling a child? Is that something you think you can do when you dress up like a priest? I think I am almost as old as you." She crossed her arms. "Child." After a moment, she resumed, "Anyways, we are well past needing a God to explain things like earthquakes and the weather." She pointed to the sky. "There's no god on a cloud up there hurling down lightning bolts."

At that moment, as if in reply, lightning lit up the sky, and the car rattled with the resulting thunder. It didn't seem possible, but the rain came down even harder. Heavy drops pounded the windshield and roof, and the ping-ping sound of hail striking glass and metal drowned out their conversation.

Joe gripped the steering wheel and leaned forward in a futile attempt to see through the torrent. "Maybe you should be more careful with your words," he said over the noise. "Plenty of mysteries remain. People still need answers and comfort. If there is no God, where do we go for them?"

"Science," she replied.

"You can believe in God and science at the same time, Jane."

"Sweet Jane," she corrected him again.

"Sweet Jane, the catechism teaches that scientific discovery adds to our admiration of God's works," he recited from some passage he'd been required to memorize.

"Tell that to Galileo."

He laughed. "Now that was a long time ago. There have been many people of faith who were scientists."

"Sure, but name one whose discoveries prove there is a God."

Like her question about God's existence, this was a familiar trope, and he was ready. "How about Georges Lemaitre?"

"Who?

"He was a physicist." Pausing for dramatic effect, he added, "And a Catholic priest."

She stared at him, smirking, as water continued to drip from her hair. "I know a little about physics, but I don't remember much about him. What exactly did he do?" Her smirk turned mischievous, suggesting she knew more than she was letting on.

"He's the one who came up with the big bang theory. You must've heard of that."

She rolled her eyes. "Wrong. That was Edwin Hubble."

"Hubble built on Father Lemaitre's work."

"Wrong again. Hubble built on Albert Einstein's theories."

A large delivery truck cut into their lane, and Joe slammed on the brakes. They lurched forward hard against their seat belts.

Unable to stop himself, he blurted, "Idiot."

She gave him a disbelieving look.

"What? He cut us off."

"That didn't seem very priest-like."

"No. I guess it wasn't."

She smiled. It was a nice smile.

"Is calling someone an idiot a sin?"

"Venial at best. No big deal," he said. Then he steered the conversation back to where they left off. "Google Lemaitre. You'll see I am right."

Still looking at him, she shook her head. "I don't go on the internet, and if I did, I wouldn't go anywhere near Google. Once they get hold of you, you're tracked for life. Let's assume you're right about Lemaitre, though," she said. "How does the big bang theory prove there is a God? Seems quite the opposite to me."

He glanced at her, noting how her eyes shined in the on-coming headlights. "Doesn't the theory say the universe came into existence in an instant? The entire universe, from nothing, in an instant?"

"Something like that, I guess," she said.

"That sounds to me like the universe began at the command of God, just like it says in the Book of Genesis."

"So, the universe started when some bearded white guy on a cloud told it to?" She laughed. "I think there may be more to it than that…or, maybe less."

"Is that how you picture God? A bearded white guy?"

"I don't picture him at all. That's how Michelangelo pictured him. I'm sure you are familiar with the ceiling."

He laughed again. She was funny. Odd, but funny. "If you don't believe in God, what do you believe in?"

"I believe in the organizing principle of the universe."

"So do I… Mine is the Holy Trinity. What's yours?"

"Entropy."

"Wouldn't that be the disorganizing principle?"

"Depends on how you look at it." She grew silent, then added, "Really, we are all just vibrations in the field."

"What does that mean?"

"It's something from Quantum Field Theory."

"I don't know what that is."

"No? You sounded so scientific before. Well, now I have a name for you. Paul Dirac."

"Never heard of him. What did he do?"

"He came up with the theory for everything," she paused, "and he was an atheist."

"Is that what Quantum Field Theory is? The theory for everything?"

"Yes. You can Google it, but I don't recommend it."

"Why don't you explain it to me?"

The mischievous grin returned. "Sure. If you drive me all the way home. It should take about that long."

He didn't bite. He wasn't sure how far he would take her. "Did you study science at Auburn?"

"No. I didn't go to school there. I went to school in California and here." She stretched out her wet sweatshirt to make the lettering easier to read.

"Georgia Tech?"

"Yes. I did postgraduate work at Tech before…" Her words trailed off, and it was like she'd gone back into a trance.

"Before what?"

She didn't answer.

"Before what?" he asked again.

She turned away and stared out her window.

"Are you okay?"

When she turned back to him, she had a confused look, as if she was not sure what they had been talking about.

"How did you know my mother taught at Auburn? Did they tell you that at the hospital?"

He gaped at her, surprised by her strange question. "I didn't say anything about your mother."

She grew agitated and twisted around in her seat.

"What's wrong?" he asked.

She leaned in close to him with wide-open eyes. "What did you do with my backpack?"

Alarmed by the sudden change in her demeanor, he thought about how he might defend himself if it came to that and prayed it would not. "It's in the back where you tossed it."

She tried to climb into the back seat, but her seat belt held her down.

"I don't see it. What did you do with it?" she demanded. Then she released her seatbelt and opened her door, filling the car with engine and wet tire noise from the surrounding sea of traffic.

"Wait, wait. You can't get out. We're moving."

"I have to go back and look for my backpack before they get it."

He wondered who "they" were but did not ask. "It's in the back seat. I'll get it for you if you shut the door."

"I have very important things in that backpack," she said as she yanked the door closed.

He pulled the car over to the shoulder and stepped out into the driving rain. The backpack was lying on the floor behind her seat. He retrieved it and held it up so she could see it. Then he placed it on the back seat in plain view and climbed in. Now he was drenched too.

He eased the car back into traffic, and the thump, thump, thump, of the beating wipers filled an uneasy silence between them. Sweet Jane curled up in her seat, eyes fixed on her backpack like her life depended on its contents. Maybe it did. Joe had no way to know. He tried to restart the conversation, but she ignored him. The sky began to lighten, but the rain showed no sign of letting up.

As they passed by the Georgia Tech campus, he turned to point it out to her and found she'd fallen asleep. He drove on, listening to the wipers, and contemplating God's plan for his strange passenger until they reached his exit.

At the top of the ramp, he pulled into a gas station. She was still out. The hospital wristband she had held crumpled had fallen into the center console. He picked it up, and as he'd guessed, it was from Grady Memorial. It had a bright orange stripe where she had torn it apart. He knew the hospital used color codes for special care units. Orange indicated she'd been on the psychiatric floor.

Printed on it was a long bar code and her information. Among other things, it said her full name wasn't Sweet Jane but Elizabeth Jane Carter. She had recently turned 32. She'd been wrong about being close to his age. He was fifteen years older, but she was no child. Calling her one had been his bungled attempt to say they were all children of God. He folded the bracelet and tucked it into his pocket.

What was he to do with her? It was a two-hour drive to Auburn in good weather. With the rain, it could take double that. If he drove her, he would not be back until well after midnight. It had been a long day. He'd left his apartment before sunrise for early morning prayers and had been going ever since. Driving her tonight was out of the question.

Maybe he could put her on a bus. He took out his phone and searched for bus routes from Atlanta to Auburn. Greyhound made the trip to nearby Opelika three times a day, but the last bus had already left. The next one was at 7:40 in the morning. He'd miss morning prayers, but Father Carlos would understand. He hoped.

Where would she stay tonight, though? With the storm, there would be no beds available at the women's shelter. Besides, something told him she wouldn't agree to stay there.

He made up his mind and nudged her shoulder. "Jane." He caught himself. "Sweet Jane."

She sprang up and moved away, pressing herself against the passenger door while staring at him with the same wild-eyed look as before. For a moment, she did not seem to recognize him. She looked around the car, and before she could accuse him of taking it, he reached into the back seat and retrieved her backpack.

She snatched it from him and opened it. After rummaging through its contents for a few frantic moments, she seemed satisfied nothing was missing. She zipped it closed and hugged it like a child might hug a favorite blanket or stuffed animal.

Her wild expression changed to a look of embarrassment as she became aware of her behavior. Actual tears, not drippings from her hair, began to run down her cheeks. "I am so sorry, Joe," she said. "This is all I have." She looked away from him and out the window. "Where are we?"

"We're still in Atlanta. We are only a few miles from where I picked you up. This is as far as I can take you toward Auburn tonight."

"Oh." She sounded disappointed. "I guess I'll find another ride." She opened the door to leave. "Thank you. I will look up your Father Lemaitre as soon as I can."

"Sweet Jane, wait. I checked, and a bus to Auburn leaves first thing tomorrow morning."

"I don't have money for a bus or any place to stay."

"I live just around the corner from here. You can stay with me tonight, and I will pay for your bus ticket tomorrow."

"Why would you do that?"

"Like I said before, God has all kinds of solutions."

She sat for a moment, watching the rain as if weighing her options. Then she pulled the door closed and rested her head against the window. "Okay."

CHAPTER TWO

Joe

As they pulled into Joe's apartment complex, the rain subsided and the dark gray blanket of clouds peeled back from the western horizon to reveal a fiery sunset. Joe parked the car and took a moment to admire the red and orange sky.

"Almighty God, we give you thanks for surrounding us, as daylight fades, with the brightness of the vesper light," he said, almost to himself.

"What is a vesper light?" Jane asked.

"It's Latin for evening, and yes, all of us almost-priests must learn Latin."

The apartment complex had been built sometime in the 1950s, and it looked its age. Reminiscent of a budget motel, it consisted of a series of long, three-story red brick buildings with white-trimmed picture windows and white steel railings. The upper floors were reached by outdoor staircases.

Joe's unit was on the third floor. It had two bedrooms, which were one more than he needed. He had lived there since arriving in Atlanta four years ago. When he signed the first year's lease, he told the property manager he only expected to be there for a year, as he planned to move to the rectory with the other diocese priests as soon as he was ordained. That claim had become an annual tradition, which was turning into a joke.

Once inside, Jane asked if she could use the shower. Then she disappeared into the bathroom with her backpack, only to reemerge a minute later asking if he could lend her some clothes because all her things were wet. He searched through his drawers until he found one of his well-worn sweatshirts and a pair of workout pants that could be tightened with a drawstring.

While she showered, he sliced up a couple chicken breasts and mixed the pieces into a salad. Joe set out bowls and utensils on the kitchen counter. The additional place setting looked strange. He couldn't remember the last time he had a guest over for a meal or for any other reason. He did not own a dining table. In fact, the only furniture he had besides his bedroom set was a sofa in the living room, a desk and chair in the extra bedroom, and two kitchen counter stools. The stools weren't even his. The previous tenant had left them behind.

The shower, that had been running the whole time, stopped, and Jane stepped out of the bathroom in a cloud of steam with her deflated backpack over her shoulder and a small bundle of clothes in her arms. She had one of his towels wrapped around her head, and she was wearing the clothes he had given her.

The faded blue shirt, with Seton Hall emblazoned in white on the chest, was one of the few he had from his alma mater, and it hung down to her knees, stopping just above where she had rolled up the legs of his sweatpants. It fit her like a dress, which was a good thing because no matter how tightly she pulled the drawstring, she could not keep the pants on her waist. He smiled. She looked like a child playing dress-up.

He watched as she peeked into each of the rooms off the hallway and then returned to the living room. "It's not much," he said.

"It is a little spartan," she agreed. "It needs pictures or something on the walls, and maybe a chair to go with the sofa."

"It's only temporary." It was a minor lie—nothing to trouble his confessor with.

She held up the bundle of clothes. "I need to wash these."

He retrieved a laundry basket from the hall closet, and she dropped the bundle in it. It looked like she had three or four changes of clothes, including the sweatshirt and jeans she'd been wearing when he picked her up.

"The laundry is down on the first floor." He motioned to the counter where he had set out dinner. "Help yourself to some food, and I'll go put these in the washing machine."

She held on to the basket. "I can't let you take my clothes."

"You can come with me, but I don't think you will make it down the steps in those pants."

She closed her eyes and shook her head. "I don't trust you with my clothes."

"I promise your clothes will be fine. I'll put them in a washer and come right back."

"What if someone takes them?"

"No one is going to take your clothes."

She loosened her grip on the basket, and he pulled it away. He carried it down to the laundry room along with his breviary. He started her clothes washing in one of the machines, then he sat on a step near the top of the stairwell and recited his evening prayers.

He was back up at his apartment in less than thirty minutes. He found her sitting cross-legged in the center of his small living room with the contents of her backpack arrayed around her, and much to his chagrin, she was smoking a cigarette.

"Please don't smoke in here."

She looked up at him with a quizzical expression, then turned away and whispered something inaudible as if she were talking to someone else. She moved the cigarette over her salad bowl and held it wavering there while continuing to whisper. It appeared she was having some kind of argument with herself.

Joe waited in the open doorway for the outcome of her internal struggle for as long as he could, but even the patience of an almost-priest is limited. "Jane, please put your cigarette out."

The interruption seemed to end the argument, and she smashed the cigarette into her half-eaten salad. Then she donned a pair of earbuds and attached them to a small tape recording device Joe recognized as a voice recorder like the kind he used to capture notes in college.

Among the other items from her backpack were a plastic ziplock bag with a collection of a dozen or so tiny cassette tapes inside. She dumped the contents out onto the floor, and Joe noticed inside the bag was another smaller bag containing a single tape. This one had a bright red label affixed to it. It appeared to be the only one with any kind of marking. She chose one of the unmarked tapes and loaded it into the player. Then she stormed into the bathroom shouting, "My name is Sweet Jane," as she slammed the door.

Joe said a little prayer to himself, as much for him as for her, and stepped further into his apartment. He left the door open in hopes the remaining cigarette smoke would find its way out. He collected the salad bowl she'd used as an ashtray and paused for a moment to look over her things.

Like Jane herself, the items strewn about the floor showed signs of both randomness and order, Soggy piles of candy wrappers and balled-up papers, lay beside ziplock bags full of items kept dry from the rain. She had protected those things but had somehow overlooked her clothes. A white plastic water bottle with UC Berkeley printed in fading blue letters caught his attention. She was a long way from California.

He poked around the bags. Their contents made him suspect she'd been living in the streets, but the absence of sleeping gear made that unlikely. One bag contained a pack of cigarettes and a lighter. Another one had toiletries, including a toothbrush and feminine items. A large one held several composition notebooks and what appeared to be an advanced mathematics textbook, and one held half a dozen prescription pill containers.

Joe picked up the bag with the pills and studied it.

"Those are my meds," she said from the bathroom doorway.

He was startled by her voice and embarrassed that she'd caught him looking through her things. He placed the bag back where he found it. "I'm sorry for being nosy. I was curious about the pills."

She walked over and picked up the bag and removed one of the containers.

"This one is called Clozaril. I take two of these in the morning and two more in the evening." She shook the vial, rattling the pills inside. "It helps with the things I see, but nothing makes them completely go away."

"The things?"

"I don't want to talk about them."

She dug deeper into the bag and retrieved another vial. "This is Prozac. I take one, or sometimes two, hmm, maybe three in the morning. It makes me friendlier and less obsessive." She scowled at him. "It doesn't always work."

"What are you being treated for?"

"I'm a psycho. Isn't that obvious?"

She got down on the floor and began packing her things into her backpack.

"Jane."

"Sweet Jane," she muttered with agitation.

"It's not obvious."

"Yeah, I'm sure you think I am perfectly fine," she mocked. Then she looked up at him. "I have schizophrenia." Then she added, "But I am getting better."

He sat down beside her. His first impulse was to ask her to pray with him, but he did not think that would go over well. "What is it like?"

She stared at him for a moment before answering. "It's hard to explain. Some days are worse than others. Right now, I am what the doctors call high functioning, meaning I can keep it together most of the time." She chuckled and added, "That has not always been the case."

"How does it affect you?"

"Lots of ways, but mostly I see things that are not there, and sometimes I lose control of my emotions."

"I haven't noticed," he said. Maybe this untruth he would confess.

"Yes, you have." She finished putting everything back in her backpack except the pile of candy wrappers, which she scooped up and handed to him. "Where am I going to sleep tonight?"

"I'll set you up out here on the sofa." Joe stood and retreated into his room, disposing of the candy wrappers on his way. He retrieved one of his pillows and an old wool army blanket he kept folded at the foot of his bed for cool nights. He set them on the sofa. She was still sitting on the floor clutching her damp backpack.

"What about my clothes?"

"I will check on them now. No smoking in here while I am gone. You can smoke out on the stairwell if you must. Understand?"

She didn't say anything.

"Understand?"

She nodded, and he headed back down to the laundry room, suspecting she would light a cigarette the moment he walked out.

After he'd moved her clothes from the washer to a dryer, he sat in one of the plastic chairs that were scattered about the room, then called the man who had helped him get back up after he'd reached rock bottom.

Dr. Caleb Montagne was a psychiatrist, a Catholic priest, and a friend. Now in his midseventies, he no longer practiced, though he kept in touch with many of his former patients, Joe being one of them.

Before he retired, Caleb was a staff physician at Saint Michael's Medical Center in Newark, New Jersey where he'd specialized in treating patients with post-traumatic stress disorders. Most of his patients were veterans, many had seen more than their share of combat in Iraq and Afghanistan. Some of them had not come home the same. They all had significant injuries—some visible and some not.

Joe had met Caleb ten years ago when he had been transported to Saint Michael's emergency room in an ambulance after the man Joe had been working for had come to his apartment to pick him up for work and found him half dead from alcohol poisoning. Sometime the day before, Joe had climbed into his bathtub with a fifth of bourbon, a razor knife, and a Bible and proceeded to drink the entire bottle, passing out before he could use the knife, but maybe not before using the Bible. He wasn't sure. He had no memory of the incident.

The hospital admitted him as an attempted suicide, which made him a psych patient, which made him Caleb's patient. There was no way Joe could have known it at the time, but that chance encounter turned his life around.

"Joseph," the old man's voice boomed. Caleb's hearing had deteriorated over the years and as his world had grown quieter, his voice had grown louder.

"Hello, Doctor." Joe said in an elevated voice. "I hope you are doing well."

"Yes. Been out working in the garden. We were blessed with a fine spring day here. How about you, my son? It's been a while since we've spoken."

"Fine, sir. Though the weather here has been more of a trial than a blessing."

"Ah, well I'm sure that will change. Tell me, Joseph, how are you sleeping?"

"Like a baby. No nightmares. None that I remember anyway."

"Good. And the other thing?"

It had been eight years, seven months, and three days since his last drink. Joe knew it almost without thinking as he shared it once a month with his Alcoholics Anonymous group.

"Not a drop." Then he added, "Outside of the sacramental wine, of course."

"Of course. Now, how are things going with the process?"

By the process, Joe knew the old man was referring to the transitional deaconship program. It is what made him, as Jane had said, an almost-priest.

All seminarians who completed formation went through the transitional deacon program. It's how priests learned the real job of being a priest, but it also served as the final evaluation step before ordination.

Even with the steady decline in church attendance, the need for priests was great. So few men heard the call anymore, and priests were retiring and dying faster than their congregations were shrinking.

Despite the need, though, the Church was cautious about who it elevated. It wasn't hard to understand why. Unforgivable acts of a few deviant priests had done enormous damage, but Joe knew those abhorrent behaviors weren't the only concerns.

Priests were men, and all men were imperfect, but some imperfections were more incompatible with the priesthood than others. Incompetency, cynicism, anger, violence, depression, mental instability, and addiction were just some of those to be identified and excluded. Once allowed into the order, they were difficult to address. Defrocking a priest through laicization was not an easy process.

Most clerical candidates completed the program in a year. The majority were young men with few real-world experiences outside of college. They were straight out of seminary. Joe, on the other hand, had been a deacon for four years. He was twice the age of the youngest man in the program and older than many of the priests he assisted.

The things he'd overcome were still part of him, no matter how hard he sought to bury them, and they were difficult to reconcile with the priesthood. He was, as he was told from the start, a special case, requiring more scrutiny and a longer and more uncertain route to ordination.

"I haven't given up yet. The calling remains strong."

"Good. And how are things with Father Carlos?"

Father Carlos Santiago was the parochial vicar to the archbishop and Joe's spiritual adviser and mentor. And, as he never grew tired of reminding Joe, he had been assigned by the archbishop himself to guide and evaluate Joe's pastoral development. In short, it was up to Father Carlos to determine when, or if, Joe would become a priest—something that seemed less likely with each passing year.

"A lot like the Atlanta weather—mostly sunny with the occasional thunderstorm."

The old man's laughter erupted from the phone's speaker.

"So why the call, Joe? Is everything else okay or is this a long-delayed social call?"

"Father, are you trying to stoke my Catholic guilt?"

"Not at all. I know you are far too busy down there to check in on your old friend."

"Ouch. You are… you are trying to stoke my guilt."

"Maybe a little. I've missed you, my son."

Joe felt the sting of a tear in his eye. Caleb had done so much for him. He'd even written the recommendation letter that had convinced the Atlanta Archdiocese to take a chance on him after Newark had turned him down. "I've missed you too, sir. I won't let this much time pass between calls again."

"Good. Now, how can I help?"

"I met someone today who I believe suffers from schizophrenia, and I need some advice on how best to help her."

"Is that so? Well, how did you arrive at your diagnosis?"

Joe laughed. "It wasn't that hard. She told me after she showed me her medications."

"Ah. That would make it easier but not conclusive. What would those medications be?"

"I think she said Clozaril and Prozac. Does that sound right?"

"Hmm. Well, as you know, Prozac is a common antidepressant, and its application is not unique to schizophrenics. Clozaril or Clozapine, on the other hand, that is a strong antipsychotic medication. It's generally not what we consider a first-choice drug, as it can have dangerous side effects and requires close monitoring."

"What does not first-choice mean?"

"It means we try other drugs first."

"I guess that should have been obvious."

The old man grunted. "It can be very effective at reducing what's known as positive symptoms. Very effective."

"I don't understand. What are positive symptoms?"

"They are the symptoms the disease adds to the sufferer's personality—things like hallucinations, scrambled thoughts, disorganization, and paranoia. You know, the ones you think of when you think of severe mental illness."

"If there are positive symptoms, are there negative ones too?"

"Yes. These are the things the disease takes away, Things like motivation, the ability to have relationships or even any personal connections. I think you know these symptoms, Joseph."

Joe swallowed. "I guess I do."

"It's the negative symptoms," the old man continued, "that make it hard for schizophrenics to function in society and why so many end up in prison or living on the streets. Do you know how much of the Clozaril she's taking?" he asked.

"I don't know the dosage, but I believe she said she takes two tablets twice a day if that tells you anything."

"Hmm. It says she's not new to the drug. We tend to start with very low doses as getting to the right level can be tricky. It can take several weeks of slow adjustment and monitoring to get to a dosage that's effective and tolerated. Like I said, there can be nasty side effects—some quite severe. So, what are your questions?"

"I only just met her a few hours ago. She was hitchhiking in a thunderstorm. I think she is homeless, though she claims to have a home about 100 miles south of here. She was wearing a hospital bracelet from Grady's psych floor."

"Where is she now?"

"I brought her back to my place to get her out of the weather."

"That's quite admirable, Joseph, and the Christian thing to do, of course, but maybe not the wisest action. You should be cautious about taking in strangers—even those in need. There wasn't a better place to bring her besides your home?"

"It seemed like the best option. I don't think she is a threat..." The use of the word threat caught in his throat. It felt like he was discussing an action with platoon leaders, and a long-buried memory sent a shiver through him. "I... I don't think she will hurt me, but I will sleep with one eye open tonight."

"She's staying with you? Now I am definitely questioning your judgment."

Joe had his own doubts. "Me too," he said. "I plan to put her on a bus in the morning, and that's why I called you."

"I don't think I can help you find her a bus, Joseph."

Joe laughed. His former doctor was enjoying exercising his rapier-like wit. "No. What I want to know is if it's okay to put someone with her illness on a bus without knowing what will happen to her when she gets off."

Caleb sighed. "Oh my goodness, I don't know how to answer that. I can't assess your hitchhiker's condition or competency based on this phone call, but what I can say is if she is taking her medication, she is doing better than many like her who live on the street."

"I don't know what to do. What do you think? Do I put her on a bus to where she says her home is, or do I drive her back to Grady?"

"I guess that depends on her. If her symptoms are not debilitating, then I think she has to decide those things. How is her behavior?"

"A little quirky… maybe a little…" Joe struggled for the word.

"Crazy?" The old man injected.

"I was searching for a more polite term."

"It's just a word. Tell me about her."

"She said she sees things that aren't there, but she wouldn't say any more about that."

"Go on."

Joe pictured Caleb sitting in a recliner in his den, wrapped in his robe, while he stroked his chin with one hand and held the phone with the other.

Joe told him about their conversation in the car and how she'd become confused and angry with no provocation. "It was like she became a different person. She thought I was spying on her."

"Hmm," was all he said.

"She's also very protective of this backpack she carries. So much so I thought she was going to attack me when she thought I took it."

"Took it?"

"She misplaced it in the car and thought I took it."

"Hmm. I think I agree with your diagnosis. It sounds like she's crazy."

"Father!" Joe exclaimed.

"You're right. I am sorry. I shouldn't joke about such things. I do agree with your diagnosis, though. It sounds like your hitchhiker is schizophrenic. The visual hallucinations could mean a severe case.

"What does severe mean? Should she be in a hospital?"

"Hard to tell, Joseph."

"Should I worry she'll kill me in my sleep?"

The old man laughed. "Schizophrenics are generally not violent." Then in a softer, more serious tone he added, "Just like combat vets."

Joe winced. "If only someone could convince Father Santiago of that."

"All things in their time as God wills."

"So, what should I do about my hitchhiker?"

"If you fear for her well-being, I suggest you encourage her to speak with a counselor. I am sure the diocese can help you find the right person."

"I will try."

"If she's taking Clozaril, she needs to be under a doctor's care. Like I said, it can have very bad side effects."

"How bad?"

"It can cause seizures and even death if too much is taken. It can also cause a reduction in white blood cells which are essential for fighting infections. That can be fatal too."

"I'll try to convince her to see a doctor."

"I have no other advice to offer. Give me a call tomorrow so I know she didn't throttle you in your sleep."

Joe laughed and said goodbye, feeling better for the talk, though still uncertain about what to do.

The dryer chimed as he ended the call. He folded her clothes and returned to the apartment to find her asleep on the couch with earbuds still in place. He set the basket of clothes down next to her backpack and readied himself for bed.

She was still asleep when he finished his evening reading and prayers. He switched off his reading light and peered through the open door. Light from the apartment complex parking lot shone through the half-closed living room blinds, illuminating her motionless form. He thought about the old man's assurances that most schizophrenics were not violent as he drifted off to sleep, thinking about threats and platoon leaders for the first time in many years.

CHAPTER THREE

Joe

He woke. Startled. Breathless. Pulse racing. His shirt was damp with sweat. He had no memory of the nightmare, but he felt the fear and agony it had left behind.

There was an unfamiliar light in his bedroom. It wasn't the usual faint streetlamp glow that seeped through his curtains, but something new. The amber digits on the bedside clock came into focus. It was a few minutes after three in the morning. The alarm would not buzz for another hour.

Pushing himself up on his elbows, he looked for the source of the strange light, and his eyes landed on a bright strip on the floor. It was coming from under his closed bedroom door. The door he was sure he had left open the night before. Jane must have closed it.

He eased out of bed and moved across the room. He could feel the adrenaline rush building as his body readied for fight or flight. Lessons drilled into him long ago by army instructors and reinforced during door-to-door night raids in remote villages on the wrong side of the Pakistan border had taught him the rush had to be controlled or it would control him. He had seen more than one soldier amped-up on their own adrenaline shot dead after charging into uncleared rooms.

At the door, he took several deep breaths and listened. He could hear nothing over the sound of his own pounding heart. A paraphrased verse from Timothy came to his lips as it had done on the thresholds of countless dark places in his past, a mantra to still his beating heart and focus his mind.

He whispered, "My God removes the spirit of fear and replaces it with love and the power of a sound mind." Then he opened the door.

He stepped into the hallway and squinted to shield his unadjusted eyes against the brilliance. Jane must have turned on every light in the apartment. He looked for her. She wasn't on the living room sofa or in the kitchen. The bathroom door was open, and the light inside was on, but she was not in there either. He found her in the spare bedroom, sitting on the floor. She was going through the things he had stored in a footlocker that had been secured with a combination lock.

When he entered the room, her back was to him, and she was inspecting something in her hand. A hint of cigarette smoke lingered in the air, and he wasn't sure what annoyed him more, her smoking or her breaking into his locker. He reminded himself about the love and sound mind from the Bible verse he'd recited and cleared his throat.

"I tried not to wake you," she said without appearing startled.

"I appreciate that, but I am not sure I appreciate you going through my things."

"Sorry. I guess we're even."

"How did you get it open?" he asked.

"Cheap lock—easy to crack. You should do something about that if you don't want anyone to open it."

He was about to respond when he heard the unmistakable sound of a handgun's slide being drawn back and locked into place. Shish, click.

"About these things," she said, turning to face him. In her right hand was his old M9 pistol. It had been many years since he'd seen it last. His commanding officer had purchased it and given it to him when he left the army, and it had remained untouched in its case at the bottom of his footlocker since it was shipped to his mother more than twelve years ago.

Without a moment's thought, Joe crossed the distance from the door to where she sat and snatched the gun from her before she had a chance to react. Despite the time that had passed, the plastic and steel weapon still felt familiar in his hand, like an often-used tool might feel in the hands of a craftsman. His fingers needed no conscious direction to find their positions on its grip and controls. He could disassemble and reassemble this pistol blindfolded. He'd done it many times.

He released the magazine and pulled back the slide to check the chamber. Empty. Joe was not surprised. He kept no ammunition in the apartment, but he knew better than to assume a gun was unloaded. Then he began to shake.

He handed her the gun and magazine. "Put these back in the case," he commanded with a tremble in his voice. Then he placed his back against a wall and slid to a sitting position on the floor. He took several deep breaths to tamp down the building panic attack.

"Are you okay?" she asked. "You're sweating."

She was right. He was drenched in sweat. His shirt, only damp moments before, was now soaked and clinging tightly to his body. Joe had not felt this anxious in years. She had no way of knowing, but opening the locker was like unsealing a tomb that he'd closed long ago. Now he would have to deal with the ghosts.

"Yes. It's just the gun and the other things." He nodded toward the items she'd removed from the locker. "They make me anxious and remind me of a time in my past that I have worked hard to forget."

She stared at him. "I guess I am not the only psycho here."

"Please put the gun away, Jane."

"Sweet Jane."

"Yeah, yeah, put the gun away, Sweet Jane."

She put the gun and magazine back in the case.

"Now put the case back in the footlocker," he said.

She opened her mouth to say something, and he raised a shaking finger to his lips to silence her. Appearing to sense how close she was to crossing a line no one had crossed in many years, she closed her mouth and put the case away.

They sat there looking at each other for a long moment until she broke the silence.

"Those are some tattoos on your chest."

He looked down and realized the elaborate images were visible through his sweat-soaked undershirt.

"They're nothing," he said. He pushed himself to his feet and retrieved a fresh shirt from his room. Then he returned and sat back down.

"You lied to me," she said.

"When did I lie?"

"You were not just a normal guy."

"Yes, I was…. Still am, for that matter."

She picked up a rectangular blue box from a stack of three she'd taken from his footlocker and retrieved an envelope from it. She drew a sheet of paper from the envelope, and holding it up to him, she read aloud.

"The President of the United States takes pleasure in presenting the Silver Star Medal to Joseph Michael Carroll, Captain, US Army, for conspicuous gallantry and intrepidity in action while serving with the Regimental Reconnaissance Detachment Team 4, Special Troops Battalion, 75th Ranger Regiment."

"Stop," Joe rasped.

"Wait," she said. "This is the good part." She resumed reading. "During combat operations in support of Operation Enduring Freedom, on 12 July 2004, in Afghanistan, Captain Carroll's team was conducting a tactical equipment drop in the Cahar Cinch region of the Oruzgan Province when they were ambushed by a numerically superior Anti-Coalition Militia force." She looked up. "Hmm, that sounds like a fancy name for the enemy."

"Please stop," he repeated.

"Just a little more." She continued. "The team took heavy fire resulting in several casualties. During the fight, Captain Carroll charged from his position to draw the enemy fire away from his pinned-down and wounded team members. He continued to lead the enemy away from the team until friendly forces were able to maneuver to the position and bring fire to bear on the ACM force. His actions saved the lives of five soldiers, three of whom were severely wounded. Captain Carroll himself, was critically injured during the action."

"That's enough," he said.

She slipped the paper back into its envelope and placed it back in the box. "You have two more. Are they Silver Stars too?"

He shook his head, "No. I only received one of those." He emitted a shaky laugh. "One is enough."

"What are the other two?"

He stood and sat back down next to her. Picking up the two other blue boxes, he opened the first one and looked inside. He handed it to her. "This medal is called the Purple Heart."

"I've heard of this one. You got it because you were wounded?"

He nodded. "Yeah. Still earning that one."

"What about the Silver Star? You still earning that one too?"

He coughed. "No. Rage and hatred earned that one, and that's all burned out now."

"Hatred? That paper said you saved your team. You were a hero."

Joe looked into her gray eyes and considered how much to share. He reminded himself that less than eight hours ago he thought she was crazy enough to kill him in his sleep. "You remember 9/11, right?"

She nodded. "I was a kid, but I remember it. Kind of hard not to."

"Well, I grew up in New Jersey, not far from New York City."

"Near where the planes hit?" she asked.

He nodded. "Yeah. My father worked in the city. I guess almost all the fathers in our town worked there. He was a building engineer."

"A janitor?"

"No. He was a mechanical engineer. He worked on things like elevators and ventilation systems. He worked in the Twin Towers."

"The ones that fell?" she asked.

"Yes. There was this park by our house from where we could see them. My dad would take my brother and sister and me to that park all the time so he could point them out and tell us about everything that went on inside them. He was very proud to take care of those buildings and the people who worked in them. When the plane hit the North Tower that morning, I couldn't see the buildings from our house, but I saw the black column of smoke rising from where I knew they were. My dad was on the tower's roof. He never came home—not even his body."

"Is that why you have that tattoo of the two towers?"

"You don't miss much, do you?"

"Well, that one is kind of hard to miss."

He'd gotten the tattoo the same day he'd enlisted in the army. He'd had to wait in line for both. It seemed every young man in his town had decided to sign up to kill the men responsible for the attack, then memorialize their anger and sadness in ink. "Yeah, I guess that was the point back then."

"That sucks. My dad died too."

"I'm sorry. How long ago did he pass?"

"It was a long time ago. I was little."

"His death must have been hard on you."

"Very hard. On my mom too." Her voice cracked.

"I pray the Lord brought you comfort."

She drew her knees up to her chin and rocked like a small child. "I told you. I don't believe in God."

He grimaced with an old pain. "I didn't much believe in Him when my dad died either."

"But you were going to be a priest?"

"Yes. It was the beginning of a long crisis. I was…." He searched for the words. "Inconsolable at my father's loss. He was a good man, a good Catholic, a deacon at our church, and I could not understand why God would take him that way and all those other people. I hated the men who flew the plane that killed him, and more than that, I wanted vengeance on all people like them."

She touched his chest and said, "Is that why you have a knight with a sword tattoo?"

He eased back from her touch and wondered how she could remember what his tattoos looked like after such a quick glimpse. "Did you look at my tattoos while I was sleeping?"

She raised her hands in exaggerated protest and laughed. "No."

"Then how do you know what they look like? You only saw them for an instant through my shirt."

She shrugged and tapped her temple with her finger. "I remember everything."

"Photographic memory?"

"Close. It's not as good as it was when I was a child, but still pretty good."

Joe thanked God he did not have that gift. For some things, being able to forget was a blessing.

"Wow."

"Yeah. It comes in handy." She closed her eyes. "The knight on your chest is holding a sword over his head. He's got a big red cross on his armor and he's standing on…" She squeezed her eyes closed like she was concentrating. "He's standing on skulls? Yikes. Definitely not priest-like."

He sighed as he recalled the time one of his seminary instructors caught a glimpse of his tattoos when Joe had removed his shirt while they were working on a mission project together. The priest had been appalled and cited Leviticus: *You shall not make any gashes in your flesh for the dead or tattoo any marks upon you.* Joe had made sure to keep them hidden after that, even after Caleb had reminded him the Church had no prohibition against tattoos, though he did say they may not approve of some of his.

"Yeah. I should have them removed," he said.

"Why don't you?"

"I don't know. They're part of who I am, I guess."

"Well, those men killed your dad and a couple thousand other people. Seems to me your feelings were justified."

"There was nothing justifiable about my feelings back then."

He pulled his knees up to his chest in the same childlike way as she.

"The day the towers fell, I turned my back on my Lord. The calling I'd felt from the time I was a small boy assisting our parish priests at the altar and learning the catechism from my father was gone, and in its place was a burning need for revenge. I left the priest formation program the very next day and enlisted in the army."

"That paper says you were a captain. Don't you have to go to a special college for that?"

"No. When I joined the army, I already had my engineering degree, and they sent me to school to be an officer."

"Engineering? I thought you were going to be a priest."

"Yes, but I wanted to be a useful priest."

She laughed. "What does that mean?"

"I wanted to build communities, not just preach. I have a degree in civil engineering."

"You can do both?"

"Sure."

"Did you kill people when you were in the army?"

He swallowed. This was one of those questions he tried to avoid. "Yes—several, I think. They are all in my prayers, and to this day the acts that took their lives remain in my confessions."

She removed the gold and purple heart-shaped medal from the blue box and held it in her palm. "You said you are still earning this one. What did you mean?"

"On that day you read about in the citation, I was shot several times. I spent a long time in a hospital bed in Germany. They fixed the physical wounds up for the most part, but I have scars. Some will never heal."

"I see. I'm sorry."

He shrugged. "It's okay. I haven't talked about these things in a long time, and I kind of feel a little better talking about them."

"What happened after you left the hospital? Did you go back to the war?"

"No. The time I spent in the hospital gave me time to think about things. I was still not ready to return to God, but I was done with vengeance. I never went back to my company. When I was well enough, I returned to the states and was reassigned to the Corps of Engineers."

He smiled. "I worked with the Pima Indians in Arizona to improve washes to control flash floods until I left the army in 2012. That's how

I got this one." He held up the last blue rectangular box. "It's called the Meritorious Service Medal, and I think I am proudest of it."

She placed his Purple Heart in its box and handed it back to him. Then she began to look around the room. Her searching became frantic.

"Jane, what's wrong?"

"Sweet Jane, Sweet Jane," she shouted. "How many times do I have to tell you my name is Sweet Jane?"

He slid back from her and placed the blue boxes on the floor. "Okay, okay. What is wrong?"

"Where did you put my backpack?"

"I didn't put it anywhere."

"Yes. You did. You took it. Where is it?"

"Sweet Jane, I woke up and came right into the room. I didn't take your backpack."

They both scrambled to their feet, and she drew near him with her fists clenched. Her eyes, that had been pools of understanding only seconds before, were now wild and terrifying. Once again, he feared he might have to defend himself. The tremors in his hands and voice that he'd just gotten under control returned.

"Where is it?" she demanded.

"Did you leave it in the living room?" His voice quivered.

Her facial expression softened, and her eyes grew less confused. "Yes." Her fists unclenched. "I think you're right." She stepped toward the door and stopped before leaving the room. "I am sorry, Joe. I don't mean to be this way." She took another step into the hallway and stopped again. "I wasn't always this way," she said in a tearful voice, then disappeared into the living room.

He held his breath and blew out a puff of air after she'd gone. Then he whispered, "Gracious Father, please fill me with your Holy Spirit to lead and guide me."

After he silently finished the prayer, he collected the items from his past that were scattered about the room. He lingered over a few before returning them to the footlocker. A collection of photographs in an envelope grabbed his attention. Most were of men he went to war with—some who never returned or did not return whole. One or two photos made him laugh as they reminded him not all his time in the army was spent, as Jane would say, killing people. He came upon a box of letters from his family, and he paused to read one from his mother. God had taken her a few months after he'd left the army and seeing her neat handwriting and hearing her words in his head cheered him some.

The alarm clock in his bedroom buzzed. Joe put the box of letters in the footlocker and re-secured it with the padlock that Jane had no trouble opening. He made a mental note to buy a better lock, then went to his bedroom to turn off the alarm. It was 4:15 a.m. He stood in the dark reflecting on the morning and thinking about what he was about to do. The bus station was on the other side of the city. With morning traffic, it would take at least 45 minutes to reach it. He was still not convinced putting her on a bus was the right decision. He glanced into the living room. Jane had her earbuds in, and she appeared to be reorganizing her backpack while listening to her tapes. He would try to convince her to let him take her to one of the church counselors instead of the bus station.

He recited his morning prayers. Then he showered and dressed. When he finished, she was sitting on a stool at the kitchen counter with a glass of water and her bag of pills. She looked like she was waiting for something.

"Are you okay?"

"I have to take my medications."

"Of course. Do you need something?"

"I have to eat before I take them, or I will get sick."

"Oh sure. Pancakes okay?"

"Yum. That would be great."

She watched with hungry eyes as he made the pancakes from an instant mix. He stacked three large golden-brown cakes on her plate and watched with amazement as she covered them with half a bottle of maple syrup and devoured them like a ravenous animal.

"I guess you were hungry."

"Starving," she mumbled in between bites.

"I am worried about you, Sweet Jane."

She swallowed the last of the syrup-drenched pancakes and looked up at him. "What are you worried about?"

"Do you have a place to stay in Auburn?"

"Of course. It's my home."

"I would like to know when you get home safe. Do you have a cell phone?"

She laughed. "No. Why would I want a cell phone? You know they can track those, don't you?"

"Who's they?"

"Everyone, anyone, the government, Google."

She took her pills and retreated to the bathroom with her backpack while he cleaned up.

CHAPTER FOUR

Joe

It was a little after 7:00 a.m. when they reached the bus station. During the ride, he tried to convince her to let him find her a counselor to talk to. He offered to let her stay with him until he could make the arrangements, but she would not consider it.

"I have to get home," she insisted. "It's very important."

When he brought up the risks with her medication Caleb had warned him about, she told him to mind his own business and refused to discuss it any further saying only, "I know how to handle my fucking meds."

The bus station was in a part of the city that looked to have been forgotten by everyone, including the politicians who represented it. They had to walk a block from where Joe parked to reach the terminal, passing. groups of shady-looking young men loitering on the street corners and in the entranceways.

Joe had spent some time on the street around men like this. He knew most were addicts of some type or another. They, as he once was, were caught in a destructive loop of dependency where everything but bare subsistence took second place to their intoxicant of choice—of need.

Despite the angry stares and menacing gestures of some, he knew most were only capable of hurting themselves. He also knew there were others among them who could be dangerous. He kept Jane moving while, as his drill sergeant had taught him, he kept his head on a swivel, praying nothing would trigger an outburst from her that might complicate things.

Inside, they found the ticket counter, and Joe purchased a one-way ticket on a bus that would take Jane to the town of Opelika, Alabama which was as close to Auburn as the line went. Jane was happy with the destination, and she assured him she knew how to get home from there.

The departure terminal was small, and though it was well lit by glowing fluorescent ceiling light panels, it felt dim and dingy. The floor tiles, furniture, and even the uniforms of the agents were all dark blues and grays that absorbed the light and made the space feel cold and institutional.

He waited with her in a crowded gate where all the seats were occupied, and travelers and their luggage were sprawled all about the dirty floor. They stood together in a corner next to some vending machines until people began lining up at the door that led to her bus.

Joe took a business card and two twenty-dollar bills from his wallet and handed them to her. "The card has my cell phone number on it. Please call me when you get where you are going, so I know you arrived safely."

She studied the card. It was nothing fancy, just a plain white business card with black block lettering in a simple font. It bore the address of the Basilica of the Sacred Heart of Jesus and his name and a phone number. "They give almost-priests business cards?" she asked.

He chuckled. "They do when you're an almost-priest for as long as I have been. I am like an office manager at the church. I do administrative things."

She wrapped the card in the twenties and slid them into her front pocket. Then she took off her backpack and retrieved the math book he'd seen the night before. "You have been very kind to me, Joe. I hate to ask any more of you, but do you think you could drop this book off at the Georgia Tech library?"

He took the book and read the title out loud, "Advances in Differential Equations and Proofs for Statistical Mechanics." He leafed through the pages. "I was pretty good at calculus in college, but this stuff looks way too advanced for me. I am impressed."

Her eyes brightened, and she gave him a crooked smile, "Like I told you, I wasn't always a nut case."

The gate agent announced the bus was ready to board and opened the door that led to the bus garage. A smokey haze drifted into the waiting area from the open door and Joe could smell the acrid stink of burning diesel fuel. A line formed at the door. She gave him a nervous hug and slipped on her backpack. He remained standing by the vending machines, watching as she handed the agent her ticket and followed the rest of the passengers through the door and into the garage.

"Safe travels and God bless, Sweet Jane," he said as she disappeared.

CHAPTER FIVE

Joe

Joe's cell phone buzzed as he reached his car. He winced when he read the name displayed on the phone's screen.

"Good morning, Father Carlos."

"Good morning, Joseph," replied the familiar, soft, but firm voice with a subtle yet detectable Spanish accent. "We missed you at breakfast."

It was customary and even somewhat expected for all priests and transitional deacons to meet in the rectory kitchen area at 6:00 a.m. to conduct their morning prayers and readings. After their liturgical obligations, they would discuss the day's plans over breakfast, then prepare for the midday Mass. Joe had neglected to call his mentor to tell him he would miss the morning rituals.

"Yes, sir," Joe snapped. Army conditioning buried for a decade had been brought to the surface by Jane's intrusion. He cringed, anticipating the reaction. Father Carlos had never been comfortable with Joe's military history which Joe knew was a big part of why his ordination was far from certain.

"I am not your superior officer, Joseph," Father Carlos replied with a reproachful tone.

"Of course not, Father. I am sorry. I meant to call you this morning."

Joe explained Jane as best he could, leaving out the morning's incident with the gun. His mentor questioned the wisdom of having a strange woman spend the night in his apartment, but in the end, agreed helping her was the right thing to do.

"Joseph, His Eminence and I have high hopes for you. We know you feel as though you have been in the wilderness for far too long, but your day will come. If you stay disciplined and endure the trials, you will get what you seek."

"I will, Father. Thank you and please thank the archbishop for his continued support and confidence in me."

As he ended the call, Joe noticed the textbook Jane asked him to return to the Georgia Tech library sitting in the car's rear seat. The school was nearby, and he had a couple hours before he was due at Sacred Heart for midday Mass. It took him only a few minutes to reach the campus.

Georgia Institute of Technology, or Georgia Tech, is one of the country's most prestigious public engineering universities. It is located on a compact, woodsy campus in the heart of Atlanta's Midtown neighborhood. The quiet tree-lined roads and walkways that meander through it and the skyscrapers that tower above it, give it an intimate, boxed-in feel. The smallness is an illusion, however, as the campus is substantial with over 40,000 students. It took Joe almost an hour to park and locate the main library.

The library was crowded with students preparing for final exams, but there was no line at the circulation desk. A pair of Black women greeted him. One was young with long braided hair and a brilliant smile. Joe took her for a student. The other was much older with short gray hair and bifocals perched on her pointed nose. The young one asked how she could help him.

He handed her the textbook. "A friend asked me to return this."

Still smiling, she scanned the book's bar code. "That's funny. We don't show it as checked out."

The older one glanced over and read the computer screen. "It says here the book was last required by a Dr. Neerja Patel in her statistical mechanics class. That class is part of the theoretical physics graduate program." She picked up the book and studied it. "It's the only copy we have. It hasn't been checked out much."

"My friend's name is Jane. Jane Carter." Remembering her name as it was printed on the hospital bracelet, he added, "She may have used the name Elizabeth or Liz. Can you tell me if she ever checked the book out?"

The young librarian was about to answer when the older one silenced her with a raised hand. The old woman looked at him with suspicion. "Are you a cop?"

"No. Nothing like that. I'm just a friend. I met Jane yesterday and helped her out, and now I am a little curious and concerned about her. I only want to make sure she is okay."

"You sure seem like a cop." She continued to study him. "If you're not a cop, maybe you're a stalker."

Joe chuckled. "No. I'm not with the police, and I'm not stalking her. I am a deacon at the Sacred Heart Catholic Church." He took out one of his business cards and handed it to her. "I'm worried about her well-being." Feeling a little irritable from the morning's events and exasperated by the questioning he said, "Never mind." Then in a gentler tone added, "I'm glad I could return the book."

The old librarian's expression softened. "Is your Jane about five four or five five, a little plump, with shoulder-length black hair and pale white skin?"

Joe nodded.

"Is she a little off?" She arched an eyebrow. "You know, maybe have some problems?"

Joe nodded again.

"If we are talking about the same young woman, she comes in here often."

"The Phantom," the younger librarian blurted.

The older librarian glared at the younger one and turned back to Joe. "The kids call her The Phantom. I tell them it's mean, but they keep doing it."

"Why do you call her The Phantom?" Joe asked the younger one.

"Because she's all pale like a ghost and creepy. And she does spooky things."

"Christal, that's enough," snapped the older one.

"Well, it's true. Sometimes she just appears among the books in the back. She's scared the hell out of me more than a few times. I almost peed my pants the last time she snuck up on me back there." She pointed at the rows of tall bookshelves.

The old woman shook her head. "She's not a ghost or phantom. I think she comes here because she has no place else to go. Most days she sits alone at a table scribbling away in a notebook with her earbuds in."

The young one continued. "She always mumbles to herself, and sometimes she yells at people when they try to talk to her. Kids who have gotten close to her say she's some kind of crazy math genius. I never believed them, but if she had this book, I guess they were right."

"She told me she was once a graduate student here. I think it would have been several years ago," Joe said.

The young one shrugged. "I don't know about that. All I know is she lives here or at least I think she does."

"You mean on campus?"

"No, I mean here. In the library."

"We think she is homeless," the older lady added. "People have seen her washing up in the bathroom."

The young one murmured, "gross" under her breath.

The older one shooshed her and continued. "We've found her asleep in unused corners. The library is open every day twenty-four by seven when school is in session, so it's not hard for street people to get in."

Joe looked around at the cavernous open area with rows and rows of tables all crowded with studying students. "Do you have many homeless people living here?"

"No. Of course not. A few wander in now and again to get out of the weather, but she's the only one we think stays here, and we are not sure she actually does."

"I'm sure she does," said the younger one. "She's The Phantom of the Library—you know, like The Phantom of the Opera?"

Joe was taken aback. He'd come to the library not only to fulfill the promise he made to return the book, but he'd hoped to learn something about Jane that would ease his concern over putting her on a bus without knowing what help she would receive at her destination. What the librarians told him had the opposite effect. His concerns had grown tenfold. He wished he'd learned more about her past, like the fact she had been living in a university library before he'd sent her on her way. He wanted to know more. He had to know more.

"Can you tell me how I can get in touch with the professor you said used the textbook in her class?"

The older librarian looked over the top of her glasses at him. "You sure you're not a cop?"

"I'm not a cop."

"If you're lying to me, I'll find out, and you'll regret it."

The younger one's head bobbed in agreement. "She's not kidding."

"I am not a cop," he said for the third time.

The older librarian sighed and tapped on her keyboard, then handed him a sheet of paper from her printer.

The paper listed the professor's name and contact information. Joe thanked them both and left.

The morning sun had risen above the trees and shone between the surrounding city buildings. Students in brightly colored summer clothing filled the walkways that connected the mix of old brick and modern glass structures. Joe took a seat on a bench and watched them pass, taking a moment to contemplate God and the mystery of people like Jane.

He recited, "The heavens declare the glory of God, the vault of heaven proclaims his handiwork."

As he finished, a young woman joined him on the bench.

She smiled and said, "I recognize that verse."

"You do?"

"Sure. Psalms 19, God's creation shows his glory. It's not the exact King James quote, though.

"That's right. I'm impressed. It's rare to meet a young person with such knowledge of the Bible. Especially someone who spots the difference between the Catholic and King James versions."

"I grew up in a church, and my daddy would agree with you about young people not knowing the Bible. He would say the King James Version was the right one, of course, but he would agree that too few know any version. He's always complaining his sermons are only heard by the old and wise when it's the young and foolish that need to hear them most."

Joe laughed. "Your daddy sounds like a smart man. Where does he preach?"

She grinned. The sun was at her back, and its light illuminated her blonde hair, forming a halo. She looked like one of the angels in Sacred Heart's stained-glass windows. "Clarkston, Tennessee. He's the minister at the Clarkston First Baptist Church."

Joe held out his fist. "My name is Joe."

She bumped hers to his. "Nice to meet you, Joe. I'm Sarah."

He showed her the paper from the library and pointed to the professor's address. "Can you tell me how to get to this building?"

She studied it for a moment. "Sure. It's one of the science halls." She stood and pointed at a signpost. "Follow the signs to the Computer Center. That building is across from the center's main entrance. You can't miss it."

He fist-bumped her again and walked in the direction she indicated.

She called after him, "Seek, and ye shall find."

Joe raised a thumbs-up, and mumbled to himself. "Now if only Dr. Patel is there to open the door when I knock."

She was, and he didn't need to knock.

The door to Dr. Neerja Patel's office was open, and she sat behind her desk staring at a computer display. She was a small, middle-aged Indian woman with mahogany brown skin, slender, manicured fingers, and long, jet-black hair with white and gray streaks radiating out from a part down the middle. He cleared his throat, and she looked up at him through thick glasses that magnified her dark brown eyes.

"May I help you?"

"I hope so. Are you Doctor Patel?"

"I am Neerja Patel, yes."

Joe introduced himself, and when he asked about Jane, he endured the same questions about his vocation and motivations as the older librarian had subjected him to. Like the librarian, the professor started out suspicious but turned helpful after Joe convinced her he wasn't from the police and was only concerned about Jane's safety.

"I know Jane," she said to his surprise. Then she reclined in her chair and gazed up at the ceiling for a moment before looking back at him through her magnified eyes. "She is a brilliant woman. Troubled, but brilliant."

"Then she was a student here."

"Oh yes, but not for a long time." She counted on her fingers. "Had to be ten years ago."

"Was she one of your students?"

"No. Not a student in the typical sense. Jane had already completed all her graduate level coursework before she came to us. She was a doctoral candidate, and I was one of her supervisors, only." She punctuated her sentences with "only" as many Indic speakers do.

"I oversaw some of her advanced mathematics studies and quantum mechanics research. What is your field again, Mr. Carroll?"

"Theology."

"That's right. You mentioned you worked for a church. Like I said, Jane came to us ready for her dissertation. She did most of her work out West." She stared at the ceiling for another moment. "Yes. The University of California, Berkeley if I remember correctly. San Francisco. She had been a doctorate candidate there."

"Do you know why she left California and came to Atlanta?"

"Her mother was an associate professor here, and when things got hard for Jane, I mean when she became sick, she came home to complete her work here near her mother. Of course, we could not offer the same facilities and opportunities for doing advanced theoretical physics as Berkeley, but we have our own specialties."

Joe furrowed his brow. "So her mother worked here?"

"Yes. For several years, only. She was with the Computer Science Department if I remember correctly."

"Odd," he said.

"How so?"

"Jane said her mother taught at Auburn and that's where she lived."

Doctor Patel rotated her seat and faced the window behind her. She appeared to stare into the building across the walkway. After a moment, she spun back around to face him. "Yes. When Jane's illness became too severe, her mother found a doctor affiliated with Auburn University who had developed new therapies for treating schizophrenia. She took a teaching position down there so the doctor could treat Jane."

"The women I spoke to at the library thought Jane was homeless and may even be living in the library. Do you know if that's true?"

Doctor Patel placed her hands on her desktop. A gold wedding band encircled her right ring finger as was the Indian custom. It shone against her brown skin. She fidgeted with it in an apparent nervous gesture.

"I heard rumors about her returning to the campus and spending a lot of time in the library, but I haven't seen or spoken to her since she's been back."

"When I picked her up last evening, she was wearing a bracelet from Grady Hospital. Do you think she is up here getting treatment?"

"I don't really know, Mr. Carroll. I've meant to find her and talk with her, but it's exam time, and I've been busy." She continued to play with her ring. "This is the first day in weeks that I have not had students sitting in the chair you are in every hour I am not teaching. I think I will go find her today and speak with her."

"She's no longer here, Doctor."

"No?"

"No. I put her on a bus back to Auburn this morning. Actually, she's headed for Opelika as the bus didn't go to Auburn."

Doctor Patel stopped playing with her ring and interlocked her long, slender fingers. She sighed and turned back toward the window. "Oh, I don't think that was a good idea, Mr. Carroll," she said without facing him. Then she turned back around. "In fact, I think that may have been a very bad idea."

Joe frowned. "I was afraid I'd made the wrong decision. Is she too sick to be on her own?"

"I don't know, Mr. Carroll. As I have told you, I have not seen or spoken to her in many years, but I do know things went badly in Auburn for Jane and her mother—very, very badly. I don't think Jane should be anywhere near that place."

"Can you tell me what you mean? What happened to Jane in Auburn?"

"I don't feel comfortable discussing Jane's personal life with you without clearing it with her. I think these things are private, only." She placed her hands back on her desk. "I feel I may have already said too much without her permission."

Joe stood. "I understand," he said and placed one of his business cards on the desk in front of her. "If I can help Jane in any way, I would like to. Please let me know if you think there is anything I can do." She looked at the card but did not touch it. He could tell she was distressed by their conversation and her level of concern troubled him. "Goodbye, Doctor Patel."

As he exited her office, she called him back. "Mr. Carroll." She stood from her chair and walked out to meet him. She had her own business card in her hand, and she gave it to him. "I do not mean to be rude. I am sure you want to help Jane, only. If I learn anything more about her current situation, I will call you, and perhaps you could do the same."

He took the card and left, feeling the same anxious guilt about placing Jane alone on a bus as he'd once felt sending young soldiers out on dangerous patrols.

CHAPTER SIX

Joe

Fifteen minutes before noon, Sacred Heart's carillon began tolling the Angelus to summon the faithful to the midday Mass. Starting as simple, well-spaced notes, the bell strikes grew in complexity and power until they reached a celebratory peal echoing off the surrounding buildings along Peachtree Center Avenue, then rolling in through the open entrance and narthex doors to reverberate off the marble floors and vaulted ceilings.

Dressed in his vestments and holding the heavy Book of the Gospels, Joe watched from the small room off the north transept as about a dozen worshippers entered the church and found their seats among the many empty pews. It was the same small procession of white-haired and bent figures he'd watched every day for years. Most were in their seventies and several he knew were even older than that. Coming to Mass grew more difficult and uncomfortable for them each day, but still they came, astonishing him with their unwavering devotion and faith.

Occupying her usual place in the frontmost pew was Mrs. Ecker, who, despite being well into her eighties, always came alone and unaided. Right behind her were Mr. and Mrs. Alverez who had lost their son in a terrible accident five years before and came to every Mass to light a candle for him and look for comfort and understanding. Joe watched them assemble. He loved them all.

Father Carlos waited in the south transept at the feet of the towering statue of Saint Joseph. Joe glanced over to him and nodded. His mentor, tall and lean, with thick, black hair and olive skin, resplendent in his emerald-green chasuble with the gold trim and gold cross emblazoned on his chest did not acknowledge the nod. Instead, he stood stern and erect like one of the Corinthian columns that separated the nave from the aisles. The musical tolling reverted to the simple well-spaced notes, signaling it was time for Joe and Father Carlos to make their entrance.

They descended the aisles in unison and met in the middle between the carved mahogany confessionals while Teddy, the church usher, closed the doors. Joe raised the Book of Gospels and made his way along the crimson-carpeted nave to the tabernacle. Several steps behind him, Joe knew Father Carlos, permitting just a hint of a smile to lighten his serious expression, glided along with his hands and eyes raised up toward the figure of the crucified Christ suspended high above them. Joe placed the book on the altar and kissed the cool wood surface, then retreated to his subservient position while Father Carlos ascended the predella.

Joe bowed and said the words that he'd learned to begin the Mass so many years ago. "Humbled, I ask for your blessing, Father."

"May the Lord be in your heart," Father Carlos replied.

Then Joe retrieved the Book of the Gospels and took it to the ambo where he placed it on the lectern and proclaimed to the attendees, "The Lord be with you."

And that's when he saw her. Jane sat in a pew near the back. He had not noticed her before. She must have come in after Teddy had closed the doors. She was a mess. She stared up at him through eyes wet with tears, hair all askew, purpling bruises on her face, and what he took for blood crusted around her nose.

The mixed responses from the worshippers of "and also with you" and "and with your spirit" did not reach his ears. He was frozen by her unexpected presence and condition. Someone coughed, and he realized every eye in the church, including his mentor's, was focused on him.

He regained his composure and continued with the Mass, worried at any point she might leave or make a scene requiring him to interrupt the holy ceremony, but she remained seated, her eyes fixed on him, in an almost catatonic stare. She did not join the communion, which he was somewhat relieved by, and when he dismissed the small congregation, she did not join the procession to the exit.

He made his way over to her. Father Carlos followed close behind.

"Sweet Jane, what happened?" Joe asked.

"You know this woman?" Father Carlos asked.

"Yes. This is the woman I told you about. The one I thought I put on a bus this morning to Alabama."

"Sweet Mary, how badly are you hurt, child?" Father Carlos prompted with genuine concern.

She did not appear to hear him at first, and Joe and Carlos exchanged concerned glances. Then she whispered, "He took my backpack."

She began to cry, and Joe sat down next to her and wiped her face with a cloth he kept in his dalmatic for cleaning the ceremonial chalice.

"Joe, he took my backpack. Everything…everything I have is in that backpack," she said in a panicked, sobbing voice.

"Who? What happened to the bus?"

"A man. He was in the garage at the terminal. I was smoking, and he came up to me looking for money."

She grabbed Joe's arms and looked at him with the same wild eyes he'd seen the night before. "I tried to help him. I gave him some money, but he wanted more. He took my backpack and ran. I followed him, and he beat me, Joe. He hit me hard and kicked me." She released his hands and clenched her fist. "He fucking took my backpack."

As one, Joe and Carlos gasped and crossed themselves.

Father Carlos backed away from the pew. "I will call the police."

"No," Jane howled. "No police. Please, no police."

Joe turned to Father Carlos, "I'll take her to the rectory where she can clean up, and we can see if she needs to go to the hospital."

"No hospital," she said. "I have to get my things back."

Joe shrugged at Carlos and coaxed Jane to follow him to the kitchen. There she sat in a wooden chair staring into space, while he used a washcloth with warm water and soap to clean her face. He had received enough field medical training in the army to know how to check for a concussion, broken bones, and signs of internal injuries. She had a few scrapes and was developing a black eye, but other than that, seemed to have no severe injuries. When he was done, her eyes, now calm, focused on him.

"Thank you."

"It's okay, Jane." He paused, expecting her to correct him, but she did not. "I think we should take you to see the police. Maybe they can get your things back."

She shook her head and took his hand in hers. "Please, Joe. No police. Can you take me back to the bus station so I can see if I can find some of my things? The stuff I want back is only valuable to me. The man who attacked me may have only wanted the backpack and dumped what was inside."

Joe sighed. "Let me go change into my street clothes." He pointed to the refrigerator. "There are bottled waters in there and maybe even a Coke or two. Help yourself. I will be right back." As he was about to leave the kitchen, he turned back to her. "How did you find me?"

She dug his crinkled business card from her jeans. "He didn't get this," she smiled.

"All done according to the Lord's will," he said.

She smirked. "There is no such thing."

He paused and considered telling her to show some respect in God's house but decided against it and left without a word.

After he changed, he found Carlos in his office. His mentor's head was bowed in prayer over an opened book Joe recognized as the Code of Canon Law—the book of all the rules and regulations of the Catholic Church along with the disciplinary guidance for those who broke them. As he watched Carlos pray, it struck Joe that this priest, who had guided and instructed him since he'd joined the diocese, was younger than he by several years, but in that light, at that moment, Carlos, who appeared to be weighing some heavy matter, seemed the older man.

His mentor opened his eyes. "Joseph, my friend, how is the young woman?" He asked as he closed the book and returned it to the shelf behind his desk.

Father Carlos Santiago was not a warm man, and it was unusual for him to refer to Joe as his friend. It made Joe wonder if Carlos was researching a rule Joe had violated in caring for Jane. Joe's face flushed with momentary anger, then he collected himself and made a note to confess this sin of doubting the motivations of this good man.

"I don't think she has any serious injuries—just some bruises, and of course, she is upset."

Carlos steepled his fingers and stared up at him. "Have you decided what we should do?"

"I am going to take her back to the bus station and see if we can recover some of her things. The man who took them was probably as troubled as she is. There are many people in need over there. Even if we cannot find her backpack, maybe I can do some good."

"What then? With the woman, I mean."

"Sweet Jane."

"I beg your pardon?"

"That's what she calls herself."

"Fine, what will we do with this…this Sweet Jane?"

"I don't know, Carlos. Father Montagne recommended I have her talk to one of the social services counselors from the center. I already suggested that to her, and I will continue to try to convince her. Maybe with God's help, we will find her things, and she can catch the next bus home."

"It is good you called Caleb. I don't know, however, if taking her back to the bus station is the right thing. I fear your involvement with this Sweet Jane is perilous."

Joe frowned. "You don't mean from a sexual perspective do you, Father?"

"No. Of course not. I know you are true in your commitment to the church and the Lord. I only fear she may bring trouble and the wrong attention to you just as you are so close to attaining your goal."

"She needs help, and I cannot turn my back on her for appearances. Jesus did not turn his back on Mary Magdalene, now did he?"

Carlos smiled. "No. He did not. You have a good heart, Joseph. As in all things, the Lord will work his way through you. Shall we pray before you go?"

They bowed their heads and Carlos asked God to grant his servant Joseph wisdom and strength and to grant Jane healing and faith. Then, he did something that surprised Joe. He told him to change his shirt and wear his clerical collar, as he thought the outward appearance of Joe's position within the church may grant him and Jane some additional protection.

Joe followed his mentor's advice and collected Jane, then they drove to the bus station and parked in the same location they had that morning. The late spring heat wave that had baked the city for over a week had not let up. The deserted streets and sidewalks offered little shade from the sun's assault. The groups of forgotten men who had slipped through society's cracks to land here like the trash that lined the curbs had all gone. Nothing moved—not even the air.

Joe put on his sunglasses and exited the car. Jane had no glasses and griped about it as she squinted against the fierce afternoon sun.

She eyed his shirt and collar. "You're pretending to be a priest again." Then she asked, "Why is your shirt gray? I thought priests wore black?"

"I am not pretending, and transitionary deacons wear gray when they wear the collar."

The empty lot behind the station appeared to be home to thirty or more people. Tents of every color and description along with crude structures assembled from scraps of wood and shipping pallets covered with tarps competed with the tall weeds to cover the red Georgia clay. Joe had visited many encampments like it, though this was the first time he'd been to this one. There were far too many of them, and their existence, along with the countless other examples of inequity and human suffering were difficult to understand in the context of God's purpose. Seminary had taught him the philosophical arguments in defense of why an omnipotent and benevolent god would permit such things, but still, he struggled with it.

When they neared the first tent, Jane bolted toward it. He caught her arm just as she yanked the flap open.

"Jane, this is someone's home."

Inside was a light-skinned Black man with a tangled salt-and-pepper beard and naked except for boxer shorts, lying on a sleeping bag and shielding his eyes from the brilliant intrusion.

"Where is my backpack?" Jane demanded.

"I don't know what you're talking about, bitch," the half-naked man replied. "Get out of my tent." He sat up and felt around until he found a bottle of what Joe took for whiskey. He chugged the contents down, then tossed the bottle aside. "What backpack?"

"You're not him," Jane said as she let the tent flap fall back in place. She pulled free of Joe's grip and stormed toward the next tent.

He caught her just before she reached it. "Wait, we can't do it like this."

The half-naked man had scrambled out of his tent and stood with one hand in his boxer shorts, glaring at them. "What's wrong with you people? You think 'cause you're white you can come down here and disturb a man in his place? I fought for this country. I deserve some respect."

Joe took a twenty out of his wallet and walked back to the man. "I'm sorry we disturbed you, sir. I am a vet myself. We meant you no disrespect." He pointed at Jane. "She's a little upset. Let me buy you dinner to make up for the interruption."

The man removed his hand from his shorts and took the money. "This don't make it right, but it helps." He glared at Joe. "You a priest?"

"Something like that."

"He's not," she said.

"Jane, please," Joe snapped.

"Sweet Jane," she screamed. Then added, "We need to find my backpack."

Joe turned back to the half-naked man, "Like I said, she's upset. A man attacked her at the bus station this morning and took a red backpack from her. We are looking for it." Joe opened his wallet again and counted the bills he had. "I will pay sixty dollars to get it back."

"Shit," the half-naked man said. "If you'd pay sixty, maybe you'd pay a hundred. Huh?"

"If we get everything back, I will give you one hundred dollars."

Jane's screaming had not gone unnoticed. A man and woman from the surrounding tents had crawled out and were watching them. The man, who was dressed in gym shorts and a sweat-drenched T-shirt stood and came over. He was much younger and fitter than Joe. His dark brown arms were muscular and covered with tattoos. It looked as if he was fresh out of the gym.

"What's going on, old man?" the fit man asked the half-naked man.

"The preacher's going to give me one hundred dollars for a backpack."

The fit man turned to Joe. "Is that right, Preacher? I got a backpack too. You gonna give me a hundred dollars?"

Jane stomped back over to Joe and pointed at the fit man. "This isn't him either." She turned to the man and yelled, "We're not buying just any backpack. We want my backpack. Someone here's got it, and we want it back."

Joe put himself between her and the fit man and forced her back a few steps.

"Hey," she said.

Joe raised his hands to show he was not looking for trouble. "She doesn't mean any harm. She's upset. Like I was telling this man…" He turned to the half-naked man. "I didn't catch your name, sir."

"Myron. Sergeant Derrick Myron. US Army."

"Nice to meet you, Sergeant. I am Joe Carroll. I was in the army too. I served in Afghanistan." Joe thought it was best not to reveal his rank. "How about you?"

The half-naked man coughed. "Vietnam. '71 to '73."

Joe nodded to him. Then turned back to the fit man. "And what's your name?"

"Call me Kay."

"Like the letter?"

"Yeah. Like the letter."

"Did you serve, Kay?"

"Yeah, I served. I served seven years in Hays."

The sergeant coughed again. "That's bullshit. Hays ain't no military base. Hays is a prison."

"You shut up, old man. You served the white man in Vietnam, and I served him in Hays. Now what's this about one hundred dollars, Preacher?"

Joe motioned with his head behind him. "This is Jane."

"Sweet Jane," she barked.

Joe turned and glared at her.

"A man took her backpack this morning, and we think he might be here."

"Is that so? What's in this backpack? Drugs? Money?"

"No. Nothing like that. Just her clothes and personal stuff."

"And my medication," she blurted.

Joe glared at her again, then turned back to Kay.

Kay smiled. "Sounds like drugs."

"Antipsychotics. Nothing anyone would want to take," Joe replied.

"Ain't that the truth," the sergeant said.

Kay looked past Joe at Jane. "What did the man look like who took your backpack?"

"Skinny, scraggly, and missing a lot of teeth. He had a Braves hat on and a puffy red coat."

"Was he white?"

"Yes."

"Tweaker Mike." Kay and the sergeant said at the same time.

"Does he live here?"

Kay nodded. "Sometimes. He's got a tarp spread between two shopping carts over there." He motioned to the back of the lot. "He's a meth-head. He's always whacked out on the stuff. I think everyone here has kicked the shit out of him at least once."

"Can you take us to him?"

"Hey," the sergeant said. "I get the reward. I get the money."

"I'll give you each fifty dollars if we get her stuff back."

Kay rubbed his chin and made a point of flexing one of his large biceps when he did. "Follow me."

The sergeant, Jane, and Joe followed Kay to an overgrown spot near a hole in a tall fence that separated the lot from the bus garage area. Next to the hole, hidden in the tall weeds, was a small shelter formed, as Kay said, from a grimy blue tarp spread between two shopping carts. Another tarp formed the floor of the shelter, and there, lying in a fetal position, was a filthy man matching the description Jane gave of her attacker.

Next to the man was Jane's zippered backpack. Before Joe knew what she was doing, Jane dropped to all fours and scrambled into the shelter and retrieved it. She punched the sleeping man in the face as she backed out and climbed to her feet.

Tweaker Mike moaned and rolled on his back, holding his bleeding nose. "Ouch. Why did you do that?" He got to his knees, then charged at Jane, but he never reached her. Kay clotheslined him as he passed and hurled him to the ground.

"Stop," Joe yelled. "Let him be." Joe squatted down next to Tweaker Mike and checked him over. Blood gushed from his nose where Jane had hit him, and he was rubbing his head where it had struck the ground. Joe tried to examine the spot, but Tweaker Mike swatted him away and crawled back under his tarp. He wedged himself against the fence and stared out at them like a cornered animal.

Joe stood and walked over to Jane. She had looked inside the pack and zipped it up as he neared. "Everything there?" he asked.

"I think so," she said.

"Okay, let's go back to Sacred Heart."

"Aren't you forgetting something?" growled Kay.

"Oh right," Joe said and opened his wallet. He took out all the money he had, and under the watchful eyes of Kay and the sergeant, he counted the bills. He must have miscounted earlier when he promised to pay one hundred dollars for the return of Jane's backpack because all he had was eighty-six dollars. "It looks like I am a little short. I'll have to come back with the rest later."

Kay snatched the bills from Joe's hand. "What the fuck do you mean you're short?" He pushed Joe and pawed for the wallet.

"Hey, hey," Joe protested. "It's only fourteen dollars. I'll get it and bring it to you later."

Kay moved toward Jane. "Tell you what, Preacher." He spit when he said the P in preacher. "I will keep that backpack until you do. And you listen here, I don't want no lousy fourteen dollars. I want five hundred dollars—minimum."

Joe stepped between Kay and Jane to negotiate, but Kay never gave him the chance. With all the speed and power of a trained fighter, Kay hit him hard in the side of the head with a crushing right hook. The army had trained Joe in close combat techniques and before that his father had taught him how to box. It was an essential skill for a skinny, redheaded Irish kid growing up in an Italian neighborhood. Joe had been in his share of fights. Some of them had been real bruisers, but he had never been hit by another man as hard as Kay hit him.

He must have lost consciousness because the next thing he knew he was on the ground, and Kay was standing over him with a muscular arm cocked to deliver another blow.

"I ain't fucking with you, Preacher. I want five hundred dollars."

Joe held up a hand and struggled to get up on one wobbly knee. He stared up at his attacker. "I'm sorry, son, I don't have that kind of money."

The cocked arm let go and Kay's fist landed square on Joe's eye, sending him back to the ground. Instinctively, Joe tucked himself into a ball, using his arms and hands to cover his head and drawing his legs in to protect his abdomen. Kay circled around him, kicking him in the back as he went.

The voice of an army instructor screamed in Joe's head. "You are out of position, soldier! Never turn away from the enemy. Get on your back and strike with your feet."

Joe rolled from side to side trying to get clear so he could kick Kay or trip him, but the toe of Kay's sneaker kept finding the back of Joe's head and kidneys, forcing him to stay covered. Just when he feared Kay meant to kill him, the onslaught stopped.

Joe risked a look to see why. Jane had the barrel of his Beretta M9 pistol pressed against Kay's temple as she dug it into the man's flesh. The sergeant, who stood next to her, wide-eyed with his hands up, urinated in his boxer shorts.

Tweaker Mike slithered out of his corner laughing and shouting in a nasally, high-pitched voice, "Shoot the fucker, shoot the fucker."

Jane's voice was menacing. "You know, Mr. Kay from Hays, I am not well. I have something called undifferentiated schizophrenia with acute bipolar mood disorder. My doctors say I have a tendency toward irrational anger and even violence. I experience severe visual hallucinations. That means I see things you can't. Sometimes those things tell me what to do. Right now, they are telling me to squeeze the trigger on this gun and pump all the bullets into your skull."

She removed the gun's barrel from Kay's skin. Its sight had cut him and there was a bloody dimple where she had pushed the weapon as if she'd tried to drive it into his brain. She backed away, holding the gun steady and aimed at Kay's face. Squatting, she whispered to Joe. "Can you move?"

"Yes," He rasped as he struggled to his feet and stared into Kay's snarling face, resisting the urge to strike him. "May God forgive and heal the anger inside you."

"Fuck that," she said, rising to a shooter's stance with both hands on the pistol. Her eyes were narrow and fixed on Kay—center mass. "You and Boxer Shorts go stand over there by Tweaker before I kill every one of you."

CHAPTER SEVEN

Barry

Dr. Barry Lieberman sat with his right leg crossed over his left in the armchair he'd placed next to the large, green Chesterfield sofa in his office at the start of the session. The blinds were closed, and the lights were dim. Soothing classical music played low in the background. Brahms: Symphony No. 4, Barry thought.

He watched the second hand of his Vacheron Constantin Fiftysix sweep around its elegant face. The luxury timepiece cost as much as a year of medical school, not that the son of Harold Lieberman had to pay for his own schooling. He'd paid for the watch, though. It was a symbol—a reward he'd given himself on the tenth anniversary of establishing his practice. He'd turned exile to this backward college town into success, and by doing so, poked his finger in the eye of the American Psychiatric Association.

His patient was a twenty-four-year-old, blonde-haired, blue-eyed beauty named Emily Baker. Her slender, long-legged body was stretched out on the sofa. Her eyes were closed, and the white silk button-down blouse that molded tight around her firm, compact breasts rose and fell with the slow rhythm of her breathing.

A saline and dextrose hydration solution dripped from an IV bag into the median cephalic vein near the elbow joint of Emily's left arm. Fifteen seconds before, Barry had injected a small dose of a hypno-stimulative drug he had custom-made to his specifications by a lab in Mexico, into the piggyback port on the intravenous line.

The drug started working as soon as it hit Emily's bloodstream, interacting with multiple neurotransmitters and dopamine receptors in her brain. It affected Emily in two seemingly contradictory ways, rendering her almost unconscious while at the same time, stimulating the centers in her brain responsible for attention and focus. It was the perfect combination for rapid, deep hypnosis. Thirty seconds after the injection, the drug had removed all distractions from Emily's consciousness, allowing her subconscious to hyper-focus on just one thing, and that was the hypnotic induction script Barry recited.

"Emily, can you hear me?"

Her response was whispery and faint, like it was carried by the breeze of her breath from a distant place inside her. "Yes. I can hear you."

"That's very good. I want you to focus on my voice and only my voice. It's all you will hear until I tell you it's okay to hear something more."

"I only hear your voice, Doctor."

"Very good, Emily. Now, I want you to imagine you and I are walking down a long, windowless corridor. You are carrying a pack on your back. The pack contains all the things you want us to talk about this week. Do you feel the pack?"

"I feel it."

"We've been walking for a long time, and your pack is growing heavy."

"Very heavy," she whispered.

"Up ahead, the corridor opens into a great room. The room is empty. No one else is around. It's just us."

"Just us," she repeated.

"You've been here before. The room is familiar to you. You are comfortable here. Safe."

"I know this place."

"At the far end of the room, there is a bank of elevators. One is waiting with its doors open. We step in, and the doors slide shut. You have grown tired from our long walk. The elevator car is taking us down to a place where you can rest. You grow sleepy as the numbers of the floors we are descending through appear above our heads. Starting with number ten, I want you to imagine the numbers counting down. Can you see them?"

She paused for a second before confirming, "Yes. I see them."

"Let's say them out loud together as they appear."

Barry started, and she joined in on the countdown. "Ten... nine... eight..."

"Good. Keep counting. With each floor we pass, the weight of your backpack grows. You are straining to keep it on your shoulders. When we reach floor number six, the pack is almost too heavy for you to bear."

Emily's face reddened and the tendons on her neck bulged as she strained against the imagined weight of the pack. She grunted from the exertion. "Seven," grunt, "six," grunt. "It's so heavy."

"You are finding it harder and harder to stay awake. When we reach the third floor, you cannot bear the weight of the pack any longer, and you ask me to carry it for you."

"Five," grunt, "four," grunt, "three... please carry the weight for me, Doctor. I am so sleepy."

"We are nearing the bottom now. When we reach the first floor, I will take the pack from you, and you will fall into a deep sleep until I wake you by telling you it's time to go back up. While you are sleeping, you will feel nothing."

"I will feel nothing," grunt, "two."

"Emily, I've removed your pack. The weight is gone now."

She stopped straining, and her face and body relaxed. Her lips parted and formed an "O," but no audible word escaped her mouth.

He watched her breathing for a moment. Then he checked her pulse and pulled back her eyelids to make sure her pupils were round and even. There was a tiny risk of a stroke with the stimulant, but that wasn't the only reason for checking her eyes. No eye movement indicated she was in a deep trance state, and Emily's eyes were motionless.

Just to be sure, because he was always sure, he pricked the back of her hand with a pin he kept for the purpose. Nothing. Emily was in a deep hypnotic trance. So deep in fact, he could cut her open and she wouldn't so much as twitch. He'd fantasized about performing vivisection on other hypnotized patients. Maybe someday he'd find the right subject and do it, but not today, not to Emily.

He checked her IV and dialed up the flow. She would receive the full 400 milliliters over the hour. The hydration solution was already flushing the fast-metabolizing drugs from her system. As always, the first thing she would want to do when she woke was urinate.

Getting the drugs out of her system was as important as getting them in. The drugs he used were not approved for use in the US, or anywhere else for that matter. Should she have an accident on her way home, it wouldn't do to have such questionable agents show up in a medical examiner's report.

Barry retrieved the black leather-bound notebook he used to keep track of their sessions and glanced at the first page before flipping to a new entry. Emily suffered from mild schizoaffective disorder, which meant she showed signs of both schizophrenia and intense mood fluctuations. In her case, bouts of depression. Her symptoms were on the mild-to-moderate side of the scale. She had minor feelings of persecution, saw momentary glimpses of things that weren't there, and was troubled by memories of childhood abuse that her parents maintained never happened. Barry was not so sure.

Her disease had not prevented her from completing her education or working for her wealthy father's real estate business, but her periodic feelings of depression could be severe. There had been times when she'd refused to leave her bed for days.

Like many of his patients, Emily had come to him for treatment to avoid hospitalization and antipsychotic medication. Auburn was a small community where everyone, especially the more privileged of its residents, knew one another and knew one another's business. Emily's parents wanted to avoid the embarrassment of her illness, and Emily wanted to avoid the weight gain associated with the usual drug therapies. Though not a symptom of her illness, Emily's vanity was extreme.

Barry specialized in treating mental illness with minimal medications and no antipsychotics. He used deep hypnosis to train patients to manage and, in some cases, alleviate their symptoms altogether. The big gun in his therapeutic arsenal was a technique he'd developed as a young resident at The Johns Hopkins Hospital in Baltimore called Disassociated Observer Exploration Therapy—DOET for short.

DOET had made him famous for a brief time. He'd published papers describing the technique in all the respected psychiatric journals and for a while, he'd been a frequent speaker at major psychiatric conferences and medical schools all over the world.

But that was all a long time ago. Barry's mood darkened when he thought about it. The little minds who ran the American Psychiatric Association had shut him down. He glanced at his $72,000 watch. Fuckers. He doubted many of those unimaginative bureaucrats had one.

A *National Geographic* magazine sat nearby with the unmistakable shape of Sugar Loaf Mountain rising over Guanabara Bay on its cover. He'd thought many times about packing it all in and heading down to Brazil where his techniques would be more appreciated or at least less regulated. He could set up in a wealthy section of Rio de Janeiro and spend all his free time on the beach. Barry ran his finger along Emily's cheek and thought about Carnaval and women who shed their clothes without hypnosis.

He'd created his DOET technique to solve the single most difficult challenge in psychiatry. Mental illness exists only in the heads of the sick, and the mentally ill are not reliable sources of information about their condition.

The solution Barry invented was inspiring. That's what *Psychology Today* had said in their May 2004 edition. Barry had figured out how to use hypnosis to create and embed a personality fragment into a patient's subconscious and use that embedded fragment, what he called the observer, as a kind of black box for the human psyche. The DOET observer's job was to stay hidden and record all the thoughts, feelings, and stimuli that the patient experienced, then play them back when asked during analysis.

The establishment of the observer personality was tricky. Using deep hypnosis, Barry created the observer in the patient's subconscious. Once the observer was defined, Barry embedded trigger phrases in the patient's mind that, when recited while the patient was under hypnosis, caused the patient's personality to switch between the observer and their own. The effects could be quite dramatic, but do it wrong, and the patient developed something akin to a split personality.

Once in place, Barry spent several sessions coaching the observer on what he wanted them to observe. When the observer was ready, Barry gave them a name. He could have called them anything, even used the same name for every patient, but he opted, instead, to use a simple pattern to create personal names for each patient's observer.

The names he used were a combination of a positive adjective and the patient's first name. For males, he'd use adjectives like strong, as in the case of Strong Steven, or capable, like Capable Curt, and for women, he tended to use pretty and sweet.

Barry brushed a lock of Emily's hair away from her forehead and leaned in close. "The little girl could not sleep because her thoughts were way too deep," Barry quoted *Alice in Wonderland* in his softest and most pleasant voice. "Her mind had gone out for a stroll and fallen down a rabbit hole. Wake up, Sweet Emily, and tell me all about your week."

The phrases served as the trigger to draw out the observer. "Sweet Emily, are you there?"

Emily's body stretched and moaned. "Yes, I am here."

"Let's talk about how Emily's week went. Shall we?"

Emily Baker's lips replied. "Okay, Dr. Barry."

"Let's begin with how she felt this week. Did she have any sad days?"

Sweet Emily described several times when Emily was sad during the week, pointing out the situations she observed that may have provoked the feelings.

Last Thursday, she relayed, two days after their last session, Emily had been overwhelmed by requests at work which made her feel inadequate. She'd obsessed on these feelings of inadequacy, causing her to feel anxious and depressed. The negative feelings peaked on Friday and were gone by Sunday.

Barry took notes in his precise, fine, block lettering, making an entry to remind himself to plant reinforcing hypnotic suggestions in Emily's subconscious for dealing with stress and denying her feelings of inadequacy.

"How about the shadow? Did Emily see the shadow this week?"

The shadow was a presence Emily sometimes detected or felt when she entered or left a room. Neither she nor Sweet Emily had been able to describe the shadow beyond a darkness in Emily's peripheral vision, as if something large just out of her sight was casting a shadow over her.

Emily was afraid of the shadow, and before Sweet Emily had been established, she refused to talk much about it. Sweet Emily, by design, had no such fear. She was eager to talk about it and based on what he'd learned from her about how Emily felt when seeing the shadow, Barry suspected it was linked to a repressed memory of some troubling childhood event. Something very bad had happened to Emily Baker when she was a small girl.

"Yes. She saw the shadow Monday evening after work."

"Tell me more about the shadow."

"She got a better look at it this time."

"Go on," he said, noting the new fact with interest.

"There might be a face in the shadow."

"This is very good, Sweet Emily. Can you describe it?"

"No. It wasn't clear, but it looked like a face."

"Try harder to remember some details. Was it a man or a woman?"

"I don't know, Doctor Barry. I didn't get a good look at it."

"That's okay. She will see it again, and when she does, you need to try harder to identify more features."

"I will try my best," she said like a small child promising an admonishing parent she will do better.

"I know you will, Sweet Emily. Is there anything else you want to tell me?"

"No, Doctor."

Barry closed his notebook and checked his watch. There were twenty minutes remaining in the session. The rise and fall of Emily's breasts and the inviting position of her long legs caught his attention. He studied her and realized he was becoming aroused. He stood and checked the door to make sure it was locked. It was always locked during sessions, but he still double-checked. Caution came easy to a disciplined mind.

"Sweet Emily, how do you feel?"

"I feel nothing, Doctor." It was exactly the response Barry expected.

"I am going to touch you now. Is that okay?"

"Yes."

"It's okay if you feel Emily's body react. Don't be afraid."

"I'm not afraid."

Moving quickly, he unfastened the buttons on her blouse and eased her bra over her breasts, exposing her pink nipples that stiffened at his touch. He kissed each one, caressing her areola with his tongue.

Barry could not recall when his sexual compulsions had pushed him over the ethical and legal line he was crossing now. He'd been getting away with it for many years, though there had been some close calls.

He didn't succumb to his urges during every session or with every patient. Some patients were much more fitting of his vivisection fantasy. There were times, though, like today, when the animal lust he felt was too strong to deny and besides, he saw no reason to deny it.

His hand moved down and slipped under her loose-fitting sweatpants. He recommended all his patients wear loose clothing to maximize their comfort and for some, his access. His fingers probed her pubic hair and mound and found her moistening vagina. She moaned and arched her back. Her conscious self was not aware of his fingers probing, but he'd given permission for Sweet Emily to feel them.

He pleasured himself while he fondled her. He considered removing her clothes and mounting her, but there wasn't time. That required an entire session. When he was finished, he cleaned himself off and returned her clothing to its proper position.

He sat in the chair studying her, thinking about Sweet Emily's claim of a face in the shadow. Barry had first learned about the hallucination four months ago, during Emily's early sessions, before there was a Sweet Emily. In all their talks and subsequent Sweet Emily observations, the shadow had always been just that—an indiscernible shadow.

This had been the first time Sweet Emily reported the shadow might have identifying features. This could be a significant breakthrough, or it could be something to be concerned about. The observers could stray and even turn on him. It had happened before. He'd keep an eye on Sweet Emily.

If it was real though, it could be quite good for Emily. Finding a root trigger for a hallucination like this was rare psychoanalytic gold. Barry had always suspected the shadow was tied to some early memory of sexual abuse. Now, maybe they would identify that and bring that memory to closure. He felt no guilt in the situation's irony. He never felt guilt or shame. That is what made him so successful. That is why he had the watch.

Checking to make sure all her buttons were fastened and clothing in place, he removed the IV from her arm and placed a Band-Aid over the small puncture wound.

"Emily?"

There was no response. There would not be. Emily wasn't there yet.

"Sweet Emily?"

"Yes."

"Do I have your attention?"

"Complete, Doctor."

He uttered another phrase from *Alice and Wonderland,* "Wake up, Sweet Emily, the white rabbit has left you, and all the magic you felt is running down your face." This phrase returned Sweet Emily to her hiding spot in Emily Baker's subconsciousness, and switched Emily back to the forefront, though still in the deep hypnotic trance state.

He gave her kidneys a few more minutes to dispose of the drugs, and then he escorted her back to consciousness.

"Emily, can you hear me?"

"Yes."

"We are going to take the elevator back up now."

"Okay."

"Your pack is light. We've unloaded everything that was in there today."

"That's good."

"The elevator door is open. We step in and the car begins to rise. It's time for you to wake up now. It's time to hear and feel the world around you."

She opened her eyes and smiled. "Hello, Doctor. How did we do?"

"Fantastic, Emily. I think we made genuine progress today. How are you feeling?"

She wiggled around on the sofa, causing him to worry she might feel something amiss with her underwear.

"Refreshed." She sat up and stretched. "Energized as always."

"Good," he encouraged. She swung her long legs off the sofa, and he stood with her. "Do you need to use the restroom?"

"Yes. You know I always do."

"You know where it is."

He waited as she disappeared into his small personal washroom. After she reemerged, he escorted her to the office door and unlocked it.

"Why do you lock the door during our sessions?"

She had asked the question before as had others. It did not worry him. "I do it with all my patients," he explained. "We wouldn't want anyone walking in while we were talking," he gave her a fatherly smile, "now, would we?" He opened the door, and they stepped out into his waiting area. Kara, his receptionist and general office manager, sat behind her desk.

Emily waved as she glided past Kara's desk, heading for the exit. "See you next week," she called over her shoulder as she opened the door, letting in the morning sun and fragrant eastern Alabama spring air.

Barry walked out with her, checking for any residual effects of the sedative. He watched as she settled into a gleaming convertible sports car.

"New car?"

"Yeah, it's a Porsche. Daddy bought it for me."

"Nice." He considered telling Kara to raise Emily's rates. "Drive safe."

Emily gave him a thumbs-up and sped off. He walked back into the waiting area and stopped at Kara's desk. She handed him a Post-it note.

"A Dr. Neerja Patel called for you."

He stared at the 404 area code. "Hmm. Looks like Atlanta. Did she say if she was with Emory?" he asked.

"Georgia Tech."

He rubbed the short graying bristles of his southern gentlemen's beard, some might call it a goatee, catching the lingering scent of Emily on his fingers. "Georgia Tech… Neerja Patel… doesn't ring a bell. Anything else?"

"Nope. Your next appointment is at two with Kyle." She wrinkled her nose when she said his name.

"Kara, that's not a nice face."

"He smells. You know he does. You make me disinfect your sofa after every session with him."

He nodded. Kyle was one of his vivisection candidates. "Yes, personal hygiene can be a problem for some of our more troubled patients."

She studied her computer screen. "Also, remember you are giving that talk to the rising pre-med kids at the university this evening."

Barry thumped his receding hairline with the palm of his hand. "That's tonight?"

"That's tonight," she confirmed.

He took the note to his desk and punched in the numbers on his phone.

A woman answered with a lyrical southern Indian accent. "This is Neerja."

"Dr. Patel, this is Dr. Lieberman. I'm returning your call."

"Oh yes, Doctor. Thank you for calling back so soon."

"Certainly. How can I help you?"

"Yes. I think it is I who can help you," she said, piquing his interest.

"Okay, Doctor. How can you help me?"

"This morning, only, I was visited by a man named Joe who was inquiring about a patient of yours."

"A patient of mine? Do you have a last name for this man?"

"Yes, of course. I have his card somewhere." The line went quiet for a moment. "His name was Joe Carroll."

The name meant nothing to Barry. "I am afraid I don't recognize that name. You said he was inquiring about one of my patients?"

"Yes. He was asking about Jane Carter."

The blood in Barry's veins turned to ice water. "This man was asking about Jane?"

"Yes. Jane Carter, only."

Barry inhaled until his lungs were full, then he moved the phone away from his mouth and released a long hiss that he was sure Neerja could hear. On a bookshelf near the sofa where he had been enjoying Emily only moments before, sat a book on Quantum Computing by Dr. Margaret Carter.

He'd almost allowed himself to forget about them. Maggie had been dead for many years now. Jane was confined up in Tuscaloosa. He'd made sure of that when he testified at her commitment hearing many years ago and every other year since at her evaluation hearings.

"Why would he be at the university asking about Jane Carter?"

"I don't know how to say this, Doctor, but she has been living here."

He rocked forward in his leather desk chair. "Jane? Jane's been living there? That's not possible."

"I was surprised myself, but people here say she has been living in the library on campus."

"In the library," Barry almost shouted.

"I know, I know," Neerja replied. "After what happened to poor Maggie, and how, pardon my colloquialism, Jane lost her mind, I thought she was in an institution somewhere."

"Yes, I thought so too." His heart thumped. How could she be out? This had to be a mistake. He tried to recall the date of her last evaluation hearing. My God, it had been over three years. Could it be he missed a hearing? The pandemic had disrupted all the normal processes. Could those fools have let her out without consulting him? "Dr. Patel, are you sure it's Jane Carter we're talking about?"

"Yes."

"Is she still there?"

"Well, you see, that's the reason I called. This Joe Carroll gentleman told me he put her on a bus this morning to Auburn."

Barry swallowed and scratched a quarter-sized scar on his neck. "She's coming here?"

"That's what Mr. Carroll said."

"Oh, this is all quite a surprise. I will keep an eye out for her. Someone needs to make sure she is okay."

"I thought that might be the case," Neerja agreed.

"Thank you, Dr. Patel. Is there anything else for us to discuss?"

"No. I don't think so. Goodbye, Dr. Lieberman."

Barry hung up and began pacing around his office. "Shit. Shit. Shit," he said through gritted teeth. They let her out, and now Sweet Jane Carter is coming here. "Kara," he shouted.

Kara opened his door, "You bellowed?"

"I need you to get a file for an old patient—someone I treated before you joined me. Her name is Jane Carter, and it's been over eight years so I think her file will be in the storage locker."

"Yeah. If she is not an active patient, then her file will definitely be out there. Is this urgent?"

"Yes, it's fucking urgent," he barked.

She retreated with a shocked expression on her face.

"Oh my. I'm sorry for that," he said in his most apologetic tone, which was an act. He was never sorry about anything. Ever.

Still looking put out by his outburst, Kara nodded. "I will go look for the files right now," she said and left.

He dug his cell phone out of his pocket and searched his personal contacts until he found Dr. Carl Walker, who was a staff psychiatrist at Bryce Mental Health Hospital in Tuscaloosa.

Dr. Walker answered in a squeaky voice that did not match his sizable physiology. Last time Barry had seen Carl, the man must have been tipping the scales at 350 pounds, all of it lard. He was a walking cardiac event waiting to happen.

"Dr. Lieberman," Carl squeaked. "Why would such a renowned hypnotist be calling a lowly shrink such as me?"

"How is the weight management plan coming, Carl?"

"Fuck you, Barry and the Freud you rode in on. Have you taken your hypnosis act to Vegas yet?"

"Very funny. Maybe if you learned more about my technique, you could get out of that nuthouse and make some real money in private practice."

"Hmm. I don't think the American Psychiatric Association would approve of the term nuthouse. Oh, but then again, you're used to the APA's disapproval." Carl made a squeaky, snickering sound. "What was that therapy of yours they shit all over? It was called Duh, right?"

"I think you mean DOET."

"That's right, Doh."

"Yeah, yeah. Look, I need a small favor."

"What's that?"

"I need you to look up an old patient of mine in the hospital's database. I need to know what her status is."

Jane had not been sent to Bryce. Barry had made sure of that. He wanted her in a secure facility, which Bryce was not. Jane had been sent to Taylor Hardin, the state's sole forensic mental institution, but the institutions were affiliated, and he knew Carl could see her records.

"There's a process for requesting this kind of information. What's the matter? No staff? I thought you were raking in the dough, or is that

DOET, treating those rich obsessives and addicts in your private practice," Carl made a piggish snort at his own joke.

"This is more personal. Something came up about this one, and I am curious what happened to her."

"Ah, old girlfriend?"

If the slob only knew. "Don't be ridiculous. I was treating her for severe schizophrenia. She was remanded to the long-term care facility there."

"Doesn't sound like you had a successful outcome."

"No. She was prone to some violent behaviors. There was a tragedy down here, and we thought it best for her to have constant inpatient care."

Barry gave Carl Jane's full name and heard Carl's fat fingers pounding on a keyboard on his end.

After a moment, Carl whistled, "Wow. You didn't tell me she was a forensics case. Hmm. Well, she didn't come here. She went to Taylor Hardin about seven years ago, and it says she was released to a community facility." He paused as if he was reading. "Looks like she's been there for two years."

"Interesting." Barry said, hiding the anger he felt for not being consulted. "You have a contact at that community facility, Carl?"

"Hold on."

Barry heard crunching on the phone and imagined Carl stuffing corn chips in his mouth while searching his computer screen for the information Barry wanted.

"Here it is," Carl's mouselike voice said, hindered by what must have been a mouthful of the chips or whatever he was crunching on. "It's the Brookhaven Behavioral Wellness Center. Desiree Philips is the name of the head facility director. She's not an MD or a PhD. Looks like an MBA with a nursing background."

Barry didn't much care about the woman's credentials. They chatted for a few more minutes before Barry ended the call and used his office phone to call the number Carl had given him.

"She walked away," Desiree Philips said when Barry asked about Jane's current status.

"I beg your pardon. What does that mean?"

"It means what I said. About four months ago. She walked away. She told some of the staff here she wanted to resume her studies in mathematics, and she walked away."

"She's a fugitive then?"

"Not really. Maybe technically. We had her symptoms under control. She was doing very well before she left. Highly functional."

Barry's right eye ticked. "I see. Well, what are you doing to find her?"

"Nothing. Like I said, She's highly functional. The purpose of Brookhaven is to get people back into life after long-term hospitalization. She's there. She's been active in a local college doing a lot of math tutoring. She even tutored a few of the staff who are pursuing higher level degrees."

"Is that so?"

"Yes. I'm sure you know, Dr. Lieberman, Jane Carter is a genius."

"Yes. She was," Barry admitted.

"No, Doctor. She is still a genius. She's not the same person who did those things years ago. She made substantial progress over the years, and we had a lot of success with her medications. Sweet Jane is not the same person who went into Taylor Hardin."

"What did you call her?"

"Sweet Jane. It's an odd quirk she has. She insists everyone call her Sweet Jane. Sometimes she sings her name."

Barry remembered the old song. He sang, "Waiting down on the corner. Sweet Jane, Sweet Jane, oh, Sweet, Sweet Jane."

"That's right, Doctor. You know the song. She would sing the whole thing. Did she do that when you were treating her?"

"Yes. It was one of her favorites." He did not sing the verse about splitting apart that always seemed to strike too close to the origins of that name. "You said she was not technically a fugitive. What does that mean?"

"It means we recommended to her caseworker out at Hardin to give her some time to return before involving law enforcement. She's at the end of her commitment. Dr. Fischer, the MD who oversees the treatment and clinical assessments here is ready to sign off on her release. We were planning to advise the panel to let her go, but unless she returns before the next hearing, that's not going to happen."

"When is that?"

"Next month. She has three weeks to come back. If you know where she is, please tell her to come home."

When the call was over, Barry placed one more call to the Lee County Sheriff's office in Opelika. Most of the senior officers knew him from the work he did with the department. His hypnosis techniques, "the show," as Carl referred to it, proved useful in helping crime victims and witnesses recall details. He had worked with the department for many years, and he was considered a friend of the current sheriff.

He spoke with a commander he knew and asked him to be on the lookout for Jane.

"Is there a warrant out on her?" the commander asked.

"I don't know. That's more your business, but I know she's strayed away from the center where she lives, and she shouldn't have. As far as I'm concerned, she should still be in a state hospital."

Barry told the commander what he knew about her coming in by bus that morning, and he asked for the department to contact him the minute they picked her up as it could be a medical emergency.

Before he hung up, the commander asked, "Is she dangerous?"

Barry smiled. Maybe they would solve his problem for him. "Hard to know without talking to her. That being said, I'm concerned, and you should be too."

After the call ended, he closed his eyes and thought about Jane. Still Sweet Jane, after all these years. She'd once been something to look at and enjoy. Raven hair, gray eyes, tanned and toned from the running she did. He could almost see her stretched out on his office sofa. It was brown leather back then. Lying there, inviting with all her clothes removed. He rubbed himself and could hear the soft, edgy rock song "Sweet Jane" playing in his head.

CHAPTER EIGHT

Joe

They made it back to the car without further conflict, but not without Jane pointing the gun at two men who approached them on the street. Joe's right eye was swollen shut and his jaw clicked when he moved his mouth. He sat behind the wheel, working his jaw until he was sure Kay's punch hadn't dislocated it, while Jane peered out the back window with the gun trained on the encampment.

"Let's get out of here," she said.

He started the car but did not pull away. "Give me the gun first."

"Why?"

"Because you are going to point it at the wrong person and get us shot. Thank God there are no bullets in it."

She pointed it at him, and he grabbed it and dropped it on the back floor.

They drove to his apartment and after returning the gun to its case, he sat on his sofa with an ice pack on his bruised face, watching her spread the contents of her backpack on the living room floor. She inspected each item and closely examined her tapes and medications.

"Missing anything?"

"I don't think so."

"Anything else of mine in there?"

She shook her head. "No."

"You should not have taken the gun."

"It's a good thing I did." She looked up at him. "You have a black eye."

"So do you."

They both laughed.

"What's on all those tapes?"

She shrugged. "Nothing much. Just notes and lectures. I like to listen to them." She looked up at him. "The Others don't bother me so much when I listen to them."

Joe assumed the Others were the hallucinations she threatened the men at the encampment with.

"I heard what you told that Kay guy. Do the Others really tell you what to do?"

"Not so much. I told him that to scare him. I don't want to talk about the Others."

"I know you say you do not believe, Sweet Jane, but you might find healing in Jesus and prayer. I have seen so many lives changed. I've seen suffering reduced and people healed through faith and prayer. I am a great example. I was broken for many years, and now, through the Church and Jesus Christ, I am whole. Would you like to try praying with me?"

She giggled in a somewhat uncontrollable manner. "Pray to who?" She spat. "I'd be better-off praying to the Others. At least they'd answer."

"God is out there. He's ready to hear your prayers."

"Oh, now he's ready." She turned to face him and crossed her legs under her. "I know you are a good man, Joe. I also know you have seen terrible things and experienced loss. God is how you handle it. It works for you."

"It works for billions of people," he replied.

"Once, I thought I understood what God really was," she said. "I understood the math, and I thought I knew what was real." She rubbed her hands over the ancient shag carpeting that covered the floor. "I am not talking about matter and energy which are just emergent aspects of our reality, but the true essence of everything. I think I can say I might have been this close," she held up her hand and brought her forefinger to within a couple millimeters of her thumb, "to understanding God even better than you, Joe."

"What do you mean, Jane?"

"Sweet Jane."

"Right, Sweet Jane. What do you mean?"

"When I was young, I loved math. I still do, but it is harder for me now. I can't focus for long without being interrupted, but back then, I was something. It's in my genes. My father was so good at it. Numbers and equations were like words to him that he could use to explain anything. He just saw the math in everything, and he taught me how to see it too."

"He sounds like he was a great dad."

"Yes. He was."

"What did he do?"

"He was a rocket scientist."

"Come on."

"He really was. We lived in Huntsville, and he worked on propulsion systems at Marshall Space Flight Center. It was amazing. He would walk me through the formulas they used to calculate pressures and stresses and all kinds of things. I was nine, and he was teaching me advanced calculus and astrophysics." She smiled a melancholy smile. "It was the happiest time of my life."

"May I ask what happened to him? It's okay if you don't want to talk about it."

"I don't mind. He's been dead for over twenty years. He had an aneurysm." She paused for a moment. Her eyes glistened. "A blood vessel burst in his big, beautiful brain when he was driving home from the lab. He passed out, and the car flipped in a ditch. Of course, he didn't die right away. That would have been too merciful for the big man in the sky. He lingered in the hospital for a few days, but they could not save him."

"I'm sorry."

She shrugged. "Me too. I prayed then, Joe. Oh, how I prayed to that God up there," she looked up. "Please, please save my daddy. But he didn't."

"I'm sure he heard your prayers."

"Yeah. Right. But what? He was too busy? Anyway, my mother was a math person too, although she didn't have my father's abilities, and she wasn't a physicist. She was into computers."

"Was she a computer programmer?"

"You could say that, but very advanced. She was more on the theoretical and hardware-design side. She worked on the systems at the space center. That's how they met. When he died, she worried I would not progress in my development. She decided to teach and in doing so, give me access to university programs while I was still in grade school. It wasn't such a stretch. She already had a PhD, and she had come from an academic culture. Both her parents were teachers here in Atlanta."

"Do they still teach?"

"My grandparents?"

"Yes."

"No. They are dead. All of them."

"I'm sorry."

She shrugged. "Everyone dies. Anyway, Mom looked for a university with advanced math and science programs within driving distance of them, and we moved here."

"She taught at Georgia Tech?"

"Yes. Did I tell you that already?"

"I think I put it together myself," he said, thinking it best not to tell her about his conversation with the professor at the university and feeling bad for deceiving her.

She thought about that for a moment then continued. "I grew up on that campus. While other girls were cheerleading and fooling around with boys, I was auditing advanced mathematics and physics classes." She looked around and appeared confused. "Where are we going with this again?"

"I think you were telling me how math brought you closer to God than religion could."

She looked down for a moment and mumbled something inaudible, then looked up at him with a strange, faraway look in her eyes. "We are all just vibrations in the field, Joe. That's all we are. That's all everything is."

"I am not sure I understand. Does this have something to do with entropy?"

She tilted her head in a classic puppy dog look. "What?"

"When I asked you what you believed in yesterday, you said entropy."

"I did? Hmm. I guess I did. Well sure, entropy does explain much."

"And I just thought it was the second law of thermodynamics," he joked.

She laughed, and it was a light, joyful laugh without the darkness and sarcasm behind most of her laughter. "That's right. You're not only an almost-priest. You are an engineer. You must have studied thermal and fluid dynamics."

"Sure did. I can even do calculus. Well, I could once. It's been a while."

She drew her knees up to her chest and gazed up at him. Her eyes glowed with an intellectual fire. Yes, she was far more than bright.

"Entropy is one of the true organizational principles of the universe. It is why we perceive time as we do, and it explains all macrophysical phenomena, including us."

"Are you saying entropy is God?"

"No. It's as a scientist named Boltzmann described, everything seeks equilibrium. All systems, be they biological or inanimate, have a single driving purpose."

Joe adjusted his ice pack. "Yes, to serve God."

She smirked, and the dark sarcastic tone was back. "Hardly. Everything. You, me, the sofa, the building, this horrible rust-colored carpeting, are all manifestations of the distribution of energy. Everything is in motion, and we are all heading to the same place."

"Heaven," he proclaimed.

"Only if heaven is a very cold, dark, and empty place. Face it, Joe. We are all just radiators."

"Seems very pessimistic to me," he said. "I still don't understand how math got you closer to understanding God."

"Maybe not closer to God," she said. "As I don't believe in him, but closer to understanding reality at the most fundamental level. That's the real purpose of science."

"Religion too," he said.

She grew silent as if contemplating a rebuttal, then without speaking, she stood and started pacing about the room.

"What's wrong?" he asked.

She tugged at her hair. "I don't know. Today has been a little overwhelming. I am feeling anxious." She began searching through her things.

"What are you looking for?"

"Cigarettes. I know I have some somewhere." She glared at him. "You didn't take them, did you?"

"No."

She continued rooting through her things, mumbling obscenities as she did, until she located a ziplock bag containing her cigarettes and a small plastic lighter. The red and white cigarette box was crushed, but she was able to salvage part of a cigarette. Igniting the lighter, she seemed ready to light up right there in his living room.

"Let's go out on the stairwell," he suggested. "I'll say my afternoon prayers while you smoke."

He grabbed his breviary, and they went outside into the early afternoon heat. They sat on the stairs, and she lit up the partial cigarette. She made no attempt to blow the smoke away from him, and he moved up a step to stay clear of it.

"What?" she asked.

"I don't like the smoke. I never understood why people do it."

She sucked in a big drag and blew a plume of smoke into the air. "Because it feels sooo good."

He was grateful she did not blow it into his face.

"How often do you pray?" she asked.

"I pray without ceasing."

"That sounds absurd, and I know it's not true. I have been with you for two days now, and I haven't seen you pray much at all."

"It's a reference from the Bible. From the book called Thessalonians. 'See that no one returns evil for evil; rather, always seek what is good for each other and for all. Rejoice always. Pray without ceasing.'"

She pointed her cigarette at the book in his hand. "Is that in there?"

"No." He held up the well-worn, black, leather-bound book with its multicolored page-marking ribbons dangling from it. "This is a special book called the Liturgy of The Hours. Some call it the breviary. It mostly contains words from a part of the Bible called Psalms."

"What's with all the ribbons?"

"They help me keep track of where I am." He fanned the pages. "There's a procedure that must be followed when using the book. It's kinda technical. You see, it has many sections containing special prayers, hymns, and readings that differ by the season, day, and even time. The ribbons are how I keep track of what to read and when."

He opened the book to the section for today's daytime prayers and showed it to her.

She flicked her cigarette into space and moved up a step to sit beside him.

"See," he said. "We are in what's known as Ordinary Season, so I am going to begin my reading from this section." He flipped the pages to a section marked by a white ribbon.

"What do you mean by ordinary?"

"Ordinary means it's not Christmas or Easter or some other special time."

"This seems very complicated."

He shrugged. "I told you it was technical. I was overwhelmed by it myself when I first started, but it's pretty easy once you get the hang of it. Though I have to admit, we spent a lot of time in school learning the procedure."

"This is what they teach in priest school?"

"Among other things."

He read aloud from the passages for the midday prayer as she looked over his shoulder. When he was done, he crossed himself and flipped to another section of the book marked by a green ribbon.

"Now this one is from the book of Psalms."

He half read and half chanted the verses. Then he crossed himself again and selected a page from a section marked with a blue ribbon. She studied him like an anthropologist might study a shaman from a primitive Amazonian tribe performing a ritual.

"Get ready, I am going to sing a song."

"Oh boy, this ought to be fun," she said.

He sang a small hymn. Then he crossed himself again, said a few more words, and closed the book.

"Do you have to pray like that every day?"

"Yes. I do it five to seven times a day, not counting Mass, which you saw this morning, the rosary, and all the other times throughout the day I ask God for strength and guidance, which," he looked at her, "I have done a lot of recently."

"No kidding. I guess you do, pray ceaselessly. Seems excessive."

"Sweet Jane, it's not excessive. It's not a burden for me at all. I look forward to my prayer time—especially the time I spend with this book."

"I don't get it."

"Get what?"

"The whole belief in God thing. I mean, you told me this morning that you killed people when you were in the army."

Her words stung him, and he winced. "That's something I prefer not to talk about. What is your point?"

"Well, you saw all kinds of suffering in Afghanistan."

"I did, and I've seen plenty of it here too. That includes the suffering of those men we dealt with this morning."

He guessed where she was going and headed her off. "You are going to ask me if God is good and all-powerful why does he allow bad things to happen. Right?"

"Yes. I guess I don't understand how you can believe in him when he lets so much bad happen. I mean if he was truly all-powerful and all good, why let all the shit happen in the world? Why not just wave a hand and make everything better?"

She was staring at him. A dark purple half-moon shaped bruise cupped her right eye, and he could see a tear form in its corner. She wiped it away before it could break loose and roll down her cheek. It occurred to him she did not wear any makeup, and he thought it unusual, since other than a few nuns, and maybe some of the elderly parishioners, he did not see many women without makeup. No foundation or concealing agent hid the blemishes on her skin or filled in the creases around her mouth and eyes. The harsh afternoon light made her bruised and unaccentuated face look older than she was, but it also revealed a fading natural beauty that he imagined was once something special before the fortunes of her life had changed.

As he studied her and considered her question, he knew what she was really asking wasn't as abstract as why God allows bad things to happen. It was why he let those things happen to her. She wanted to know why God took her daddy away, and why he gave her a debilitating and stigmatic illness that prevented her from doing what she loved.

It would not do for him to spout the philosophical arguments as to why moral and natural evils existed. She was not seeking explanations as old as Saint Augustine about free will giving man the capacity to commit evil or to hear how he and the Church believed, as she did, that natural events in the world were governed by the laws of physics as defined by God. She did not want to hear how nature's adherence to those laws, not God's intercession or lack thereof, caused natural evils like car accidents, hurricanes, and earthquakes.

"I cannot tell you why God allows bad things to happen to us. All I can say is, as a Christian, I believe in His goodness, and I have faith that we are all part of his purpose, even if we are unable to comprehend the fullness of that purpose."

She considered his words for a minute, then she stood and said, "I got to pee," and went back inside his apartment.

They did not talk much the rest of the day. She slept on his sofa while he made some phone calls. One was to Father Carlos to let him know they recovered her backpack and were safe at his apartment. He told him about their dealings with the men in the encampment but omitted the more harrowing details, making a note that his omission constituted another lie which he would need to confess. His next time in the confessional promised to be longer and more interesting than usual. He told Carlos he planned to drive her home to Auburn in the morning and endured his mentor's protests and warnings.

She was still sleeping when he went back out on the stairs for evening prayers. He ordered a pizza before he began, and just as he finished, a heavy man smelling of pepperoni and sweat labored up the three flights to deliver it to him.

Hungry, they wolfed down the whole pie. Afterward, there was little for them to do, so they took a walk around his complex, and she talked about living in California. He wanted to know if she went to the beach often, and she explained Berkeley was in San Francisco where there were not many beaches—at least not the kind for swimming.

She said she liked to run when she was there and would run along the bay near the Golden Gate Bridge. They avoided any more talk of God, and by the time they returned to his apartment, the sun was setting, and he knew she had completed both her graduate and undergraduate degrees in mathematics and physics but, as Dr. Neerja had already told him, she had been unable to finish her PhD.

"It's where it all fell apart," she'd said.

The next morning, he woke before the alarm for the second day in a row, but this time it was from his own cries. Maybe it was the memories resurfaced by Jane going through his things, or the feel of the gun in his hand, or the violence of the day before that triggered it.

Whatever had brought it on, he found himself back on that cold, predawn hilltop where he'd feared he'd lost his soul so many years ago.

By God's grace, he'd not thought of that place since giving himself over to the Church. But here he was, sobbing and drenched in sweat from a nightmare that was more recall than subconscious fabrication with the image in his head of a dead Afghan child clutching an ancient AK-47 in his fine, dirty hands and his tiny chest ripped open by bullets fired from his rifle.

He rolled off the bed and kneeled in prayer, begging for forgiveness, and once again pleading for his own healing. After he was done, he stumbled to his feet and made his way to the kitchen where in the dark, he located an unopened fifth of bourbon stashed in a remote corner of his small pantry.

It was the first item he placed in the pantry when he moved in. It was there not to drink, but to serve as a constant challenge to his faith in God. It was his own temptation from Satan that he would overcome as Jesus had in the desert. Not once in four years had he been tested— not in all that time had he come for the bottle. Not until tonight, and with the bottle in his trembling hands, he prayed again for strength.

The cap seemed to come off on its own and he raised the open bottle to his nose, breathing in the bitter smell of the liquor. A smell that was at once wonderful and revolting. He raised the bottle to his lips. This was it, years working with Caleb, years of prayer and restraint about to be washed away by the amber liquid. He could already taste it. He could almost feel the burning in his throat and the warmth in his stomach, and the blissful numbness that it promised to deliver.

"No!" came a shout from the sofa.

Joe had forgotten Jane was there, and startled, he almost dropped the bottle. "Sweet Jane," he called.

"No!" came the reply.

He considered the bottle for a moment and then dumped its contents into the sink and turned on the faucet to wash its stench away. "You shall not put the Lord, your God to the test," he said and went into the living room to check on her.

She was still asleep and appeared to be having her own nightmare. He considered waking her and noticed she had her earbuds in. The microcassette deck was on the floor beside her, and its red power light glowed.

He got down on the floor and removed a bud from her ear and pressed it close to his own. He could hear a woman's voice.

"Now Jane, sweetheart, when you type this next section about Shor's Factoring Algorithm, please make sure you spell Shor's name correctly. It's S H O R, not S H O A R…"

The voice went on to dictate what sounded like complex technical information including a description of formulas with the requisite Greek letters used in such expressions. The use of the term sweetheart intrigued him. Could this be Jane's mother? Was she dictating something for Jane to write?

At that moment, he realized Jane's eyes were open. She was staring at the square patch of light projected on the ceiling from the window, but he could not tell if she was awake.

He placed the earbud on the pillow next to her head. "Sweet Jane," he whispered.

"My name is Jane, you bastard," she whimpered. Then she closed her eyes and seemed to fall back to sleep.

CHAPTER NINE

Joe

It is an almost arrow-straight, 110-mile shot on Interstate 85 from Atlanta to Auburn. They waited until Atlanta's notorious morning traffic had subsided some before setting out from Joe's apartment at a few minutes after ten. This had allowed him to attend the morning prayer session at Sacred Heart which also gave him an opportunity to smooth things over a little with Father Carlos.

He'd left Jane alone in his apartment when he went and found it impossible not to worry about what she was doing while he was gone. It turned out he had nothing to worry about. He'd returned to find her still asleep on the sofa with no hint of cigarette smoke in the air and no evidence she'd tampered with his footlocker, which he had moved to his bedroom for safekeeping.

After a quick pass through a Dunkin' Donuts drive-through— coffee for Joe and a bag full of chocolate donuts and a bottle of water for Jane, they were on their way. She devoured the donuts, then removed a composition notebook and a mechanical pencil from her backpack and began writing. Whatever she was doing, it had her complete attention. She ignored all his attempts at conversation. When he tried to ask her what she was working on, she shushed him. They'd driven over ninety miles, and the only sounds she had made were inaudible mumbles and the occasional curse that followed the snap of broken pencil lead. She did not say a word until they pulled off the highway for gas.

"Where are we?" she asked.

"We just crossed into Alabama. We need gas."

"I was hoping you were going to stop soon. I have to pee real bad," she said as she put her notebook back in its large ziplock bag and shoved it into her backpack.

"You should have said something. I would have stopped earlier."

"I guess I was a little absorbed in the work. I haven't been able to focus like this in a long time. I might've wet my pants if you hadn't stopped."

"Well, then I will be sure to thank God for that blessing. What are you working on?"

She shrugged. "It's a math problem. It's part of something called the Millennium Prize."

"I never heard of that. What is it?"

"It's a contest that was started back in 2000 to solve seven possibly unsolvable math problems. The prize for solving any of the seven is one million dollars. The one I'm working on deals with the Yang-Mills Mass Gap. It's a kind of mathematical proof of Quantum Field Theory. Though it's not really necessary."

"Why isn't it necessary?" he asked, intrigued.

"Most physicists think Quantum Field Theory is already settled science, so the proof is not considered all that important, but it has kept me occupied for the past few years. It was the first thing I started working on when I started getting better."

"Well, now I have all kinds of questions," he said as he brought the car to a stop alongside a gas pump.

She opened her door. "I need to go to the bathroom first." Before she got out, she said, "That Tweaker Mike guy took all the money I had. Can I borrow some more from you? I'll pay you back when I win the million dollars."

He laughed and gave her one of the fresh twenties he'd withdrawn from an ATM that morning.

She stuffed the bill into her pocket and asked, "Do almost-priests make a lot of money?"

He laughed louder this time. "No. I draw a small salary for my office work at the parish. My parents left me some money, so I have enough to get by until I am ordained."

"Do priests make a lot of money?"

"No, but they don't have many expenses either."

"Oh. Well, I will pay you back."

"Of course, when you win the million dollars."

"Right," she said. Then she jogged toward the store. A bearded man with skin tanned dark from too much time under the southern sun was sitting propped up against an ice freezer holding a cardboard sign with NEED HELP scrawled in black marker. The man stood and met Jane at the door. She stopped, shifting her weight from one foot to another and talked with him before going inside. The man noticed Joe watching him and nodded. He touched his eye to show he saw Joe's bruise and smiled, revealing several missing teeth.

The gas pump clicked, indicating the tank was full. Joe debated going inside to check on Jane but decided to wait for her instead. He leaned back on the car and watched the dark-skinned man peer into the store through the door. Joe's phone rang and its screen showed Father Carlos as the caller. It was almost noon, and Joe knew his mentor must be calling moments before he was due to conduct midday Mass and wondered at the timing of the call. He touched the display to answer.

"Good morning, Father."

"Joseph," Carlos spoke in a hushed urgent tone with Sacred Heart's bells tolling the call to Mass in the background.

"Yes, Carlos. Is something wrong?"

"I don't know. That's why I am calling. Are you okay?" His mentor sounded distressed and unusually concerned about his wellbeing.

"Yes, of course. Why do you ask?"

"A man called here looking for you as I was preparing for the Mass. He said his name was Dr. Lieberman. He said he heard you were helping an old patient of his."

"Jane?"

"Yes. Joseph, he seemed quite concerned about her and you."

"Me?"

"Yes." Carlos's voice lowered even more. "He said you might be in danger."

"Why would I be in danger?"

"He said this woman, this Jane you are with, she was committed to a forensic mental hospital, and she should not have been released."

The gas station's door slid open, and Jane stepped out. She had a plastic bag in her hand, and she handed it to the dark-skinned man. The man looked inside and gave her a hug. He removed a bottle of water and guzzled its contents down while Jane lit two cigarettes. She handed the man one, and they stood near the store entrance smoking. They were both laughing and talking as if they were old friends, and Joe was so taken by their apparent familiarity he almost forgot Carlos was on the phone.

"Joseph, are you still there?"

"Oh. Yes. I am sorry. What is a forensic mental hospital?" he asked, but he had a feeling he already knew the answer.

"It's where courts send people with mental health issues who commit crimes. Dr. Lieberman said she was sent there eight years ago."

The cadence of the tolling bells in the background changed, and Joe knew it was time for the priest to make the procession to the altar. One of the other deacons would be holding the heavy book of the gospels and waiting in Joe's place for Carlos to join him in the church's center aisle.

"Joseph," Carlos whispered, "I have to go. I will call you after Mass. Be careful, my friend. This Dr. Lieberman said she could be quite violent."

Jane was still smoking and carrying on with the dark-skinned man. After what they'd been through, Joe could not imagine her being a danger to him, but she'd threatened others with a gun—a gun that was never loaded, he reminded himself.

"Okay, Carlos. I will be careful."

Jane noticed he was watching her. She smiled and waved. He waved back. She finished her cigarette, then took several from her pack and handed them to the man. Joe climbed back into the car and waited for her while considering Carlos's warning.

He thought about how to ask her about this Dr. Lieberman. She would wonder how the doctor connected her to him, and Joe knew the only answer was Neerja Patel. Revealing that would mean admitting he'd talked to people at the university about her, and he thought she might view his prying as a betrayal. Of course, he could not simply ignore what Carlos had told him. Maybe he'd learn more when Carlos called back. Joe was still thinking about it when she climbed into her seat, humming to herself and smelling of cigarette smoke.

"Do you know that man?" he asked.

"No. Why?"

"You seemed like old friends."

"He asked me for money, but he said what he really wanted was a sandwich." She paused for a moment then added, "And a beer."

"I see. I would think after what happened to you at the bus station you would be more cautious around strange men." Joe meant strange transients, but he felt that was not a very Christian thing to say.

"He was nice. He saw the bruises on my face and asked if I was all right. He wanted to know if you hit me." She looked at him. "I said no."

"That's good."

"He had a Georgia Bulldogs shirt on, and I told him he was on the wrong side of the border, and that made him smile."

"Well, you sure seemed to connect with him, and it was very nice of you to buy him something to eat."

"Technically, you bought him something to eat."

"Yes, and I want the full twenty back when you win the million dollars."

Smiling, she pushed back a lock of her black hair and peered at him through those translucent gray eyes in a way that stirred him such that if not for his convictions, might challenge his vow.

She turned and looked out the window as he navigated the car back onto the highway.

After a few moments she said, "Have you ever lived on the street, Joe? No money, no place to sleep, worried about the basics like where to get food and even where to go to the bathroom. Have you?"

Joe swallowed. He'd spent many nights sleeping in doorways and underpasses, cold, wet, and only concerned where his next bottle would come from. "I've had more experience with that than you might think, Sweet Jane," he rasped, unable to conceal the pain in his voice.

She studied him for a moment, seeming to process the secret he'd shared. "Then you know how it feels. That man's name was Rodney. He said he wanted beer, but what he really wanted was someone to treat him like a person."

Joe swallowed again and felt a little ashamed. Here was Jane, who professed to have no faith in God, teaching him the Gospel. He thought about reciting some passage from scripture but settled on crossing himself and saying a silent prayer of thanks for the lessons of the Lord. They drove on in silence for the remaining 25 miles until they reached the small college town of Auburn, Alabama.

At a stoplight near the center of the town's business district, Joe asked the question he'd never thought to ask before. "Where am I taking you?"

"Here," she said.

"No. I mean what address. Where is your home?"

She looked around for a moment. "It's been a while. It's close." She pointed to a restaurant where groups of college-aged men and women were distributed around the outdoor tables and waiters and waitresses shuttled between them. "I used to eat there with my mother."

"Okay. How do we get to your house?"

She guided him through the busy streets until they reached a residential area away from the main campus but still close enough to be an easy bicycle ride or long walk. Jane had told him her mother used to ride her bike to class.

Her directions led them down a street lined with pecan trees and aging mid-sized homes. Several were run-down and needing significant repairs with sagging gutters and overgrown lots, but there were many well-kept homes too, with newer high-end cars in the driveways and signs of recent renovations. She had him stop in front of one of the more dilapidated structures.

Like most of the homes on the street, it appeared to have been built during the first half of the last century. From the outside, it looked to be about the perfect size for a mother and daughter. Joe guessed it had two bedrooms upstairs and maybe a bathroom. He figured there was a kitchen, living room, and perhaps a dining or sitting room on the main floor. Some of its faded sky-blue siding had pulled away and was dangling into the wild remains of shrubbery that formed a border between it and the overgrown lawn. A covered front porch Joe imagined may have once hosted a pair of rockers had flaking white posts and handrails. Ample dark windows were trimmed in mildew-stained white with navy blue shutters, also in need of paint. An ancient rusted For Sale sign hid in the tall weeds. Obviously, no one had lived there in many years.

"Home sweet home," she said. "Boy, it looks like shit."

"This is your house?"

"Yep. At least it was. I'm not absolutely sure now."

"You're not sure?"

"Well, there are still some legal things to go through, but I am here to fix all that."

She turned to him. "Thank you for bringing me here." She stuck out her hand, and he shook it. Then she retrieved her backpack from the back seat, opened her door, and scrambled out.

"Wait," Joe called after her. "I can't just leave you here." He turned off the car and got out. He caught up to her and followed her along the walkway and up the weathered porch steps to the front door where she dug out a single, worn brass key from one of the side pockets of her backpack.

She held it up to him. "Here goes nothing."

The key fit into the dead bolt lock. She wiggled it for a moment, then the tumbler turned, and the door pushed open.

He followed her inside and tested a light switch in the entrance hallway. He was not surprised to find the power off. The interior floors were bare except for a layer of dust—no rugs and no furniture. The sounds of their movements echoed throughout. A staircase facing the front door rose from the center of the main hall to the upper floor. What appeared to be a dining room opened off one side of the stairs and a similar-sized room on the opposite side was accessible through a pair of closed French doors.

Joe tried to open the French doors, but they wouldn't budge. "These are locked," he said.

"Keep out of there," Jane snapped in a harsh tone. Appearing to realize her reaction had stunned him, she added, "It was my mother's office. I am not ready to go in there yet."

They made their way into the living room, which was illuminated by bright sunlight streaming in from large windows that ran along the back wall and overlooked a weed-choked yard.

Jane gazed out the window for a long moment. "That was once my mother's rose garden."

"How long has it been since you've been here?" Joe asked.

"Seven years, ten months, and eight days, but who's counting?" she said in a low, wistful voice.

"Where have you been all this time?"

"I told you," she said without turning to face him. "I got sick."

"I know you got sick, but where have you been?"

She leaned her head on the window and stared into the tangled mass of the ruined garden.

"What happened to your mother? I don't think we ever talked about her. Is she still alive?"

Jane did not answer at first. Then she mumbled something inaudible under her breath and whirled around to face him, her eyes wild and her face contorted in building anger. "Don't talk about my mother. It's none of your fucking business what happened to my mother!" she shouted.

He stepped toward her, planning to put his arms around her. "Jane, please calm down. I did not mean to upset you."

"Sweet Jane!" she screamed.

"Yes. I know. I keep making that mistake."

She stormed up to him. "Why?"

"Why what?"

"Why do you want to know about my mother? Why do you need to know? What would you do if you knew? Would you make me go back? I won't go back." She began to pace around with her hands gripping the straps of her backpack. "I won't go back!" She screamed in his face. "You can't make me."

He tried to wrap his arms around her, but she pulled away and ran down the hall. She stomped up the stairs, and somewhere above him he heard a door slam. Her practiced motions made him guess it wasn't the first time the old house had witnessed that scene.

Joe waited for her to return, and when she didn't, he explored the rest of the main floor, avoiding her mother's office. Like the lights, the faucets didn't work either. No power, no water—he could not leave her like this. If this was her house, she could not stay here without water or power. He would help her get that situated. He was not sure what he'd do if this was not her house. "In for a penny, in for a pound," he said to himself.

Digging out his cell phone from his pocket, he brought up the app he used for prayers when he did not have his breviary and performed his midday obligation. It was past 1 p.m. when he finished. Father Carlos should have completed Mass by now. He was about to call him when he heard Jane come down the stairs.

"Joe," she called.

"Yes, Sweet Jane."

"I am sorry."

He found her sitting on the bottom stair smoking a cigarette. It looked as if she had been crying. She was writing or drawing something in the dust on the floor with her finger.

"Are you okay?" he asked.

"I don't know. There's a lot for me to process here. I am a little overwhelmed."

She continued to draw something in the dust. It looked like a mathematical formula.

$$i\hbar \frac{d}{dt} |\Psi(t)\rangle = \hat{H} |\Psi(t)\rangle$$

"What are you doing?"

"Smoking. Sorry. I know it bothers you."

"No. I mean what are you writing on the floor?"

She looked up at him and then back down at the formula etched in the dust. She seemed surprised by the marks as if she had not been aware of making them. She laughed.

"Look at that. Just a doodle. It's a form of a famous equation by a physicist named Schrodinger. You might have heard about his cat."

"His cat?"

She giggled. "Yes. There's a famous exchange between Schrodinger and Einstein involving a hypothetical situation where a cat, Schrodinger's cat, can be both alive and dead at the same time." She looked up at him. "That's kinda right up your alley, isn't it?"

"I don't know what you mean."

"Sorry, bad joke on the whole Jesus Christ resurrection thing."

"Yeah, I get it now," he said. "So tell me more about this equation."

She smiled that vow-challenging smile at him. "I will if you buy me lunch."

CHAPTER TEN

Barry

Barry had set out early that morning. It was a three-hour drive from his home to the Brookhaven Behavioral Wellness Center in Tuscaloosa. He had an 11:00 a.m. appointment with Desiree Philips to discuss how, as she had put it, they let Jane Carter *just walk away*.

It was a mindless drive with all but the last ten miles on the same highway. He punched the address of the center into his navigation system, set his cruise control to five miles over the speed limit, and thought about the call he'd had yesterday afternoon with the priest.

After getting the phone number for Joe Carroll from Neerja Patel, Barry had discovered it belonged to a church in Atlanta. The woman who answered the call told him Joe had taken the day off, and she'd connected him with a Father Carlos Santiago, who, she said, was the closest thing to Joe's supervisor.

When he got Father Santiago on the phone, Barry learned Jane had been at the church, but the priest had been unwilling to provide any information about her current whereabouts. He wouldn't even disclose if Jane had left Atlanta. All Santiago would agree to do was take a message.

Barry had tried to frighten the priest in hopes of getting more information by telling him the only message he had for Joe was Jane was a fugitive from a forensic mental hospital and might be dangerous. Barry pressed for Joe and Jane's contact information. He told Santiago Jane might kill somebody if the police did not catch her soon. Barry even told him the Church might have legal trouble if Santiago did not tell him how to reach them, but the recalcitrant priest would not budge.

Barry had no reservations about lying to a Roman Catholic priest or anyone else for that matter. He'd spent over twenty-five years probing and manipulating the human psyche, and Father Santiago was just another psyche to be probed and manipulated.

Dr. Barry Lieberman did not believe in God, guilt, or morality for that matter, only self-interest. In Freudian terms, he didn't have much of a superego. He was too well acquainted with the psychological and physiological processes that formed what a layman may call a conscious, and a foolish priest might say is a soul, to subscribe to such artificial behavioral constraints. From Barry's perspective, Nietzsche was right—morality made us cringing, cowardly, and submissive creatures. Barry was a nihilist, plain and simple.

Jane Carter's file peeked out of the leather computer bag on the passenger seat next to him. Kara had dropped it off at his house last evening after she had spent all of yesterday afternoon digging through boxes of old records looking for it. Her efforts were somewhat incidental, however, as he needed no file to remember Sweet Jane. He scratched at the oval scar on his neck. He would never forget her. She had made sure of that.

As unnecessary as the file was, it provided some useful reminders of the progression of her disease, even if it was light on specifics. The bulk of it comprised narratives of their forty-six sessions. He had crafted the narratives in such a way to frustrate legal discovery. Only he knew their secrets. Nothing in them was falsified, but he had omitted important details about his techniques, and of course, he also neglected to mention how entertaining their sessions had been.

Without those details, any other physician would conclude Barry had delivered quality care using sanctioned psychotherapeutic techniques. His treatment had been effective in reducing Jane's symptoms. Her condition had been improving right up to the point of the setback and its tragic consequences.

The file indicated Jane Carter presented severe symptoms of schizophrenia. These included frequent visual hallucinations, feelings of persecution, and extreme delusional thinking which centered on her obsession with perceived reality and quantum mechanics. It showed Barry had used a combination of hypnosis and cognitive behavioral therapy to surface the root causes of Jane's illness and had coached her on how to manage her symptoms. It also indicated, in accordance with Jane and her mother's wishes, Barry had not prescribed antipsychotic medications. The file made no mention of DOET.

When Barry first met Jane, she and her mother, Maggie, were still living in Atlanta where Jane was under the care of psychiatrists from Emory Mental Health, and the prognosis was not good. After a year of treatment, Jane's condition had only worsened. The Emory doctors had said she would soon require regular inpatient care. They told her mother it was time to face facts—Jane would be in and out of mental hospitals for the rest of her life.

The Emory people had followed the typical, unimaginative diagnostic and therapeutic protocols. They had tried different medications and varied doses with minimal success. Jane claimed the medications they prescribed interfered with her cognitive abilities, making it impossible for her to perform complex mathematics which impeded her ability to complete her doctorate. After a while, she quit taking the pills and, not surprisingly, things got worse.

Maggie Carter had contacted him after learning about his drug-free treatments. The APA had already condemned his Disassociated Observer Exploration Therapy and Johns Hopkins had sent him packing. It had been three years since an old family acquaintance who happened to be an alumnus and large donor to Auburn University, had convinced him to set up a practice in the small town where the family friend assured him there were plenty of wealthy people in need of therapy. The friend had been right, but Barry had grown bored with treating run-of-the-mill depressives and substance abusers. Jane was a welcome challenge, and Maggie was stunning.

He desired Maggie from the first moment they met. She was not only attractive, but she was also smart and confident. No one told Margaret Carter what to think. Looking back, that had been her undoing.

Maggie had done her own research and concluded as she had told him, "She didn't give a shit what the doctors at Emory said about him. She wanted him to treat her daughter." She'd been convinced by the old article in The New York Times that had called him *a visionary whose technique was a much-needed innovation in a field whose treatment options had changed little since the 1950s.* A framed copy still hung in his office.

Of course, the *Times* had written that before the American Psychiatric Association issued the bulletin calling into question his use of drug-induced deep hypnotic trances and the unknown effects of the observer construct. He squeezed the steering wheel until his knuckles whitened. With a few taps on a computer keyboard, some bureaucrat had redefined his therapy from revolutionary to quackery. Barry had threatened the primacy of antipsychotic medications and psychiatric establishment dogma, and they had shut him down for it.

"Well, fuck them," he said out loud. He glanced at his watch. He no longer gave a damn what the APA, the psychiatric profession, the media, or all of human fucking kind thought of it or him.

Soon after their first meeting, Maggie and Jane had moved down to Auburn, and he and Jane began meeting every Monday afternoon. At first, Jane had been difficult to hypnotize. She fought it, and it took many sessions for him to build the Sweet Jane observer persona. Like constructing a house on difficult terrain, every psychological brick had to be laid with care in her subconscious. In the end, though, brick by brick, Sweet Jane grew. It was only when it was too late that he'd discovered how much.

Like her mother, Jane was a beautiful woman. She had a small, athletic body, maybe a little too firm for his liking. Back then, he tended to be attracted to the more classical, curvy female form. For that reason,

Maggie had been more his type, but that had not prevented him from sampling Jane.

It was difficult, but he kept his urges under control during the early observer building sessions, though not out of any sense of decency—he didn't even know what that was. He kept them in check to ensure Jane was reaching a trance state suitable for his needs.

Getting there with new patients was always a challenge, and it was especially difficult with Jane. The eager patients sometimes faked trance state to try to please. That could be dangerous, and he was always on the lookout for such deceptions. The skeptical ones like Jane, on the other hand, were guarded and denied the trance state. They had to be worn down. They all eventually were, but until they were, their hypnotic trances tended to be fragile. Patients like Jane clung to consciousness, and until a path down to the deep state was found, they were too easy to wake and too risky to use.

After Sweet Jane was established, though, their sessions became routine, mostly. Once Jane was under, he would surface Sweet Jane and question her on what had troubled Jane since their last session. Using the information from the observer, he'd plant what he called "tuning suggestions." These were little coping techniques he'd ask her to try when she'd become anxious or experienced hallucinations.

There were other times, however, when the mood took him, and he would use their sessions for his own needs. The memories of these times with her came flooding back, and he shifted in his seat as he became aroused.

Jane's auditory and visual hallucinations were the most well formed of any patient he'd ever treated. Most schizophrenics suffer from some inability to discern imagined thoughts from reality. It's one of the defining characteristics of the illness. Some sufferers believe they are persecuted by nonexistent government or spiritual entities. Some see aliens around every corner or are tormented by fictional characters. Jane saw versions of herself which she called Other Janes or simply the Others.

Jane had created an elaborate delusion to explain the hallucinations based on her extensive knowledge of quantum physics and something known as the multiple world interpretation of quantum wave theory.

Over their many sessions, Barry had learned more about physics, and in particular, quantum wave theory than he'd ever cared to know. He never quite understood everything she talked about, but he'd understood enough to know how the theory supported her delusion.

Quantum wave theory had been invented in the early part of the 20th century by an Austrian physicist named Erwin Schrodinger. According to Schrodinger, the subatomic particles that make up everything in the universe really don't exist in the way we think of them. They are not discrete physical things but are, for lack of a better term, interpretations of vibrations in the quantum fields, much like how sound is just the interpretation of vibrations in the air.

Another physicist named Hugh Everett described how Schrodinger's theory required the existence of multiple adjacent realities. Everett theorized that since our reality is based on one interpretation of waves moving through quantum fields and there must be a near infinite number of possible interpretations, there had to be a near infinite number of realities or, as Jane put it, universes.

Jane had come to believe the Other Janes appeared to her because of some quirk in her brain that allowed her to connect with other instances of herself existing in adjacent Everettian universes.

Barry struggled with Schrodinger's and Everett's theories. He believed they were irreconcilable with real-world experiences. He'd debated these things with Jane during many of their sessions, pressing her on how it could be that particles could shift from one universe to another based on their position in the wave and yet there was no evidence of such shifts in the real world.

On more than one occasion, he'd rapped his knuckles on his desk to show it was hard and real, and then he did it again a second later to show it was still just as hard and real. How could that be if the particles that made up the desk might not exist in our reality from one point in the wave to another?

She'd laughed and told him there had been thousands of experiments proving what he thought was impossible was happening all the time. She said he was thinking on too simple of a scale. A small percentage of particles in the desk were guaranteed to move out of this universe between raps, but the number of particles in the desk and in him and in the surrounding environment was on the order of one followed by dozens of zeros. There were plenty of particles to share with alternate universes in any given instant without impacting the solidity of the desk.

From out of nowhere, a tractor trailer appeared in front of him, forcing him to hit his brakes and veer into the other lane. Barry laid on the horn as he sped past the slow-moving truck. In his rearview mirror, he glimpsed the driver giving him the middle finger. "Asshole."

Barry cared little about the science. The only thing that had interested him was how Jane had used it to rationalize her hallucinations. That was unique.

Jane perceived the appearances of the Others as random, complaining she had no control over when or how many Other Janes would cross over from their universe into hers. She used to say it was like having an alternate universe walkie-talkie in her head and no way to control when it was on and what channel it was tuned to.

But Barry, using Sweet Jane, figured out most of the appearances were not random. They were triggered by frustration and stress, feelings Jane had experienced often as the disease and its treatment affected her academic pursuits, and he set out to use Sweet Jane to fix it.

Before Jane, Barry had never encountered a patient who saw multiple versions of their self as recognizable separate beings. He'd had plenty of experience with a condition known as Dissociative Identity Disorder or multiple personalities. In fact, he had conceived of the idea for his DOET treatment by using hypnosis to surface the alternate personalities in Dissociative Identity Disorder cases, but sufferers of that disorder never experienced their other personalities as separate visible beings as Jane did.

Barry's experience with alternate personalities had taught him to be cautious, as he knew once an alternate personality took root, it was almost impossible to eradicate. He had a rule when building the observers—they were never to "switch" and dominate the patient's personality unless under his hypnotic control, and they were never to be known to anyone else but him. Observers were to remain, as he said in his writings, *absconditum, et observet somnia*—hidden spies, his spies, there to observe and report, not participate.

Barry broke the stay-hidden rule with Sweet Jane. The nature of Jane's hallucinations had led him to try something he should not have tried. He had allowed Sweet Jane to surface in Jane's conscious mind, becoming an alter ego that Barry directed to help Jane deal with her frustrations and curtail the appearances of the Others. In essence, he had camouflaged Sweet Jane as an invisible Other who would act as a guiding voice in Jane's head to help her with the precipitating stressors. Then he used their sessions to instruct Sweet Jane on how to manage Jane's thoughts. His intent had been to use Sweet Jane to control, and with time eliminate, the appearances of the Others, and then put her back in observer mode.

Sweet Jane had other ideas, though. She became a distinct personality, and he lost control of her. He didn't realize how much he'd lost control until it was too late, and she had turned on him. Sweet Jane had started out as his Eliza Doolittle and had become his Frankenstein's monster.

I know what you've been doing to us. After eight years, that phrase still echoed in his head.

"I know what you've been doing to us."

It's what Sweet Jane had said during their last session.

Barry shuddered from the memory. That session began like any other session. After he'd sedated her and stepped her down, he began with his usual opening question. "Sweet Jane, will you come out and talk to me?"

"Yes. I am here."

"Good girl. How was our Jane this week?"

"Not so great, Doctor Barry. I don't think she can hold it together much longer."

"What happened?"

"She's been stuck in a loop, obsessing over a mathematical proof. It's all she thinks about. It gnaws at her night and day, making it hard for us to concentrate on anything else. She thinks about it so much she forgets things, important things, like turning off the stove or buttoning her shirt. It has Mother so afraid she won't leave us alone. Soon we won't even be able to help Mother with her book."

Maggie had published a handful of textbooks in her field of computer science. At the time of her death, she had been working on a book on artificial intelligence and quantum computing. Jane was helping, and Maggie had planned to list her as a coauthor—a mother-daughter thing.

"What about the Others?" he had asked. "Have they appeared this week?"

"All the fucking time. We see them everywhere."

"We've talked about this, Sweet Jane. You need to help her relax and reduce the frustrations she feels. That's the only way we will stop the Others."

Sweet Jane had laughed, and the laugh had startled him. He had never heard an observer-personae laugh before or express such anger.

"Doctor, you don't give a shit about Jane."

He'd been taken aback. "What do you mean by that? Of course, I do."

"I know what you've been doing to us, Doctor. I know you fuck us when we are here. Don't you think I can feel that tiny dick of yours sliding in and out of us?"

He'd almost cried out when she'd said it. He'd jumped to his feet and began pacing. "What is this? Some new delusion?"

She'd laughed again. This time it was a sinister laugh.

"Delusions don't leave bruises. They don't leave panties bunched up and wet. They don't leave scrapes inside you."

He had always been careful, but there were times when animal drive overcame prudent caution. Other patients had claimed similar things over the years, and in those cases, he'd been able to deflect the charges by claiming the accusers were experiencing false memories and maybe even side effects from the hypnosis. He'd had some close calls, and he'd done what he needed to do to get out of them.

"It is time for Sweet Jane to sleep now and Jane to wake," he'd said in the calmest voice he'd been able to manage.

"Oh, she's not asleep, Doctor. If I'm awake, she's awake."

He tried to ignore her. "It's time to wake Jane."

"I know what you are doing to us," she'd hissed again.

"I am going to count down from five now, Sweet Jane. When I reach three, you will begin to feel very sleepy. When I reach one, you will sleep, and you will forget this session."

"I know what you are doing to us."

"Five... four."

"I know what you are doing to us."

"Three... two."

"I... know... what... you... are... doing... to...."

"One."

She had gone as he had commanded, but she had not gone far. He knew she was still there. He had to remove her, had to kill the Sweet Jane persona, but he never got the chance.

"Exit now." The voice on his navigation system startled him. He had been in such deep thought about Jane it was a miracle he'd not caused an accident. The exits for Tuscaloosa were on him before he knew it, and he almost passed them by. If it wasn't for the insistent urging of the car's navigation system to "exit now," he might have wound up in Mississippi.

CHAPTER ELEVEN

Joe

The outdoor tables were all taken at the restaurant where Jane said she had gone with her mother. They settled for an inside booth by a window. Spread out on the portion of the large table not occupied by the plates and cups from their lunch were two paper placemats with their local advertisement sides flipped over and their blank sides turned up. Their blank sides, however, were no longer blank, as from the moment they'd slid into the booth, Jane had used a pen borrowed from a waitress to scrawl formulas and diagrams to illustrate the wave theory of quantum mechanics and the work she was doing on the Millennium Prize.

Joe's head was still spinning from all the math. It had been over twenty years since he'd last looked at a calculus problem, and he doubted he'd be any less confused had it been yesterday. Jane was a different person while she explained the steps in the mathematical proofs. Confident and clear, her words streamed out with no hint of agitation or doubt, and at no time did she pause, as she often did during their other conversations, to mumble to herself or gaze about. At one point, he'd interrupted her, calling her Jane instead of Sweet Jane, and she did not correct him. It occurred to him this was the true Jane—the one hidden behind the illness.

He studied one of the diagrams she'd drawn. It showed a series of undulating waves and at the crest of each wave, she'd placed a neat little circle. He tapped one of the circles with his finger. "So you are saying the electrons that orbit the nucleus of atoms that make up everything do not exist as particles like we were taught in high school. Instead, they are actually part of these waves, and they only appear as particles where the waves reach these high points?"

She pushed away a lock of hair that had fallen across her pale face like the wing of a blackbird and shrugged. "Yes, it's referred to as wave-particle duality, but it's more than just the electrons. It's all particles. That includes the quarks and leptons that make up the rest of the atom."

"I thought those were protons and neutrons."

She shrugged again. "Protons and neutrons are made from quarks and leptons. It's all described in the standard model. We can discuss that on the next date."

He raised his eyebrows at her flirtatious comment.

"Back to waves and particles," she said. "It's technically not right to say the particles only exist when they reach the right energy level. They are more likely to be real," she made air quotes with her fingers, "at those points, but the weird thing is they don't appear as particles at all until they interact with other particles; it's like the waves only behave as particles when they need to be particles. That's called the measurement problem."

He sucked the remaining soda from his glass, making a loud slurping noise as he drew in the last drops. "Wow. I think that blew my mind. I mean particles are only real when they are needed?"

"As bizarre as it sounds, it's true. There are experiments that have been done since the early 1900s that demonstrate how light and electrons behave one way when they are measured as waves and another when they are measured as particles."

"What are the waves made of? I mean, this all sounds familiar. Isn't it what Aristotle called the ether? I thought that idea was abandoned long ago."

She grinned at him. "Well, you wouldn't be the first to make that comparison. Current thinking is the waves are ripples in energy fields, and the fields themselves are made of particles at what we could think of as a neutral energy level."

"Wait a minute. You said particles don't exist until these energy waves reach a certain level, and now you are saying the waves are made of those particles."

"No. I said particles don't appear real to us until we go looking for them, and they are easier to find at certain energy levels. They are not detectable in their neutral energy state. They need to be excited."

"Excited?"

"That's the vibration part."

"Okay. Now I am lost. Waves are made of particles that are not particles until they are."

"Exactly. You are not so lost. You know what a field is right? I mean in terms of graphs and math." She pointed at one of the graphs she'd drawn with intersecting lines forming four quadrants.

He took a bite out of a pickle spear and shrugged. "Sure. It's an area where any point can be reached through coordinates X and Y. Unless, of course, it's three-dimensional, then you need a Z coordinate."

"You got it. And if we add the time dimension, we need a T coordinate, but we will leave that one for another discussion."

He smiled. "Our next date."

"Right." She smiled back. "If we stick to three dimensions, we can think of a field as a cube or a matrix."

He nodded.

"In basic Quantum Field Theory, the universe is made up of overlapping matrices with all the points in each matrix having a range of possible energy values and an average base or neutral value physicists refer to as a vacuum."

"I thought a vacuum was when there was nothing at all."

"There may be no such thing as nothing. What we call it is not important. What's important is the fields are made of potential particles that are only recognizable as particles at the points in the fields with energy values other than the neutral value."

"Other or greater?

"Good catch. Other. We might say values below neutral are antiparticles."

"Antimatter?"

"Could be. Though not all particles result in matter so not all antiparticles result in antimatter, but let's not go there right now. For reasons we don't understand yet, the values in the fields exhibit certain harmonic properties, meaning they vibrate like guitar strings when they are plucked. These vibrations are continuous, but they are not uniform throughout the universe. We say they are local.

"Local?"

"Yeah." She spread her arms. "Like here. The matrices are vibrating here differently than they are vibrating in, say, the space between the Earth and Mars or back at your apartment." She slid her water tumbler toward him and flicked her finger against the glass causing the water inside to ripple. "The vibrations are like the waves in this glass. That's why it's called quantum wave theory and why these equations are important." She pointed to two formulas he now knew were called the Schrodinger and Dirac equations. "They describe the vibrations."

He looked up from the placemats and noticed one of the waitresses was staring at Jane. He surmised it wasn't every day the waitress saw a quantum-physicist lecturing aspiring Catholic priests over burgers and Diet Cokes.

"So, the waves are changes in the values in the matrices, and everything we see, feel, smell, and hear are really just those changes."

"Exactly. We are all just vibrations in the field or fields, if you will." She snatched up a french fry from her plate and munched on it while reclining in her seat with a somewhat smug expression on her face.

"Okay. What causes the vibrations?"

Her eyes gleamed, and she pointed at him with what was left of the french fry. "That's a good question, but a better question might be what causes the vibrations that cause us?"

"That's easy. God," he blurted.

She leaned forward. "I don't believe in God, and neither should you. You are far too smart."

He shook his head. "I see God in all of this, Jane." He waved at the placemats and waited for her to correct him with her usual admonishment to refer to her as Sweet Jane, but it never came.

"Oh my gosh. Where? Can you show me?" She pretended to search the placemats. "No. You can't because all that is here is randomness and probabilities." Perhaps sensing she had overstressed her anti-God point she added, "But I have to admit it seems like there needs to be more to the explanation."

"Ah, am I detecting some spirituality in the cynic?"

"No. Not the way you define spirituality."

"Whatever do you mean by that?"

"You falsely believe in an anthropomorphic superbeing who has some grand plan for everything."

He smiled. "Only if by that you mean I believe we are made in the image of an all-loving and all-powerful God who has a plan for us all."

She gestured at the placemats then folded her arms across her chest. "There is no plan in these models—there's just random fluctuations. Einstein was wrong. It is a big dice game."

He knew she was referring to the famous quote by Albert Einstein that "God does not play dice with the universe."

"Everything you are saying only confirms there are mysteries that science cannot explain by theories and math alone."

She threw up her hands. "Quantum theory is the most successful scientific theory of all time. It's been proven by countless experiments. So it's not just math."

"And yet, you said it yourself, there's something missing in the explanation. I think your exact words were, 'the important question was what causes the vibrations that cause us.'"

She stared out the window for a moment. "Yes. I'll admit it. There's something missing." She turned back to him. "Have you ever heard of the Upanishads?"

Surprised by the question, he dropped the french fry he had been holding. "You mean the texts from the Hindu Veda?"

"Yeah."

"Sure, I studied them in college."

"They teach them in priest school or was that some odd elective course you took when you were studying engineering?"

He laughed. "I took a couple classes in eastern theology in seminary. They were required. What do the Vedic Upanishads have to do with all this?"

"Erwin Schrodinger, the father of quantum wave theory, studied them, and he wrote and lectured often about how some quantum phenomena seemed to agree with their tenets."

"Schrodinger was a Hindu?"

"No. He was an atheist like me, but he and several other founders of quantum physics struggled with what their theories said about reality."

Out of the corner of his eye, Joe noticed the waitress who had been staring at Jane had inched closer to them and was listening to their conversation.

"What did Schrodinger believe?"

"He wrote in his essay *Mind and Matter* that the ancient Indian philosophers thought the true nature of reality was hidden from most humans. They believed we are all part of a single consciousness which is kinda like saying we are all part of the same universal energy field. Schrodinger found parallels in how the ancient Hindus viewed the human experience of reality as an interpretation limited by our senses and how quantum physicists see reality as the interpretation of the vibrations in the energy fields, also limited by our senses."

Joe thought for a moment. "From what I recall from my classes, it sounds like Schrodinger believed in what is known as Advaita Vedanta. In this philosophy, there is a single consciousness called the Brahman. We humans are all part of this single Brahman, and according to the belief, we falsely perceive ourselves as individuals."

She blinked at him. "I should have known better than bring this up with you."

"Do you want me to go on?"

"Please."

"We only perceive ourselves as individuals because we experience the Brahman through a vale called the Maya which acts like a filter that only passes what the human Atman, or soul, can experience. The Hindus say the Atman is misled by the Maya into a false interpretation of reality and only through a process they call Moksha, or liberation, can the Atman know the Brahman."

"Now it's my turn to be confused," she said and leaned in close to him. "What do you think, Joe? Could all the math and physics point to the Brahman that the Hindus have known about for thousands of years? Is the math how we penetrate the Maya as Schrodinger believed?"

Joe took a breath. The conversation had taken an interesting twist, one he was much more equipped to take part in. Just as he opened his mouth to answer, the waitress who had been watching them stepped forward.

"Jane? Is that you?" she asked.

Jane looked away and tried to hide her face with her hand. "I'm sorry you have me confused with someone else."

"No. I don't. It is you. I know it's you. They let you out?"

Jane grabbed her backpack. "You have me confused with someone else," she repeated as she exited the booth. "I have to go to the bathroom," she said to Joe as she rushed past the waitress and disappeared deeper into the restaurant.

The waitress turned to Joe. "I know that is Jane Carter. I cannot believe she came back here."

"Why? What do you mean by that?" Joe asked.

"You don't know?"

"No."

At that moment, Joe's phone buzzed. It was Carlos Santiago returning his call. "Excuse me. I have to take this," he said.

Appearing agitated, the waitress hurried off.

"Hello, Carlos, how was Mass?"

"Joseph, thank goodness. Mass was fine. Is everything okay?"

Joe had expected Carlos to be annoyed, but the priest sounded worried and once again, unusually concerned about his wellbeing. "Everything is fine, Father. Why the concern?"

"Joseph, the doctor I spoke to you about earlier, he wants you to call him as soon as you can. Can you take down a number?"

Joe picked up the pen Jane had been using and wrote the phone number on a napkin which he tucked in his breast pocket.

"I will call him as soon as we hang up," he said. Out the window, he watched as three police cars from the Lee County Sheriff's Department pulled into the parking lot with their lights flashing.

"Joseph, Dr. Lieberman told me Jane had been committed to a state mental hospital."

"Yes. You told me that when you called earlier. You said it was a forensics hospital. Do you know why she was sent there?"

"Is she with you?"

"Not at the moment."

"Joseph, the doctor said Jane was sent there for murdering her mother."

Joe took a breath. Jane had been evasive, and even hostile, when he'd asked about her mother—but murder her? It didn't seem like something the brilliant young woman he just shared lunch with would be capable of.

"That can't be right," he said. He angled around in the booth to watch the officers enter the restaurant. They were met by the waitress who'd recognized Jane. She pointed toward the restrooms at the back of the restaurant, and all three of the officers moved in that direction.

"I have to go, Carlos," Joe said.

"No. Wait, Joseph. The doctor said Jane is dangerous. She's a killer. You need to call the police."

"That won't be necessary. The police are here, and it looks like they are going to arrest her. I have to go, Father. Pray for us," he said as he exited the booth to follow them.

"God be with you, my friend."

Joe caught up with the three policemen outside of the women's restroom. The officer who appeared to be in charge was a tall, lean Black man wearing a lieutenant's bar on his collar. Joe recognized the fit-ordered military look about him and wondered if he had been in the army. Fort Benning, where Joe had attended Ranger school, was less than fifty miles away, and the lieutenant looked as if he just stepped off the base.

"Lieutenant," Joe called as he walked up to the group.

All three officers turned to face him.

"You have a good eye for rank. You military or a cop?"

"Ex-military."

The waitress, who had followed close behind Joe, said, "He was with her."

The two deputies who bracketed the lieutenant put their hands on their sidearms.

Joe put his hands up. "Whoa, officers. I am no threat." He wished he had heeded Carlos's earlier advice and wore his ministerial collar. It might have put the men at ease. Of course, the outward appearance of priesthood had done nothing to calm the man at the homeless encampment. "My name is Joe Carroll. I am a friend of Jane's. What's going on?"

"What happened to your face, Mr. Carroll?" the lieutenant asked.

"I had a disagreement with a troubled man."

The two deputies chuckled, but the lieutenant's face remained hard, and his eyes focused on Joe's.

"Her face is bruised too," the waitress said.

The lieutenant's eyes narrowed.

"Same problem, different man," Joe said.

"Mr. Carroll, Ms. Carter is a fugitive from a state facility. I have to take her into custody so she can be returned to that facility or something else can be worked out. Do you understand?"

"Yes, sir. I only want to make sure she is not harmed."

"I have no intention of harming her."

Joe nodded at the two deputies who still had their hands on their weapons. "What about these men?"

"My deputies don't mean her any harm either, but we have been advised by medical authorities that she can be violent. We don't want anyone hurt."

Joe decided to try to seek some common ground between them. "Lieutenant, were you in the military?"

"Yes, sir. I was in the army for twenty years. I retired with the rank of master sergeant two years ago, and the Lee County Sheriff's Department decided that qualified me to be an officer." He grinned.

"Any combat?"

"Two tours in Iraq and two in Afghanistan. So yes. I saw my share."

"Me too. I was in Afghanistan for over four years."

"Retired?"

"No. I couldn't stay the twenty. I resigned and went to seminary school. I'm in the process of becoming a priest in Atlanta." It wasn't as good as the collar, but Joe hoped mentioning his connection with the church would engender some trust.

"You can become a priest after combat?"

"It's not easy, but I am trying."

"The Almighty works in mysterious ways," the lieutenant rasped.

"Amen to that," Joe agreed, then looked each of them in the eye. "Officers, I've only known Jane for a few days, but I don't believe she is a threat to anyone."

The waitress who was still standing behind him said, "She killed her mother. She beat her to death with a fireplace poker."

Joe turned to face her. "The Jane I know would never do such a thing." At least he did not want to believe she would.

The waitress looked past him to the lieutenant. "Yeah, well she did it. They said it was gruesome too. She smashed in her mother's skull. The police caught her walking down the street covered in her mother's blood with the poker in her hand. We don't want her here."

Joe crossed himself and said a quick prayer. Then he turned back to the lieutenant. "Soldier to soldier, what if I gave you my word, as a man of God, that I'd bring her to the police station? Would you consider falling back to the parking lot and letting me talk to her?"

"Mr. Carroll, we cannot just leave. She's a fugitive." The lieutenant looked around and Joe followed his gaze. The restaurant was about half full and most of the patrons were staring at them. He leaned in close to Joe, "Besides, I remind you, the medical authorities said she could be a threat to others." He nodded toward an empty booth back by the door. "My men and I will sit over there and let you bring her out. If she agrees to go to the station, you can drive her, and we will follow. That's the best I can do."

After the lieutenant and the deputies moved to the booth, Joe knocked on the restroom door. There was no answer, and he knocked again.

The waitress who was hovering nearby said, "She's the only one in there."

Joe opened the door and poked his head inside. "Sweet Jane, are you okay?"

No answer. He stepped into the small, white-tiled bathroom. There were two enclosed stalls. The door on the one nearest to him was closed. He knocked on it. "Sweet Jane, are you in there? Are you okay?"

Still no answer. A warm breeze floated through the air carrying traffic noises. The top sash of the double-sashed window centered above the two stalls was open. He tried the stall door. It was locked. He climbed up on the toilet in the open stall and looked down into the locked one. It was empty. Jane must have climbed out the window. He pushed up the lower sash and stuck his head out.

The window overlooked a narrow alley, and it appeared to be about six feet down to the road. Joe looked to his right. In that direction, the alley intersected with a busy street which was the source of the traffic noise. In the other direction, the alley continued toward what looked like a vacant wooded lot. Jane was half limping and half jogging toward the lot. She must have injured herself when she jumped from the window.

"Sweet Jane!" he shouted.

She stopped and glanced back. Then she quickened her pace, but it was clear she was in too much pain to move fast.

He wormed his way through the window, clutching at a drainpipe that ran along the outside wall until he pulled his legs through and twisted around. As he dropped, he saw the waitress peek through the bathroom door. He hit the ground and chased after Jane.

"Sweet Jane, please stop."

She ignored him and kept hobbling toward the lot, but he was gaining on her and was only about twenty feet behind. She cleared the alley and was a short distance from the trees when a deputy crossed in front of him and tackled her.

She screamed as they tumbled to the ground. The deputy lost his grip on her, and she rolled on her back and began kicking at him as she pushed herself along the tall grass toward the trees. One of her kicks caught the deputy in the face, which seemed to enrage him. He grabbed her around the waist and threw her onto her stomach. The violent move caused her backpack to rip and its contents flew out into the weeds. She began to wail like one of the police sirens Joe thought he could hear in the distance. The deputy put one knee on her back and twisted her left arm behind her while pinning her right arm underneath her. He was fumbling for his handcuffs when Joe reached them.

"Officer, officer. You're hurting her. Please stop."

The deputy's sweat-glistened face was as bright red as Jane's ruined backpack, and a dark red stream of blood gushed from his nose where Jane had kicked him. He shouted through gritted teeth with spit flying everywhere. "Stand back, sir. Stand back."

Jane's face was forced into the dirt by the weight of the large man on her back. Her cries were muffled, and Joe realized she was gasping for air.

"She can't breathe," he yelled. "Please, let her up."

"Get back, sir."

Wanting only to calm the man down, Joe made one of the biggest mistakes of his life. He put his hand on the deputy's shoulder. "Please let her breathe, son."

Those words had just left his mouth when he felt a sharp pain in his neck where a pair of darts sunk deep into the skin below his right ear. He was aware of his bladder releasing as he hit the ground. All his major muscles seized from the 50,000 volts that flowed through the fine metal wires that ran from the gun-shaped taser device held in the lieutenant's outstretched hand to the probes embedded in the tendon under his jaw.

"Stay down, soldier," the lieutenant commanded.

CHAPTER TWELVE

Barry

The navigation system in his car led him to a neighborhood near where the Black Warrior River became the first of several narrow man-made lakes that divided Tuscaloosa into north and south. The Brookhaven Behavioral Wellness Center was on the lake's south side in a wooded residential area near the main branch of the small city's library.

The center occupied all of a nondescript, single story professional building on a quiet street off the main road beside the lake. Other than a basketball court and a few picnic tables, there was nothing about it that suggested it was anything other than a large medical office. No sign confirmed the navigation system's declaration that he had arrived at his destination. He was sure those passing by had no idea the building housed psychiatric patients transitioning from long-term institutional care to independent living.

Places like Brookhaven did not advertise, as it would make fulfilling their purpose almost impossible. These facilities had to be located in or near residential areas to prepare their patients for non-institutional living, but the stigma with mental illness resulted in most communities shunning the centers and their occupants. Better to fly under the radar than risk the not-in-my-backyard cries during zoning board meetings.

The main entrance led to a small lobby where a young man with long, dirty blonde hair drawn back in what Barry knew was called a man bun and dressed in a wrinkled button-down shirt and a neon-blue tie greeted him.

"May I help you?" the young man asked.

"Yes. My name is Dr. Barry Lieberman. I have an appointment to see Desiree Philips."

"Uh oh. You must be important if you are here to see the big boss. I will let her know." He pointed to an open area where a few chairs had been arranged around a table covered in magazines. "You can wait over there until she comes to get you."

Other than the young man, who Barry deduced was a resident, there appeared to be no security. A trickle of people who he guessed were residents or maybe visitors came and went without stopping at the desk. It looked more like a college dorm than a residential psychiatric care facility.

The more he watched, the more he realized the receptionist was only there to receive deliveries and handle the occasional stranger like himself. It was obvious "walking away" as Desiree had told him Jane had done, required nothing more than just that—walking away.

After several minutes, a tall no-nonsense-looking woman with dark brown, almost black, skin and close-cut gray hair appeared at the desk. She was wearing a businesslike taupe-colored pantsuit and a white blouse. Man bun pointed Barry's way, and he rose to meet the woman as she glided across the lobby.

She extended her hand as she reached him. The custom of shaking hands had died out some since the pandemic, but he wasn't about to embarrass her by refusing the gesture. He wondered if it was some kind of test. She was, after all, a behavioral science expert, even if she wasn't an MD.

"It's nice to meet you in person, Dr. Lieberman. I am Desiree Philips," she said, releasing his hand.

"It's nice to meet you too, Director."

She gave him a brief but brilliant smile that came and went like a flash of white lightning at midnight. "No need for such formalities. You can call me Desi. Everyone else does. I'm still surprised you drove all the way up here. I'm sure we could have told you everything you wanted to know over a video meeting."

"I am sure, but I have an appointment at Bryce Hospital today, and I thought it would be good to discuss Jane in person."

The claim of an appointment at Bryce was true enough. He had arranged to meet Carl there after he finished at Brookhaven. The meeting with Carl, however, had nothing to do with why he had elected to make the long drive instead of meeting over video. He made the drive because he was reinserting himself into Jane's psychiatric evaluation chain, and he wanted to be face-to-face with Desiree when he demanded Jane be returned to the state, then made it clear to her he was to be contacted before she was ever released again. Which would be never if he had his way.

Desiree pointed toward a hallway. "I have the team assembled. They are waiting for us."

He followed her to an office with big windows overlooking the parking lot with a desk and a small, round conference table. A large, middle-aged white woman and a younger, fitter Hispanic man were sitting close to one another at the table, leaving room for him and Desiree. The large woman looked uncomfortable wedged between the arms of an office chair, and the Hispanic man was absorbed in something on his phone. Neither looked up when they entered the room. A speakerphone sat on the table between them, and a red light glowed on the phone, indicating it was connected to a call.

"This is Dr. Barry Lieberman," Desiree announced as she took one of the empty seats and motioned for him to do the same. She pointed at the heavyset woman, "This is Diane Spencer. She is Jane's counselor. The man next to her with his nose in his phone is David Lopez. He is our on-site psychiatric nurse and medical coordinator."

Diane smiled up at them while David nodded and made a show of putting his phone away.

"On the phone," Desiree continued, "is Sheila Weber from the state and Dr. Carl Walker from Bryce Mental Health Hospital. Sheila is responsible for patient community placement at Taylor Hardin and Dr. Walker is part of the team at Bryce that provides psychiatric care to our residents."

Barry nodded and in his most non-confrontational professional voice said, "Hello, everyone. It's good to meet you all. I treated Jane for a year before the incident with her mother."

"Thank you, Dr. Lieberman," Desiree said. "Those of us familiar with Jane's case know about your involvement." She turned her attention to the phone. "Dr. Walker, on the other hand, is new to us. It's my understanding, Doctor, that you have taken over Jane's case from Tom Reynolds. Is that correct?"

"That's true," Carl's high-pitched voice whined from the phone. "I just took on Jane's case."

Desiree frowned. "Can you explain what prompted the change? Jane has been working with Dr. Reynolds for a long time. They had good chemistry. Dr. Reynolds had worked wonders with her. She would never have come to us if it wasn't for him." She leaned forward toward the speakerphone. "I don't mean any offense, Dr. Walker. We were caught a little off guard here."

"None taken. It's pretty simple, actually. Tom Reynolds retired, and I had room in my caseload."

Barry knew all about the change. It had been a stroke of incredible luck. Reynolds had only retired two months ago and until yesterday, no Bryce physician had taken over Jane's case. Why would they? Jane was gone. She was no one's patient until Barry had talked Carl into listing himself as her doctor for when the police tracked her down and brought her back—something Barry hoped would happen soon.

Carl continued in a reassuring tone, "I have familiarized myself with Jane's file, and I plan to speak with Dr. Reynolds as soon as possible."

"That's encouraging," Desiree said. She turned her attention to Barry, giving him a long, uncomfortable stare. "Perhaps you could explain to the team your current concern with Jane's case."

"Yes, of course. Like I said, I was once Jane's physician."

The heavy woman glanced at a file folder she had open in front of her. "That was almost eight years ago, correct?"

Barry worked to conceal his detest for her. He loathed people who let themselves go. It was all he could do to tolerate Carl. "Yes. Thank you. That's correct." He smiled at her, then launched into the summary of his and Jane's relationship that he'd practiced during the drive. "When I was treating Jane," he glanced at the woman, "eight years ago, I observed firsthand her behavior grow dangerously erratic as her psychosis became quite severe. Her hallucinations were dominating her attention, and she had formed several complex delusions related to her field of study. These delusions led to internal conflicts that often boiled over into violent outbursts."

He took a deep breath, then removed his glasses and used a sleeve to wipe tears from his eyes. The heavy woman and the Hispanic man were staring at him. It was a masterful performance.

"Are you okay, Doctor?" the Hispanic man asked.

"Yes. I am fine. It's difficult to talk about Jane without thinking about her mother. Maggie, that was Jane's mother's name, was a lovely woman, and I feel partially responsible for what happened to her."

"Why is that?" the Hispanic man asked.

"I knew back then Jane was losing her ability to manage her internal struggles, and I had become increasingly concerned she would harm herself or another." He sniffled and looked at Desiree. "Which, of course she did. I had urged Maggie to have Jane hospitalized, but I could not convince her."

He summoned another pathetic sniffle, and the heavy woman handed him a pack of tissues she'd removed from her bag.

"I've spent the past eight years thinking about what I should have done differently. Had I tried a little harder to convince Maggie, maybe she would still be alive, and things would be different for Jane. That is why I am here. I knew back then Jane needed to be in a managed setting, and Maggie lost her life because I failed to act on that. My current concern, as you put it," he raised his voice, "is, I once misjudged the severity of Jane's delusions with disastrous consequences, and I am here to make sure you don't do the same." He slapped the palm of his hand on the table.

The heavy woman jumped. "Dr. Lieberman, please. Jane has been with us for over two years. She has been an exemplary resident and has showed no tendency toward violence. When she does present symptoms, they tend to be mild, along the lines of transient hallucinations and brief periods of minor confusion and depression, all brought on by stress. We've been able to control those through stress-reduction techniques and a moderate medication schedule."

She looked to the Hispanic man and then Desiree for agreement. "None of us have known Jane to be delusional or to be impaired in any meaningful way by her symptoms. She is brilliant and engaging, and she has been functioning well in the community."

Desiree chimed in. "The incident with her mother took place eight years ago when Jane was in her mid-twenties. I don't have to tell you schizophrenia often moderates with age. Isn't it possible the disease reached its worst at that point? On top of that, she's received constant care ever since. We think it's time for Jane to restart her life."

Barry pulled Jane's file from his bag and set it on the table. He opened it and retrieved a document. Holding it up he said, "This is a copy of Jane's commitment order I am listed as her evaluating physician. It also sets the terms for rescinding this order, which includes a court hearing where a judge is to consider the psychiatric evaluation of her physician. That would be me."

"We had a hearing," interrupted an authoritative woman's voice on the phone.

"That might be so, but I was not asked to assess her, nor was I part of that hearing," he responded with an angry edge. "Worse, I was not even notified she had been released. Forget about the order naming me as her physician—I should have been notified for my own safety."

The heavy woman sighed. "Jane is not dangerous."

Barry glared at her. "Says who?"

The phone cracked with the authoritative woman's voice, "Excuse me."

"Go ahead, Sheila," said Desiree.

"Dr. Lieberman, you have not examined or even spoken to Ms. Carter in years. You can hardly make the case that you are still her physician. She has been under the care of our staff here at Hardin and Bryce Mental Health for over seven years now. Her physician of record was changed to Dr. Reynolds several years ago. Dr. Reynolds wrote the assessment that was presented during Ms. Carter's hearing. He indicated Ms. Carter no longer presents a danger to herself or others and was ready to move to an unsecure residential facility for transition to outpatient care, and the court agreed with his assessment."

Barry interrupted her. "Even if I am no longer Jane's physician, I should still have been notified."

"As I said, Doctor," Sheila's tone was controlled but firm, "we determined Ms. Carter no longer poses a risk to herself or others. She had responded well to our programs here. We filed our recommendation with the circuit court as part of the state's efforts to reduce overcrowding at state institutions during the COVID-19 health emergency. I consulted with our legal team yesterday afternoon when Desiree requested this meeting, and it is their opinion we are in full compliance with state laws and procedures."

"Sheila," Carl's voice came from the speaker. "No one is suggesting your team did anything wrong. Given the case history, however, I think we can all agree Dr. Lieberman has legitimate concerns. Dr. Reynolds wrote in Jane's file a few months before he retired that she still suffered from some delusional thinking along with minor paranoia. I agree this does not sound severe, but he wrote that there remains a possibility of Jane having violent reactions if her delusional thoughts were challenged."

"I don't believe it for a minute," the heavy woman said.

"Dr. Reynolds never voiced any concerns about Jane leaving Hardin," Sheila said, then added, "quite the contrary."

"I would have voiced them if anyone had called me," said Barry. "Besides, all of this is moot. We are no longer talking about whether she is fit to live in a community house like Brookhaven." He turned to Desiree. "She is no longer here. You people let her walk out almost four months ago, and it is highly unlikely she has received any treatment since."

"Is that true, Desiree?" Sheila demanded.

"Yes. I intended to bring that up here, Sheila. Dr. Lieberman is correct, Jane is no longer with us."

The phone went silent for a long moment, and then Sheila's authoritative voice said, "Well, that changes everything."

CHAPTER THIRTEEN

Barry

Bryce Hospital is the largest and oldest inpatient mental health facility in the state of Alabama. Established during the Civil War as the Alabama State Hospital for the Insane, it was originally housed in an architecturally magnificent building designed for 300 patients and representing the state-of-the art of Victorian age "moral" mental health care. But that was a long time ago, and despite its promising beginnings, the hospital spent most of its history as a notorious example of mental patient warehousing. During the 20th century, Bryce Mental Hospital grew to be one of the largest institutions of its kind in the world, housing over 5000 patients in such abominable conditions that by the 1970s, it was considered the worst hospital of its kind in the United States and perhaps the western world. But that was a long time ago too, and now the institution is once again housed in a modern facility designed for 300 full-time residents and considered the state-of-the art in mental healthcare.

Barry met Carl at his office, and they had gone to a local barbeque place for lunch. Carl loved barbeque, and it showed. Barry picked up the tab. It was the least he could do for Carl's support on the call with Sheila, and now they sat in Barry's BMW in a lot across from the old Bryce Hospital structure. The university had purchased the building over ten years ago and had spent those years renovating it. Someday, it would become the university's new performing arts center and a museum for mental health treatment in Alabama. Barry chuckled when he thought of the irony.

Reflecting on the differences in architecture between the elegant Italianate classical structure before them with its towering cupola along with grand, columned balconies and the nondescript brick and steel modern replacement where Carl worked, Barry said, "They sure don't build them like they used to."

"That's for sure," Carl agreed.

"It's one of the last of the old Kirkbride designs," Barry lamented.

"I, for one, am glad to see it go," Carl said. "I spent my first few years after residency in there. It was a mess. The roof leaked. There was almost no air-conditioning, and it had this smell to it."

"Smell?"

"Yeah. It smelled of old antiseptics and something else that is hard to describe. Maybe it was the residual stink of having so many people crammed in there—many of them suffering from extreme disease. And just think of the treatments they received if you could call them treatments."

"Those were the days," Barry grinned.

Carl emitted a high-pitched, squeaky chuckle. "They practiced some seriously barbarous stuff in there." He gestured toward the windshield.

"No doubt. With an institution this size, they would have tried everything. I'm sure some of what they tried would seem horrific by today's standards."

"You know my granddaddy worked in there," Carl said.

"Is that so?. What did he do?"

"He was an orderly."

"That's a title you don't hear anymore. I guess we call them nursing assistants or techs now."

"I think the job my granddaddy did was closer to a prison guard than a nurse. He was a mean old son of a bitch, always eager to whip my ass for raiding his raspberry bushes. I think he enjoyed hurting people. My daddy told me he used to talk about how he had to control the lunatics. I think that meant he'd beat them and tie them up. That kind of stuff was pretty common back then. I actually have an old straitjacket my granddaddy took from here when they had the big release."

"The big release?"

"Oh yeah. In 1974, the courts ordered more than half the patients released and the end of the work farm."

"I am sure I can guess, but what was the work farm?" Barry asked.

Carl waved his arms toward the windshield again. "This entire area was one large farm. The patients worked in the fields and the hospital fed them the crops and sold the surplus."

"Really?"

"Yep. Damn amazing to think about. Can you imagine forcing patients to work as part of their treatment today?"

"Early form of occupational therapy," Barry quipped.

Carl snorted.

"It must have been something. Did you see the farm?"

"Yes, but I was a small boy when it shut down. I don't remember much of it."

Barry had trouble imagining Carl as small. "When was that?" he asked. "Late seventies?"

"Yep."

"Your granddaddy keep anything else?"

"Oh sure. His old house is filled with stuff from the asylum."

"He's still alive?"

"No. He passed about five years ago. The old goat lived to 93. Daddy never got around to selling the house. He passed last year himself, and now it's my problem. I've been sorting through the old stuff to see what the museum might want."

"What kind of stuff?"

"All kinds. It's like he was building his own little asylum in his cellar. Pretty creepy. There's some heavy old oak and metal chairs, a couple big metal desks, a bunch of cabinets, some carts, and even a hospital bed. There were quite a few documents and photos too, but I already sent them over to the committee compiling the collections. I haven't sent them the best stuff yet."

"Like what?"

"Geez, you wouldn't believe it. There are straightjackets, harnesses, wrist and ankle restraints, surgical equipment, all kinds of odd crap." Carl stared out at the building. "There's even a funky old leather muzzle to keep patients from biting, which looks like something a sadomasochist might use for weird sex." He snorted a laugh. "I guess the most interesting thing is an old electroconvulsive therapy machine."

"You're kidding me!"

"No. I think it's from the 1960s, maybe earlier. It's like something Dr. Frankenstein would use during a lightning storm to animate the monster."

Now it was Barry's turn to laugh.

"Yes, sir. It's a serious zapper—nothing like the puny ECT devices we use today."

"Ever see it work?"

"No. Not on a person anyway, but I've plugged it in once or twice to see what it does. It's downright medieval."

"Man, I'd love to see it."

"When are you going back to Auburn?"

"Tomorrow morning."

"If you are free this evening, you could come out to Granddaddy's place and take a look. Then we could go to dinner. There's a fine barbeque place near there with great ribs."

Barry eyed a small red stain on Carl's shirt. "We just had barbeque. You are still wearing some of it."

Carl followed Barry's eyes down to the stain. "Shit." He spit on his fingers and tried to rub the stain out with it. "That wasn't barbeque. Come out tonight, and I will take you for the real stuff."

Barry mulled over for a moment whether seeing Granddaddy's asylum collection was worth watching Carl wolf down another rack of barbequed ribs. The artifacts alone may not be interesting enough to endure such horrors, but Carl was proving useful with his Jane problem so he would spend the evening looking at the implements of his profession's dark ages with someone he would like to use them on. "That sounds great."

"Okay, then. I will text you the address. I can meet you out there when I am finished with my afternoon rounds. Six work for you?"

"Works fine."

Two young women dressed in athletic shorts and tight-fitting half tank tops ran past them. Their tanned skin glistened with sweat and their long, blonde ponytails bounced behind them. Barry watched Carl watch them pass.

"Roll Tide," Barry said.

Carl nodded. "Oh yeah. One of the benefits of being located on the campus is the scenery."

"What does Jackie think about the scenery? She ever worry you may do more than appreciate it?" Jackie was Carl's wife. With his mousy voice and elephantine bulk, it still surprised Barry Carl had convinced someone to marry him. Of course, Jackie was no prize herself, being roughly Carl's size and having an uncanny resemblance to him. The first time Barry had met her he thought she was his sister. He still wasn't so sure his first impression was wrong.

Carl waved his hand. "Jackie would find me having an affair, especially one with a young coed, hysterical." He laughed, but his tone betrayed the pain of a lifetime of rejection from the opposite sex. "My dear wife doesn't believe any woman could possibly find me appealing. That certainly applies to her. Then again, if she believed I was messing around, she'd probably beat me, and believe me she could, and then get her asshole brother, a very successful and vicious divorce lawyer, to take everything I have."

Barry chuckled then said, "Well, let's hope she never finds out about Miami."

Carl froze and stared at him with a terrified look on his pudgy face. The year before the pandemic struck, the two of them had attended a psychiatric convention in Miami. The event hotel had been full of physicians as well as a myriad of pharmaceutical and medical sales reps. Most of the attendees were men, well-to-do, and horny. It was, as they say, a target-rich environment for the world's oldest profession whose representatives had been drawn to the conference like moths to a floodlight. The hotel and surrounding bars were swarming with dozens of attractive young women in sleek little evening dresses who for the right price, would do just about anything with anyone, even Carl.

Barry watched the jogging coeds for a moment, then in a wistful tone he said, "That was some night."

Carl put up his hands. "We agreed never to talk about that night again."

"I mean, some of the things those girls were doing with you were about the most deviant and downright disgusting things I've ever seen or even heard of. I feel dirty just thinking about it."

"Then don't, and let's stop talking about it. Besides, as I recall you made them do it."

Barry placed his right hand over his heart feigning shock. "Moi?"

"Goddamn right, you."

"I only made suggestions. Those girls just found you irresistible."

Carl snickered. "Yeah, right. After you convinced them to let you hypnotize them."

"Hmm. They did seem particularly susceptible to those techniques, didn't they? You know, though, I suspect they were not as deeply under as they appeared. I mean, they disregarded my suggestion not to charge you."

"No kidding. That little party cost me $2,000 and a year off my life from fear that Jackie would notice the missing cash."

"You are really afraid of her, aren't you?"

"Damn right I am, and I've got good reason to be. She is my size and twice as strong."

Now Barry laughed.

"Can we stop talking about this?"

"Okay. What should we talk about?"

"I want to know a bit more about Jane Carter," Carl said. "Why are you so eager to have her returned to Hardin? That place is not much better than this one was."

Barry turned in his seat so he could face Carl. "Have you ever treated a patient that frightened you?"

"I am not sure what you mean."

"I mean someone who you felt might actually do you harm—besides your wife."

Carl didn't reply for a moment, seeming to consider the question. "I guess there's been a few times in the ER where things have gotten out of control and security has had to step in. I'm sure nothing like the big urban hospitals see, but we've had a few incidents. It kind of comes with the territory. I mean, dealing with troubled patients is in a psychiatrist's job description, right? Besides that, I have treated patients whose delusions made them a hazard, mostly to themselves, but I cannot recall any of them threatening me in any meaningful way. Of course, I've been spit on about a dozen times, and even punched, but those cases were extreme manifestations of those patient's behavioral disorders. So, no. I don't think I can say I have ever been afraid of one of my patients."

"You're lucky," Barry said. "Jane Carter scares the hell out of me."

"I guess I can understand after what happened with her mother," Carl said. "Did you talk to her after the incident?"

Barry studied him for a moment, forming the right story to draw him in. He didn't like it, but he needed the slob's support to get his hands on Jane, and he wanted her back in his hands. "The Lee County Sheriff's Department called me that afternoon and told me what had happened to Maggie. They told me they had arrested Jane for Maggie's murder."

"Why did they call you?"

"Jane asked for me. The police said she was being uncooperative, and the only thing they had gotten out of her was my name. I thought nothing of it at the time. We had developed an intimate patient-doctor bond, and it made sense that she would want my help."

Carl nodded.

"They asked if I'd come to the Lee County jail and talk to her, and of course, I did. When I arrived, I discovered she wasn't uncooperative—she was unresponsive."

"Catatonic?"

"That's what I believed at first. They told me they had found her in the middle of the street brandishing the fireplace tool she had used to bludgeon her mother and screaming at the top of her lungs."

"That doesn't sound catatonic."

"No, no. They got the poker away from her and put her in a police car. Apparently, they were not very gentle as when I examined her at the jail, she had multiple abrasions and contusions on her face and arms. They said she fought them like a wild cat until they put her into a holding cell, and then she went into a corner and, to use their phrase, 'zoned out.' That's how I found her."

"Akinetic Catatonia."

"That's what I thought. She was displaying all the usual characteristics. Her eyes were open, and her gaze was fixed, but now that I look back on it, her body wasn't right. You would expect someone suffering from Akinetic Catatonia to be a bit twisted up, but she wasn't. She was sitting with her back propped up against the wall, staring at the door like she was waiting. I should have been more cautious."

"Why? What happened?"

"I convinced them to let me in the cell with her."

"Did she recognize you?"

"Yeah. And then some. When I reached her, I began looking her over, noting the injuries I mentioned. I was in the process of examining her when her eyes met mine and all hell broke loose. The wild cat the police had described was back, and she was all over me. Punching, scratching, biting." He lifted his jaw and pointed to an ugly quarter-sized scar near the top of his neck. "See this?"

Carl leaned in closer. "That looks nasty. Pretty close to the external jugular too."

"She bit me and tore out a sizeable portion of skin. Luckily, she did not reach the vein, but she could have."

"My God. This sounds like quite an extreme psychotic episode."

"There certainly was psychosis involved, but there was premeditation too."

"What do you mean?"

"She ambushed me. She had the police call me. Then she faked the seizure, and when I got close, she tried to kill me."

Carl laughed. "You're sounding a little paranoid. Maybe you should come back to the hospital. I could write you a script."

"Believe what you want. I know what she did. She tried to kill me."

"Barry, you said it yourself. Her schizophrenia had taken a significant turn for the worse. Apparently, her delusions had gotten the better of her, and she was under an enormous amount of stress. A catatonic seizure would not be unusual in this case, and neither would it be unusual for the sufferer to react violently to being disturbed.

"No. No way. I know what I saw and felt. She's a real-life, Hollywood-style psycho, and until I am convinced otherwise, I believe she is dangerous. They never should have let her out of Hardin, and I mean to see her put back where she belongs."

"What if her condition has truly moderated like Tom and the people at Brookhaven say?"

"The people at Brookhaven are idiots. Besides, if she is well, she should be in jail for killing her mother and assaulting me."

Barry watched Carl chew on his words like he was chewing a spare rib.

After a long moment, Carl looked at his watch. "Oh geez. I have to get back. I've got afternoon rounds."

Barry stared at Carl, trying to make him feel as uncomfortable as possible. "She's a killer, Carl. When they catch her, I want to be part of her evaluation, and I sure as hell want to be part of any future release decision."

Carl nodded. "I understand."

"Then you will help me?"

"Yes. If they bring her back to Hardin, I will make sure she is evaluated at Bryce, and I will make sure you are part of that." He paused. "As long as you promise never, ever, to bring up Miami again."

Barry grinned, then put the car in drive and guided it toward the parking lot exit. "Deal."

Carl took out his phone. "I'll text you Granddaddy's address. What did we say? Six?"

"Yeah. I'm looking forward to it," Barry said with an element of genuine enthusiasm. "I can't wait to see this collection of yours."

CHAPTER FOURTEEN

Joe

The holding cell was a small ten-foot by ten-foot cube with light-gray cement block walls. A large window with thick safety glass filled half of one wall, and an oversized steel door took up the other half. Joe was lying on a metal bench that, with the addition of a thin, plastic-covered mattress, served as a cot. Through the window, he could see a well-lit corridor with three identical window-door pairs arranged on the opposite wall. Two of the three windows were dark. He could not see into the cell with the light on, and he wondered if Jane was in that one.

The puncture wounds under his jaw from the taser's darts itched, and so did the stiff Day-Glo orange coveralls they'd given him to wear after his bladder had released all the Diet Coke he'd drank while Jane walked him through quantum wave theory. It was still surreal to him. He did not remember being tased or being arrested. All he remembered was seeing Jane struggling with a deputy, then the next thing he knew, he was sitting in the back seat of a police car, handcuffed and drenched in his own urine with no clue why. They had taken him to the local emergency room first. The deputies told him it was standard procedure for tased suspects. He was still struggling with the suspect label. The hospital staff was familiar with the process and were not surprised by his wet pants.

"Don't worry, sugar. It happens often," one of the nurses told him. "If your bladder is full, there's no holding it in when that electricity goes through you."

The doctor confirmed the nurse's assertion, and he told Joe, like the urination, some memory loss was not uncommon. After shining a flashlight in Joe's eyes and listening to his heart, the doctor pronounced him humiliated but uninjured by the experience. The lieutenant showed up with the coveralls and they loaded him back in the car and brought him to the cell.

Joe stared into the fluorescent light panel above him, wondering how the diocese would react to his arrest when a loud buzzing sound interrupted his contemplation. The door opened, and the lieutenant came through carrying a pale blue, plastic tub with the words Property of Lee County Sheriff's Department stenciled on it. Joe pulled himself into a sitting position. The lieutenant placed the tub on the bench next to him. Inside was Joe's laundered clothes, his wallet, cell phone, and pocket breviary. Joe retrieved the breviary and kissed its worn leather cover.

"Thank you for this," Joe said, holding up the book. "I was worried I lost it."

The lieutenant eyed him for a moment, then rubbed the stubble on his chin. "I am trying to decide what to do here. Normally, I'd let a man who interfered with an arrest stew in a cell in the county jail for a couple days until we got around to a bail hearing, but when we ran your identification through the network, we learned some interesting things about you, Captain Carroll." He emphasized the word captain.

Joe looked up at him, "I am no longer in the army."

"No. I know, sir. You mustered out a good ten years ago, and I was able to confirm you are indeed, employed by the Catholic Church in Atlanta."

Joe wondered if they had called Sacred Heart. It was inevitable Carlos would learn about the incident, but Joe would have preferred he learned about it from him instead of through a call from law enforcement. "If you spoke to my parish, you know I was telling the truth about my involvement with Jane."

"We confirmed your story, but you should not have interfered with my deputy."

"Like I told you at the hospital, I was only trying to help calm the situation."

"I am inclined to believe you, but from where I was standing it looked different. Get dressed Mr. Carroll, and then we can talk."

Joe looked at the big window and the security camera that peered through it. "Here?"

"No. Grab your things, and I will take you to the restroom."

Joe followed the lieutenant out the door and down the hall. He stopped at the cell with the light on and looked in the big window. Jane was curled up on a bench identical to the one he'd been lying on. Her eyes locked on his and she came to the window.

The lieutenant turned around. "Mr. Carroll, the restroom is this way."

"Can I speak with her?" Joe asked.

"After we talk."

Jane shouted, "I want my backpack, Joe. I need it." Her voice was muted by the thick walls and heavy window glass.

The lieutenant pointed down the hall at a door. "The restroom is right there."

Joe mouthed the words, "I will be back."

Jane pounded on the glass and screamed, "Joe, don't leave me here. I need my backpack."

He crossed himself and said a quick prayer for God to grant her peace and him strength, then he turned away and made his way to the restroom.

After he changed into his clothes, he rejoined the lieutenant in the hall and handed him the tub that now contained the orange coveralls.

"That's better," said the lieutenant. "I did not like seeing a war hero in those coveralls."

Joe grimaced, "I am no hero, Lieutenant.

"That's not what your record says, Captain."

"Please, I don't use that title anymore. I am just Joe now—a servant of God."

They made their way to a small, windowless cube with a nameplate that read Lt. Melvin Cooper affixed to the wall beside its doorway. The little office had barely enough room for a desk and two visitor chairs. The lieutenant closed the door and took his place behind the desk. His wide-brimmed campaign hat hung from a hook on the back of the door. The walls were bare, and except for a phone, computer, and a single green, ceramic coffee mug with the words *BE ALL YOU CAN BE* emblazoned in yellow letters, the desk was bare as well. Joe eased into one of the empty chairs.

"I've spoken to the sheriff, and we've agreed not to pursue charges against you for interfering with law enforcement," the lieutenant said.

"Thank you. What about Jane, um, Ms. Carter? What's happening with her?"

The lieutenant steepled his long fingers against his crooked nose, which looked to Joe as if it had been broken more than once. He seemed uncertain how to answer the question. "Normally, I would not discuss another individual's case with anyone other than their lawyer or their people, but I am guessing you are Ms. Carter's only people."

Joe nodded. "I think that's probably right."

"I assume you know about Ms. Carter's past?"

"Only what I heard at the restaurant. Did she really kill her mother?"

The lieutenant nodded. "'fraid so."

"I still can't believe it. She's a little odd, and she can get intense when she's upset, but I can't see her killing anyone, least of all her own mother."

"It happened a few years before my time here, but the reports I read say it was an open-and-shut case."

"Did she go to prison?"

"No. No prison. The only time she spent behind bars was a couple months in the county jail."

"Here?"

"Nooo. This isn't the jail. This is the Lee County Sheriff's Department. The accommodations at the jail are much less posh than our little holding rooms."

"If that's the case, I don't want to visit them."

"No. You most certainly do not. Anyway, Ms. Carter never stood trial for her mother's murder. She was found incompetent during a pretrial hearing and was committed to the state mental facility up in Tuscaloosa. That is until two years ago when she was moved to a low-security facility as part of a pandemic release program. She was there right up until they lost track of her about four months ago."

"Lost track of her? Is that why she was arrested?"

"Technically she's been detained, not arrested."

"Detained?"

"Yes. She has not been accused of committing a crime. When she left that low-security facility, she violated the terms of her release. Now the state hospital wants her back."

"So now what?"

"As I understand it, she will spend the night over at the jail and be transported up to Tuscaloosa tomorrow morning."

"Can I visit with her?"

"I don't see why not, but there is a notation in her file about an incident that happened the last time she was in custody. She attacked her psychiatrist. I don't want a repeat of that, so we will be very cautious. A deputy will stand right outside the holding room while you visit with her, and we will be watching. We good?"

Joe had seen Jane upset to the point where he thought she might attack him. She never had, but he thought she'd come close. He'd grown fond of her in the short time they'd been together, but he had to admit to himself he did not know her enough to challenge the lieutenant's concerns.

"Affirmative." Something about the lieutenant made Joe use military jargon. It felt comfortable, like putting on old clothes.

"She had a backpack with her. She's very attached to it and the things inside it."

"All her personal items will be handed over to the people in Tuscaloosa. I'm sure they will be returned to her."

"There are some things that she needs."

"What would they be?"

"She has medication, cigarettes, and a few items that seem to comfort her."

"I will see to it that her medication is turned over to the nurse at the jail and she gets what she needs. As far as cigarettes, we don't allow smoking in the facilities, but she may be able to smoke outside depending on how processing goes. I will make sure she gets a smoke on the way over."

"What about the other things?"

"What are they?"

"She has a small tape player and some tapes she listens to when she sleeps. Also, she has some notebooks that are important to her."

The lieutenant drummed his fingers on the desk for a moment then pushed a button on the desk phone.

A cheery woman's voice answered. "Good morning, Mel. Miss me so soon?"

The lieutenant cleared his throat. "In a meeting here, Charlene. You know the woman we got in three?"

"I do. That would be Ms. Jane Carter."

"That's the one. Could you bring me her personal property?"

"You know I'd do anything for you sweetie." She emphasized anything. "I'll bring it right over."

The lieutenant punched the disconnect button and turned his attention back to Joe.

"She seems friendly."

"She sure is." The lieutenant leaned over the desk and said softly, "I think she is a little sweet on me."

Joe smiled. "No Mrs. Lieutenant Cooper at home, I take it?"

"No. I was married to the army for twenty years and never found a woman willing to compete with that. How about you?"

"The Church doesn't allow it."

"Oh. Right. You're a priest."

"An almost-priest, as a friend of mine would say."

At that moment, there was a knock on the door and the lieutenant shouted, "Come."

A tall, curvy woman with light-brown skin and long black hair entered the office carrying a blue tub similar to the one the lieutenant had used to transport Joe's things. Her uniform struggled to contain her chest and thighs. She placed the tub on the lieutenant's desk and flashed him a gleaming smile. In the same cheery voice from the phone conversation, she said, "Here's Ms. Jane's property."

"Thank you, darlin'."

She turned and looked down on Joe. "Hello. I don't think we've met before."

Joe stood and introduced himself.

"You're the religious man Mel tased."

"Unfortunately, so," he said.

"Oh my." She looked him over. "You're too cute to be a preacher."

Joe smiled, and the lieutenant growled. "Charlene."

"I spoke to a nice lady at Sacred Heart Church up in Atlanta about you."

"That would have been Agnes. She works with me in the parish office."

"She was very nice. I'm sorry Mel tased you. Are you okay?"

"Charlene!" Mel growled again.

Joe laughed. "Only thing hurt was my dignity."

"Oh, we get a lot of that hurt dignity stuff," she said.

She turned back to the lieutenant. "Is there anything else I can do for you?"

"Not right now."

"Well, I'll look forward to when I can do something for you."

"Thank you, Charlene."

She hovered for a moment, and as she turned to leave, the lieutenant said, "Charlene, were you here when Ms. Carter was arrested for murdering her mother?"

"You know I was. We talked about it."

The lieutenant rolled his eyes. "Yes. Thank you for reminding me. Mr. Carroll here…"

"Call me Joe."

"Joe," the lieutenant corrected, "would like to hear what you think about the case."

She leaned on the desk and turned her gleaming smile on him. "It was a long time ago," she said. "But I remember it like yesterday. I was working dispatch when we got the call, and I was here when they brought Ms. Jane in. I remember how shaken up and sad she was. She didn't seem like no violent murderer to me."

"How did she seem?" Joe asked.

"Lost and scared, and maybe a little crazy. She couldn't stop crying, Kept begging everyone to help her mother. Of course, her mother was already dead, but she didn't seem to understand. She didn't know why she was under arrest, and when we finally got her calmed down enough to talk to us, she insisted she didn't do it."

The lieutenant shook his head and waved his hand dismissively. "I've only been in law enforcement for five years, but I know everyone claims they didn't do it."

"Yeah, I know," Charlene said. "But she seemed different. She didn't feel like someone who would kill her mother if you know what I mean. And she was so sure…" her voice trailed off.

"Sure of what?" Joe asked.

"Said her doctor had been the one who attacked her mother. She was emphatic."

"Careful, Charlene," the lieutenant said.

She pooched her lips. "Right. She was a hot mess, but not like a killer—more like a confused child. She cried and cried, and when she wasn't crying, she was talking to herself. I mean really arguing with someone who wasn't there. It freaked a few of us out."

"What about the doctor?" Joe asked. "Did anyone ever look into him?"

The lieutenant leaned over his desk and lowered his voice. "We need to be careful about how we talk about Doc Lieberman. He's, umm, well connected here."

"Uh-huh. That's a truth," Charlene said.

Joe didn't understand. "Connected?"

"We use him from time to time to help with witnesses. He, uh, he… what does he do, Charlene?"

"He hypnotizes them. It's really spooky too. Makes them remember things."

"That's right," the lieutenant continued. "He works with the city police and us. He plays tennis with the sheriff."

"Ah," Joe said.

The lieutenant nodded. "You'd be doing me a favor by watching how you throw his name around."

"Roger that," Joe said and turned his gaze back to Charlene.

She spread her hands. "Besides, the way I understand it, he had a solid alibi, and Ms. Jane was covered in her mother's blood. That I'll never forget. I helped clean her off."

"She did it," the lieutenant said.

Charlene shrugged. "I guess."

"She did it."

Charlene shrugged again. "Is there anything else you two fine gentlemen need?"

"No, thank you," Joe said.

"That will be all, Charlene."

She wiggled her fingers and left the office.

The lieutenant reached into the tub and withdrew Jane's battered backpack. He handed it to Joe. "Is this what you're looking for?"

A large rip had been torn in the pack's fabric. Joe put his hand through the hole. "Where's all the stuff she had in it?"

The lieutenant slid the tub toward Joe. "This is everything we found."

Joe searched through the items in the tub. He retrieved a plastic bag with several pill vials and held it up. "These are her meds."

"I'll get those to the nurse," the lieutenant said.

Joe nodded and continued searching. He found the microcassette tapes not in their bag but lying on the bottom of the tub. He stacked ten of them on the desk. The tape player was still in its bag, and he set that next to them. Three notebooks, also no longer in their bag, were mixed in with the other items. Joe thought there had been four. He set the three aside and continued searching. "I think some things are missing."

The lieutenant shrugged. "Most of the stuff went flying when the bag ripped. This is all we found."

Joe continued sorting through the items. He set aside a bag with the semi-crushed remains of the pack of cigarettes she had bought that morning and a plastic lighter.

"She can't smoke where she is, and she cannot have the lighter. Give me that bag, and I will ensure she gets the cigarettes when she is where she can use them."

Joe slid the bag over to the lieutenant and took one more look through the items for anything that might bring some comfort to Jane. A small shield-shaped patch caught his eye, and he picked it up and smiled.

"Looky there," the lieutenant said grinning. "Is that a Ranger patch?"

"Yeah."

"Wonder where she got that?"

"I have my suspicions."

Joe found an empty ziplock storage bag in the tub, and he filled it with the tape player, tiny cassette tapes and the patch.

"I'd like to bring these things to her."

The lieutenant looked over the pile and nodded. "I don't see anything there that will be a problem. She will have to give them up again at the jail when she is processed, but I will make sure she gets them back and has them when they transport her up north."

The lieutenant made another call to arrange for a deputy to monitor Joe's visit with Jane. Then he led Joe back to the room where Jane was held. As he approached the room's window, Joe searched for her. She was sitting cross-legged on her cot and jumped to her feet when she saw them approach. Joe held up the plastic bags containing her things and smiled. She smiled back.

A young, lean deputy with deep-black skin and a military haircut that screamed Marine stood at attention outside her door.

"At ease, jarhead," the lieutenant barked. He turned to Joe. "Deputy Jeremy Tyrell here is one of our up-and-coming officers. I know he looks like a grunt fresh out of Parris Island, but don't let that fool you, he's actually got a brain under that high and tight hairdo."

"Thank you, sir. Manners like yours are why the marines are always happy to rescue our army brothers when the real fighting starts."

"Careful, jarhead." The lieutenant growled and pointed at Joe. "This is Mr. Carroll. He's going to spend a few minutes with the subject in this room. You will monitor things and render assistance to Mr. Carroll if the subject, Ms. Carter, poses any threat."

"Threat, sir?"

"I don't expect any problems, but Ms. Carter has a history of violent outbursts. Just keep an eye on them. Once Mr. Carroll is done, you will drive him back to his car." The lieutenant looked at Joe. "I assume your car is at the restaurant."

"If you guys didn't tow it, it's there," Joe said.

"We didn't tow it." The lieutenant turned back to the deputy. "His car is over at Stripes."

Deputy Tyrell nodded at Joe and said, "No problem."

The lieutenant punched in a code on a keypad on the wall beside the door and a loud buzz reverberated from the lock. He pushed open the door and stared at Jane who was standing in the center of the room with her arms folded across her chest in a defiant pose. "Ms. Carter, I am going to let Mr. Carroll spend some time with you before we take you across the street for the night. Do you understand?"

"I understand I'm being held illegally against my will."

"No, Ms. Carter, we went over this before. You are being detained until we can transport you back to the Taylor Hardin facility tomorrow morning. Now, before I go, do you need to use the restroom?"

She shook her head.

"Okay. I'll be going." He paused next to Joe on the way out. "You got fifteen minutes and then we need to take her."

After the lieutenant left, Joe held out the items he'd brought from her backpack. "They wouldn't let me bring everything, but I thought these things would make you more comfortable."

She took the items and sat on the bench. "There's only three notebooks," she said. "I had four."

"I know. Your backpack was damaged when the deputy tackled you, and some of your things spilled out. I'll go look for the notebook as soon as I can."

She dumped the bag containing the tapes out on the bench and began sorting through them. Picking up the Ranger patch, she held it out to Joe. "This is yours. I kinda took it from your apartment to remember you by."

"It's okay. I want you to have it."

She smiled and set the patch aside while continuing to look through the tapes. "Were these the only ones you found in the backpack?"

Joe looked at the tiny cassettes she'd stacked on the table. He was certain he had brought them all. "Are you missing some?"

She grew agitated, snatching up each tape, examining it, and shoving it back into the ziplock bag.

"Jane, are you missing tapes?"

She glared up at him. "Sweet Jane. How many goddamn times do I have to tell you my name is Sweet Jane? And you know what tape's missing." She popped off the bench and got into his face. "You let them take it, didn't you? Didn't you?"

Eyes wide and wild, she appeared to be on the verge of losing control, then, as quickly as it had come on, the storm in her eyes subsided. She slumped back down on the bench and put her head in her hands.

"I am so sorry, Joe. I can't help it. Sometimes I just can't help it."

He sat down next to her and put his arm around her. "It's okay. I will help you. God will help you. I promise."

She leaned into him and sobbed. "I am missing a very important cassette. I need it to show everyone the truth. It's marked with a piece of red tape. Do you know which one I am talking about?"

Joe remembered seeing it before. "Yes. I think I do."

He held her for several minutes and prayed for peace and healing for her. She stopped sobbing and straightened up.

"Damn, I need a cigarette," she said.

Joe laughed. "The lieutenant promised me he would find a place for you to smoke."

"I don't want to go back to Hardin. It's awful there."

"I will do whatever I can to help you."

The door buzzed, and the lieutenant stepped in.

"We have to take Ms. Carter now."

Jane gathered up the notebooks and placed them in Joe's hands. "Can you keep these safe for me?"

"Don't you want them?"

"No. I am done. I finished on the way down here. Of course, none of it matters without the fourth book. Be careful, there's a million dollars in those books."

"I'll find the other book and keep them all safe."

"Please help me get out of Hardin. Tell them I will go back to Brookhaven and won't leave."

Joe wasn't sure what Brookhaven was, but he made a mental note to find out.

The lieutenant held the door open.

They hugged, and Joe walked out. As he passed the lieutenant, he paused. "Remember, you promised to let her smoke."

"We'll take good care of her."

In the doorway, he turned to Jane. "We are all part of God's plan. Everything will be right in the end."

She half smiled and half smirked and said, "We are all just vibrations in the field, Joe. Somewhere it is already right."

CHAPTER FIFTEEN

Joe

Deputy Tyrell drove Joe back to the restaurant. It was the first time Joe had ridden in the front seat of a police car. It was much nicer than riding in the back. It was also nice not to be handcuffed and drenched in his own urine. The young deputy was friendly and talkative. Joe learned he had left the marines two years ago after deployments in Syria and Sudan and was now pursuing a criminal science degree at the university. One day, Tyrell confided to Joe, he hoped to join the FBI and leave Opelika behind.

Joe's car was parked in a small lot across from the restaurant's entrance. After the deputy dropped him off, he leaned against the front fender contemplating the day's events and watching a steady flow of customers coming and going through the double doors, one painted orange and the other blue. The sun hovered above the small town's skyline. It would be dusk soon, and the fading light would make searching for Jane's things difficult.

The restaurant was in the middle of a row of buildings that branched off from the main street. The empty lot where he and Jane had been arrested was at the opposite end of the row. He pushed off his car and made his way across the street. The lot was a small overgrown parcel of land that was about 150 feet wide and 150 feet deep. It looked as if a house or business had once stood on the property but had been demolished and removed a long time ago. The remnants of a foundation and driveway were visible beneath the bramble and tall grass.

Joe walked back to the narrow alley that ran behind the restaurant and paused where he believed Jane had run into the lot before she was tackled by the deputy. The army had trained him in what they called tactical site exploitation and he surveyed the area like he might have surveyed an Afghan goat pasture. The process would be the same, except of course, he was not searching the lot for a weapons cache. He looked for a spot to act as the center point for a spiral search pattern, which was the best pattern to use when searching an open area by yourself.

Jane had made it about twenty feet into the lot before the deputy tackled her. Joe scanned the tall grass until he spotted an area where the grass had been crushed by the struggle. That would be his center point. He walked over to where the two had landed and where he had been tased. Reasoning the tape and notebook would have traveled no more than a couple dozen feet from where they were ejected from the backpack, he picked out a tall, thin pine sapling about 25 feet away for the western boundary of his search area. The road that separated the lot from the alley would be his eastern boundary.

Just as he'd been trained, he got down low and crept around the search center in an ever-widening circular pattern. Picking his way through thorny bushes that tore at his bare arms and stung his fingers, he probed the tangled grass with his eyes while murmuring a short prayer to Saint Anthony, the patron saint of lost articles.

On his third circle, he found a plastic bag containing a toothbrush, tube of toothpaste, a bar of soap and a small bottle of shampoo. The notebook was found on the next rotation. It had been caught in the limbs of a small hardwood. With his attention on the ground, he'd almost missed it. He continued the pattern, checking his progress against the center point to make sure his course remained circular. Every few feet he picked up and discarded a piece of litter or debris left over from whatever had once stood in the lot. He came across an empty bottle of Southern Comfort whiskey. His hands trembled when he picked it up, and unable to overcome the compulsion, he put the opening to his nose and sniffed. The tangy, fruity smell filled his mouth, and he fought back the urge to put his lips on the rim. His eyes watered as he beat back the demon that rose up from those dark places within him. "God, when will you free me of this?" he shouted as he pitched the bottle into the air.

Joe reached the outer markers of the search perimeter without finding the cassette. The sun had set, and the sky was purpling. Soon it would be too dark to see anything. He took out his phone and turned on the flashlight feature, then retracing his steps backward, he inched along with his phone close to the ground. About halfway to the center point, near where he'd almost succumbed to the demon, the red tape on the small cassette Jane had begged him to find caught the phone's light. Joe snatched the cassette up and put it in his front pants pocket. Then he took his breviary from his back pocket and sat down in the matted grass where Jane and the deputy had fallen, and, using the light from his phone, read his evening prayers.

On his way back to his car, he noticed the restaurant was still open and decided to stop in to get something to eat. It was almost 10:00 p.m., and the place was full of young people who Joe assumed were all students.

The hostess sat him at a small table away from the crowd. The staff had changed since lunch, and no one appeared to recognize him. The waiter commented on his black eye saying something like, "Dude, I hope the other guy looks worse." He appeared disappointed when Joe told him he hadn't laid a glove on the other guy.

Joe studied the cassette while waiting for his food and wondered what was on this particular one that made it more special than the others. Jane had said she needed it to prove everyone wrong. Wrong about what, he did not know. Whatever was recorded on it was important to her, and he'd see she got it back.

The lieutenant had told him they were taking her up to Tuscaloosa first thing in the morning. He wondered how early that would be. He was over two hours away from home. It did not make much sense to drive all the way back to Atlanta tonight if he was going to return early in the morning.

He took out his phone to search for a hotel. He hadn't looked at the incoming calls since the lieutenant had returned it to him. There were three missed calls, two from Carlos, and one from Caleb. Joe dreaded calling Carlos. His mentor was already rattled by the incident at the homeless encampment. It would not be lost on the doubting priest that in three days, Joe had experienced more temptation and violence than the other members of the Sacred Heart clergy experienced in their entire lives. His mentor would not come out and blame him for the events, but he knew Carlos would believe Joe's approach to helping Jane was more in keeping with a soldier than a shepherd. Caleb, on the other hand, would be less worried about whether Joe behaved like a priest than if he remained sober. Of the two, he would rather talk to Caleb right now, but it was too late. The old man would have turned in hours ago. He took a deep breath, prayed for understanding, and selected Carlos from the missed call list.

Carlos answered on the third ring. "Joseph. Thank God. We have all been worried sick about you."

"I'm fine, Father. No need to worry."

"We received a call from a sheriff's department in Alabama. They spoke to Agnes. They told her you were involved in some kind of incident, and you were being questioned. They wouldn't tell her any more than that. What is happening? Are you in some kind of trouble?"

"No. I am not in any trouble, but they arrested Jane."

"Arrested her? What did she do?"

"It's what that doctor told you. She left a state hospital without permission."

"Where are you now, Joseph?"

"Still in Auburn. The police are taking Jane back to the hospital in Tuscaloosa tomorrow morning. I need to see her before they do so I'll be staying the night here."

"We won't see you at morning prayers then?"

"I'm afraid not. I need to make sure she is okay before I leave here."

"I believe your heart is in the right place, Joseph. I really do, but perhaps it would be best to let the proper authorities take care of Jane.

She must be a very troubled person. You have obligations that cannot be neglected. You mustn't let this—this…." Carlos paused like he was searching for a word, "obsession with this woman jeopardize what you have worked so hard to achieve."

Joe held back the anger he felt by his mentor's use of the word obsession. He knew Carlos meant well and was only trying to guide him, but at the same time, he wondered if this was some reference to his battle with alcoholism. After taking a few breaths, he decided it wasn't Carlos who was worried about his addiction, it was he. The demon was near. He'd almost succumbed to it last night at his apartment and moments ago in the empty lot. He'd passed those tests, but it had been close. He might not pass the next one. He said a silent prayer for strength.

"Joseph?" Carlos's soft Latin voice interrupted his prayer.

"Yes. I am sorry, Father. You're right of course."

They spoke for several more minutes. Carlos told him he had spoken to Caleb, and the old man had expressed concerns about Joe's well-being. Joe promised to call Caleb, then he told Carlos everything that happened that day including his being tased and held by the Lee County Sheriff. The story of course, only exacerbated the priest's concerns, but Joe knew any attempt to gloss over the events would be construed by his doubting mentor as deceptive and untruthful—not traits the archdiocese looked for in a priest. Before they hung up, Carlos asked Joseph to pray with him, and they recited prayers for strength and courage in troubled times. They prayed for Jane and recited verses from Romans, Isaiah, and Philippians. Joe ended the call feeling invigorated with the spirit and some remorse at thinking ill of his mentor.

As he pocketed his phone, he noticed an attractive young waitress was standing off to the side watching him. He smiled and motioned her over. She was a small, dark-haired, olive-skinned woman who appeared to be in her late twenties—a little older than the students who filled the noisy half of the restaurant.

"I heard you praying, and I didn't want to bother you," she said. She avoided his gaze and seemed more than a little nervous.

Joe knew public prayer outside of a church appeared odd to most people. "I hope I didn't make you feel uncomfortable."

"Oh no. Of course not," she said as she stepped forward and collected his plate and utensils. "Can I bring you anything else?"

"No, thank you. Just the check please." As she turned to go, he remembered he had not paid for his and Jane's lunch. "Come to think of it, there is something else," he said. "I was in here earlier with a friend, and she…" he searched for a way to explain it. "Uh, she had to go with the police. I guess we both had to go. We left in such a rush, I didn't pay our check for lunch, and I would like to take care of that now."

"Oh. I heard about that. Let me go see what I can find out."

A few moments later a short, stocky man with the same Mediterranean complexion walked over. Where he had hair, which was only on the sides of his head, it was the same color as the waitress's. He looked to be in his mid-fifties. He was dressed in tan pants and a clean white shirt, and he wore a blue and orange striped tie with the Auburn University logo embossed on its tip. When Joe saw the tie, he said "ah" to himself as he realized the restaurant's name, Stripes, was related to the university's football team, the Auburn Tigers.

The man was smiling when he reached the table. "Good evening. My name is Charlie Rossini. My daughter told me you were part of the excitement we had here at lunchtime."

Joe nodded and returned the smile. "Yes. I am sorry for whatever trouble that may have caused. The situation could have been handled better by everyone."

Charlie motioned at the empty bench across from Joe. "Mind if I sit down?"

"Please," Joe said and introduced himself.

Charlie slipped into the empty seat. He had two restaurant checks in his hand. He placed them on the table in front of him but did not slide them over to Joe.

"I am curious about what happened today—about Jane. I don't mean to pry into your business, but I know a little about the situation. It was big news around here when Dr. Carter was murdered. I knew her. I knew Jane. They came in together often. I also know about Jane's illness. I have a little experience with that sort of thing."

Joe smiled and told Charlie what he knew about Jane going AWOL from the hospital. He confessed to only knowing her for a few days and gently asked what Charlie knew about her and her mother.

"Like I said, they were in here often. Jane was quiet and a little off, but there were times when she would talk, and you could tell how smart she was. She knew her numbers."

"She still does," Joe said.

"I bet she does. Back then, the waiters would play a game with her when they brought the check. They'd hand the check to her mother and ask Jane how much it was without showing it to her. She would always know the exact price including the tax. She even caught our mistakes here and there. I guess that wasn't such a big deal when it was only her and her mother, but sometimes they were here with bigger parties, like when her mother would bring her graduate assistants or other students and colleagues with them, and she would still know the exact price on the spot. It wasn't like she calculated it on some paper before the check arrived either. She just remembered what everyone ordered, remembered the prices on the menu, and did the math in an instant. It was very impressive."

"Yes. She is special." Joe patted the notebook he had retrieved from the empty lot. "This is full of some pretty hairy equations she has been working on." He grew silent for a moment. "I have only known her for a few days, and I have seen her intense and even fierce, but I find it hard to believe she would kill her mother, or anyone for that matter. Did you ever see her fight with her mother or show any hostility toward her?"

Charlie laughed. "Hardly. Like I said, Jane was odd and said some off-the-wall things, but she was always kind to her mother. They were friends. No—they adored each other. Anyone could see they shared a special bond. Dr. Carter was very, very proud and protective of Jane and Jane of her mother."

Joe shook his head. "I guess only God knows why such things happen. It's hard to understand how such tragedy can be part of His plan."

Charlie nodded. "Ain't that the truth. My daughter suffered from schizophrenia too."

"The one who waited on me?"

"No. That's Anna. She helps me out now and again when things get busy, but she has a good job with Microsoft. She's a computer genius. In fact, Anna was one of Dr. Carter's students. She had a twin, Elizabeth. We called her Beth."

Joe picked up on the words "had" and "called." "Beth passed away?"

Charlie's smile faded. "Yes. She took her own life. Been almost six years now."

"Oh. I am so sorry."

Charlie cleared his throat, and his voice grew a little hoarse. "Thank you. She was a smart girl too, not like Jane, of course, but smart. She and Anna were very competitive. They drove each other to do better in school, tennis, everything. They had similar interests and both of them went to the university. That made me quite proud as I am an alumnus who still bleeds orange and blue." He spread his arms. "As you can see by the restaurant's décor."

"And the name," Joe added.

"The kids like it. Especially during football season."

"So, tell me some more about Beth. Did she study computers like her sister?" Joe prodded, sensing Charlie wanted to talk about her.

"Beth never finished school. She got sick in her second year, and she had to withdraw. It took us a long time to get the right treatment for her and find a doctor she trusted. When we did, she started getting better. She still struggled, you know, but she had her good days, and for a while it seemed she had more good days than bad ones."

Charlie took a napkin from the dispenser on the table and wiped his eyes.

"She started working here at the restaurant and began socializing with some friends again. She even talked about going back to school. We were hopeful, then one day she came home from her doctor's appointment, went in her room, and swallowed a fistful of her pills."

"Her pills?"

"Yeah. Like most schizophrenics, Beth took medication. Her mother would set out pills for her to take in the morning after breakfast and in the evening after dinner. The doctors told us it was very important that Beth took the right dosage of her medicine every day, and Marie, that's my wife, made sure she did. On the day she died, Beth took the pills from the kitchen up to her room and swallowed every pill in the bottle."

He wiped his eyes again.

"We figured she must have swallowed twenty or thirty pills. After she did, she called for her mother and told her what she'd done. I was here as usual, and Marie called me in a panic. I told her to take her to the hospital to get her stomach pumped. I rushed there to meet them, but it was too late. By the time they pumped her stomach, the drug had already entered her system. She had terrible seizures in the emergency room and died."

"May God bless and comfort you, Charlie. I am so sorry."

Charlie held up a finger while he composed himself. "No. It's me who is sorry. I normally don't go around telling strangers about my pain, but there's more to this story. You see, Beth and Jane had more in common than schizophrenia."

"Did they know each other?"

"No. Not really. I'm sure they ran into each other here and there, but Jane is several years older than Beth, or older than what Beth would be. They were not friends, but they saw the same doctor."

"Dr. Lieberman?"

"Yes. Lieberman, a vile son of a bitch," Charlie growled. "Beth started seeing him about six months after the murder."

Joe was startled by Charlie's reaction. "Why do you speak so harshly about the doctor?"

"I didn't like the man from the start. He felt like a used car salesman, if you know what I mean. Sleazy and manipulative. The kind who always talks in a soft, reassuring way and seems to agree with everything you say, but in the end, only wants to close the sale. Nope, I couldn't stand him, but Marie, Marie begged me to give him a chance, and when Beth started to improve, I had to admit I had been wrong about him." He grew quiet for a moment and stared at his reflection in the dark window, then almost under his breath he said, "But I guess it turned out I wasn't."

"What do you mean?" Joe prodded.

Charlie turned back from the window. "Remember I said it took a long time for us to find the right doctor for Beth?"

Joe nodded. "Yes. Someone she could trust."

"Trust is important, especially for schizophrenics like Beth with paranoia problems. Beth didn't trust anyone." He paused and dabbed his eyes again with the napkin. "Not even me, but she came to trust that son of a bitch."

"What did he do?"

"I couldn't prove it, but I believe he was abusing my daughter during their sessions."

"Abusing?"

"Sexually. I think the bastard was raping her."

Joe quietly gasped. "Did she tell you that?"

"No—not directly. But she would tell Marie that she had pain in her feminine parts after her sessions with him, and one time Marie found blood in Beth's underwear."

Joe wasn't sure what to make of the man's claim. "If the doctor was raping her, wouldn't she have told you?"

"Not if she didn't know."

"How could she not know?"

"He uses a form of deep hypnosis in his treatment. It's his own process. He's kinda famous for it." He paused. "And notorious. Lots of other doctors and experts have accused him of quackery and even fraud, but there are many others, including former and current patients, who claim he is a genius. If you Google him, you'll see what I mean. We were a little uncertain about it when we first brought her to him, and he let us sit in on one of their sessions so we could see what it was all about."

"I didn't realize psychiatrists used hypnosis for treating schizophrenia."

"Neither did I until we saw it for ourselves. When we sat in on the session, he had us wait in his lobby until he put Beth into what he described as a deep hypnotic trance, then he called us in to observe. She was lying on his couch with an IV in her arm."

"What was the IV for?"

"He said it reduced anxiety and helped her focus."

Joe made a mental note to ask Caleb why a psychiatrist would use an IV during an office therapy session. "Do you know what he was putting in her?"

Charlie shook his head. "Nah. Marie kept up with all that."

"What happened during the session?"

"Beth was out. I thought she was sleeping, but he said she was in a deep hypnotic trance. She was technically conscious, he said, but she was not aware of her surroundings. She didn't even know we were in the room, she never knew, and she only responded to his voice. It was pretty darn creepy. He called her Sweet Beth."

Joe sat upright. "Sweet Beth?"

"Yeah. Isn't that odd? Apparently, Liberman's technique involved creating an alternate personality inside Beth that he used to probe Beth's thoughts."

"Like a split personality?"

"Yeah. Just like that."

Joe wanted to call Caleb right then. He never heard of such a thing, and he wondered if Lieberman had given Jane the name Sweet Jane. "Did Beth suffer from, you know, multiple personalities?"

"No. At least not before she started seeing Lieberman."

"How did he use Sweet Beth to treat your daughter?"

"Lieberman asked Sweet Beth questions about how Beth felt and what the voices in her head said." Charlie coughed and shook his head like he was trying to deny the memory. "That's about it. He said it gave him insight into why she thought the things she did so he could treat her."

"This all sounds very unusual to me. I have a close friend who is a psychiatrist. I will have to ask him about it."

Charlie dabbed his eyes. "I guess it helped Beth. Marie was sure happy with the results, but I was never really okay with the technique. I didn't like the thought of her lying on that sofa in that dark office with that man, especially when I saw how much control he had over her while she was hypnotized. It was clear to me he could do anything to her, and she wouldn't resist and wouldn't remember. Then when she started complaining about the pain and Marie found that blood, I lost it."

"What did you do?"

"I went to see him. I wanted to kill him, but I didn't lose my temper. Marie was sure that bastard was helping Beth, so I stayed calm. I told him about Beth's complaints and what Marie had found. Do you know what he said?"

"What?"

"He said it was possible she was doing it to herself, maybe even masturbating in her sleep. He said just because she was sick didn't mean she didn't have sexual desires. Her illness kept her socially isolated for so long. She hadn't had a boyfriend in years. She was just doing what was natural."

"You didn't believe him."

Both Charlie's hands fell heavy on the table with a thud. "No. I still don't. He had her under his control, and she had obvious signs of abuse."

"Did he explain why it seemed to only happen after her visits with him?"

"Yeah. He said something about the sessions may have aroused her. Can you believe that?"

"No. It all sounds very wrong. What happened next? Did you go to the police?"

Charlie rumbled his lips. "Not officially. I spoke to a few cops. They are in here all the time. They told me Lieberman had connections in both the county sheriff and city police departments."

The lieutenant had said the same thing. "Did she see him again?" Joe asked.

"Yes. Marie and I wanted to believe him. We wanted Beth to get better." The distraught father seemed to be pleading for Joe to understand. "We wanted Beth back, and like I said, she seemed to be responding well to his treatment. But we kept a close eye on her, believe me."

"And?"

"She didn't complain of any further issues. Imagine that. I confront him, and it all stops." Charlie stared at him. "Everything was just fine right up until the day she died."

Joe thought hard about his next question. He didn't want to accuse the doctor of engineering the man's daughter's death, but Charlie had led him to the conclusion. "You think he did something when she was under hypnosis to make her take all those pills?"

Charlie's eyes flashed with anger before cooling back to sadness. "Yes. I do." His voice cracked, and a tear rolled down his cheek.

Joe did not know what to do. He wanted to console this man. He wanted to pray for God to ease his pain and show them the truth, but all he could do was sit in silence until Charlie regained his composure.

Charlie studied the balled-up napkin he'd been wiping his eyes with and smiled. "Wow, I usually don't go on like this. Anna told me you were praying over here. Are you a pastor or just very religious?"

Joe smiled. "I guess I'm a little of both, though I haven't been ordained yet."

"You'll make a good priest. You're easy to talk to."

"Thank you, and God bless you and your family," Joe said. Then he added, "And especially Beth."

Charlie nodded and picked up the checks. "No charge for these. You had a rough day."

"You don't need to do that," Joe said.

"It's my pleasure," he said as he slid out of the booth. "Say a prayer for me." He paused and took a breath. "And for my daughter too."

"You bet I will. Would you like to pray with me now?"

Charlie shook his head. "No. Thank you. I wouldn't feel comfortable doing that here—these kids," he motioned toward the crowded part of the restaurant, "wouldn't understand."

Joe nodded. He knew he was right. "Sure."

Charlie turned to walk away, and Joe raised his hand to stop him.

"Do you think Dr. Lieberman could have made Jane kill her mother like you believe he made your daughter take those pills?"

Charlie stared at him for a long moment. "It was obvious to everyone that Jane loved her mother. Something made her kill her," he said. Then he rapped his knuckles on the table and walked away.

CHAPTER SIXTEEN

Barry

"You got her?" Barry almost shouted into his phone as he exited his car in the gravel driveway of Carl's granddaddy's house. He reached into the back seat and retrieved a bag containing two bottles of wine he'd stopped to purchase at a liquor store near his hotel.

Carl and his wife, Jackie, were standing on the top step of the old house's front porch, watching him. He nodded at them and pointed at the phone pressed against his ear. He wondered how the old porch step planks supported the weight of the bovine couple.

"Yes. We picked her up this afternoon," the man on the other end of the call said.

"That's great news," Barry said.

"We've been in contact with the state, and we'll be returning her to Hardin tomorrow morning."

"Tomorrow morning? Did you say you are bringing her to Hardin tomorrow?"

"Yes, first thing."

"That's a relief. Thank you, and I owe you one."

The call over, Barry pocketed his phone and made his way up the cracked and age-stained concrete walkway to a large two-story farmhouse with a steep peaked roof, ornate scrolled trim, and weathered clapboard siding that may have been white once but was now a dirty gray.

"Good evening, Doctors," Barry said as he reached the couple. Jackie was a medical doctor too—a pediatrician. As Barry recalled, the two of them had met at a tedious-sounding lecture on pediatric psychiatry. They'd probably found each other at the refreshment table. Carl had confided in him that Jackie loved children as long as they belonged to someone else. She had no interest in having any of her own. Carl had wanted children but lost the battle and was forced to settle for dogs. They had three.

"Good evening to you," Carl returned the greeting. Standing on that porch, grinning, with his ruddy complexion, blonde hair and dressed as he was, in jeans, plaid short-sleeved shirt, and work boots, he looked more like a dairy farmer than a board-certified psychiatrist.

Jackie smiled but said nothing. She too had a ruddy complexion, blonde hair and was wearing jeans and a plaid shirt. Damn if they didn't look like twins.

Barry gestured at the farmhouse. "This is quite something. How old is it?"

Carl came down the steps to meet him. "It was built in the 1900s. They call it a Folk Victorian style."

Barry handed Carl the wine. "I wasn't sure what you'd prefer. I settled on a nice Chardonnay. I thought it would go well with the beautiful spring weather."

Jackie came down the steps to meet them and took the wine from Carl. Eyeing the labels, she said to Barry, "This is perfect and very nice of you. I'll go see if I can find some glasses." She retreated up the steps and disappeared into the house.

Barry continued to take in the structure and surrounding landscape. "It sure is a big place," he said.

"It used to be part of a large family farm." Carl pointed to an empty field. "There once was a barn over there, but it burned down about twenty years ago. The fire almost took the house too. Every fire truck within thirty miles was out here hosing the house down while they let the barn burn to the ground."

"Your granddaddy was a farmer too?"

"No. He didn't own the entire farm. He owned the house and the barn and six acres. He did garden, though. He had an enormous garden over there." Carl pointed to another empty field. "Let's go inside, and I'll show you his collection from the asylum."

The front door led into a two-story entrance foyer dominated by a steep staircase rising to the second floor. A large living room was visible through an arched opening on Barry's left, and a smaller sitting room opened off his right. A threadbare Persian-style throw rug covered the foyer's dark wood floorboards which creaked under Carl's bulk. The interior, like the exterior, was clean and maintained, but appeared not to have been updated since the middle of the last century. Faded cream-colored wallpaper with light green stripes covered the plaster walls. Some of the seams were lifting with age. Antique dark wood furnishings upholstered in various shades of browns and golds filled the rooms.

Noting how all the furniture was polished and dust-free, Barry asked, "Does anyone live here?"

Carl shook his head. "No. It's been empty since Granddaddy passed. We pay a couple from Guatemala to do general maintenance and upkeep. He takes care of the yard and does minor repairs, and she dusts the place and makes sure no critters get inside."

"Critters?"

"Yeah. We had a raccoon living in here last fall. It got into the attic through a busted roof vent. Some bats too. What a mess."

Barry followed Carl down an arched hallway that led to the rear of the house. "Why do you keep it?"

"Because his brother is an ass," answered Jackie from somewhere down the hall.

They made a left into a 1950s-style kitchen. Jackie was standing next to a large, modern stainless-steel refrigerator that looked out of place among the ancient avocado cabinets and chrome-rimmed Formica counters.

"John's not an ass," Carl objected. "He only wants to make sure we get what this place is worth."

Barry looked at Carl then Jackie, feigning confused interest.

Jackie snorted, then explained. "Carl is the executor of his dad's estate, such as it is, but he has to have his brother's consent to sell the real estate."

"John gave us the okay to sell Dad's house, didn't he?"

"Yeah, but it took a year before he agreed, and he only did because we told him he would have to pay for its upkeep. Now we need his permission to sell this money pit." She spread her arms and laughed. "Why anyone is worried we won't get what this palace is worth is beyond me."

"It's one of the oldest homes in the area," Carl protested.

Jackie smirked at him.

"It's a landmark," he continued, sounding defensive. "It's even in the county's historical registry."

She made an unattractive farting sound with her lips and handed them each a glass tumbler half filled with the wine Barry brought. "There are no wine glasses. I guess we'll have to make do with these. At least they are clean."

Carl took a gulp of his wine and said, "Barry doesn't want to hear about our problems. Let's go see Granddaddy's asylum." He led them to a door in a corner of the kitchen that led outside.

"It's outside?" Barry asked.

"No. It's in the cellar. The door to the cellar is outside."

They followed Carl out the door and down some shaky wooden steps to the backyard. He led them to a pair of large green wooden doors that were set on top of what looked like a grass-covered hill rising from the ground to the house. The paint on the doors gleamed as if it had just been applied.

"Mateo has been busy," Jackie said, noticing the fresh paint on the doors.

Carl handed her his wine and said to Barry, "Mateo is our Guatemalan maintenance man."

"El Salvadorian for Christ's sake," Jackie said.

"What?" Carl said, giving her a questioning look.

"They are from El Salvador. You never get that right."

Carl shrugged and said "whatever" as he struggled to fit the key into the rusty padlock that secured the doors. After a few grunts and curses, he got it unlocked and heaved opened the doors, letting them fall on the grass with a loud thump, likely marring the new paint. Beneath them was a dark rectangular opening with concrete walls and concrete steps leading to an underground doorway set in the foundation.

They followed Carl down the steps.

"I don't think I have ever seen a basement you enter from the outside," Barry said.

"Oh?" Jackie said in the annoying, superior tone Barry had already grown tired of. "You need to visit more old farmhouses. They are quite common."

Barry smiled at her, but he didn't know how Carl tolerated it. If she was his wife, he was certain he'd have talked her into swallowing her own tongue within the first week of marriage.

Carl opened the lower door, and they stepped inside. The room was dark except for the rectangle of light let in by the open door. Carl felt around on the wall and flipped a switch, illuminating several bare light bulbs in fixtures mounted on the massive wood beams supporting the house above them.

Barry noted the drop in temperature. It was much cooler than above ground. "It feels good down here. It's almost cold."

"That's kind of the point," Jackie said. "The house was built pre-refrigeration. This was the refrigerator."

The cellar was one large room divided by two rows of rough, bare wood columns rising from the concrete floor to the overhead beams. The walls were composed of irregularly shaped stones that had been cut and mortared together. Despite the abundance of high-wattage lighting, the room was still gloomy and in places, dark. Little of the harsh overhead light reached the room's edges, but in the center of the room, it shone brightly on what looked like an exhibit in a medical museum.

Barry drained the last of the wine from his glass and stepped into the light. A heavy, steel tubular hospital bed with a black vinyl mattress gleamed under the naked bulb. What looked like leather wrist and ankle restraining straps were fastened at the head and foot of the bed frame. On one side of the bed was an old intravenous drip stand complete with a glass bottle, and next to it was a shiny steel cart with a black box the size of a small suitcase resting atop it.

"What is this?" Barry asked, pointing to the black box.

"Open it," Carl replied.

Barry unsnapped the metal clasp that secured the lid and flipped it back, revealing a silver metal electrical panel cluttered with switches, dials, and indicator lights. Printing on the panel identified the device as a model B-24 ECT unit manufactured by the Medcraft Electronic Corporation. A headset with contact electrodes instead of earphones was wrapped in what looked like several feet of wire and stowed in an adjacent compartment along with a coiled standard wall plug.

"Ah. Look at this antique. Electroconvulsive therapy is such a misunderstood procedure."

Carl nodded. "True. People only know what they've seen in old movies. Then again, back in the day, when machines like this were used, the process was a bit… um, jarring." He attempted a diabolical laugh, but with his high-pitched voice it sounded like a child's giggle. "This unit could deliver quite a jolt. I'm told it was not uncommon for patients to break bones and teeth during the process. It's much different today. The charge is more focused, and the patients are under general anesthesia."

"The procedure seems very barbaric to me," Jackie said. "Sending electric current through the brain for what? Your profession doesn't even know why it works, or if it does."

Carl shrugged. "Sometimes there is no other option. You have a patient who is not responding to the medications, you wire them up to this and hope the seizures it causes will trigger a sort of reset in the brain that relieves their symptoms. It takes several sessions, but I've had a great deal of success treating depression with it."

She snorted. "Reset? Hope? Those don't sound like medical terms to me."

"I'm not in the mood to debate the neuroendocrine hypothesis with someone who treats booboos and tummy aches."

"I'll take babies over babblers any day, sweetie."

Barry removed the headset and studied it. He placed it on his head, adjusting it so the electrodes fit snugly against his temples and wondered what it must feel like to have current run through his frontal lobes. "I don't do ECTs myself, but I have referred several patients to those who do. I bet this old model delivers quite a shock. I've had a few patients who I would have liked to have used this on."

"That's awful," Jackie said, emitting another piggish snort-laugh.

"You'd have to know those patients," Barry said. Still holding the headset, he turned to face Carl. "You told me earlier you think it still works."

"It lights up when it's plugged in, but I've never tested it on myself," he cast a sidelong glance at Jackie, "or anyone else."

Jackie glared at him.

"You want to give it a shot, Dr. Lieberman? I could wire you up," Carl offered, making a snorting, piggish laugh indistinguishable from his wife's.

Repulsed by their laughter, Barry thought he'd like to wire the both of them up. He returned the headset to its compartment and shut the machine's lid. "No. That's quite all right." He turned his attention to the other side of the bed where another metal cart sat. This one held a tray with about a dozen old surgical instruments arrayed on it. He picked up a small surgical bone saw, studied it for a moment, and returned it to the tray. "Probably not sterile," he quipped.

"I think not," Jackie agreed.

Next to the cart was a freestanding iron coatrack and hanging from it was a white canvas straitjacket and the sadistic looking head-restraining system Carl had mentioned earlier.

Barry examined the head restraint. It consisted of a series of interconnected leather straps and buckles. One strap went under the wearer's jaw and over their head, connecting to another strap that encircled their forehead. The head straps attached to a collar that went around the wearer's neck, and the whole system was attached with small chains and fasteners to a wide strap that was buckled to the bed. "Looks like something Hannibal Lecter would wear."

"I'm sure they still use things like this at Taylor Hardin," Carl said. "We use less sadomasochistic looking versions of them all the time at Bryce. Sometimes it's necessary to immobilize a patient's head, especially when the patient is trying to bite you," he bared his teeth and bit at the air near Jackie's face.

"There are times I'd like to use one on you," Jackie said, snorting.

"Barry doesn't want to hear about our sex life, honeybuns."

Jackie continued to snort, and Barry imagined pigs copulating in the mud, one of them wearing the head restraint.

"Speaking of Taylor Hardin," Barry began, "That patient we have been discussing is being returned there tomorrow morning."

"She's been found?" Carl asked.

"Yes. I just received the news from an acquaintance in the Opelika Sheriff's Department. That was the call I was on when I pulled into the driveway. They picked her up this afternoon."

"Carl told me about her. You must be very relieved," Jackie said.

Barry put on his best caring smile, the same one he used on his patients. It took exceptional acting skill to get right, given he cared about nothing. "I am, but I am also concerned about her." He glanced at Carl. "I want to make sure she gets the best care, and I would like to talk to her. I want to try to help Jane—maybe even begin treating her again if that is possible."

Carl stared at him for a moment, and then, seeming to notice Barry's glass was empty, turned to Jackie and asked if she wouldn't mind returning to the house for more wine. She scowled at him, then drained her own glass and trudged toward the steps. Carl followed her across the room but veered away before reaching the steps to retrieve a couple of heavy metal chairs from a cache of hospital office furniture. He paused by the exit for a moment to make sure Jackie was gone before returning to the bed where he dropped into one of the chairs and motioned for Barry to take the other.

Barry lingered at the instrument tray. "What's on your mind?"

"I know I promised to help you, but I am a little concerned about your obsession with this woman," Carl replied in his squeaky voice.

"Obsession, Doctor Walker? Is that your clinical assessment of my behavior?"

"No, not exactly, but you do seem, well, obsessed with her."

Barry considered his host for a moment. The two men had met many years ago when Barry had taught a short seminar on medical hypnosis at the university. Carl had attended the classes and had been curious about Barry's work. He hung around after the classes, peppering Barry with questions about subconscious manipulation and the ethical and unethical uses of the technique. They had become friends of a sort, though. Barry had always looked down on Carl, thinking him a man of mediocre intellect and inferior upbringing. Barry came from old family money. His father had been something like royalty in Baltimore. He thought of Carl, with his southern upbringing and inferior education, as a bit of a rube, and since Barry practiced in Opelika, he considered himself an expert on rubes.

"Did I mention this afternoon I knew her mother? That we were involved, if you know what I mean?"

"Romantically?"

"Yes. We'd even discussed a long-term commitment, but it was difficult on Jane. You see, Jane had developed a bit of a fixation on me. She misinterpreted our patient-doctor relationship and began to see her mother as a rival for my affection."

"She was jealous of her mother?"

"Quite so, and now when I look back, I fear the stress of that arrangement may have exacerbated Jane's psychosis."

Carl half coughed and half laughed. "I guess so. My God, Barry, there're all kinds of ethical issues with that situation."

Barry eyed the surgical tray and imagined using some of its contents on Carl. "You are not in any position to lecture me on ethics and women."

Carl raised a finger and shot a nervous glance over his shoulder toward the steps. "Hey, you want my help? Then you best stop with that now."

Barry found the threat as amusing as it was empty. Carl was afraid. He was always afraid, which made him easy to control. "Yeah, yeah," he said while waving his hand. "So now you know why I am, to use your word, obsessed with Jane, I owe it to Maggie to take care of her."

"And you think keeping Jane locked up in Hardin is the way to do that?"

Barry ignored the comment and picked up a scalpel from the instrument tray. The stainless-steel handle felt cool in his hand, and it had the weight and balance of a prior age's machined-metal manufacturing that modern plastic scalpels lacked. Its edge flashed in the bright light from the overhead bulb. He ran the edge across the tip of his finger making a tiny incision that leaked a small crimson dot. He dropped the scalpel on the tray and put his finger in his mouth. "Still sharp."

Carl grimaced. "Those blades are not clean. I hope your tetanus is up to date."

Barry shrugged, then took a seat in the chair opposite Carl. He stared into the fat man's eyes until Carl lowered his gaze. "Jane will be at Hardin in the morning. How do we get access to her?"

"You already took care of that when you convinced me to take on the case. I am her physician now. I will call over there tomorrow afternoon and get things rolling."

"Will you be able to have her brought to Bryce or will they insist you go there?"

"Hardin is secure. They will require me to go there. At least initially. Bryce's facilities are much better though, especially our imaging and on-site lab. I'll get them to transfer her to us so I can update her brain scans and adjust her medication. I should be able to do that right away. It will be part of the evaluation. The Hardin folks aren't going to push back. They don't want her. They want her released to Brookhaven, but they won't do that without my sign-off."

Barry studied Carl's round, fleshy face and multiple chins, thinking about the right words to use. Word choice was important for control as it was in all forms of hypnosis, especially the most subtle forms. "A solid plan, Dr. Walker," he said. "We will take a thorough look at her." *We. They were treating her together.* "If it turns out Dr. Reynolds was right and her disease has moderated, I will reconsider my position," *After all, he only wanted the best for her, didn't he?* "But we must be careful." *We are a team.* "She's very smart. Probably smarter than both of us, and plenty smart enough to manipulate people who don't know her like I do. I'm not going to let that happen." *I'm just looking out for you.*

Jackie had snuck up behind them. They both flinched when her voice broke the fragile trance. "Manipulating you two doesn't sound so hard."

She filled their glasses, and they all laughed. Carl's laugh sounded more like a nervous squeak. Barry took his glass and left his hosts who started to bicker.

He wandered around the cellar inspecting the other asylum artifacts. Most of it was furniture and tools. Carl explained there had been a well-equipped machine shop on the grounds for maintaining the facility, and much of its hand tools as well as an ancient drill press wound up here. Several unusual ornaments were propped near the door. Barry brushed the cobwebs from them. They appeared to be Christian crosses. He lifted one for a closer look. It was about two feet tall, painted black, and felt as though it was made of iron. He brought it back to where Carl and Jackie were still arguing about something.

"What is this?"

Carl and Jackie stopped their argument and looked at him. "Grave marker," they said in unison.

"The asylum had its own graveyard," Carl added.

In the better light, Barry could see a palm-sized oval badge affixed to the center of the cross with markings on it. He squinted at the markings, searching for information about a decedent. "There's no name on it—just a number."

"It's an index number. It corresponds to an entry in a journal where the dead patient's name and specifics about their death were recorded."

"Hmm. Why would your granddaddy take these?"

Carl shrugged. "I don't think he took them from graves. I think that one and the others were all part of unused stock. He probably took them for scrap metal."

"Or maybe he was a crazy old coot," Jackie said.

"That diagnosis is possible too," Carl admitted.

Barry propped the marker against the wall near where he found it. "Regardless of his mental state, your granddaddy sure amassed an extraordinary collection. I find the whole place very interesting." With the right company, Barry thought, he could have some real fun with some of these things. He turned to Carl. "I expect to be shuttling between Opelika and here often over the next couple months. Would you consider renting this place to me?"

Jackie snorted then said, "Yuck. You would really want to stay in this old place?"

"Beats the Hampton Inn."

"I don't know about that. There's no TV, no Wi-Fi," she said.

"But it does have AC," Carl offered. "Daddy had it installed when Granddaddy got sick."

"Sounds perfect," Barry said.

"I'm hungry. Let's go to dinner, and we can discuss it over barbeque," Carl said as he hefted himself from the chair.

CHAPTER SEVENTEEN

Joe

Joe sat at a picnic table in a pleasant little area he discovered at the end of a walkway in the rear of the Opelika Best Western Hotel. It was early. The eastern sky glowed with the anticipation of an unbroken dawn. The nighttime cacophonic chirping of what had sounded like a million crickets had subsided to an occasional lone chirp accompanied by the soft cooing of a morning dove. *Chirp, chirp, coo, coo.*

It was warm. The still air was redolent with the smell of jasmine and hung heavy with moisture that condensed on every surface. He held his breviary above the tabletop to keep it dry and read its pages by the yellowish glow from a mercury lamp that shone above the walkway.

Joe gave thanks for the morning and the blessing of another day, and as he'd promised, he prayed for Charlie and his daughter. When he finished, the sky was orange and a brilliant sliver of sun appeared between the trees. Traffic noises replaced the chirping and cooing. He stood and stuffed the leather book in his back pocket then retrieved his phone from his front. It was 5:50 a.m. there in the central time zone, which meant it was ten before seven in Newark, New Jersey, and Caleb would have been up for hours.

"Good morning, Joseph." The old man's loud voice seemed even louder in the morning calm. "How are you doing, my son?"

"Very well, Doctor."

"Ah, it's Doctor this morning. Something tells me you have medical questions."

Joe laughed. The old man saw right through him. "Maybe a few," he admitted.

Greetings behind them, the old man got right to the point. "Before we get to your questions, Carlos tells me you've been having some adventures. He said there was some violence involved." His voice softened. "How are you dealing with it?"

The concern in the old man's voice was unmistakable, and so were the questions not asked. Are you having nightmares and, most importantly, are you drinking? Self-medicating was how Caleb usually referred to it.

"I am okay, blessed as always. I'm sleeping well." That was a small lie, but the nightmares were nowhere near as bad as they once were and besides, as far as he knew, he'd slept through the night last night. "I'd be lying if I told you there weren't times in the past couple days when I wanted a drink. The craving is always there, but this week I've felt more tempted than usual."

"How have you resisted it?"

"God has made me strong," he said, and thought to himself, I pray He makes me stronger.

"That's good, son, but I am worried about you. Up until recently, your life has taken on a stable rhythm. Disrupting that rhythm could trigger some old memories and feelings that you've struggled with in the past. You need to be cautious and seek help if those things become a problem again. You know what I am talking about."

"I do."

The old man was right, of course. Joe had settled into a comfortable routine since moving to Atlanta, some might even call it a rut, but he was closer to God than he'd ever been, and, until two nights ago, he hadn't spent a minute back on that hill in Afghanistan. Joe didn't want to talk about that right now, though. He hadn't called Caleb for analysis and therapy for himself though he knew he was about to get some.

"Good," Caleb continued. "Now, tell me about these adventures. When we last spoke, you had picked up a schizophrenic hitchhiker—a woman named Jane, if I recall. Correct?"

"That's right," Joe confirmed, then told him everything that had happened since their last conversation, which seemed like a month ago instead of only three days.

Caleb made him repeat the details about the attack at the homeless encampment and his arrest by the Lee County Sheriff's Department, saying, "The violence—the violence is very worrisome." He pressed Joe on how he felt about the events and how he coped with his feelings. Was he anxious? Was he depressed? What were his physical reactions? Shakes? Tremors? Details, details, the old man pressed. He made Joe talk about the guilt, pain, and even happiness he'd felt while going through his old army things with Jane, and most of all, Caleb pressed him about how he felt handling the firearm.

The probing was familiar. They'd spent many long afternoons in the old man's office at Saint Michael's covering the same ground. Back then, there had been times Joe resented Caleb's aggressive interrogations, but he grew to understand and appreciate their purpose and to love the man. Joe had shared the most painful events in his life with Caleb—things he'd shared with no one else, and Caleb had used the information to help Joe find his way out of the darkness. He'd taught him how to recognize and deal with his severe PTSD and to replace the half liter of Wild Turkey he was consuming every day with prayer and meditation. "Let's confront your memories, Joseph," Caleb's voice reverberated in his head, "then you can put them behind you,"

The questioning slowed, and the dialog shifted to small talk as it did at the end of all their sessions. Joe knew when the old man began complaining about the Yankees, he'd completed his analysis. Now it was Joe's turn to draw out of Caleb his assessment of Joe's emotional state. Had his war-damaged psyche held up? Or had some psychological line been crossed, indicating their years of repair work had begun to fail?

"It's like old times," Joe said. "I feel like I am sitting in that comfortable old leather chair in your office, discussing my dreams again."

Caleb laughed. "Mea culpa. Mea culpa. You can take the psychiatrist out of his office, my son, but you can't take the psychiatrist out of the man."

"Or the patient off the recliner it seems," Joe responded, then not wanting to hurt Caleb's feelings, added, "I am forever grateful for all the help you've given me, and as always, I welcome your guidance. What do you think? Am I coming unglued? Do I need to return to therapy?"

"I don't know. Do you feel you need more therapy?"

"No."

"And if the nightmares return?"

"I will call you. Do not worry, Father. I have my faith, and the meditation techniques you taught me. My heart is as healed as it can be in this life. I can't undo the things I've seen and done, but I trust in the Lord and know it's all part of a greater plan."

"In minibus Dei," Caleb agreed. "What are you going to do now? Is the adventure over?"

"I'm not sure. I need to find out more about what's next for Jane and how best to help her."

"And you don't believe the authorities can do that?"

"I don't know. I guess they will in their way, but I cannot reconcile the Jane I know with the person they say she is. I know there are mentally ill people who must be kept in hospitals. I just don't believe she is one of them. She's odd and driven by something, but she is also brilliant and caring. She seems quirky—but not psychotic. I have a lot of empathy for her. I mean, there was a time when people thought I should have been locked up."

The old man cleared his throat. "Joseph, as you know, these things are not black-and-white. The severity of certain conditions may ebb and flow. Someone suffering from schizophrenia may be high functioning one day and experience episodes of debilitating symptoms the next. You said the police told you she had been living in a community facility?"

"The lieutenant said low security, but I think he meant a halfway house."

"Well, that's good. That means her doctors agree with you. They would not put her in a facility like that if she posed any risk to herself or others. This may only be a setback—not uncommon. They will probably observe her in the hospital for a month or two, then return her to the community facility."

"That makes me feel a little better," Joe said. "But there's something else bothering me about all this."

"What's that?"

"She was seeing a psychiatrist here in Opelika when she allegedly killed her mother, a doctor named Barry Lieberman."

"That's interesting. Carlos told me he had spoken to a doctor named Lieberman," Caleb said.

"Yes. Same one. At the time, Jane told the police she didn't kill her mother, but this doctor had."

"Did anything support her claim?"

"No. The police told me they investigated the doctor and didn't believe he had anything to do with it. They also said this Dr. Lieberman does a lot of work with the police departments around here and has friends in high places."

"No higher than yours, I'm sure." Caleb laughed at his own joke.

Joe chuckled as much from the old man enjoying his joke as at the pun itself. "Though I am sure that is true, I am concerned about the conflict of interest."

"Well, it's not uncommon for psychiatrists to work with law enforcement. Heaven knows I've helped the Newark departments out a few times."

Joe had no idea. "Really?"

"Sure. No organization deals with the mentally ill more than the police."

Joe knew that had to be true. "What do you think about Jane claiming this doctor killed her mother?"

"I don't know any of the facts, Joseph. I think if the police ruled him out, it's more likely Jane was experiencing a delusion or might have just lied. Those things happen, especially with people suffering from schizophrenia."

"I know that is a possibility, but I spoke to a man last evening who told me his daughter had been a patient of the same doctor, and the man suspected him of doing terrible things to her."

"Go on."

"He told me the doctor used hypnosis to treat his daughter."

"Clinical hypnosis is commonly used in therapy sessions. I've used it myself. In fact, Joseph, we discussed using hypnosis for your condition if I recall."

"Yes. I remember that, but the man said Dr. Lieberman used a controversial technique he called," Joe searched his memory, "DOET. Does that sound right?"

The phone went silent for a few moments except for the old man's raspy breathing.

"You know, I do recall reading about that technique," Caleb said reflectively. "This Dr. Lieberman was quite famous for a while. He wasn't in Alabama back then, though. If I remember right, he was a big shot at Johns Hopkins. Now that I think about it, I seem to remember the controversial nature of his therapy got him in trouble with the APA. Maybe that's why he is down there now instead of Baltimore."

"Did he lose his license to practice?"

"I don't know. I don't think he would have been treating this man's daughter if he had. He was probably asked to leave Johns Hopkins to avoid entangling them in his controversy. What did the man tell you about this DOET that has you concerned?"

"Well, for one, the man told me as part of the therapy, Dr. Lieberman creates an alternate personality in the patient."

"Yes. I remember there being a lot of concern about that. It seemed like he was actually creating a disassociated identity disorder in his patients."

"What is that?"

"Multiple personalities."

Joe grew excited. "Yes. That's exactly what this DOET therapy does. This man's daughter was named Beth, and Dr. Lieberman used hypnosis to create another personality inside her named Sweet Beth. I don't think it's a coincidence my friend Jane, who had been treated by the same doctor, insists on being called Sweet Jane. Do you?"

Caleb grunted. "Perhaps not."

"Do you think it's possible this doctor gave Jane that disorder you described?"

"I guess it's possible, Joseph. It was one of the concerns with this DOET technique. What about this man's daughter? How has the Sweet Beth personality affected her?"

"She's dead."

"Mary Mother of Mercy," Caleb exclaimed. "How did she die?"

"She took her own life."

"Oh, God bless the poor man and the soul of this girl."

"Yeah, well there's even more to the story. This man is convinced Dr. Lieberman used hypnosis to make his daughter do things she would not normally do. He said he and his wife believed the doctor may have been sexually abusing their daughter during their sessions."

The old man gasped. "Did they report their suspicions to the police?"

"No, but the man confronted Lieberman."

"What did the doctor say?"

"He convinced him it was all in his daughter's head and part of her illness. The man's daughter continued seeing Lieberman until she committed suicide."

"Oh my," Caleb barked. "What a tragedy."

"Yes. The man believes Lieberman somehow convinced his daughter to kill herself to cover up the sexual abuse. It made me wonder if Lieberman could have done something similar to have Jane kill her mother."

The phone grew silent again. After a long moment Caleb said, "I don't think that's possible, Joseph."

"It's not possible because it's not something a doctor would do?"

"No. No. The medical profession is not immune from evil. It's just not how hypnosis works. It's not like the movies. Hypnotic suggestions can be powerful, but they are only suggestions. The person being hypnotized must receive the suggestion and subconsciously agree with it. Hypnosis cannot be used to make a person do something they don't want to do."

"What about these other personalities? Could he have used them somehow?"

"That, I don't know about. It does seem very troubling, but I find your theory of mind control hard to believe. Hypnosis just doesn't work like that. Don't get me wrong, someone as knowledgeable about hypnosis and psychology, as Dr. Lieberman could do great harm. He could confuse and upset an individual, especially a troubled individual, but I don't think he could control them like you are describing. The alternate personality thing, well, that is interesting. I know it got him in some kind of trouble, but without being able to talk with these women, I'd say their actions were their own. In my opinion, it's more likely that the father of the poor woman who committed suicide is still grieving and needs an answer for why his daughter took her life."

"And you think he's found an answer in blaming Lieberman?"

The old man breathed a heavy, raspy sigh into the phone. "Grief is a powerful emotion. It makes us hurt, and it clouds our judgment."

"You think because I can't imagine Jane doing something as awful as killing her mother, I may be looking for answers too?"

"Perhaps. You care about this woman and in a way, you are grieving too."

After the call, Joe lingered at the picnic table contemplating Caleb's words until the sun had risen above the trees and all traces of morning's glow had been pushed aside by the new day. It was almost 7:30 a.m. when he took the card the lieutenant had given him out of his wallet and punched the number into his phone.

"Mel Cooper. Go."

Joe smiled inside. The lieutenant was as hard and no-nonsense as they came, just like all the master sergeants Joe had ever known.

"Good morning, Lieutenant. It's Joe Carroll."

There was a long pause, and Joe added, "I'm the man you tased yesterday."

"Oh sure. You feel'n okay, Captain? Those tasers can leave you with muscle aches for days."

"I'm fine. I'm calling because you said I would be able to see Jane Carter this morning before she was taken north."

"Yeah. I remember. Let me check."

After a few bursts of keyboard tapping punctuated by a curse or two, the lieutenant said, "She's scheduled to leave in an hour. Meet me at the main entrance here at eight, and I'll walk you over. You won't be able to spend much time with her, but I'll get you in."

Joe returned to his room. After leaving the restaurant last night, he had found an open Walmart where he purchased a few things including a fresh shirt, inexpensive personal travel kit, and a new red backpack for Jane. He placed the notebooks and the cassette tape in the new backpack, gathered up the rest of his things, and went down to the front desk to check out.

Google maps led him to the Opelika Sheriff's Department with a quick detour through a Dunkin' Donuts drive-through for coffee. It was a few minutes before eight when he let the officer seated at a desk behind a glass window in the lobby know he was there to meet Lieutenant Cooper.

Ten minutes passed before the lieutenant emerged from the door that led into the department's office area. Not a single wrinkle or unintended crease appeared on his uniform, and every buckle, pin, and piece of leather from the top of his broad-brimmed campaign hat to his glossy, black shoes gleamed. He gave Joe a grin and pointed to the doors leading outside.

"They are ready for us, but we have to hurry. They run a tight ship over there, and they won't wait long."

Joe held up the new backpack. "Will it be okay if I give her this?"

"Should be fine. As long as there are no weapons or contraband inside."

Joe unzipped it and showed the lieutenant its contents. "Nothing like that. Only a few notebooks and a small cassette tape."

"Looks okay, but believe me, they'll check it right thorough at the jail."

Joe followed him across the street to the Lee County Detention Center where, as the lieutenant said, a stern-looking woman in an equally crisp uniform searched the backpack. The lieutenant tried to make small talk with her, but she would have none of it.

"I need your weapon, Mel," she demanded, thrusting an outstretched hand, palms up, at the lieutenant while a large, pink-faced police officer stood beside her smiling.

"Yolanda, as much as I like the thought of you handling my pistol, I left it at the station."

She scowled at him and waved them through.

"That one's all business," the lieutenant said, then laughed.

Another officer met them beyond security and led them to a small room where Jane was sitting at a table. They let Joe enter the room alone. The lieutenant told him the room was under video surveillance, but there were no microphones so their conversation would be private. Joe had expected Jane to be shackled and dressed in prison overalls, but she was unbound, holding a new Lee County Sheriff's water bottle, and dressed in the same jeans and sweatshirt she had been wearing the evening he had picked her up in the storm.

All things considered, she looked pretty good—rested even. Her hair was pulled back into a short ponytail. With her bangs out of her face, the bruising around her eye from where the homeless man had punched her was more visible, but the deep purples had begun to fade to reds and yellows. Her eyes were clear and bright and not wild. Her facial expression was sullen when he first entered, but she smiled when they made eye contact.

He put the new backpack on the table. "I think it's the same size as your old one."

"Thank you," she said. "That was very sweet of you."

"How are you doing?"

She shrugged. "As good as can be expected, I guess."

"How are they treating you?"

"I hate to admit it, but they've been nice to me. They even took me outside where I could smoke a couple times and gave me a cell to myself. So, it's been okay. Better than the last time I was here."

"Were you able to take your medicine?"

"Yeah. The nurse here made sure I got my pills. They won't let me have the bottles, but I guess where I'm going, I'll get what I need."

She stood and inspected the backpack. She opened it and took out the notebooks, finding the tape in a plastic bag beneath them. She studied it for a long moment then let out a deep sigh. "You found it."

"And the other notebook. Don't forget that. It's worth a million dollars, right?"

"Yes. And the notebook."

She stepped around the table and gave him a long hug. It surprised him. Her body felt good against his. Too good. As gently as he could, he pried himself from her embrace.

"What's a matter?" she asked. "Am I making the almost-priest nervous?"

"No, child," he said. But he had found it difficult to pull away, and that troubled him.

She grinned that mischievous grin. "Someday I'm going to show you I'm not a child," she said, then her expression became sad. "I don't want to go back to Hardin. I promise if they let me go back to Brookhaven, I won't leave again."

He nodded. "I know. If I can help with that, I will."

She turned her attention back to the notebooks and the tape. "Will you hold on to these things for me? I don't know what will happen to my stuff at Hardin. They'll go through it, and I need to make sure the tape is safe."

"What's on the tape?"

She handed it to him. "My mother's last words. They led me back here, and someday, they will free me."

"What does that mean?"

She put the tape in his hand. "It means I need to make sure it's safe. Will you keep it for me? Just until they let me go back to Brookhaven. Then you could send it to me. Or better yet, bring it yourself." She smiled. "That is, if you are not afraid of this child."

He laughed at her flirtation, worried he enjoyed it. "I will make sure it gets back to you. What about the notebooks?"

"Joe, I know I'm crazy, but I am thinking clear again. Clearer than I have in a long time. What's in these books is real. No delusion." She stacked them on the table, "They will win the Millennial Prize. I have to get them to Dr. Martin."

"Who's he?"

"Dean of Mathematical and Physical Sciences at UC Berkeley. He'll know what has to be done to submit them for consideration. Please hold on to them for me. A million dollars won't do me any good in the funny farm."

She laughed as if she found that hilarious, and he could not help but laugh with her. A knock on the door ended the moment. The lieutenant stepped in and announced it was time to go.

Jane shouldered the empty backpack. "Promise you will come visit me, Joe?"

"I promise. As soon as I can." Then he added, "I will pray for you, Sweet Jane."

"As long as it makes you feel better." She winked at him. "Just think, almost-priest Joe, in some other universe I might be praying for you. Take good care of my things," she said over her shoulder as she disappeared through the door.

CHAPTER EIGHTEEN

Carl

"What is she doing?" Carl asked the stern-faced nurse standing beside him at the window overlooking one of the common areas where Taylor Hardin's low-risk patients spent their days.

Jane was sitting at a table near the center of the room writing on a sheet of letter paper. Her eyes did not stray from her work and her fierce scribbling was only interrupted by an occasional brush of her hand to push aside a swoop of her black hair. Several crumpled sheets were scattered about the tabletop, and a few were on the floor. About two dozen other patients were in the room with her. A small group sat at another table playing cards. Another group sat watching a large-screen TV and the rest, like Jane, were by themselves. Most of those were sleeping.

"Writing," she said in a deep voice Carl envied.

Carl scowled and studied the nurse. She was a tall, boney, white woman with brown hair pulled back in a tight bun. She was taller than him and had hard, angular features that were almost masculine. Judging by her lack of breasts and pronounced Adam's apple, he thought she might be transgender. A plastic ID card clipped to the breast pocket of her plain blue hospital scrubs identified her as Miranda Hopewell, RSN.

"I can see that. What is she writing?"

"Math formulas. She works on math problems all day long. Same as she's done for years."

Carl raised his eyebrows. "Really?"

"Uh-huh. It's the most unusual obsession I've ever seen, and I've seen my share." She nodded toward a young man in a corner who was walking in a small circle. "Take David over there. If you watch him, you will see he executes the same ritualistic movements over and over again."

Carl watched as the young man walked in a series of tight circles, then sat down on a couch and shuffled his left foot and then his right, then crossed his left leg over his right and then his right leg over his left, then sat as still as if he were carved from stone. After a few minutes, he repeated the entire sequence again.

"His symptoms appear severe. Are they triggered or persistent?" Carl asked.

"Triggered by any change in his immediate environment. He just came into the room. He will go through that ritual until he is comfortable—usually takes about thirty minutes or twenty cycles. After that, he will sit alone on that couch until we take him to lunch. If anyone approaches or attempts to sit next to him, he will repeat the pattern. I've seen him do it ten times in a day. When he gets comfortable, he is gentle and even conversant, but if someone or something interferes with his ritual, he will get violent, which is why he's here. He beat his grandmother to death."

"Hmm. Medications don't help?"

"He doesn't tolerate them well."

Carl turned his attention back to Jane who wadded up a sheet of paper and dropped it by her feet. "Has anyone checked the math she is doing? Are the problems real or part of some delusion?"

"Not me. It's become way too advanced for me, but we've had people look at it. It's real. I'm told it's mostly calculus and something called linear algebra. Lots of Greek symbols."

"What do you mean it's become too advanced?"

"When she first arrived here, I mean years ago, she did a lot of simple arithmetic and algebra. Back then, she would sit for hours doing basic multiplication and division problems—those I could understand. She seemed to be timing herself in computing large numbers, and she would get very frustrated if the answers did not come fast or if she got things wrong. Doctor Reynolds told me she tests herself with the math. He said she has benchmarks for her cognitive abilities based on the problem complexities, and they worked together to get her medication right based on how well she hit her benchmarks."

Jane wadded another sheet and dropped it at her feet. About a dozen of the crumbled balls littered the area by her chair.

"She keeps crumbling up the papers. Is that a sign she is having difficulty?"

"Not necessarily. She may be finished with whatever problem she is doing. She never keeps the work. I haven't noticed her acting out like she does when she's frustrated."

"Acting out?"

Miranda shrugged. "You know. Vocalizing, throwing things, acting aggressive to others. She's done none of that. In fact, she was socializing with a few of the other patients this morning. Some of them get curious about what she is doing, and they will come and watch her. When she is frustrated, she will chase them off or stop working until they leave. Yesterday, she had a group at the table with her, and she seemed fine."

"Interesting."

"I heard you are taking over for Tom. Are you going to see other patients here like he did or just Jane?"

"Just Jane. I've been asked to determine if she can return to Brookhaven."

"I sure hope so," Miranda said, looking down on him with a smile that did nothing to make her look more feminine. "She doesn't belong here. I mean, I don't think she ever belonged here. We have very few women patients. Most women confined by the state don't come to Hardin. They go down the street to your hospital, and they rarely stay longer than six months."

Carl nodded. He treated many of them. Most were drug addicts with lifelong histories of emotional and physical trauma. Almost all of them, in his opinion, were hopeless cases. Their negative behaviors were permanent and untreatable. Once they got out, most ended up on the street.

"The few who do come here," she continued, "live in isolation. It's not safe for them." She gestured at the window. "These are our least aggressive patients, but all of them are here because, well, you know why. For a while, Jane was our only female patient. Can you imagine that? Locked up in here and being the only woman?"

Carl knew exactly why Jane had been kept at Hardin. Barry had somehow convinced the state mental health administration to make her a special case. He was beginning to suspect his assessment the other evening was correct. There was something more to Barry's interest in this patient beyond a sense of personal obligation to her mother. This was no place to keep someone you cared about. No, something odd, possibly aberrant was at play. He grew increasingly suspicious of what he believed to be an obsession of Dr. Lieberman's.

"That's what I'm here to determine. I am having her transferred to Bryce for a couple months so I can do a full workup on her."

Miranda nodded. "Yes, I was told about the plan yesterday. Everything's been prepared. She'll be brought over this afternoon. I hope you decide to let her go back to Brookhaven, but if not, you need to keep her at Bryce. This place is a prison pretending to be a hospital. She does not need to be imprisoned. She needs care."

Carl gazed through the window. Miranda's opinion was meaningless. She was only a nurse. He nodded in Jane's direction. "I'd like to introduce myself to her and explain what we will be doing at Bryce."

"That will be fine. I will have her brought to a private examination room unless you want to go in the day room and talk to her." She gave him a sly smile, letting him know she could sense his discomfort.

Carl studied the room, his eyes moving to the multiple cameras that were monitored by the Alabama Board of Corrections officers located at security stations throughout the building. "What about the other patients? How will they react? Will it be safe?" His squeaky voice made him sound pathetic even to his own ears.

"You'll be fine. I will go in with you." She pointed to a large Black man dressed in tan slacks and a blue polo shirt that stretched tightly across his muscular chest and arms. The man was talking with a patient. "That's James. He's the day room supervisor. He keeps an eye on things. He'll make sure no one attacks you," she chuckled.

Carl nodded, and she pressed a button on an intercom station mounted on the wall. "James, I'm bringing in a guest."

James looked over at them, smiled, and gave a thumbs-up.

Miranda led Carl through a security door, and they made their way over to the table where Jane sat. She glanced up at them as they approached and returned to her scribbling, seeming not to care why they were heading her way. Most of the other patients ignored them as well, but Carl was aware of a few eyes tracking him as he crossed the room.

"Good morning, Jane," Miranda said as they reached the table.

"Sweet Jane," Jane replied.

The nurse turned to Carl. "She prefers to go by the name Sweet Jane."

"Sure thing," Carl said. "How are you doing this morning, Sweet Jane?"

Jane's gray eyes locked on him with a predatory intensity, and he noted a slight twitch in her facial muscles below her right eye that he speculated might be mild tardive dyskinesia.

"Who the fuck are you?"

"Now, Ms. Sweet Jane," the nurse said with an overdone southern drawl. "There's no need to get testy. This is Dr. Walker. He's here to help you."

Carl pointed to one of the empty plastic chairs that ringed the table. "Is it okay if I sit down?"

"Suit yourself."

Carl took a seat. He glanced at the paper Jane had been scribbling on. As the nurse had said, it contained a series of complex math equations. "What are you working on there?"

Jane crumbled up the paper and dropped it on the floor. "Nothing."

"It looks like something to me. Do you enjoy solving math problems?"

She furrowed her brow. "I don't know. Do you like breathing?" she asked in a calm, nonchalant manner, like she was asking him if he took cream in his coffee.

He wondered if her response was some kind of threat, but there was nothing threatening in her tone or posture. She had a smirking are-you-serious look on her face. "Of course, but what does that have to do with liking math?" He asked.

"You don't just like to breathe, Dr. Walker. You are compelled to breathe to stay alive. It's essential to our existence. That's how I feel about math. I don't just like doing math. I *have* to do it." She tapped out a beat on the table with her pencil.

"Can you remember how long you've had this compulsion?"

She stopped tapping. "It's not a compulsion. At least not in the way you mean it."

"How do I mean it?"

She looked up at Miranda who had remained standing. "Is he serious?"

Before Miranda could answer, Jane looked back at him. "I've been analyzed by men like you for over a decade. Do you think you are the first one to suggest my need to express my thoughts mathematically may be a symptom of my mental illness rather than an ability?"

"I didn't mean it that way."

"Sure you did. What I do with math is not repetitive, ritualistic, unwanted, or harmful in any way."

Carl recognized the medical definition of compulsion.

"It's not a compulsion," she continued. "It's just, it's just… the way I sort things out."

She looked away and mumbled something inaudible, then her eyes returned to his, and Carl thought he detected a hint of uncertainty or confusion in them. He'd seen the look many times before in patients who were struggling to discern hallucination from reality, and he guessed Jane was hearing or seeing something he could not.

"Okay, Jane."

"Sweet Jane," she barked.

"I'm sorry. Sweet Jane. We seem to have gotten off on the wrong foot. Let's start again. My name is Carl Walker. Like Miranda said, I will be helping with your treatment, and I wanted to introduce myself."

Jane stared up at Miranda. "Where's Tom?"

"Dr. Reynolds retired, honey. Dr. Walker is your new doctor."

"Retired? No one told me that." Carl thought she looked worried and maybe even hurt. "When?" Her voice cracked a little as if she might be on the verge of tears.

Miranda shrugged. "It's been a while now. Do you know when he left Dr. Walker?"

"He's been gone for three months, Jane. I mean Sweet Jane. He lives in Florida now. Spends all his time golfing."

"We might be able to arrange for you to speak to him one day," Miranda offered. "I know he keeps in touch with some of his other patients,"

Carl nodded. "That's right."

Jane shifted her attention back to him. That almost imperceptible tick under her right eye appeared again.

She folded her arms across her chest, and her facial expression changed from worry to anger. "I don't know you, and I don't want your treatment. I want Tom back."

Carl weighed how to respond and decided a direct approach was best. "Unfortunately, when you walked away from Brookhaven, you violated the terms of your release. Now, the state has asked me to look after you. In short, I have been asked to determine if anything has changed in your condition and if you can return to Brookhaven." He looked around the room. "I assume you would prefer that rather than remaining here."

That got her attention. She looked into his eyes and gave him a slow nod.

"So, what do you say? I know you and Tom had a good relationship. Give me a chance. Maybe we can become friends too."

She sat silently with her arms still tight across her chest, hugging herself. After a moment, her expression softened, and the hostility that radiated from her like heat from a smoldering fire cooled.

"When can I have visitors?"

Miranda stepped in. "We've discussed this before. The rule is no visitors for the first thirty days."

"I've been here for years."

"Uh-huh, but you left and came back."

"Who do you want to visit you?" Carl asked.

"Sweet Jane has a boyfriend," Miranda interjected.

"He's not my boyfriend," Jane snapped. "Don't talk about me like I am a child."

"I'm sorry. I did not mean to upset you."

"I will see what I can do about this rule," Carl said, recognizing an opportunity to initiate a bond. He looked up at Miranda. "What about phone or video calls? Are they allowed?"

Miranda nodded. "Sweet Jane talks to her friend every evening. Isn't that right Sweet Jane?"

Jane ignored the question. "What do I have to do to convince you I am well enough to return to Brookhaven?"

Carl folded his hands in front of him and leaned forward in his chair, knowing his body language combined with his size and the white lab coat he wore communicated dominance and authority. "First, I am having you transferred to Bryce where we can spend some time together.

"Bryce? You mean I'm getting out of here?"

"Yes. At least for a while."

"Maybe forever if you cooperate," Miranda added.

Carl glanced up at the boney nurse, a little annoyed with her speculation. He looked back at Jane and nodded. "That's right."

"What does it mean to cooperate?" Jane asked.

"It means we will talk frequently, and you will participate in some group sessions with the counseling staff. Also, we'll be running some tests, and I don't want to fight you about them."

"What kind of tests?"

"Nothing you haven't been through before. We'll check your blood and urine to make sure your medication is not interfering with any of your functions and maybe take some pictures of your brain."

"And after that you'll decide if I come back here or return to Brookhaven?"

"Yes."

"When do we start?"

"Today. This afternoon."

She stared at him with a flat expression on her face.

"Is that okay with you?"

She nodded. "I will do whatever you want me to do to get out of here."

CHAPTER NINETEEN

Barry

"Who invented hypnosis?" the nurse with the green eyes and red hair asked.

Barry smiled at her. They were sitting together in the Bryce Hospital cafeteria. He had struck up a conversation with her and the other nurse at the table, a curvy blonde with large breasts and pale blue eyes while they were in the serving line. The blonde, after telling her red-haired friend how famished she was, remarked she wished she had the willpower to stay on her diet. Barry, overhearing the conversation, asked if she had ever considered hypnosis, which led to the pair asking him to join them.

"No one really invented hypnosis. People have been hypnotizing themselves and one another for as long as there have been people."

"Really?" the blonde said, holding a ketchup-coated french fry.

"Yes. The first hypnotists were probably ancient Neanderthal shaman who hypnotized their clans with their spirit magic."

Both women laughed, and the redhead said, "You're kidding."

"No. It's true. The best hypnotists have always been religious leaders. Take faith healing for example. The practice of laying on hands is definitely a form of hypnosis. The priest or rabbi brings the devotee to a trance state through rhythmic chants or prayers and plants the suggestion in the devotee's mind that by his touch, they will be relieved of their suffering."

Barry held his hand up. "You're healed, and poof, you are." He chuckled, but it came out like a snicker.

"Does that ever work?" the french fry-wielding blonde asked.

"Sure. In some cases. The mind can be convinced to ignore pain and manage around symptoms—even severe ones." He took a sip of his iced tea. The redhead was looking at her phone, but the blonde was hanging on his every word. "It can be a cure in cases where the illness is behavioral, like some addictions, or when the symptoms are purely psychosomatic."

The redhead looked up. "Can anyone be hypnotized?"

He considered her for a moment, wondering how many sessions it would take before he could get her deep enough to peel those scrubs off her slender body and run his tongue along her pale, freckled skin. "Some people find it more difficult to enter a trance state than others, but we all enter trance states on our own all the time. I'm sure the two of you have each experienced multiple trance states this week."

The redhead smirked. "I don't think I've ever been in a trance state."

"Sure you have," he said. "Trances are nothing more than periods of hyperfocus when our internal thoughts, you know, our subconscious, dominates our perceptions. I'm sure you can think of many times when you've been deep in thought, and you've lost track of what's happening around you." Or what's happening to you, he thought.

"Like when you are daydreaming?" the blonde asked, her blue eyes fixed on him.

"Exactly. Or when you are absorbed in a good book. Your normally dominant conscious mind, the part aware of your physical surroundings, takes a back seat to your inwardly focused subconscious mind. That's a trance."

The blonde looked down at the remaining fries on her plate. "Could hypnosis stop me from craving these french fries?"

He smiled at her. It wouldn't take long to get this one deep, he thought. "Very possibly." He took another sip of his iced tea and scanned the room. Carl was sitting alone at a table in a far corner with a stupid grin on his face, wriggling his fingers at him. "Well, ladies, you'll have to excuse me. I must join my colleague." He looked at the blonde. "If you want to talk more about hypnosis and appetite control, I will be in town for a while. Maybe I could help you."

"How do I get in touch with you?"

He retrieved a pen from his sports coat breast pocket and wrote his name and cell phone number on a napkin. "Call me. We will set something up."

He took his tray and made his way over to Carl's table.

"You seemed to be enjoying yourself over there," Carl squeaked.

Barry shrugged. "One of them wants me to hypnotize her to help with weight management. Care to guess which one?"

Carl glanced over at the two nurses who were now laughing like high school girls. "Probably not the rail thin redhead."

"You would be correct."

Carl's plate was heaped with several slices of brown meat Barry guessed was meatloaf and a mountain of mashed potatoes. All of it was covered in a thick, brown gravy. He gestured at the food. "Maybe I should be helping *you* with some weight management."

"Fuck you."

"Only trying to help."

"Okay. Then fuck you very much."

Barry leaned in over his tray. "Did you see Jane?"

Carl shoveled a forkful of mashed potatoes into his mouth and swallowed without chewing. "Yes, I did. I just returned from talking with her. We spoke for about a half hour. She's an interesting individual. Not at all what I expected."

Not what he expected. As if Barry gave a shit about what Carl thought. "How so?" he asked, doing his best to conceal his revulsion for Carl's eating habits and disregard for his opinions.

"In our brief conversation, she did not exhibit significant psychopathic symptoms. Based on what you told me about her, I expected her to be more hostile and disoriented. If I had to make a call right now, my gut assessment," he patted his pachyderm-sized midsection, "and I have a rather large gut, would be she strikes me as very functional. I know you don't want to hear this, but my first impression is she doesn't appear dangerous. She seems competent enough to go back to Brookhaven." He patted his midsection again and belched. "But that's only my gut talking." An ear to ear grin split his face and for a moment, his enormous head resembled a jack-o'-lantern.

Barry wasn't interested in Carl's assessment. Jane was dangerous to him. She knew things. Things that could be dismissed as delusional as long as her mental competency was in question, and he had no intention of ever letting it be deemed otherwise—not by that idiot Reynolds and certainly not by his oafish friend who he was using to get access to her. "You think a thirty-minute conversation is enough to make that call?" he asked, finding it harder this time to conceal his contempt.

"No. Of course not. I plan to observe her for a few weeks, but she seemed quite lucid. A little irascible maybe, but lucid."

"Lucid?"

"Yes. Her thinking was organized. She didn't ramble. She struck me as bright and engaging."

"You detected no symptoms of her schizophrenia, then? No signs of psychosis? They were hard to miss the last time I spoke with her."

"Nothing significant. She may have experienced some mild paracusia during our talk."

Now that was interesting, Barry thought. "She was hearing voices? Did she tell you she was hearing voices?"

"No. She just got distant for a moment and seemed to be engaged in some form of internal dialog."

"You don't consider such hallucinations significant?"

Carl gave an exaggerated shrug, and one of his chins bulged around his jawline. He looked like a turtle retracting its head into its shell. "Could be, and then again, it could be nothing. Depends on whether it's debilitating or not. You know as well as I do over ten percent of the population hears an occasional voice, and all of us talk to ourselves from time to time."

Barry couldn't believe it. Carl, the rube, was lecturing him on psychiatric diagnostics. He imagined thrusting his fork through the fat man's forehead deep into his prefrontal lobe, though he was certain the tines on the cheap cafeteria utensil would not penetrate the brain case's frontal bone. No. He'd need an auger for that or better yet, a drill. An interesting fantasy, he thought. He pushed the images out of his mind and drew the last of his iced tea through his straw, careful not to make any repulsive slurping noise.

"Anything else?"

"She has a slight tick under her right eye. It may be mild dyskinesia, but it could be about a dozen other things too. We'll have to watch it. I'll order lab work and wire her up for an EEG as soon as she gets here."

"When will that be?"

"This afternoon. They may be bringing her now."

"Then what?"

"The staff will get her situated. We'll get her on a routine. You know—meds, groups, evaluations. The typical stuff. It will be familiar to her."

Carl pushed his tray aside and leaned in closer. "I need to know something."

Barry could smell the meatloaf on Carl's breath. "What do you need to know, Doctor Walker?"

"If after I complete my very thorough evaluation, I conclude Tom was right and her condition no longer warrants secure inpatient care, are you going to be okay with that?"

The scar on Barry's neck itched, but he did not scratch it. Carl would see that as a tell, an outward manifestation of Barry's true thoughts. "Of course, I will be okay with it. Why wouldn't I be?" But he wouldn't be okay with it—not even a little. He wanted Jane Carter right where she was, right where he had put her. Out of sight, and out of mind, rotting away behind Taylor Hardin's thick walls and razor wire. Only then could he go back to his Wednesday afternoons with Sweet Emily and Thursdays with Sweet Charlene and once again forget about Sweet Jane.

"That being said, if you are even half the mediocre psychiatrist I think you are, Carl, you will conclude Tom was a fool and she should remain right where she is."

Carl leaned back. "We shall see."

"I want to see her."

"I know you do. How do you think she will react? She could attack you again." Carl squeaked, then snorted the obnoxious piggish laugh.

"I don't know. I'm hoping she will be glad to see me." He lied. Carl was right. She would not be pleased to see him and left alone, she may very well attack him again. "It's been a long time."

"And after all these years, now you are so eager to see her. I have to tell you Barry, there's something not right with your..."

"Obsession," Barry finished Carl's sentence.

"Well, I'm not sure what else to call it. You've left your practice and moved into Granddaddy's old farmhouse so you can be close to this woman who you have not seen in over five years. What would you call it?"

Barry waved his hand in a dismissive gesture. "We've been over this. I neglected my responsibilities with her. I know that. We don't need to cover it again. I am staying here until I know things are right."

"And by right you mean keeping her locked up."

Carl's overexaggerated sense of ethics and, Barry almost gagged, compassion, was going to be a problem. A big farm animal-sized problem. Barry looked over at the two nurses who were still carrying on. The blonde met his gaze and smiled back at him. He stroked his beard. Yes. Carl would be a problem. He needed a backup plan. He returned the smile. Maybe he just found one.

He turned his attention back to Carl. "Unless I am convinced otherwise."

Carl pulled his plate back in front of him and resumed shoveling mashed potatoes into his mouth with mechanical intensity. After he'd reduced the mound to nothing, he looked up. "Let me get her routine established, then I will see what I can do to bring you in."

CHAPTER TWENTY

Joe

It was a few minutes after eight in the evening. To the west, the sun made its slow descent through the hazy summer sky, still well above the distant skyline of Buckhead. It was late June in Atlanta, and nightfall was two hours away. Joe sat on the top step of the stairwell outside his apartment door and watched the sun's slow progress while he listened to Jane tell him about her day as he'd done every evening since he'd stood in the doorway of the Lee County Detention Center watching her being driven away.

That had been over a month ago. Since he last saw her, he'd spent some time researching Dr. Lieberman and his DOET technique, but he had not learned much more than what Caleb had told him.

Almost all the information Joe could find about Lieberman through Google was ten years old. As Caleb had said, Lieberman and his techniques were celebrated for a brief time before they were rejected. Lieberman had engaged in a public battle with the American Psychiatric Association, which at its height included heated debates on social media and even cable news stations. As Caleb had surmised, the scandal had cost Lieberman his position at Johns Hopkins, but not his medical license.

After the DOET controversy, Joe could find little about Lieberman aside from mentions about his association with Jane and her mother in articles related to the murder. Joe was surprised when he discovered some people speculated Lieberman was in a relationship with Jane's mother. There was also a smattering of positive articles about the teaching he was doing at Auburn University and awards he'd received from multiple law enforcement groups, including one from the Lee County District Attorney's office. Other than those few stories, media interest in Lieberman ceased when his DOET technique was discredited.

Nothing he read linked Dr. Barry Lieberman to claims of patient sexual abuse or deaths. At first, it appeared to Joe that Caleb's doubts were correct. The restaurant owner's grief over losing his daughter, combined with his distrust of Lieberman's unorthodox treatments, had led Charlie to believe the worst about the doctor. That was until Joe learned how Jane felt about Lieberman.

Joe had brought up the doctor during one and only one call with Jane, and he promised never to ask her about him again. The mere mention of Lieberman's name evoked a severe, visceral reaction from her, starting with a profane tirade about Joe spying on her and ending with sobs and her insistence that he never, ever, bring the monster's name up again. She'd called him the monster—not Doctor or Barry or Lieberman—just the monster.

Jane's reaction made it clear. There was something to Charlie's suspicions, no matter what the internet said or didn't say. Joe knew it. One day, he would find a way to get Jane to open up about it, and maybe he could help both her and Charlie. Carlos would never understand this need. In fact, Joe knew if he consulted his mentor, the priest would advise him to stop thinking like a hero and start thinking like a shepherd.

With each call, Joe had learned more about Jane's life in a mental hospital. He never told her how much experience he had with the things she talked about. Maybe, as part of that opening up process, he'd share how similar they really were. They both used their faith to overcome the darkness in their lives—his in God and hers in science.

She had been ecstatic when she was moved from Taylor Hardin to Bryce. "It's much better here," she told him. "I have my own room with my own full bathroom. It's almost as nice as Brookhaven," she'd said.

"Much better than the cell they had me in at Hardin. They don't lock us up at night here, Joe."

"Mornings are always the same," she'd told him. "Up at eight, wash, breakfast, meds, back to the unit for free rec." Free rec, he'd learned, stood for free recreation time which ran from nine until ten during which she could stay in her room, make phone calls, or sit in the common area she called the day room because that is what they called it at Taylor Hardin. She spent this time working on puzzles and math problems or watching TV with the rest of the nutcases, as she called the other patients.

After morning free rec, a psych tech named Jody led them through physical therapy, which usually meant stretching and yoga exercises. She'd told him half the patients could not or would not participate, but Jody still tried to coax them to join. "They would never try this at Hardin," she'd said. "The psychos at Hardin would riot if anyone tried to make them get down on the ground and roll around on yoga mats." When they were done with physical therapy, they would return to their rooms until noon when they would head back to the cafeteria for lunch.

The afternoon schedules varied a little. On Mondays and Fridays, she'd attend a group discussion session from one until three. The sessions were led by a therapist she called Dr. Homeless because he wore faded T-shirts and jeans and had long, stringy hair and a scruffy beard. Joe laughed to himself when he remembered her saying, "Joe, I swear the guy looks like he crawled out of one of those tents by the Atlanta bus station."

She felt the group sessions were a waste of time. "They're like every other group session I've ever attended. There's usually twelve of us. We sit in a circle, and Dr. Homeless makes us talk about our feelings and our thoughts. It's always the same shit. Someone's always bitching about something they hate about the hospital or talking about how the world's out to get them."

Joe was familiar with such groups. Years ago, at Caleb's urging, he'd joined a group for veterans dealing with PTSD where he and several other vets from the Iraq and Afghanistan wars would open up to each other about what they were going through. It wasn't always pleasant, but unlike Jane, Joe felt such groups helped him. He derived comfort in knowing his feelings and struggles were not unique. It made him feel less alone. It's also where he learned how many combat vets, like him, struggled with addiction, and how he first got involved in Alcoholics Anonymous.

On Tuesdays and Thursdays, she'd meet one-on-one with the psychiatrist who was treating and evaluating her. A doctor named Carl, who she described as a large man whose mind seemed to be as out of shape as his body. She said he was okay, but she wished the doctor who had been treating her before she'd been released to Brookhaven was treating her now. "Tom understood me. He really helped me. Carl is just going through the doctor motions like all the rest."

Despite her lack of enthusiasm for Dr. Carl, she did not think the rest of the staff were bad. Jody was helpful and empathetic—much better than most of the techs she dealt with at Hardin. "They are like prison guards there," she'd said. Besides Jody, she liked a nurse named Sandra who talked to her and filled the empty hours between afternoon group and dinner. They had become friends.

Other than her talks with Sandra, the afternoons were much like the mornings—hours of free rec time, meds for those who needed them, and group activities. Jody would organize games, and when the weather was good, some of them would go outside and wander around the small fenced-in yard where, as she put it, the crazies were allowed to roam.

Except for the time they spent on the phone, Jane had told him, evenings and weekends were the worst for her. That's when many of the patients would have visitors, and some got passes to spend the weekends with their families.

Once a week, Joe called the hospital to inquire about visiting her, but each time he was told the same thing by the same woman in the same syrupy, southern accent. "I'm so sorry, sugar. Ms. Carter is unable to receive visitors at this time. Please check back in a week." Each time, he would break the bad news to Jane, and infuriated, she would report the next day that Dr. Carl had promised the restriction would be lifted soon. Dr. Carl never told her when or explained why it was taking so long other than "hospital rules."

Since their first conversation after she'd been returned to Taylor Hardin, her demeanor on the calls had gone from despair and anxiousness, to resignation, to relief and even hopefulness with her transfer to Bryce. Tonight, however, there was nothing hopeful in her manner. The anxiousness was back. More than that, she sounded frightened and on the verge of some kind of breakdown.

For the first time, he saw actual signs of the severe illness that had tormented her for so long.

"I feel myself slipping away, Joe. I think I must be phasing in and out too. Can you still hear me?"

"Of course I can hear you. You sound fine." Lies were coming too easy now, and he made a silent commitment to be more honest. She sounded anything but fine—nothing like the fierce and brilliant woman who climbed into his car on that stormy evening a month ago. "What do you mean phasing in and out?"

"I come and go. Just like the Others. From one universe to another."

Her words sounded like nonsense. He did not know how to respond.

"They've been fucking with my meds. I swear he's doing it just to screw with me. They all like to screw with you here."

"Who? Dr. Carl?"

"Yes. He says he's worried the Clozaril is harming me, but I think that's bullshit. He wants me to fail the evaluation. They all want me to fail so they can put me back in that awful place."

Joe tried to remember what Caleb had told him about her medication. Something about white blood cells. "Maybe he's seen something wrong in your blood work."

"No. That's not it. They draw my blood every week, and they tell me it's been fine."

"And Dr. Carl didn't tell you why he's worried?"

"He said he was altering the dosage because he's concerned about neurological damage, but I think he's full of it. I don't trust him. He's nowhere near as smart as Tom. Tom got it right. My meds were working. I was getting better."

What could Joe say? The doctor must be concerned about something. All he could do was try to reassure her and let her know she was in his prayers, but he did not think that brought her much solace. He decided to keep his prayers to himself.

"Sweet Jane, perhaps you should trust the doctor."

"I can't. I can't."

She sounded like she was crying.

"Tom got my meds right. They worked. I can't keep them away without them."

"Keep who away?"

"The Others. I see them again. Phasing in and out. They won't leave me alone, and I can't think clearly anymore. The math is so slow, Joe. So slow."

"Who are these Others?"

Her voice became hushed like she was afraid someone would hear her. "They are me, but not me. So many versions of me. Phasing in and phasing out. Torturing me with their whispers. But they are afraid too, Joe. They see me and each other, and they are as tormented as I am." Her voice grew even quieter. "We should not know of each other, Joe. We are all just vibrations in the field, and our waves should never, never intersect. Never!" She screamed the last word, but Joe had a feeling she was not screaming at him.

He moved the phone away from his ear and ran his fingers through his hair. "Please calm down. Is there someone there who can help you? Where is Sandra?"

"She's gone for the night."

"Is there someone else?"

"There is always someone else. They are always watching me."

"Do you want me to talk to them?"

"Who? The Others?" She laughed. "Now that would be fun."

"No. The people who are taking care of you."

"No one takes care of me. They watch me."

He didn't know how to respond. He'd never heard her so despondent.

"Joe," she said in a whisper.

"Yes."

"Do you still have my tape?"

She often asked about the little cassette marked with a piece of red vinyl tape, but she would never talk about what was on it.

When Joe had searched for information about Dr. Lieberman, he'd found many articles about Margaret Carter's murder. They all had similar headlines, "Daughter Kills Auburn Professor Mother," "Genius Daughter Kills Genius Mom," and "Killer Genius Daughter Too Insane to Try." None of them told him more than what he'd learned from Charlene and Lieutenant Cooper, at least nothing more about the murder.

Among the articles he'd found was one about Jane and her mother that was published a couple of weeks before the murder. It was part of a series of stories done on women in science and technology, and it described how the two of them were working together on a book on artificial intelligence and quantum computing. Joe wasn't sure what that was, but he assumed it had something to do with the science Jane talked so much about.

According to the article, Margaret Carter had written three other books. Jane had helped with two of them, but this one would be the first where Jane would be listed as a coauthor. The article described their writing process. Margaret would record her thoughts on tape, and Jane would listen to the tapes and transcribe them into a word processing program, but Jane did more than type what her mother dictated. She inserted sections that explained the math and physics behind the technology and advanced programming.

The article's author had spent an afternoon with Jane and her mother and wrote, "The two were an amazing team who were as beautiful as they were brilliant." Nothing was mentioned about Jane's illness or any hint of problems between them that in two weeks would lead Jane to bludgeon her mother to death with a fireplace poker. On the contrary, the author gushed over their "very special closeness," writing, "Mother and daughter share the same thundercloud gray eyes that sparkle with adoration and pride when they describe each other's contributions."

The article explained the small voice recorder cassettes Jane carried in her backpack but not why the one with the red tape was so special or why Jane needed it "to make things right." He wanted to help her, and he thought knowing what was on the tape might help him do that, so he had tried to find a machine that would play the small tape. He didn't have one, nor did anyone at Sacred Heart. He'd toyed with ordering one online, even going as far as putting one in a shopping cart, but he couldn't press that "buy" button. He thought it would be too much of an invasion of Jane's privacy. If she wanted him to know what was on the tape, she'd tell him. If not, he had no right to listen to it. Every time she asked about it, though, he wondered if there was something recorded on it that might explain what happened between her and her mother and maybe even Dr. Lieberman.

"Of course, I still have the tape. It's in a safe place along with your notebooks."

"Are you sure the tape is safe?"

She never asked about the notebooks—just the tape.

"I got to have it back. When will you bring it to me? You promised. Remember?"

"Of course, I do. I will bring it when I come."

"You say that, but you never do."

He sighed. "The hospital people tell me I cannot come yet. You know that. We talk about it every week. I could mail you the tape."

"Noooo!" she wailed. "It could get lost in the mail. You need to bring it to me."

"I will. As soon as I can."

"You always say that. I don't think you will ever come."

"I'll come. I promise. As soon as the hospital says it's okay."

The phone went silent.

After a few moments he asked, "Are you still there?"

"I don't want you to come," she said in a sorrowful voice.

"Don't be like that, Sweet Jane."

"No. I don't want you to come."

"Why?"

"I don't want you to see me like this."

"Like what?"

"Crazy."

"You're not crazy."

She laughed and sobbed at the same time. "Right. All sane people phase in and out of their universe."

"Will you pray with me?" He had to try.

"That's your answer for everything."

"Well, I am an almost-priest, after all."

She laughed, and he felt relieved.

"You know," she said. "One of these versions of me may be sleeping with a less priestly version of you."

He fought back a chuckle. "Let's not talk like that, Jane."

"Sweet Jane," she quipped.

Better, he thought.

They continued to talk for another thirty minutes. The psychotic episode, if that's what it was, seemed to pass, and she talked about what was discussed during her group sessions and about something she watched on TV about how stars were formed. She thought the program was marginally interesting but superficial, as it was targeted for general audiences and not theoretical physicists.

As usual, the call ended with them talking about all the things she wanted to do when she got out. She wanted to go back to her home in Auburn and maybe plant a garden. She wanted a dog, and she talked about teaching one day. Of course, she would have to finish her doctorate, but she was close. "I think I can do it now," she said, then she added, "as long as I can stay in phase."

After the call ended, Joe took out his breviary and began to say his evening prayers, but he found it difficult to concentrate on the liturgy. His heart was not in the reading, which troubled him almost as much as Jane's deteriorating mental state. For the first time since he committed himself to the priesthood, the obligation felt more like a burden than a comfort. He shuddered to think what Carlos would say of his preoccupation with Jane over God. His mentor's soft Latin voice filled his head, "Joseph, this woman is putting all you have strived for at risk."

Joe closed the book and watched the sun disappear behind the Buckhead skyline until the first stars twinkled to life. The gloom of twilight reflected his mood. There seemed little he could do for Jane except pray for her, and tonight he could not even do that.

CHAPTER TWENTY-ONE

Carl

Carl belched, and the greasy taste of the morning's bacon and onion omelet, mixed with the stale bitterness of the vending machine coffee filled his mouth. He tossed the half-empty cup in the trash can and popped two berry-flavored Tums tablets to cleanse his palette. It was all they were good for, as they would do little to douse the five-alarm fire in his chest.

His acid reflux was raging this morning, burning away the squamous cells of his esophagus. As an MD, he knew all too well the damage his gluttony was inflicting on his body. As a psychiatrist, he knew his destructive eating habits were symptoms of the depressive mood disorder that weighed down his will as sure as gravity's force pulled his 350 plus pounds to earth. To tell the truth, he'd tried every serotonin inhibitor in the PDR catalog and in the end, none of them were better antidepressants than bacon.

He shifted his position, trying in vain to get comfortable in an office chair intended for someone half his size. The chair squealed in protest. He was alone at the unit's central nurses' station. All the belching and squealing, not to mention the continuous flatulence, had driven away the psych tech and nurse who'd been there when he'd arrived.

The station was perched on a raised platform in the center of the unit's common area. The patients called it the control tower or just the tower, no doubt due to its height and fortified appearance. It was home base for the unit's staff and wandering doctors like Carl. From its modest height three feet above the surrounding room, its occupants had a 360-degree view of the common area and most of the rest of the unit.

From his seat, Carl had a clear line of sight to Jane. She was lounging on a sofa in the corner with that blonde-haired nurse again. Those two had become almost inseparable. He'd seen them huddled together for hours, talking and giggling. They were at it early today. Mornings were when Jane usually sat by herself scribbling math formulas like she had done at Hardin when he'd first met her.

Of late, however, the scribbling had become less urgent. The staff reported some mornings she didn't write at all. She was talking to herself more, arguing with some invisible adversary, and she was growing belligerent with the techs and other patients. Not with this nurse, though. If it were any other patient or any other nurse, Carl would welcome the congenial interaction, but there was something not right with this nurse's interest in Jane. She was not part of the unit's team. She'd shown up several weeks ago and had visited Jane every afternoon since. Now she was here in the mornings too.

Carl had looked her up. Sandra Tally, BSN, worked in radiology, which was located on another floor about as far away from the unit as you could get and still be in the building. At first, he'd assumed the two had become friends when Jane had gone for her CT scans. Nothing but a chance meeting resulting in a nice friendship, but then he'd realized Sandra was the same nurse Barry had been flirting with in the cafeteria.

That had made him a little suspicious, but he had chalked it up to coincidence. That is until he drove by Granddaddy's house two weeks ago and saw a strange car parked in the drive next to Barry's BMW. The car had a hospital parking tag dangling from the rearview mirror and a pink heart-shaped sticker on the back window that proclaimed in flowing script, "Nurse Life." It didn't take much to figure out who the car belonged to—just a picture on his phone and some small talk with the guards who monitored the employee parking gate.

He'd asked Barry if he was sleeping with the young nurse. "Jesus, Barry. She can't be much older than 25. She's half your age. You must be hitting the Viagra pretty hard."

Barry had laughed at what he called Carl's lurid speculation and claimed, "I'm treating her for an eating disorder. We are not all sexual deviants like you, Dr. Walker."

It was always there, the ever-present threat of the Miami hooker incident. It was like a leash around his neck that Barry was quick to tug on whenever Carl pried into Barry's business or denied him a favor.

No matter what Barry said, Carl knew he was screwing Tally. That on its own didn't bother or surprise him. Barry wouldn't be the first old doctor to bed a young nurse. Of course, if, as Barry claimed, she was his patient, it was unethical as hell. Though that wasn't his concern either. Carl couldn't care less who Barry screwed—ethical or not. The thing that concerned Carl was Barry appeared to have involved his new girlfriend in his obsession, like how he had sucked in Carl.

Obsession was what it was. Carl was now sure of that. When it all started, he had no reason to doubt Barry's motives for pushing to ensure Jane's continued institutionalization. After all, Barry had treated her for over a year and had been there at the breaking point when Jane's psychosis took its tragic turn.

It wasn't hard to believe she needed to remain hospitalized. Most severe schizophrenics needed long-term care, and most never got it. The sins of the mental health industry's past made it almost impossible. Laws passed in the 1970s to address the failures of asylums like the old Bryce Hospital often prevented families and caregivers from compelling the severely mentally ill to seek inpatient treatment. It was just as well though, the system was overwhelmed as it was. The numbers were too great. There were not enough suitable places for the sick to go. For most of these hopeless people, the only long-term care facilities available were prisons.

Carl, like every other mental health professional, knew the truth, and that's why he was willing to believe Barry when he claimed Jane Carter was one of those hopeless people who would never be able to live on her own. He even believed him when he said she was dangerous— at least at first.

That was before he'd had time to form his own opinions of her condition and before he'd spoken to Tom Reynolds. Now he was not so certain. He treated several patients with worse symptoms who did okay as outpatients. They had jobs. Some had significant others. They weren't on the street, and they weren't hurting anyone. Sure, it was clear by Jane's file that early on she'd been prone to intense psychotic episodes, but that was during the acute phase of her disease and during a period of extreme stress. All the recent entries in her file, however, suggested the severity of her disease had peaked shortly after she'd been committed, even before Tom put her on Clozapine, which according to Tom's notes had a transformative effect on her.

It was the Clozapine that prompted Carl to call Tom. He'd begun to suspect the medication was behind her facial tic, even though the drug was not known to cause tardive dyskinesia, which was what he had thought was causing the involuntary movements.

He wanted to hear from Tom how the drug had helped her and ask if he had observed any adverse effects. Tom didn't provide much more information about the drug's effects on her than what was in the file, but he said some things about Barry that confirmed Carl's belief that his friend might not have Jane's best interests in mind.

Tom had been Chief of Psychiatry at Bryce before he retired, which meant he had been Carl's boss, though Tom had never paid much attention to the management part of the job. He used to tell Carl and the rest of the staff that he was a shrink, not a bureaucrat.

It had been several weeks since Carl reached Tom on his cell. His old boss, had been fresh off the golf course and was sitting poolside sipping a margarita while staring at the bikini-clad trophy wives of his new golf partners. The call lasted for more than an hour. It started with Tom pumping Carl for news about hospital politics and gossip. Like Barry and Tally, someone at the hospital was always screwing someone else, in both literal and figurative ways. For a man that claimed not to be a bureaucrat, Tom knew the inner workings of the hospital well and everything there was to know about its senior staff. He seemed to enjoy detailing to Carl all the ways they were failing at their jobs. Eventually, they got around to talking about Jane.

Carl had brought Jane's file up and went through the entries Tom had made over the three years he had treated her. His old boss hadn't looked at Jane's file in over six months, but he remembered most of the details. She had been his special project, a genius and onetime math phenom left to rot in Taylor Hardin.

"She was still hyper symptomatic when I first met her," Tom had said. "Hallucinating almost nonstop, fighting with staff and other patients. She must have spent half the time she was in Hardin in isolation."

Carl had asked him, "How did you turn her around?"

"The usual things. I built a relationship with her and gained her trust, then we just worked the symptoms. You know how it is. The environment made it hard, though. That place is all about containment. I started working on getting her out of there as soon as she became my patient. I still can't believe it took three years to get through all the paperwork bullshit and even then, I only pried her out because of COVID."

"Your notes say you attributed much of her improvement to the changes in medication."

"Oh yeah. The Clozapine worked a damn miracle on her. She began improving as soon as she started taking it, and we spent a few months dialing in the dosage until she became stable. Hell, more than stable— high functioning—brilliant, as a matter of fact. She does math that would make your head spin."

They'd finished going over her file, and the call was about to end when Tom had asked, "Carl, how did Jane get assigned to you, anyway? As I recall, you don't typically get involved with the Hardin patients, do you?"

Carl thought about claiming it was the luck of the draw, but Tom still talked to people at the hospital and would find out Carl had asked for the case. No point in lying. "A friend of mine asked me to. He treated her back in Auburn. You know... when she did what she did."

Carl heard ice rattle and pictured Tom in a deck chair under an umbrella rocking a glass back and forth.

"Lieberman?"

"That's him."

"Carl," Tom's voice had become low and almost forceful.

"Yes?"

"Whatever you do, don't let that bastard anywhere near Jane."

Carl's heart had skipped a beat at Tom's warning. "I don't understand." But deep down he did.

"Don't let him near her. That's all I'm going to say."

The call ended with Tom angry and Carl sure of one thing. There was much more to Barry's obsession with Jane than some remorse over missed signs and a dead lover. A lot more, and he thought Tom knew why and wasn't telling.

Whatever it was, it was bad enough for Barry to want her locked up forever. It didn't matter how high functioning she'd become or what math she could do. Barry was out to prove she was irredeemable, and he was using Carl to do it.

From the start, Barry had pushed to take part in, if not dictate, Jane's treatment. He wanted to hear about every symptom and every conversation, including what Jane said in group-sessions and in her and Carl's individual sessions. Barry insisted on weighing in on everything from her medication regiment to her visitation privileges. He wanted her to have no visitors, which included no boyfriend from Atlanta. He even wanted Carl to stop her from talking on the phone with him—something Carl refused to do.

"For God's sake, Barry. She has to have some reason to get out of bed in the morning,"—he had told him.

Carl had fended off Barry's requests—no, his demands—to see Jane by claiming he needed more time to get a routine established for her before reintroducing her to her former doctor, which even Barry admitted would be disruptive. After the call with Tom, though, Carl had no intentions of ever allowing Barry to see Jane—at least not while she was his patient. *Don't let that bastard anywhere near her.*

It took him two weeks to work up the courage to tell Barry what he'd decided. He never mentioned the call with Tom. He told him Jane was his patient, and he did not think, given their past, allowing him to see her would have a positive outcome for her. He had been prepared for Barry's wrath and possible blackmail threats, but to his amazement and relief, Barry had accepted the decision and even said he thought Carl was right. Carl had been stunned.

That's when he began suspecting there was more to this nurse's motives. He'd confronted Barry, asking him why his eating disorder patient was spending so much time with Jane.

Barry had feigned surprise, saying, "She is? My, my, that is an odd coincidence."

It was bullshit, of course. The son of a bitch was using this nurse to get to Jane. Carl knew it, and Barry knew he knew it. What Carl did not know is what Barry hoped to achieve.

He'd tried to get Jane to tell him what she and Tally talked about, even going so far as to probe whether Tally was asking about Jane's treatment. His inquiries had not gone well. Jane was defensive about her relationship and lashed out at him saying, "First you fuck with my meds, and now you don't want me to have any friends."

She was right about the meds. He had more than halved the dosage of Clozapine, and the change had a dramatic negative impact on her symptoms. She was wrong, however, about his motives. He had not changed the dosage just to fuck with her.

Her facial tic was not tardive dyskinesia as he'd first assumed. Clozapine had many side effects, but tardive was not one of them. Tom never observed the tics, and after talking to him, Carl had decided the drug was not the cause. Then he wired her up to an electroencephalogram, and the results made him suspect the medication again. Tiny electrical bursts in Jane's brain called myoclonic seizures were to blame. CT scans showed no obvious brain damage or abnormality to explain the problem. Clozapine was known to provoke such seizures.

Given how well Jane had done on the Clozapine, he'd decided to leave her medication as it was and monitor her, but Barry had challenged the decision. "You know it's the long-term effects of the drug. Are you going to let her keep seizing? It's only going to get worse. Before you know it, she's going to be on the floor with the techs shoving a bite guard in her mouth."

Barry had been relentless and Carl had dropped the dosage to see if the tic went away, and so far it had, but not without costs. The tic might be gone, but Jane's psychosis had worsened. Carl wasn't sure it was a good trade. The seizures were mild, and Jane had functioned well on the drug. As Tom had written, it had a transformative effect on her, and Carl realized that now that he was denying her it, the transformation was reversing.

A suspicious thought crept into Carl's mind that left him cold despite the acid fire raging in his chest. What if Barry hadn't pushed for the medication change out of concern over Jane seizing? What if the reemergence of her positive symptoms had been the objective all along?

Barry was so adamant in his position that Jane should never be allowed to leave Hardin, but Carl had found little in her behavior to support that position. That is—until he'd altered her medication. Now her condition was deteriorating, which bolstered Barry's argument.

The suspicious thoughts arced between the dots. Of course, Barry had known changing Jane's medication would destabilize her. That was his intent. The nurse was there to report on the decline. That had to be it. The fucking guy was a master manipulator. He'd built a multi-million- dollar practice around manipulating people through hypnosis. That's what he was doing with this nurse, and in an odd way, Carl suspected, he'd done the same to him. Barry had hypnotized him somehow.

"Well, I am awake now, you bastard," Carl said to himself as he tapped on the station's computer keyboard. Jane's file filled the screen. He brought up the treatment plan and moved the cursor to the medication order. After a few more clicks, he'd restored the dosage to where Tom had it. He would monitor the seizures. Next, he brought up the section on visitation restrictions and set them to none. Jane's isolation was over. The boyfriend could now visit. He chuckled when he imagined Nurse Tally relaying that news to Barry.

CHAPTER TWENTY-TWO

Jane

The door to her room, like every other patient's room, was open. Patients were not permitted to close their doors. Only nurses and doctors could, and they only did so when they wanted to ensure no one could see what was going on inside. It was okay. She preferred it open. She'd spent too many years locked inside a room at night. A room they lock you in isn't a room—it's a cell.

This room wasn't a cell. It was your typical hospital room, except it was designed for mental patients which meant it contained nothing one could use to hang or cut oneself. She had looked when she thought suicide was her only option. No way they were going to put her back in that prison. No way.

She'd been in enough mental hospital rooms to know they were all about the same. They all had a bed, usually a platform twin with no springs, a wardrobe with fixed shelves and no hangers or rods, and a bathroom with a shatterproof mirror and no lock on the door. This room had a window with unbreakable glass of course, and a cushioned visitor's chair. She'd hoped every day to see Joe sitting in that chair, but he'd never come, and now it was too late.

Cool air flowed from the vent in the ceiling over the window, causing the closed blind to sway front to back. The air hissed as it rushed through the vent and a rhythmic tapping came from the blind striking against the window frame. Other than the hissing and tapping, the room was quiet. The whole unit was quiet, as it was well past lights-out, and all the nut cases were asleep. Except her.

She lay on her side and stared out the open door into the day room. The rows of fluorescent lights in the ceiling were all dark, but she could still see the shadowy shapes of empty tables and sofas illuminated by the glow from a single bank of ceiling lights above the control tower. The tower was never dark, and it was never empty, but it soon would be if everything went according to her and Sandy's plan.

Jane had met Sandy a few days after she'd arrived when she'd gone for her first CT scan. She had never had one before, and she had been curious about the procedure. Sandy explained CT stood for Computed Tomography and said the machine used X-rays and computers to create detailed cross-sectional views of internal body structures. Jane had been fascinated by the large rotating machine, and Sandy seemed to enjoy answering her questions.

The two met again when Jane had gone for a follow-up scan. This time, Carl had ordered a contrasting agent be used, and Sandy explained how the chemical injected into her blood interfered with the X-rays, causing the blood vessels in her brain to appear darker on the images. The tech who was to take Jane back to her room had been delayed that day, and the two of them sat and talked for over an hour until the tech arrived.

Soon after that, Sandy began visiting Jane during her afternoon breaks. Jane had forgotten what it was like to have a girlfriend to hang out with. She hadn't had one since she'd left Berkeley. They talked about everything from science to men. Jane even told Sandy all about Joe, though she had to admit Joe was not her boyfriend, and as he was trying to become a Catholic priest, her chances of changing that were not good. They had laughed a lot about that.

At some point, Sandy learned the reason for Jane's stay at Bryce. She could not believe Jane would be sent back to Hardin. She had been shocked when Jane told her she'd been locked up there for five years.

"That doesn't make sense. I thought Hardin was only for men. I had no idea there were women there," she'd said.

"There's a few," Jane had told her. "Really mean and crazy ones."

"Why were you there then, girl?" Sandy never called her Sweet Jane or for that matter Jane. She just called her girl. Jane didn't mind, even though Sandy was several years younger than her.

"I may have been a little crazy once. I mean, more than I am now."

"Jesus, how did you survive? Were you ever, you know?"

"Raped?"

Sandy had taken her hand and nodded.

"No. Not at Hardin anyway."

"Oh girl, what does 'not in Hardin' mean?"

Jane had refused to explain. "It's not important. Nothing like that happened at Hardin. I was left alone a lot there. It's an awful place."

"I'm so sorry."

Jane had shrugged. "Forget it."

"Well, girl, you don't seem crazy to me. Even if you root for the wrong football team."

Sandy had gone to school at the University of Alabama on the same campus that surrounded the hospital, and though Jane had never attended Auburn, she'd been to more than a few Tigers' games—hard to avoid when you lived within walking distance of Jordan-Hare Stadium.

Sandy never missed an opportunity to work the Bama-Auburn rivalry into their conversation. To which Jane would reply with "Go War Eagles!" prompting the inevitable, "Roll Tide!" response.

But Jane was crazy and becoming crazier. She could feel it. It was getting harder every day to act normal. Carl had fucked with her meds, no matter how much she pleaded with him not to. "Call Tom, please," she'd begged. But no. Carl changed them, and now it was only a matter of time before they sent her back to Hardin.

"I'm not going back there," Jane had told her friend. "No matter what they say. I'm not going back."

"What will you do?"

"I'll kill myself before I let them put me back there."

That's when Sandy offered to help her escape. "No. We won't let that happen. I'll help you get out of here. We'll bust you out if we have to."

From that moment on, their conversations changed from hospital gossip and boyfriends they did not have, to figuring out how to, as Sandy put it, bust her out.

At first, it sounded easy. Bryce wasn't Hardin. Hardin had what Jane thought was like an army of armed guards who were positioned at security checkpoints throughout the building and who watched everything through security cameras. Tall fences with barbed wire surrounded the grounds, and every door was locked, including the patient rooms. Bryce, as near as Jane could tell, had very little security. Sure, there were guards, but it didn't seem like there were many, and they didn't seem half has frightening as the ones at Hardin. From Jane's perspective, one was a prison, and the other was a hospital. Easy. Jane had walked away from other hospitals.

Except the more they talked about it, the more difficult it became. Sandy knew much more about the security at Bryce than Jane. After all, she worked there and had access to most of the facility. She told Jane that Bryce was not your average hospital. It was the main Alabama state mental institution. People like Jane were sent to Bryce against their will, which meant they had to be kept in. Which meant there was plenty of security even if it wasn't in your face like it was at Hardin.

First, Jane would have to get past the control tower. That part they thought would be easy. Then, she had to get downstairs and out of the building. Again, not difficult, but impossible without being seen or setting off an alarm. After that, it got hard.

Bryce had fences surrounding it too. Though not crowned with barbed wire, they still would not be easy to climb, and there were two of them. An inner one surrounded the hospital buildings, and an outer one surrounded the park-like grounds that helped make the parents of the students from the nearby Bama campus forget what the hospital was for and who was in it.

Once past the fences, Jane would have to avoid the police, university security, and maybe even some of the Hardin security force until she could get away from the area. She would need a ride.

She wasn't sure what she would do once she was free. Maybe she would hitchhike back to Atlanta. Joe would help her, and if he wouldn't, well, she would get her things from him and return to the hidden space in the Georgia Tech library where she'd stayed after leaving Brookhaven. She had ways to get her pills there. Tom had helped her before, and she was sure he would help her again. She'd call him when she got to Joe's. She would get the crazy under control and return to Auburn to finish what she started.

The hands and face of the wristwatch Sandy had given her glowed. It was ten minutes before one in the morning. Almost time. She threw the blanket back. She was already dressed in jeans and a sweatshirt. On her feet were the bright orange slip-proof socks with the rubbery nubs on their soles that had been given to her when they brought her over from Hardin prison. She'd be going shoeless. Her sneakers were locked up in a storage room somewhere. Laces were dangerous. The socks would have to do.

As she'd done every night since she and Sandy had first devised the plan, she climbed out of bed and crossed the tiny room to the door. Careful to remain in the shadows, she peered out at the control tower.

She'd learned from Sandy that the hospital was divided down the middle into two wings known as green wing and blue wing. It was easy to know what wing you were in by a stripe that ran down the center of each corridor. The blue wing had a blue stripe, and the green wing had a green stripe. It was simple. Jane's room was on the third floor in the green wing and belonged to what the staff called the Green 3 unit.

Green 3's floor plan formed a capital H with the day room sitting in the horizontal bar of the H and two long corridors forming the vertical bars. The corridors were named by their compass orientation with the tower being the center point. Patient rooms ran along the outside east and west walls, and the unit's cafeteria, group rooms, therapy rooms, and other special-purpose rooms were located between the corridors.

Jane's room was the second room on the east corridor south of the control tower. Bright green letters on her door identified it as SE2. They had put her there to make it easy to monitor her, but it worked both ways.

The night nurse and tech sat at the tower's desk in the same spots they occupied every night. The nurse, Jane did not know her name, stared into the computer monitor with the same intensity she always did, while the tech, Alex, reclined in his chair reading the same book he'd been reading since Jane started watching them.

Neither of them moved for several minutes, then, at precisely 1:00 a.m., just as she knew he would, the tech stood and raised his arms in an exaggerated stretch. Break time. Jane watched him descend from the tower and disappear down the northeast corridor toward the staff break room. If he stuck to his routine, he wouldn't return for thirty minutes.

The rest of the plan was less certain. At ten minutes after one, Sandy would call the tower's desk phone and tell the night nurse that her sister was a patient in room NW15 which was all the way on the other side of the unit, far from Jane's room. Pretending to be panicked and overcome with concern, Sandy would tell the nurse her sister had left her a message saying she was going to kill herself.

Jane wasn't quite sure how such an imaginary attempt was plausible given the suicide-proof environment, but Sandy had assured her the nurse would have no choice but to go check on the patient. Unknown was whether the nurse would wait for Alex to come back from break, or, as they hoped, leave the tower unattended. Jane checked her watch. She would find out in five minutes.

She stepped back into the room to retrieve her backpack from its hiding place behind the visitor's chair. The chair didn't provide much concealment, but it made the pack less conspicuous. She'd spent the day worrying a nosey nurse or tech would notice it and ask why it was packed. Looking at its deflated form now, she thought her concerns had been unwarranted.

The pack contained the few things she'd been allowed to keep in her room, mostly just her old clothes. The rest of her things had been taken from her at Hardin, and she assumed stored away somewhere. She listed in her mind what she'd lost: her mother's cassette tapes, the small cassette player for playing them, a super-bright LED headlamp she'd "found" at a campground, a toothbrush, a bar of soap, a small bottle of shampoo, deodorant, some tampons, an umbrella, a scientific calculator, a raincoat, a hat, a pair of good running shoes she'd scored at a Goodwill in Birmingham, the nasty little knife a woman she met at a shelter had given her, some notebooks that now may be worth a million dollars—no wait, she reminded herself Joe had those, the army patch she'd taken from Joe's locker, a bunch of plastic bags to keep things dry, and of course, her pills and cigarettes. It didn't seem like much to be all the possessions of a 32-year-old woman with an IQ once measured at above 180, but they had been important things to her. Important enough for her and Joe to have almost died getting them back from those vile men at the homeless camp.

Well, the most important thing was Joe had the tape with the red label. He better.

She stuffed her pillow in the pack before strapping it to her back. Sandy said she would need the pillow to get over the fences. The pack no longer looked or felt as empty. As she cinched it tightly to her body, she was thankful for the lack of imagination and inconsistency demonstrated by whomever decided the laces in her sneakers were deadly, but the long nylon straps holding the pack to her back were not.

A shimmering figure greeted her when she turned back toward the door. Though not unexpected, the apparition startled her. "Fuck, I don't have time for you right now."

The figure was her, or at least one of a near infinite number of versions of her that must exist in this exact moment. Somehow, the two of them were occupying the same quantum reference point or at least partially. The other Jane was not solid. She was more like a three-dimensional holographic image floating in space, like something out of science fiction. The image was at times clear and other times blurry. She believed the image's instability was due to the Others phasing in and out of her quantum frame.

Jane moved toward the door, and the figure moved with her, floating along like a ghost in an old movie. "Go away," Jane hissed through clenched teeth.

"Where are we going, Sweet Jane?"

"Quiet," Jane whispered, worried the control tower might hear them.

"Quiet," the apparition mimicked her.

Jane stomped her feet and balled her hands up in fists like a frustrated child. "Stop it."

"Stop it," the ghost echoed.

She called these visitors the Others—meaning Other Janes. They had first appeared to her when she was deep into her studies of quantum physics at Berkeley, but they didn't start calling her Sweet Jane until she'd made the mistake of talking about them with the monster.

When they first appeared, she'd been terrified, and she'd focused her considerable intellect on finding an explanation for them. Something other than madness. By then, she was well acquainted with Hugh Everett's Multiple World Interpretation of Quantum Wave Theory, which allowed for the existence of a near infinite number of universes containing all possible variations of quantum configurations. She grabbed on to Everett's theory like a drowning woman clinging to anything that will float.

Based on the theory, she reasoned an anomaly in her brain was somehow allowing her to interact with her near-identical twins in those variant universes. Deep down, she knew this was impossible, but nevertheless, she came to accept her brain contained some kind of biological holographic walkie-talkie that could communicate with other identical walkie-talkies in different universes at the same moment, all of which would only exist in the heads of Other Janes.

The problem with her walkie-talkie was that its tuning was imprecise and random. She and the Others tuned into each other with no rhyme or reason. Most times, like at this moment, she connected with only one of them, but there were times when her walkie-talkie picked up multiple Janes. Sometimes rooms full of them, all phasing in and out. During those times, she felt the most insane.

It was impossible for her to function with all the Other Janes floating about, their voices filling her head. It could be so overwhelming and terrifying that she'd cry out and even scream, but she was careful not to do that when people were around, which took all her will, making her seem withdrawn and even catatonic. But she knew better than let her guard down when too many Janes were about. She'd lost control a few times in Hardin, and they'd locked her in isolation for days.

Puzzles and math problems helped. It seemed if she could keep her mind occupied, the walkie-talkie would not engage, but when her concentration wavered, her mind's holographic projector activated, and the Others appeared. The meds Tom had prescribed interfered with the communication somehow, and though the pills did not prevent her from ever seeing the Others, they did make them appear less frequently, and then, only one at a time.

But Carl had fucked with her meds, and now she was picking up the Others all the time again. She glanced about the room. Only the one for now. Okay, she could deal with that.

Ignoring the Other, she crept back to the doorway in time to see the night nurse descend the control tower steps and head down the northwest corridor toward the patient who was not attempting suicide. It was now or never. She took a breath and darted from the room. Now she was on her own, except for the Other who she was sure was following behind.

Jane padded down to the end of the southeast corridor where a glowing red exit sign marked the stairwell. She put her hands on the door's push bar and closed her eyes. She and Sandy had spent weeks devising the plan and talking about this very moment. This was the point of no return. Jane could back away from this door and return to her room now with no one knowing, or she could push the bar.

Pushing the bar would commit her to the plan. When she pressed it, the door's alarm would go off, waking every patient on the south side and summoning the hospital security guards. Once the alarms sounded, Jane would have to get down the stairs and out the ground floor exit door before the guards got there. If a guard was near any of the stairwell doors on the lower floors, her escape would come to an abrupt end, and they would send her back to Hardin.

A faint blue light flickered from somewhere off to her right. The Other was still with her. "We will get caught, Sweet Jane," it said and placed a shimmering arm across the bar.

"You don't know that."

"We will get caught, stupid girl."

Jane squeezed her eyes shut. "Bullshit. You're not even real," she said as she pushed the bar.

The alarm let go with a piercing high-pitched wail as Jane barreled through the door. She plunged down the steps, heart pounding, terrified security guards were rushing up to meet her. Holding her breath, she flew past the second-floor door, bracing for a guard to burst through. Her orange socks never touched the last three steps to the ground floor landing. She hit the exit door push bar like an Auburn defensive lineman hitting an Alabama guard.

"Go War Eagles!" she shouted over the door's alarm as she burst out into the hot Tuscaloosa night.

The southeast fire exit deposited her in the rear of the hospital near a loading dock. The area was lit up like noonday by bright lamps installed on the building and nearby poles. Sandy had showed her pictures on her phone of the dock. A tall chain-link fence surrounded it, separating it from an access road leading from the hospital's service entrance. The fence was too tall for her to climb, but she and Sandy had planned for it. She ran toward the automated gate delivery trucks used to enter the dock.

Sandy knew many people at the hospital, including a young man who worked in security and would hit on her at a local bar she and a few other nurses frequented. Jane's friend had used her charms, which may or may not have included sleeping with the man, to get him to tell her the gate security code. Sandy had said the man was hot and only

235 | DANIEL BURKE

giggled when Jane had pressed her on how she'd gained the code from him.

Jane had memorized the six-digit code. It was not hard. Even with the Others clogging her brain, she still remembered everything. She punched the digits into the gate's keypad while her eyes scanned the dark windows of the guard house. No one was there. Why would there be? There were no deliveries this early in the morning. She hit the pound key after pressing the last digit as Sandy had told her to do, and the gate slid open with a loud rattling sound that almost drowned out the sound of her pounding heart.

She forced herself through the widening gap and almost panicked when her backpack caught on the gate. She wiggled free and raced across the access road to another chain-link fence. This one separated the hospital buildings from the grounds. The psych techs would sometimes take groups of patients through a gate to the green space beyond, but that gate required a badge, and Sandy could not get one. Jane had to climb.

When she reached the fence, Jane realized why Sandy had told her to pack the pillow. The fence wasn't very tall, but unlike the chain-link fences she remembered climbing over as a child, the wire on this fence extended above the top rail, creating sharp pickets. It wasn't like that razor wire on top of the fences at Hardin but getting over it without the pillow would've been painful.

She took off her backpack and pulled out the pillow. She zipped the pack and tossed it over the fence, then she covered the pickets with the pillow and climbed. Years of institutionalization and the extra pounds that accumulated as a side effect from her medication made the climb more difficult than she'd imagined, but inside her soft exterior remained an athlete. She dropped to the cool grass on the opposite side.

Shouts came from somewhere behind her in the loading dock area and looking back, Jane could see two guards jogging toward the gate which was now retracting. The lights from the dock did not reach the fence. The grounds beyond them were in darkness except for a few streetlamps that ran along walkways. She would avoid those. She retrieved the bright white pillow from the top of the fence, snatched up her backpack, and ran as fast as she could to the outer fence that separated the grounds from a wide street Sandy told her was called University Boulevard.

At the outer fence, Jane paused long enough to scan the boulevard for police or hospital security before using the pillow to scramble over. She dropped onto the sidewalk that paralleled the boulevard as a gray car unexpectedly pulled up to the curb. The driver's face was concealed by, of all things, a dark ski mask, and his hands were either ghost white or he was wearing white gloves that glowed in the light from the streetlamp. Jane was about to run when the rear door opened, and a familiar voice shouted from inside.

"Get in, girl!"

Not pausing for a second, Jane tossed the pillow and backpack inside and dove into the back seat right into the waiting arms of her new best friend. The rear door slammed closed as the car raced away.

Jane hugged Sandy while staring at the back of the masked driver's head.

This had not been part of the plan. "Sandy, what are you doing? Aren't you afraid of getting in trouble?"

"No way. We got this." Sandy laughed. "We got you."

"Whose car is this?" Jane asked, still panting from exertion and fear.

"Mine, silly," Sandy said as she wrapped her arms around Jane and pulled her close.

Jane stared at the stranger's eyes in the rearview mirror. She thought she recognized them. "Who is he?"

"A friend," Sandy said while holding her tight. "Girl, your heart is about to beat out of your chest."

Sandy released her grip for a moment and opened her purse. She withdrew a pill vial, removed its cap, and turned it over in her hand. Three pills poured into her palm—a small, round yellow one and two larger, oval white ones. Sandy chose the yellow one for herself and handed the two oval ones to Jane. Sandy popped her tablet in her mouth and washed it down with a sip from a water bottle.

"Take those, sweetie."

"What are these?"

"Valiums," Sandy said while holding out the water bottle. "I take them when I get anxious, and girl, you are super anxious."

Pills had been part of Jane's life for so long she popped them in her mouth without thinking twice, then took a long swig from Sandy's water bottle. Settling into her friend's arms, she stared at the man's eyes in the mirror as the car sped along.

"Where are we going?"

Sandy nodded toward the front seat. "He has a house out in the country about ten miles from here."

A blue shimmer appeared to Jane's right as one of the Others came into view. "Who is he?" the Other said.

"I don't know," Jane said.

"You don't know what?" Sandy asked.

"Who he is."

"He's my friend. He's your friend too. You'll see when we get to his house."

The Other said, "Why the fuck is he still wearing the mask and what's with the latex gloves?"

"Why doesn't he take off the mask?" Jane asked.

"I'm sure he will when we get off the main roads. Now relax."

"You are a stupid girl, Sweet Jane," the Other said.

"Yes. You are a stupid girl," said another Other who appeared in the passenger side of the front seat.

"A very stupid girl," said a third Other who appeared at her feet on the car floor.

Jane stared out the window, trying to ignore the taunts from the Others. She didn't want Sandy to know they were there. They'd left the Alabama University campus and were driving past dark fields full of short, leafy plants Jane thought might have been soybeans.

With each mile, she felt more relaxed, and had even stopped worrying about the strange man wearing the ski mask. The Others must have figured out she was ignoring them because they had all gone.

Those pills must be working. She slumped down into Sandy's lap and stared out the rear window into the night sky. Stars shone through an opening in the clouds. She hadn't seen stars since she sat on Joe's stairwell listening to him pray. Her thoughts turned to him. If only things were different. She reminded herself that there were plenty of universes where they were.

A familiar voice came from the front seat. "Is she asleep yet?"

Jane was sure she knew that voice, but thinking was getting harder, and she couldn't remember who it belonged to. All she wanted to do now was sleep.

Sandy stared down at her and smiled. "Almost. Those pills must be powerful. What were they again?"

The familiar voice said, "A special benzo mix I get from Mexico. I knew it would work well on our girl."

Benzo mix? Hadn't Sandy said they were Valiums, and what did he mean by our girl? Were they talking about her? Was she their girl? Maybe so. It didn't matter. She was floating on a cloud, and the Others had gone away. Nothing bothered her now except maybe the strange man's voice. She was sure she knew that voice.

It was becoming impossible for her to stay awake. She gave up trying, and as she drifted off, she heard Sandy say, "She's out." At least Jane thought it was Sandy.

Then from somewhere she heard the voice say, "Good night, Sweet Jane."

That's when she realized who the voice belonged to.

CHAPTER TWENTY-THREE

Barry

Carl's granddaddy's house was only ten miles away from Bryce Hospital, but it felt much more remote, especially on a moonless, overcast night such as this one. There were no streetlights along the empty asphalt roads, no lights from neighboring homes, and no passing cars. It was dark. So dark in fact, Barry would have missed the turn into the gravel driveway had the headlights not caught on a half dollar-sized reflector affixed to the mailbox.

Barry parked the car and caught Sandra in the rearview mirror watching him.

He peeled off the ski mask and grinned at her. "How is she?"

Sandra looked down. Jane was sleeping in her lap. She brushed a lock of Jane's hair away from her face. "Sleeping like a baby."

"Good. Now we have to get her inside."

He exited the car and opened the back door. Sandra slid out from under Jane and climbed out. Barry, still wearing the gloves, reached down and pressed his index and middle finger against Jane's neck. Her pulse was slow and strong. Not quite the runner's pulse she had years ago, but he guessed it was not much higher than 60 beats per minute.

"It's so dark," Sandra said.

Barry was prepared. He was always prepared. He took a small LED head lamp from his pants pocket and stretched its band around his head. The small light shone with intense brightness disproportionate to its size.

He reached under Jane's arms and pulled her out of the car.

"Grab her legs."

Sandra took her legs, and they carried her around the back of the house.

"Where are we taking her?"

"You'll see."

Sandra stopped, and Barry almost pulled Jane's legs free of her grasp.

"What's the matter?"

"I don't want you to hurt her."

"Sweet Sandra, I am not going to hurt her. We went through all this trouble to bring her here so I can help her. Don't you remember what we discussed? How the medication she's been prescribed is harming her?"

"What are you going to do to her?"

"I'm going to talk to her and coach her subconscious to help her deal with her psychosis. Not much different from the way I help you."

"I am not psychotic."

"No, but you do suffer from major depression and anxiety which is why you need my help with your eating and other..." he grinned, "urges."

She flashed a deviant grin back at him, "I'm feeling one of those urges right now."

"Let's get Jane comfortable, then we can discuss that urge. Let's set her down by the cellar entrance." He shined his headlamp on the doors so Sandra could see.

They set Jane down in the grass, and Sandra molded into him. She kissed him hard and moved her hand down to his crotch. He grabbed her wrist and pulled her hand away.

"Not yet. We have to get her down to the cellar."

"I still don't understand why you couldn't treat her at the hospital."

He took a deep breath to gain control of his emotions. His control over her was still fragile. If he made her angry, she might rebel against the suggestions he'd placed that had convinced her to help him in the first place. He couldn't have that. He'd never get Jane down the cellar steps without her help.

He pulled the latex gloves from his hands and stuffed them in his pocket. He ran his fingers through her hair and caressed her cheek and neck. Then he kissed each of her eyelids and said three times in a soft even tone, "Remember, you are in control." She didn't know it, but these intimate gestures and words were part of the rapid hypnotic induction pattern he'd established during their sessions.

"Yes, I am," she said. "I am confident, and I am powerful."

Her affirming response told him she was in a receptive mode. Sandra was in a trance, albeit not a very deep one, but her will was pliable and as long as he was careful, he could convince her of just about anything.

"Sweet Sandra, are you ready to help me help Jane?"

She nodded. "Yes, of course, silly. Why would you ask?"

"Good. I have to open the doors."

He withdrew a key ring from his front pocket and selected a shiny new key. from the tarnished collection. The key went to the new padlock he'd purchased to replace the old rusty one Carl had used to secure the cellar doors. He unlocked the padlock and swung open the heavy wooden doors. Then he descended the steps and opened the lower door. He looked back, and his headlamp illuminated Sandra peering down at him from the opening.

"Come on down."

"It looks creepy. Are there lights in there?"

Barry stepped in and turned on the lights, then looked back up the stairwell. "Yes. It's fine. Come down and see."

She descended the steps and came through the door, blinking in the glare of the high-wattage lights.

"Wow. It's like a hospital room. Who put all these things down here?"

"Dr. Walker's grandfather."

"It's so incredible. Where did this stuff come from?"

"The old Bryce Hospital."

Sandra made the face you'd make if you smelled something awful. "The insane asylum?"

"The very one."

"Now I am so fucking creeped out." She inspected the bed and the old medical equipment. "This stuff is really old." She handled one of the leather and steel wrist restraints attached to the bed. "You're going to chain her to this bed down here?"

"Chain is an awful term. We will restrain her for her own good. I may not be here when she wakes up, and we don't want her injuring herself trying to climb out of that bed in the dark, do we, Sweet Sandra?"

Sandra released the restraint and stepped away from the bed. "I guess not."

"Let's go get her before she wakes up," he urged.

Sandra folded her arms and did not move.

Again, he reminded himself how fragile the trance state was. "Remember, everything is under your control. Let's talk about your concerns."

"I don't like that we are putting her down here. Let's take her to the room we use in the house. There's a bed there, as you know," she grinned.

"This place has everything I need to care for her. It will only be for a couple days. I promise Jane will be fine."

She unfolded her arms and came to him. Once again, he ran his fingers through her hair and caressed her cheek and neck, then he kissed each of her eyelids and said three times in a soft even tone, "Remember, you are in control."

Sandra smiled and pushed her lips over the top of his in a fierce kiss. She dropped to her knees and unfastened his pants then took his erect penis deep into her mouth and worked it back and forth in her throat until he came with an intensity that made him dizzy. She was undoing the buttons on her blouse when he regained his composure.

He glanced at his watch and fought to hide his irritation. There was no time. He zipped up his pants and pulled her to her feet.

She frowned. "What about me?"

He buttoned her blouse. "Later. I promise. We need to get her down here before she wakes up."

They returned to where they had left Jane. As before, he grabbed her under her arms and pulled her up while Sandra took her feet. He had Sandra turn around and hold Jane's legs at her knees almost like she was giving her a piggyback ride, then she went first down the steps with him following.

Once down, they placed Jane in the bed and removed her clothes. Sandra wanted to know why, and he had had to manage her through it, but in the end, Jane lay naked on the white sheet he'd covered the mattress with that morning. He studied her pale body. It glowed under the bright lights. Her once firm, athletic physique had softened and turned somewhat plump. She looked a lot like her mother lying there, and he was overcome with erotic memories of Maggie.

After he and Maggie were done having sex, he'd often insist on turning on the lights so he could see her lying naked among the rumpled sheets, as Jane was lying now. Maggie had been a beautiful, curvy woman. Her shape had reminded him of the women in the French paintings from the 19th century he so adored, painted when pale, soft curves were valued above tanned, firm abdominal muscles. Now Jane's body had taken on those same classically seductive characteristics. She looked like she was waiting to be painted by Manet.

It was difficult for him to control his urges. He almost reached out to caress her breasts when he reminded himself that Sandra was watching. He slipped the latex gloves from his pocket and pulled them back over his hands.

"What now?" Sandra asked.

"There are clean sheets in that cabinet over there." He pointed to a large, gleaming white cabinet with glass-paned doors standing against a far wall. "Grab one so we can cover her."

While Sandra retrieved the sheet, he opened a drawer on a nearby surgical cart and retrieved a sealed plastic bag containing a urinary catheter along with some medical tape, lubricant, and disinfectant. The catheter was not an artifact of the old asylum. It was new and sterile.

He'd brought it and the other supplies from his Auburn office three days before.

He placed the items on a tray near the bed and went to work inserting the catheter in Jane's urethra. His hands trembled some as he parted her vulva, and he could not resist probing her vagina with one of his fingers.

"What are you doing?"

"Catheterizing her. What does it look like? I assume you've done this procedure?"

"Yes. Of course."

Barry stepped away without finishing and took the sheet from her. "Why don't you take over, and I'll get the collector set up."

After they finished, he covered Jane with the sheet and secured her wrists and ankles in the restraints while Sandra watched from across the room. Then he inserted an IV line in her arm and connected it up to a bag.

"What are you infusing her with?"

"It's just saline solution to keep her hydrated."

After he finished, they climbed out of the cellar, leaving Jane sleeping in total darkness. He closed and locked the doors and they headed back to Sandra's car.

"It's getting very late," he said. "The sun will be up in a few hours, and you have a plane to catch in the morning."

"Cancun," she whispered. "Too bad you can't come with us."

"I have Jane to take care of now. Besides, I'm sure your friends don't want an old man tagging along."

He guided her toward her car without turning on his headlamp.

"Too bad you left your car at my apartment. Now you have to come with me." She put her arm around his waist and squeezed.

At her car he opened the back door. "I'm going to sit back here so I can stretch out."

"Not fair."

"You want me to have some energy when we get to your place, don't you?"

"Hmm. I guess so," she giggled. "Take your nap. You'll need it, old man."

He pretended to sleep to avoid conversation as she drove back to Tuscaloosa. Her apartment was on the outskirts of town, several miles from the hospital. The complex was new and still under construction. It contained three five-story buildings each housing maybe forty apartments. Two of the buildings had tenants. The third building was in the final stages of construction and vacant. Sandra lived in a one-bedroom unit on the fourth floor of one of the occupied buildings.

Barry had parked his car in an unlit section of the parking lot near the construction equipment. When they pulled into the lot, he directed her toward his car. "I'm parked back by the new building."

Jane's backpack was on the seat next to him. He'd been loosening the straps on it while Sandra had been driving and had created a large loop which would be plenty big enough for what he planned.

Sandra steered toward his car. "Why did you park way over here? There are no lights."

Exactly, he thought, *and there are no security cameras either,* but he said, "Got to get my steps in."

She pulled her car up next to his. "I thought you were going to come in. You owe me. Remember?"

He did not answer. Instead, as soon as she put the car in park, he lifted the backpack and threw the strap he'd lengthened over her head and around her neck. Then he pulled back with all his strength. The action had been smooth and lightning fast—so fast, she'd had no time to react before the inch-wide strap began digging into her flesh and cutting off the oxygen flow to her brain.

She tried to twist away from him, and at one point her foot landed on the accelerator, causing the engine to scream as it redlined. He continued pulling as hard as he could, and she clawed at the strap and tried to reach his arms with her hands, but she could not get to him. After a couple minutes that felt to Barry like hours, her foot slipped off the accelerator and the engine stopped screaming.

He'd never done this before. He knew it would take time—longer than what it took in the movies, but the fight she put up and the effort required to keep her airway closed surprised him. She continued to struggle for a good five minutes before she began to go limp, and it was at least another minute before he was sure she was unconscious. He kept the strap pulled tight until his strength gave out.

After he was sure she was dead, he dropped the pack and checked her carotid pulse. Nothing. Just like he felt. Nothing. He reached around her and turned off the ignition, then he sat back in the seat to catch his breath. It was much easier to convince the people he needed to kill to take their own lives.

Before he got out, he considered Jane's pack and the pillow she'd brought from the hospital. They would give the police ample evidence to link Jane with the killing. Poor Sandra, another victim of the insane psychopath, Jane Carter. He frowned his best theatrical frown and walked to his car.

CHAPTER TWENTY-FOUR

Jane

She regained consciousness like a swimmer ascending from a plunge into a deep, dark lake. Thoughts, murky at first, like water clouded with the sediments churned up from a muddy bottom, grew clearer as she rose from the depths. She remembered getting into the car with Sandy and the masked driver. She remembered taking the pills Sandy had offered, the comfort of her friend's embrace, and the feeling of floating before she felt nothing at all. Then she remembered the voice, and like a swimmer completing her ascent, broke the surface. Awake.

Were her eyes open? She thought so, but if they were, she was in a place of total darkness. Darkness so complete Jane knew this must be what it was like to be without sight. Could she be blind? Maybe the pills Sandy had given her had done more than make her sleep. Maybe they had blinded her. She went to reach for her eyes, but when she tried to move her hands, she discovered straps around her wrists prevented her from raising her arms more than a few inches. She tried to move her legs and found they too were strapped to the bed.

She fought against the restraints. The blackness echoed with the sounds of chains rattling against the metal bed frame. As she struggled, she became aware of a stinging pain in the place where she urinated and the feeling that something had been inserted inside her. Jane had never felt anything like it before. *Ouch. What is that?* She relaxed and the strange hurt stopped, but she recognized a more familiar sting in her arm. It sure felt like an IV needle. *Shit.* She was back in the hospital. They had caught her, and they must have put her in isolation. *Fuck.*

"I'm awake," she shouted. "Turn on the fucking lights! You hear me? I'm awake. Turn on the lights, you bastards!"

There was no response.

"Help!" she shouted as loud as she could.

Struggling seemed useless, and the IV and whatever was inside her made it painful. She tried to relax. She even tried some of the breathing exercises she remembered from the yoga the well-meaning psych tech had tried to get her to do.

If she was in a hospital, someone would be monitoring her and notice she was awake, although she did not appear to be connected to any monitoring devices. There was no blood pressure cuff on her arm, no EKG leads on her chest, and no power lights on nearby electronics. That was the most unsettling thing—a hospital room with no glowing switches or buttons. Something wasn't right.

Again, she worried she might be blind.

"Please talk to me," she pleaded.

A familiar silver-blue shimmer appeared out of the darkness and an Other materialized. Jane seldom welcomed such visits, but she welcomed this one.

"At least you haven't abandoned me. I hope things are better in your universe."

The Other floated in the darkness, gliding about in tentative, random movements as if uncertain of her boundaries.

"What do you see?" Jane asked.

"Nothing. It's dark. Where the fuck are we?"

The Other faded and disappeared only to reappear a moment later closer to the bed. At least Jane thought it was the same one, but she could never be sure.

"What do you see?"

"Now I see a stupid girl strapped to a hospital bed. You should've never taken those fucking pills."

"Fuck you."

Another shimmering Other appeared, floating above her near where she imagined the ceiling must be.

"What do you see?" Jane asked the new arrival.

"A stupid girl strapped to a hospital bed."

"Stop!" Jane screamed. "I don't need your bullshit either."

"Why would Sandy have brought us to a place like this?" the Other floating above her asked.

"I don't know," Jane replied. "Something must have happened while I was sleeping. Maybe the police caught us. I guess I am back at Hardin." She rattled her restraints. "But this seems a little much, even for them."

"What about the voice? It's him, isn't it?" the Other closest to the bed asked.

"I don't know," Jane said.

"It's him," both Others said together.

"Quiet!"

She pulled against the restraints. The IV needle in her vein bit at her, sending a sharp pain through her arm. "Fuck. That hurts," she said through gritted teeth.

"Then stop moving, stupid girl. We need to think our way out of this," the first Other said.

"Be more Jane than Sweet Jane," said the second Other.

Jane closed her eyes to block them out, knowing they never went away that easily. She thought back to a time when there was only Jane and no Sweet Jane, back when visits from the Others were infrequent and, she thought, manageable. She had been in the home stretch of finishing her doctoral thesis, "Quantum Mechanics at Macro Scale and Its Application to Computing and Telecommunication," and was presenting portions of it during lectures and conferences to prepare for its defense. It was during those final months of intense research and calculation the occasional visits from one or two Others had turned into gangs of them appearing almost nonstop. They overwhelmed her. It was like her quantum wave walkie-talkie had become stuck on conference call.

Of course, she knew back then, even at her craziest, the Others couldn't be real. They were hallucinations, products of her diseased mind, not alternate versions of herself from other points in the quantum wave. They had to be. The scale of interactions required to perceive such macro-phenomena across different states in the quantum wave were almost unimaginable. It didn't matter, though. Knowing they could not be real didn't prevent them from being real to her.

That's when pretending they weren't there or hiding her interactions with them from other people stopped working. She began having problems in public. She'd even been escorted off a university stage after engaging with the Others in front of a perplexed and alarmed audience. No doubt that video was still on the internet somewhere. And just like that, speaking invitations dried up, and her doctoral adviser began expressing more concern about her mental health than her thesis. In less than a year, she'd gone from brilliant Jane Carter to crazy Jane Carter.

After that, she left Berkeley and returned home. She saw many doctors—the best her mother could find, and they'd tried a variety of approaches, including different types and dosages of antipsychotic medications. Some of their treatments were even successful at reducing the frequency of the visits from the Others but not without side effects. The medications all clogged her mind up. She could function, she could even pretend to be normal, but when she was on those medications, she couldn't do the math. Working through equations felt like navigating familiar roads in a dense fog. She knew the turns were out there, but she could not find them.

At that point, she and her mother began to lose hope, as it seemed no therapy or medication existed that would give her back what she'd lost. Doctors advised her mother they had to lower their expectations. She would never complete her dissertation. There would be no PhD, no professorship, and no research fellowship. According to the doctors, all the things she and her mother had dreamed of were now unattainable. In time, they said, maybe if she stayed on her meds—the meds that made her dull, and stuck with the therapy sessions, the ones that taught her better ways to pretend the Others weren't there, Jane might lead a decent life. Decent for who, they never said, but decent.

Jane's mother could not accept the prognosis. She was desperate for treatment options, and that's when she discovered the monster. Of course, she did not know he was a monster when she found him. It would be another year before they figured that out.

One of the Others appeared at what she imagined was the foot of her bed. The silver-blue shimmer radiating off the Other did not penetrate the blackness. None of the Other's aura reached her invisible surroundings. No reflection on the metal bed frame or the chains that bound her to it. No glow on the thin bed sheet she knew covered her by its cool feel on her bare skin.

"He was always a monster," the Other said

"There was no way Mother could have known that."

"You knew it."

"Not at first. He seemed fine at first. Better than the other doctors."

"Stupid girl."

Jane had been recently discharged from a two-month stay at Emory's psychiatric hospital when her mother arranged her first meeting with the monster. She had been there recovering from what the counselors called a crisis. That was the polite term for "losing it." This particular crisis occurred in a crowded Atlanta subway car. She'd been on her way back to the small home she and her mother shared near Piedmont Park when the Others overwhelmed her.

They were everywhere—mixed in with the other passengers. All of them talking to her at once. All of them making comments about her appearance and her discomfort at being around so many people with their prying and judgmental eyes. She'd ignored the Others for as long as she could, but at some point, she'd snapped. She had a vague recollection of being dragged from the train by two police officers while screaming at the top of her lungs for the Others to go away. After that, she spent a few terrifying days in the psych ward at Grady Hospital before being transferred to Emory.

Emory is where her mother had found the monster. Not at the hospital itself, but in a magazine article she had read while in the waiting room of Jane's psychiatrist at the time. The article, titled

Gaining Insights into Psychosis with Disassociated Observer Exploration Therapy was in a seven-year-old copy of the *American Journal of Psychiatry*. In it, the monster described his technique for understanding and treating psychotic symptoms without antipsychotic medications.

It was the very treatment they'd been hoping for, something to get rid of the Others without the drugs.

"You can't get rid of us," the Other floating above her said.

Jane ignored her.

It didn't matter that by then, the monster had been censured by his own profession, that other more recent articles challenged the efficacy of his therapies and warned benefits of his Disassociated Observer Exploration Therapy did not outweigh its risks. Mother researched him and found he was still treating patients at Auburn University, and most importantly, the patients he treated claimed he was making them better.

Mother was a thorough researcher who wasn't satisfied by a collection of positive internet reviews. She tracked down a half dozen top psychiatrists and questioned them about the monster's techniques. Half thought the treatment was a scam or even dangerous, but the other half thought it was revolutionary. After that, she spoke to the monster himself and to the patient references he provided. The monster's therapy was controversial and expensive, but according to his patients, worth the risk and money. Mother had been desperate for hope. They both were, and the monster had offered it.

"She was as stupid as you," the Other at the foot of her bed said.

"Don't say that. Mother was smart. She had no way of knowing what would happen."

"The Emory doctors knew. They warned her, but Mother wouldn't listen," the floating Other said.

"Shut up. They didn't know what he would do. They just didn't agree with his methods."

It was true. The doctors who'd treated her at Emory had tried to talk her mother out of switching treatments. They had told her to give the Haloperidol they'd prescribed a chance. They had felt they had stabilized her during her stay and advised she stick with the treatment plan they'd devised. The monster's methods had been discredited. They even called him a quack.

"If Mother had listened, she'd still be alive, and we might have had a life," the Other at the foot of the bed said.

"Shut up!" Jane shouted into the blackness.

Her first session with the monster was on an unusually cold mid-October afternoon, the heart of football season. His office was located near the Auburn University campus, and all the storefronts were festooned with Halloween decorations and so many "Go Tigers" and "AU" banners Jane's mother had remarked they must be required by law.

Most of their first meeting was spent talking about her past. They talked about her completing high school two years early and starting college when she was only fifteen. He'd expressed the same admiration for her early start as everyone else who'd heard the story and asked the same questions about what it had been like to attend classes where she was so much younger than the other students.

She'd told him the same thing she told everyone. She'd practically grown up on the Georgia Tech campus, so taking her first courses there was almost like homeschooling. After all, her mother was part of the Tech faculty, and Jane had attended a private school for gifted children near enough to the campus that she'd walk to her mother's office every day after school. She'd already audited most of the advanced math classes before she'd enrolled.

He wanted to know about her time in California attending Berkeley. How did she enjoy living there? Did she feel alone? Did she have friends? How were her grades? What degrees did she complete?

That was all they talked about during their first meeting. After 45 minutes, he looked at his expensive watch and told her he looked forward to seeing them again in a week when he said they would begin talking about why she'd left Berkeley. She'd become his patient.

They made the long drive to Auburn every Monday for the remainder of the year. The first several sessions involved little more than talking about her past and no hypnosis. Her mother attended those early sessions with her, and Jane began to notice the monster flirting with her, and to Jane's astonishment, her mother flirted back. Her mother dressed nicer for those visits, and she began spending a few minutes in the parking lot freshening her makeup and brushing her hair before they went in.

Jane did not begrudge her mother's apparent crush. Not at first, anyway. The monster wasn't a bad looking man. He was fit, dressed nice, and seemed up on many topics, including a superficial understanding of her mother's field of computing.

"It was disgusting how she fell for him," the Other at the foot of her bed said.

"She was lonely, and he fooled her. He fooled us both."

Things started out well enough. The Others continued to visit her, but they did not gang up on her as they did on the train or during the episodes she'd had back in California. The monster began to introduce hypnosis into their sessions. She remembered telling him she doubted he could hypnotize her. She didn't believe in it. *How wrong she'd been.* He'd smiled and told her they'd see. Even after he'd done it, Jane didn't believe it, but her mother was still attending the sessions and assured her—she had been hypnotized.

Those first few times, he used what he called standard shallow medical hypnosis. "Wading in," he'd called it. The monster had not taken her deep. That would come later. He'd just brought her to a point where she was receptive to the suggestions he made for how to manage the Others' visits and techniques for controlling the random thoughts that he said she perceived as mind fog. Nothing appeared out of the ordinary or weird about it. The therapy actually seemed to help. The visits from the Others grew less, and her mother, who by then was seeing more of the monster than Jane, was convinced.

Before she knew it, they were looking for houses near the university, and her mother was meeting with the head of the Department of Computer Science and Software Engineering. They left Atlanta at the end of the fall semester in time for her mother to begin teaching at Auburn when classes resumed in January.

Jane coughed. Her mouth felt as dry as old leather. She rattled her bindings and called out. "Come on. I'm thirsty. I need something to drink."

There was no response. The room was as silent as it was black. She'd think herself deaf too if she couldn't hear the racket the chains made against the metal bed frame.

The Other at the foot of the bed stared at her and shook her head. "Stupid girl."

"Fuck you."

It continued to go well for the first couple months. Nice, even. Their new home was larger than the one they had in Atlanta. She and her mother spent the weekends scouring local shops and estate sales for furniture and odds and ends to fill the empty spaces of their home. Jane had things under control enough to work as a tutor and research assistant in the university's physics department. She spent every Monday afternoon in the monster's warm office on his oversized leather sofa where they continued what he called hypnotic enhanced cognitive behavior therapy, and the Others kept their distance. Her mother no longer sat in on their sessions.

Soon, the monster began to hang around the house more. He and her mother would go out on Friday and Saturday nights. Sometimes, her mother wouldn't come home until well past midnight. Jane would sit up waiting for her, watching from the big window in her bedroom that overlooked the street. She'd watch them walk to the door. The monster's arms around her mother's waist, both of them laughing.

"She was such a slut," the Other floating above her said.

"No, she wasn't. She was in love."

"With a monster."

"She didn't know."

Things started to change in the spring. That's when they began what the monster called deep hypnosis sessions. Her first deep session was in late March. She'd entered his office to find an IV bag set up next to the sofa. He'd explained the drug would make her more comfortable and allow them to achieve the deep trance state necessary for his DOET treatment. "You were a fool to let him do that to you," the Other at the foot of the bed said.

"Shut up."

Throughout the rest of the spring and into the early summer, she would show up for their sessions and leave with no recollection of what had transpired. All she could recall was lying down on the big brown sofa, maybe the sting of the IV needle penetrating her arm, and then waking with his soft voice reciting the familiar words, "You are climbing a ladder in the dark. Your hands and feet move from rung to rung. Above you is the glow from a welcoming light. You climb up into the light, and then you recognize a familiar face. Your mind is clear, and your body feels refreshed. Now, open your eyes."

It was in early May, after several of these deep hypnosis sessions, that she first noticed something new when she'd see the Others. She began hearing a voice in her head when the Others appeared. The voice said her name was Sweet Jane, which Jane found amusing at first. Sweet Jane would argue with the Others. She'd command them to go away. Sometimes, the arguments between Sweet Jane and the Others were so intense and distracting, Jane could not move.

More than once, she'd emerged from the paralyzing argument with her chin and blouse wet from drool and frightened students and colleagues staring wide-eyed at her, asking if everything was all right. One time, the EMTs got involved, and that was the end of her research assistant gig.

The monster told her mother the episodes marked a severe advance in her disease known as catatonia. It was no longer safe for her to drive, and he'd advised she not spend time in public alone.

It was okay, her mother had told her. They had been working together on her mother's latest book. Losing the job at the university would give Jane more time to work on her parts and to transcribe the tapes her mother used to record the chapters.

Then, sometime in late May, Jane started to wake from the Monday sessions feeling like her clothes were not on right. Sometimes her shirt would be untucked. Sometimes her panties would feel out of place, and sometimes, they'd be wet. Bruises began to appear on her inner thighs and she felt scratches inside her.

"He's raping us," Sweet Jane would whisper in her head during the cab rides home.

The memory made her want to vomit. Jesus, when was someone coming? She'd been awake for at least an hour. "Help!" she yelled again into the blackness,

Her plea echoed off the invisible walls. If she was in a room in Hardin, it was like no place she'd ever been in before, and she'd seen plenty of isolation rooms. This had to be some kind of special place. Maybe it was punishment for her escape.

"It's a fucking dungeon," the Other floating above her said.

During her early years at Hardin, she'd been locked up alone often. Back then, the Others would swarm her, and she'd get confused and lash out at a tech or a guard, and they'd lock her away. She'd even been strapped to a bed once or twice, though never with chains, and never naked with something shoved inside her.

Her first few years at Hardin had been pure hell, the worst years of her life, but things got better when Tom became her doctor. He'd been the only doctor she'd seen at Hardin who seemed to want to help her get well. She became comfortable with him, let her guard down, told him secrets. Not all of them, but things she had told no one else, not even Joe.

His reaction to some of the things she'd told him had been frustrating. Like when she told him how Sweet Jane had popped into her head after the deep hypnosis sessions with the monster. Tom had brushed it off like it was normal to wake up with a new person inside you. She couldn't get him to admit he saw any malpractice in what the monster had done. That's when she realized doctors, even the good ones, protect each other. Tom used to say to her, "Being Sweet Jane is your choice. It's up to you to let her go or keep her, no matter how she got there."

It was the way she believed Tom took the monster's side with the origin of Sweet Jane that prevented her from telling him about the rapes. She'd come close, even mentioning her clothes felt out of place and she felt uncomfortable after her hypnosis sessions with the monster, but Tom never seemed interested in learning more about what Jane knew happened during those sessions. After a while, when she'd realized Tom either did not believe her or, as she suspected, was unwilling to cause problems for another psychiatrist, she stopped bringing it up.

"Help me, you fuckers," she screamed.

She should have played the tape for Tom. She'd wanted to, but she had been too afraid he'd take it and give it to the guards who ran the place, the blue-suited prison people. She didn't trust them. She barely trusted Tom. If she'd lost the tape, then she'd have nothing to prove what the monster had done to her and to her mother. No. Tom was a good doctor, but he was one of them, and they always protected each other. Didn't they?

The Other at the foot of the bed said, "Always."

The Other floating above her said, "You should have told Joe. Joe would have believed you."

She knew that was true. Joe would have believed her, and he would have helped her get the monster. If only she hadn't gotten caught, she would have made it back to Atlanta. She would have made it back to Joe.

"I didn't want him to know."

"Know what?"

She clenched her fists. "You know what. I didn't want him to know what that monster did to me."

Jane had only told one other person what he'd done. That's how she'd killed her mother. She'd told her mother the Barry Lieberman her mother thought she knew was not the real Barry Lieberman. The soft-spoken, intelligent man with the fit body and well-groomed appearance who claimed to care so much about her daughter, who would take her to expensive restaurants, and even spend the occasional night, was a monster. She'd shown her mother the bruises on her inner thighs, the scratches, and the redness around her vagina. It had broken her mother's heart.

A thin, vertical sliver of light appeared out beyond the end of the bed. Unlike the unreal glow from the Others, it reflected off the polished steel of the bed frame.

"It's about fucking time," she said.

She heard a loud thump from somewhere above her as if something heavy had been dropped, and the light went out.

"Shit. Hey, I'm thirsty! I need water!" she shouted.

After a moment, the sliver glowed again, but now it seemed to waver as if its source was moving.

"Come let me out of this fucking bed," she said.

"Hush," said the Other at the foot of the bed.

"Stupid girl," said the floating Other who moved toward the wavering light.

A door opened and a fierce white light as bright as the afternoon sun shone in her face. She squinted her eyes to ward of the stabbing brilliance. The light hovered in the air as it moved toward her. She could not see what emitted it, but she assumed it was a flashlight or one of those LED head lamps. She'd had one of those. It was locked up somewhere with the rest of her things.

"What the fuck?" she said. "Turn on the lights."

The floating light illuminated her bed and some of the surroundings. She was naked beneath a thin white sheet lying on what she assumed was a hospital bed with heavy-gauge steel tubular railings unlike anything she'd seen before. It struck her that it looked very old.

The light shone on the IV bag that dangled from a polished chrome stand that looked as old as the bed, and it lit upon what appeared to her to be an ancient electrical device.

The bindings on her wrists and ankles appeared to be made of thick leather with metal buckles that made them look like oversized dog collars. Shiny chains connected them to clamps on the heavy bed frame. It was like something out of an old horror movie.

Her heart pounded from fear. She wanted to scream, but she was gasping, almost panting, for air. She felt her bladder let go, and out of the corner of her eye, she saw a plastic tube turn yellow with her urine. Now she knew what was inside her.

"Where am I?" she managed.

The light did not answer.

She smelled something, a pungent, musky smell like a man's cologne. It was familiar. Yes. She'd smelled that cologne many times before. It was the monster's cologne.

"What are you doing to me, Barry?"

The light bobbed, and she heard a soft chuckle and caught a glint of polished white teeth.

"Where is Sandy?"

The light moved in close to her, and she could feel breath on her cheek.

"Don't you remember? You killed her."

"No, I didn't," Jane sobbed.

Then a hand brought up a syringe and injected something into a port on the IV rig.

"No," she whispered in a dry, hoarse croak.

"No!" the Others exclaimed.

There was a faint buzzing in her ears, and the floating light enveloped her. She felt fingers pressed to the vein in her neck. Then she was falling. The feeling was not unpleasant. Down she went. It was as if she was a diver again, descending back down into the deep, warm lake. And then there was nothing. Nothing but the monster watching her go.

CHAPTER TWENTY-FIVE

Carl

Carl arrived at the hospital that morning to find the staff in a state of near panic. Jane Carter, his patient, was missing. Police and hospital security had searched every square inch of the hospital and the grounds. They'd been at it since 2 a.m., and no one had called or texted him. He'd stormed down to the medical director's office and now was pacing in front of her closed door.

He pounded on the door with his club-like fists.

"I'm on a call," came a muffled shout from the other side of the door.

He pounded again. Harder this time. *Thump. Thump. Thump.* The door flew open and a red-faced Meredith Barstow, MD, MBA, stood glaring at him from behind beige and gold tortoise shell horned-rimmed glasses. She was tall, and her magnified brown eyes looked straight into his. An espresso-colored strand of her otherwise perfectly salon-styled and dyed hair dangled in front of her right ear.

"I said, I am on a call," she hissed.

"I need to know what happened to my patient and why no one called me," Carl squeaked.

She sighed. "Come in and close the door. I'm on with Darryl."

She sat down behind her desk and motioned for him to take a seat in one of the two visitor chairs. She angled her computer monitor so Carl could see the screen. A video image of Darryl Forbes, the Vice President of Hospital Operations, stared back at him. Darryl was a middle-aged Black man with a powerful build that was going soft. He looked like he may have been an athlete when he was younger—maybe a football player. Now, all that muscle was turning to fat. In a few more years he'd look like a Black version of Carl.

"Good morning," Darryl's deep voice boomed from a speaker on Meredith's desk.

Carl could tell by the video Darryl was in his office which was a short walk down the hall. He didn't understand why they were meeting over video, but it was just as well. Carl had planned to pound on Darryl's door next when he was done with Meredith, and now he was saved from that indiscretion.

"Hello, Darryl," Carl said, trying to lower his mousy voice an octave or two. "I'm sure you are aware one of my patients escaped last night."

Meredith peered at him over her glasses. "We prefer not to use the word 'escape.' We are not a prison."

"I'm sure the folks up the street at Hardin will be glad to hear that as they were pretty clear Jane was to be secured at all times," he replied, his voice returning to its natural squeal.

"I've already spoken to the head of operations at Hardin," Darryl responded. "We've agreed to hold off on assigning blame for now while we focus on getting Jane back to where she belongs. I suggest the three of us do the same."

Carl put up his hands to show he was not seeking conflict. "Okay, but someone should have called me. She's my patient for God's sake. I had her transferred down here. I vouched for our security. What the hell happened?"

"You're right, Carl," Meredith said. "Someone should have called you. I will look into that." If she was trying to sound apologetic, it didn't work. "Now that you know, can you think of anything that might help the police find her? Does she have family near?"

Carl shook his head. "No family. There is a man in Atlanta who she is close to. I think he may be involved. I know he's asked to come visit her several times."

Meredith's finely plucked eyebrows raised above her glasses. "Sounds promising. Do you know his name?"

"I'm not sure. Joe, maybe."

"Joe. That's all you got?" Meredith asked with an edge in her voice.

"For Christ's sake, Meredith, the man wasn't coming to see me. I'm sure the police can get his information from the front office. I think he's called here every week since Jane arrived."

"Anyone else?" she asked. "Did she have friends on the unit who might know?"

Darryl's voice burst out of the computer speakers. "Think about it. Anything we can tell the police will help."

He was about to tell them about the radiology nurse but caught himself. Gas in his lower intestine was building, causing a sharp pain in his abdomen. He willed his sphincter closed to prevent what would be a noxious release. A worrisome thought almost broke his concentration. If the nurse, Sandra Tally, knew, then Barry was most certainly involved. He grew suspicious. Could Barry be behind Jane's disappearance, and if so, why?

"Carl? Does she have any friends on the unit?" Meredith asked again in a reproachful tone like a teacher asking a question of a daydreaming student.

Carl glanced up to find her magnified eyes studying him. She looked like an owl on the hunt, and he was the mouse. "Sorry, I was thinking about the question. No, no one she's mentioned. She spends most of her time alone." His answer was not entirely untrue. Jane did spend most of her time alone, that is, when she was not talking to Sandra Tally. The police would find that out soon enough when they interviewed the unit staff. He glanced at his watch. It was almost 10:00 a.m. Tally should be in by now.

"I have patients to see."

Meredith continued to stare at him.

He avoided her gaze and stood.

She shook her head and turned her attention back to Darryl's video image. "Carl is leaving."

Darryl cleared his throat. "Carl?"

"Yes?"

"I read Ms. Carter's file. Is she, you know, a threat to anyone?"

"I don't think so."

"Really? You do know she murdered her mother," Meredith said.

"That was a long time ago. If you read her file, you know her previous physician cleared her for community living. She was in Brookhaven for two years. I was going to recommend she return there once we dialed her meds back in."

Meredith bristled. "I read the file." Her tone softened. "She was Tom Reynolds's patient before he retired."

"Reynolds cleared her? That's a relief," Darryl said. "I'll be sure to let the press know that before they claim we allowed a psychopathic killer to escape."

"She's not a killer," Carl said, staring at Meredith. "At least not anymore."

After he left them, Carl didn't go back upstairs. Instead, he followed the labyrinth of first floor corridors until he reached the radiology department, only to find Sandra Tally was not there. The radiology tech seated behind the service window informed him she was on vacation. She'd be gone for a week. He'd said he thought she went to Cancun.

Carl was not sure what to make of her absence. Maybe she really was sprawled out on a beach in Mexico. Maybe her absence is what triggered Jane to leave.

He walked back to Meredith's office and pounded on her door again. This time Meredith shouted, "Come in," and he opened the door.

She stared up at him. Her owl eyes blinked. "You're back."

Carl glanced at her monitor. "Are you still on with Darryl?"

"No. What now?"

"I was wondering—I know, as you said, we are not a prison, but we have security. I mean, there are fences, cameras, security guards. How did she do it? How did she get out?"

Meredith sighed. "Shut the door." She waited until he had and said, "She had help."

"Help?"

She tapped on her keyboard and turned the monitor toward him. "Keep this to yourself. Got it?"

He nodded.

A video window appeared on the screen showing a nighttime scene shot from high up, looking down on what Carl recognized as the narrow fenced-in park surrounding the hospital. Most people thought of it as the grounds, but he knew security referred to the green space as the buffer zone. It hid the hospital and its occupants from the street, and it was supposed to slow runaway patients down. On the other side of the zone was a wide sidewalk and then University Boulevard. The trees and shrubs in the park appeared as dark areas in the grainy picture but the sidewalk and boulevard were lit up by bright lamps that ran along the multilane street.

"This was taken at 1:10 this morning by one of our security cameras."

Small white numbers showed the time in the lower left corner of the image. The seconds were counting up. There was no other motion in the picture. Carl had mistaken it for a still photo until he noticed the changing time.

"I don't see anything."

"Watch."

After a few more seconds, a person with a backpack strapped on their shoulders appeared in the video running through the park.

"Jane," Carl whispered.

The video showed her run to the fence separating the park from the sidewalk. There she took off her backpack and removed a pillow. Then she tossed the backpack over the fence, placed the pillow on top of the fence and scrambled over. So much for the buffer zone slowing her down.

"She used the pillow to cover the fence wires."

"Yeah. I get it," Carl said. "Not surprising. After all, she is a genius. I have seen nothing that indicates she had help though."

"It's coming."

On the other side of the fence, Jane collected her backpack and then appeared to study the street as if she was trying to decide where to go, when a gray car pulled up to the curb in front of her. The car's rear passenger door flew open and Jane dove in. Then the door slammed shut, and the car continued along the street until it disappeared from the image. The car had not been in the picture for more than ten seconds, and the image quality was not all that great, but Carl knew he'd seen the car before.

"Okay, it looks like you are right. She did have help. Do the police have this?"

"Yes, of course."

"I didn't notice. Was there a shot of the license plate?"

Meredith shook her head. "Not from that camera. The police are reviewing the images from our other cameras."

Carl felt the gas that had been building in his overworked digestive system escape. Meredith wrinkled her nose.

"For God's sake," she said. "Open the door."

"Sorry. I'm going now."

He backed out of the office.

"Leave the door open and make yourself available if the police want to talk to you."

Carl rushed back to his own office and plopped down in the special oversized chair he'd insisted Meredith purchase for him. His heart pounded so hard he worried he might go into cardiac arrest. He took his pulse—over 100. Jesus, he was going to have a heart attack. Sweat seemed to be gushing out of every pore. It ran down the sides of his nose, stung his eyes, and drenched his armpits. He removed his lab coat and loosened his tie. What the hell was Barry up to? Damn, he knew the son of a bitch was obsessed with this woman. He knew the obsession was unhealthy, even psychotic, but he couldn't imagine him being part of something like this.

He dug his cell phone out from his pants pocket and selected Barry's number from the contacts list. "Be calm," he told himself. Coming right out and accusing Barry of helping Jane escape would put Barry on the defensive. He might refuse to talk about it. He might even hang up. After all, Carl didn't have any proof Barry was behind Jane's escape. It wasn't his car she'd gotten into, but he was almost certain the car belonged to Sandra.

After several rings, the call went to Barry's voice mail.

Carl took a deep breath before blurting out, "Barry, it's Carl. We need to talk about Jane right away."

He tossed the cell phone on his desk and leaned back in his chair until he was staring up at the ceiling tiles. He could think of no rational explanation for Barry helping Jane escape. Carl wondered if he might have been wrong about Sandra working with Barry. Maybe Barry's relationship with Sandra, whatever that might be, had nothing to do with Sandra's friendship with Jane. Maybe it was only a coincidence. No way, he thought, Barry had to be behind it. But why? Why was he so obsessed with this woman? Maybe there was no rational explanation for it because Barry was no longer rational.

Tom Reynolds's words came back to him: *Don't let that bastard anywhere near her.*

It occurred to Carl if Barry had helped Jane escape, she might be with him at Granddaddy's house. There was only one way to know for sure. He launched himself out of the chair and snatched up his phone. He redialed Barry's number. The call went to voice mail again. Not bothering to leave a message, he hung up and opened his office door. He expected to see several stern men in police uniforms bearing down on him, and he was relieved when he found the corridor empty.

Before Meredith had shared the security video with him, Carl had been eager to talk to the police—anything to help find Jane and return her to the hospital. Now, he wasn't so sure. What was he supposed to say when they asked if he knew who might have helped Jane escape? Yes. He's an insane friend of mine who happens to be staying at my house. He needed to talk to Barry before he said anything. More than that, he needed to make sure Barry didn't have Jane at Granddaddy's house. He gathered up his courage and headed for the elevator.

Carl made it out of the hospital without being stopped by the police, though he bumped into several staffers who wanted to know what was going on up on Green 3.

It took a little over twenty minutes to reach Granddaddy's farmhouse. When he got there, he was somewhat relieved to find the only vehicle in the gravel drive was the battered pickup truck and landscaping trailer belonging to Mateo.

Carl took this as both a good and bad sign. On the drive over, he'd worried he would find Sandra's car there and Jane holed up inside, but with neither Sandra's nor Barry's cars in the driveway, that seemed unlikely. He was relieved. Explaining to Meredith why his missing patient had been found at his property would not have been pleasant. Then again, with Barry gone and not answering his calls, it made Carl suspect Barry's involvement even more.

He hefted himself up and out of his car. The steady roar of a lawn mower came from behind the house. He followed the walkway around to the back to find Mateo guiding a large riding mower along the remains of the pasture fence that separated Granddaddy's backyard from the overgrown fields beyond.

The maintenance man had gotten an early start. It was not yet noon, and it looked as though most of the yardwork was already done. The flower beds had been weeded, the front lawn had been mowed, and Mateo was about done with the back. Carl watched him maneuver the machine close to the sagging fence posts. Mateo looked his way and raised a gloved hand in greeting as he steered toward him.

The mower sputtered to a stop a few yards from Carl, and a grinning Mateo dismounted while he removed his yellow leather work gloves. He offered Carl his hand.

"Good morning, Dr. Walker."

Carl shook the man's callused, brown hand. "The place looks nice as always. You must have been here for hours."

"Sí. Yes, all morning."

"Have you seen the man who is staying here?"

"Sí. I saw him earlier this morning while I was unloading. He came from," Mateo appeared to grope for the right English word before giving up and motioning toward the cellar doors. "From there."

"He was in the cellar?"

"Sí. He came out of there and got in his car and left."

"Did he say anything to you?"

"He say good morning and then he drive off."

"Was anyone else here? A woman?"

"No, but I found this when I was cutting the grass." Mateo dug into his pants pocket and produced an orange sock with white anti-slip nubs on its sole.

Carl took the sock. Bryce Mental Health was printed in white lettering on the ankle, but he hadn't needed to read it to know where the sock was from. He'd seen countless of them on the feet of patients, and he even had brought home a few pair for his wife because she'd said they were comfortable.

His chest began to burn as he studied the sock and then stared at the cellar doors.

Mateo was watching him. "Is everything okay, Doctor?"

Carl ignored the maintenance man as he continued to stare at the doors, stomach acid pushing past his lower esophageal valve.

"Doctor?"

"Oh. Sure, Mateo. Everything's fine. I'm going to look around a bit. You have a good day."

"Gracias. You as well."

Carl tucked the sock in his pocket and walked over to the cellar doors. He'd kept them locked with the same tarnished old padlock his Granddaddy had used. The lock had to be at least thirty years old. The only key to that lock was on a ring in his desk at home. He knew as soon as he neared the door the key in his desk would no longer work because the lock had been replaced by a shiny new one. Barry must've cut off the old lock.

"Ah, shit," he groaned. He wondered if Barry could be hiding Jane down there. Carl could not imagine Jane agreeing to be locked up in a cellar, especially one as creepy as Granddaddy's, no matter how much she wanted to get away from the hospital.

He tugged on the lock in a futile gesture. Mateo might have something to cut it off with, but he wasn't sure he wanted to go down there. At least, not yet. He made his way over to the back door that led to the kitchen. It was locked, but Carl kept a spare key hidden under a garden gnome next to the steps. He retrieved the key and let himself in.

"Anyone here?" he called, as he stepped inside.

There was no response.

All the first-floor rooms were empty. He glanced out the sitting-room windows that overlooked the gravel drive. Mateo was loading his mower onto the trailer. He paused at the bottom of the stairs leading to the upper floor and called again. "Hello. Anyone here? Jane? Anyone?" He heard no reply, and he ascended the steps like a mountain climber negotiating a difficult pass.

He hated this staircase. There was something wrong with its pitch. It was too steep. His know-it-all wife had told him it was because the ceilings in the old farmhouse were higher than most modern ceilings, ten feet instead of nine or eight, and the steeper angle was necessary to keep the stairway from dominating the room. *Blah, blah, blah.* Whatever the case, as a boy, Carl dreaded coming down them. Once, he'd tumbled down the entire flight. His injuries hadn't been severe, a sprained wrist and a goose egg knot on his forehead, but he was much older and far fatter now.

Barry's things were in what had been his granddaddy's bedroom. It was the largest of the four and the one nearest to the bathroom. The enormous bed where his granddaddy had spent the last months of his life looked like it had never been slept in. Not a single wrinkle was visible on the bedspread, and the pillows were placed at precise equal distances from the edges. Several pressed button-down shirts, slacks, and two light-colored sport coats hung in the closet. There was a toothbrush and other toiletries in the bathroom. Everything was neat and organized as anyone who knew Barry would expect it to be.

The two bedrooms that ran along the back wall were empty. They were unfurnished when Carl had taken possession of the house, and there had been no reason to change that. The bedroom on the opposite end of the hall from the room Barry occupied had been where Carl's father had stayed while caring for Granddaddy. It contained a smaller bed and heavy oak and metal desk furniture that had been taken from the old Bryce Hospital. How they got it up those stairs, Carl could not imagine.

It appeared Barry had been using the room. His expensive leather bag sat open on the desk as well as a laptop computer. An upholstered armchair Carl did not recognize sat next to the bed, and next to it, to his astonishment, stood an IV stand. Barry had said he was seeing patients, Sandra Tally being one. Perhaps this is where he was treating them.

Carl tapped a key on the laptop. The sign-on screen appeared. There was no point in wasting time trying to guess Barry's password. Whatever it was, Carl was sure it would be complex and cryptic. He moved on to the leather bag. The document pouch contained a single file folder. On the folder's tab, a black marker had been used to write the name Sandra Tally in precise block lettering.

He slid it out and skimmed through it. The file contained about two dozen pages of session notes written in the same precise lettering. The pages were dated. The oldest was from seven weeks ago and the latest was from last night. Based on the dates, it looked as if they were meeting twice a week. The early sessions were short, lasting only 30 minutes, and the notes contained general background information about her family and childhood.

He carried the file over to the window where the light was better. Down in the drive, Mateo was closing up his trailer. Carl watched as the yardman bent and picked something up. Mateo studied it for a moment, then looked backed at the house before putting whatever it was in his pocket.

Thinking about the sock, Carl wondered what it might be. He thought about opening the window and calling down to ask, but he let the thought pass. He took a seat in the chair by the bed and continued reading.

Barry had begun hypnotizing Sandra during their third meeting, and he introduced what he referred to as medicated deep hypnosis during their sixth. That explained the IV rig. By this time, the sessions were lasting well over an hour and Barry's notes described the establishment of an observer to assist Sandra in overcoming self-esteem and confidence issues that made it difficult for her to manage her appetites for food, alcohol, drugs, and men. "Everyone has issues," Carl said to himself.

By the tenth session, Barry had written the observer was in place and he'd made the curious note that Sandra's subconscious was now being managed.

The last entry was brief because there was no session. Barry's notes simply stated: "Appointment canceled by patient."

Carl closed the file and took it back to the desk. He was slipping it back into the bag when he heard a noise at the door. When he looked up, Barry was glaring at him, and Carl almost lost control of his bowels.

"Can I help you find something, Dr. Walker?"

CHAPTER TWENTY-SIX

Barry

It had not surprised Barry to find Carl at the house. He'd ignored several calls from the fat man, and it was inevitable he'd come around.

Carl was an oaf, but he wasn't stupid. Now, as Barry stood watching Carl going through his bag, the question was what to do about it. Well, not really what, more how. He'd pondered this question for days. How to get rid of Carl without implicating himself and triggering a search of the cellar.

He wanted tonight and tomorrow with Jane. No. He needed the time with her. Then he'd dispose of her and head back to his office, and his patients, and his sofa, leaving the police with a nice mystery.

"Did you find what you were looking for?" he asked in the most nonthreatening tone he could muster.

Carl jumped, and for an instant, Barry let himself think maybe he will have a heart attack and the problem will solve itself, but no such luck. The oaf didn't keel over.

"Jesus, Barry. You fucking startled me," Carl squeaked.

Barry held up the paper cup he was carrying. "Had I known you were coming, I would have brought you coffee." He took a sip and made a sour face. "Just as well, though. It's ten miles to the closest Starbucks, and it's always cold by the time I get back." He drained the rest of the coffee into his mouth and dropped the empty cup into a wastepaper basket.

"You know, most of the time I like how out of the way this place is, no one around to pry into your business." He glared at Carl. "But there are times I miss being able to run out for a cup of coffee without it taking a fucking hour. What are you doing here?"

"Looking for you. I must have called you a half dozen times since this morning."

Barry retrieved his phone from his pocket and made a show of looking at the missed calls. "Oh. I must have had the sound turned off." He stared at Carl, whose forehead was glistening with sweat. "That doesn't explain why you are going through my bag."

Carl shrugged. "I was curious about what you were doing up here with Nurse Tally." He retrieved the file he'd been trying to push back into the bag. "It says in your notes here you had achieved a state of management over her subconsciousness. What the hell does that mean?"

"It means I was helping her. Please put the file back where you found it. It's confidential. I should not have to tell you that. Honestly, if we weren't friends, I would consider filing a complaint."

"A complaint," Carl made a piggish snort. "To whom? It's my house."

"To the AMA for one. You have no right to read a patient's file without prior consent."

Carl laughed and shoved the file back in the bag. "You are going to raise an ethics complaint against me? That's rich."

Barry shrugged the insult off. "Why all the calls? What's so urgent?"

"You know what."

"No. I don't," Barry lied with such ease it almost sounded true to him.

"You have Jane here."

Barry laughed. "Don't be ridiculous. She's at the hospital where you should be."

"No. She escaped last night, and there's video of her getting into a car I happen to know belongs to that nurse you're banging—the one whose subconscious you are managing."

"That's absurd."

"Is it? Explain this then." Carl reached in his pocket and pulled out what looked like an orange rag. He tossed it in Barry's direction. It fell short.

Barry bent down and picked it up. "A sock?"

"Yeah. Jane's sock. It was in the yard by the cellar."

"How do you know it's Jane's sock?"

"Who else could it belong to?"

"I don't know, Carl. It's a sock."

"Look at what's written on it."

Barry stretched it out and examined the wording. "Bryce Mental Health? So what? You work at the hospital. Half the things in this house are from Bryce Hospital." He nodded toward the desk.

"Not that Bryce Hospital."

"She's not here, Carl."

"Okay. Then why did you change the locks on the cellar doors?"

"My, you have been busy this morning. I was curious about the asylum things down there. For Christ's sake, the whole reason I wanted to stay here was to explore the cellar. I couldn't find a key, so I cut off the old lock and put on a new one. I had every intention of giving you the key when I left."

"Okay, then you won't mind if we go take a look, will you?"

Barry grinned. "Let's go."

He stepped out of the doorway and motioned for Carl to lead the way. At the top of the landing, Carl paused and grabbed the handrail like he was preparing to repel down the face of a cliff.

"What's the matter, Carl? A little acrophobia? You know, I could help you with that."

"These fucking steps. I hate these fucking steps."

It amazed Barry how often he benefited from pure serendipity. The old adage, "chance favors the prepared mind" was so true. Barry was always prepared, and since he had no sense of empathy to hold him back, preparation often meant an ability to act with absolute disregard for others.

Carl leaned his bulk forward to take that first step, and when he did, Barry took the opportunity that had presented itself and shoved his fat friend hard from behind causing him to pitch forward and tumble down all fifteen steps.

Three hundred and fifty-six pounds of blubber makes a heck of a racket when tumbling down a flight of stairs. Carl hit the bottom with such force he busted through the ornate wooden spindles that wrapped the landing platform and landed with his head and most of his upper torso wedged between the broken spindles. His legs remained on the last three steps and the rest of him projected out of the staircase wreckage suspended above the entryway floor.

Barry descended the steps in no great hurry. "Carl," he said as he stepped around Carl's twitching legs, "what happened?" Carl was lying face-up. His eyes were open and moving from side to side. Wet gurgling and wheezing sounds along with a mix of blood and saliva bubbled from his mouth. Barry sniffed. It smelled as though Carl had shit himself when he fell.

"Whew," Barry waived his hand in front of his nose. "Carl. You stink. You always stink, but now you really stink."

He walked around the broken guard rail and knelt next to Carl's face.

The fat man's terrified eyes followed him, and the gurgling sound grew louder. Blood spat from Carl's mouth as he struggled to say something, but the words were faint and inaudible over the gurgling.

Barry leaned closer. "I can't hear you."

Gurgle, "'elp me."

"Oh. Of course." Barry studied his friend's position. Carl's head projected out over the landing about a foot and a half above the floor, held there by muscle, tendon, and that evolutionary wonder that allowed animal kind to emerge from the primordial sea. "Yeah. I think I can help you," he said. Then he stood and placed both hands on the injured man's sweaty forehead and pressed down hard until he heard Carl's cervical vertebrae snap—he guessed C5 or maybe C6.

Carl's legs continued to twitch for several seconds, the muscles acting on their own chemical stimulus, no longer receiving signals from Carl's brain. Barry stepped back and wiped the dead man's sweat from his hands. Then, he took his phone from his pocket and called 911.

CHAPTER TWENTY-SEVEN

Joe

The meteorologist on the morning news program said records would be set today. Atlanta, she'd said, would once again earn its nick name of Hotlanta. Joe had listened with interest to her explanation of the heat index which measured how humidity impacted the body's ability to cool itself. She'd said the index provided a better indication of how hot the day would feel, and today it would be off the charts bad.

She was right. By the time Sacred Heart's bells tolled for the midday Mass, the temperature had reached 100 degrees and the humidity was so high after walking the short distance from the rectory to the sanctuary, Joe's clerical collar was damp and the dark gray button-down that had been starched and pressed crisp this morning now clung to his sweat-moistened skin. He'd Googled the heat index on his phone as he'd walked. It was above 136 degrees. It felt so hot it wasn't merely uncomfortable—it was dangerous.

He'd spotted two homeless men napping on the concrete benches surrounding the ancient live oak tree in the rectory's courtyard. Like the men, the tree's leaves were withering in the heat. He'd prayed for them and all the people living in the streets and in the many encampments around the city, adding an extra prayer for those in the camp where he had been attacked. Jesus had called the poor blessed as their poverty on earth secured spiritual wealth in heaven, but he knew promises of a better afterlife provided as little comfort to these men from the terrible heat as the sprawling tree's wilting leaves.

As he entered the great church and donned his vestments for the day's Mass, once again he found himself reflecting on the riddle of suffering. It presented such a challenge to those trying to reconcile their faith with the realities of the world. Even he struggled to answer why an all-powerful and loving God would allow so much suffering. The answers provided by the catechism were hard for many to understand and could seem callous. Attributing all human suffering to the price for Adam's sin seemed more fitting of a vengeful and petty God—not the merciful Lord Joe loved.

He pushed such thoughts out of his mind as he took his place at Sacred Heart's ambo to read from the Gospel. Now was not the time for a crisis of faith, albeit a small one. He looked out over what was a larger group of worshippers than he was accustomed to seeing at a Friday Mass. Most weekdays, Joe preached to a near-empty church with only a handful of regulars gathered in the front pews, but today the pews held many new attendees.

As Joe read, he studied the new faces. There were more men than women, and the majority were Black, which made them stand out as Sacred Heart's parishioners were predominantly Hispanic and White. He guessed many of the newcomers lived on the street. He knew most had only come to escape the terrible heat, but he was glad they had. If the church could not provide answers to these people, at least it could provide air-conditioning.

Today's reading was from the book of Matthew. In a clear voice, he read, "Jesus said to the disciples, the Kingdom of heaven is like a net thrown into the sea, which collects fish of every kind. When it is full, they haul it ashore and sit down to put what is good into buckets. What is bad they throw away. Thus it will be at the end of the age. The angels will go out and separate the wicked from the righteous. and throw them into the fiery furnace, where there will be wailing and grinding of teeth."

The parable of the net and the portrayal of Christ as a fisher of men's souls had always struck him as hopeful, but today the words struck him as hard. Looking out at the newcomers, he couldn't help but wonder if the message of such winnowing was out of synch with a world seeking less judgment and more tolerance. Maybe the Church was fading because its core message of forgiveness depended on a long list of wrongs to forgive, and today's society no longer agreed with the inventory of transgressions.

Jane had challenged him on this very question during many of their calls. Calls that had become as much of a regular part of his evenings as vespers until they abruptly ended four nights ago. He knew she was angry he had not found a way to visit her, and he suspected that was why she'd stopped calling.

As he read, his eyes landed on one Black face sitting alone in a pew midway down the nave. This was not an anonymous face driven inside from the summer inferno. Joe knew this face. It belonged to Lieutenant Melvin Cooper. Their eyes met, and the lieutenant grinned. Joe smiled back. He was glad to see the man but also unsettled by what his presence might mean.

After the reading, Joe relinquished the ambo to Father Santiago and took his formal place below the priest. He kept his eyes on the lieutenant. A small bead of sweat at Joe's hairline broke free and ran down his face as he listened to his mentor deliver the homily. The Lord's house was cool. Anxiety over what the lieutenant's visit could portend and not the summer heat had broken his sweat.

The lieutenant remained in his pew throughout the ceremony. He did not receive communion, neither did most of the newcomers, but Joe noted he had risen for the credo and prayers. His clear, drill sergeant baritone voice rose above the rest during the recitation of the Lord's Prayer and the singing of the hymns. His singing was so distinctive, in fact, that Joe caught several parishioners glancing back at him.

After the Mass, Joe and Father Santiago led the congregation out into the fiery Atlanta streets. Few parishioners paused for goodbyes, opting instead to hurry for the air-conditioned shelter of their cars. Most of the newcomers remained sprawled about the pews where they would be permitted to remain until evening.

Joe and Father Santiago stood a few steps inside the vestibule until all of those who were going to leave had made their way out onto Peachtree Street. Joe pulled the great oak door shut and turned to see Father Santiago shaking hands with the lieutenant.

"That was a beautiful service, Father," the lieutenant was saying. "I'm not Catholic, but I am washed in the blood and attend church every Sunday."

"That's fine, my son. We welcome all believers here at Sacred Heart. What denomination are you if I might ask?"

"Why, I am a Baptist, Father. Born and raised in the south where I was never far from the good Lord's teaching and my nana's switch."

Father Santiago put his arm around the lieutenant, "Well, we love our Baptist brethren here, especially those who can sing as fine as you, though it is rare to see one attending Mass, outside of a wedding or funeral. What brings you to our church today if it's not this terrible heat?"

The lieutenant nodded toward Joe. "I have come up from Opelika, Alabama to meet with Captain Carroll."

Joe winced.

"Is that so?" Father Santiago said, casting a sidelong glance over at Joe with a raised eyebrow. "Although we thank the Lord for the captain's service, around here we prefer to call him Deacon Carroll or Joseph after our dear saint."

"Of course," the lieutenant said as he released his grip on Father Santiago's hand. "Would it be possible for me to have a word with Deacon Carroll?"

The troubled priest dipped his head. "By all means. I will leave you two."

Joe stared at the lieutenant who was watching Father Santiago walk away. He was about to ask why he'd come when, as soon as the priest was out of earshot, the lieutenant made the question unnecessary.

"Where is she?" the lieutenant blurted in a hushed, angry tone.

"Where is who?" Joe replied, though as soon as he said it, he knew who the lieutenant must be talking about. "Jane?" he added before the lieutenant could reply.

"Yes, Jane. Come on, Joe. Where is she?"

Joe was dumbfounded. "She's missing?"

The lieutenant crossed his arms. "You know damn," he caught himself, "I mean, darn well she's missing."

"No. I do not. I don't even know what you mean by missing."

"She escaped. Two nights ago. If you know where she is or helped her in any way, you are an accessory to a crime."

Joe shook his head. "I have not talked to Jane in almost a week."

The lieutenant stepped closer. "Don't lie, Joe. I came here as a courtesy before telling the Alabama State Police about your relationship with her. When they find out, they will have the Georgia Bureau of Investigation question you. If you lie to them, they will…"

Joe cut him off. "Tase me?"

"Arrest you."

"I am not lying, Mel."

"You sure she's not waiting for you at your home?"

Joe stared at him for a moment. It was not unreasonable to believe Jane would come back here. "Follow me," Joe said. He led the lieutenant back through the church.

"Where are we going?"

"To see if Jane is at my apartment."

Joe stopped at the tabernacle steps. "I need to go into the sacristy to change out of these robes. You can come with me, but this is holy ground. I ask that you treat it that way and stay as far from the altar as possible when we make our way back."

"I'll wait for you here."

"Aren't you afraid I will call her?"

The lieutenant glanced up at the large carving of the tortured Christ on his cross, looming down at them from its place high up in the half dome of the apse. "No. I trust you."

Joe followed his glance and smiled. He touched his knee to the marble floor and crossed himself before ascending the steps. It took him less than five minutes to remove his vestments and store them. He found the lieutenant leaning against a choir column, watching the collection of men and women slumbering in the pews.

After a brief stop at the parish office so Joe could let Agnes know he was leaving, they took the lieutenant's car to Joe's apartment. As they entered his complex, Joe's mouth grew dry and his palms sweaty. He was not sure what they might find. It would not be unlike Jane to break into his apartment.

He said a small prayer at his door. He was glad, and at the same time disappointed, to find it still locked and the apartment unoccupied. Inside, he led the lieutenant into each of the empty rooms.

"Well, that's all there is. It's not much, and as you can see, she isn't here," he said after completing the walk-through.

The lieutenant took a seat at one of the kitchen counter stools. "You really have no idea where she is?"

"No. Like I told you, I have not heard from her in several days."

Joe opened the refrigerator. "Water?"

"Sure."

Joe brought two plastic bottles of water to the counter and placed one in front of the lieutenant. "Glass?"

"No."

Joe pressed his bottle against his forehead. The vents in the ceiling were hissing with the sound of rushing air, but what they were blowing didn't feel much cooler than the super-heated air outside.

"AC's not doing the job," the lieutenant said as he took a long sip of his water.

"Roger that," Joe said. "Can you tell me more about what happened with Jane?"

The lieutenant shrugged. "There's not much to tell. I received a call this morning from a chief deputy I know in the Tuscaloosa Sheriff's Department. He told me Jane Carter was missing. He said they got a call at two this morning. They have video of her leaving Bryce Hospital sometime after one."

"Did she just walk out the front door?"

"Nope. She left the building via a fire exit."

"It was that simple?"

"Not exactly. Somehow, she got the key code for a gate, made it over two security fences, then got into a waiting car and rode off. She had help."

"And you think I was that help?"

"I did."

"So now what?" Joe asked.

The lieutenant shrugged. "I go back to Opelika and look for more unruly priests to tase."

"I mean about Jane. What happens now?"

"She'll turn up." The lieutenant looked around the living room. "Probably here, though she might leave when she realizes you have no air-conditioning."

"I have air-conditioning. It's just not very effective."

The lieutenant downed the rest of his water. "Ain't that the truth." He looked Joe in the eye. "When she comes here, you need to call the police. She's a fugitive now. If you don't turn her in…"

"I know," Joe said. "I'll be arrested."

"Yes, and something tells me that your boss won't like that. I assume that priest I was talking to is your boss."

"I guess you could think of him that way, and no. Father Carlos Santiago would not like to hear about me being arrested again."

"He did not seem to appreciate your military career as much as I do."

"No. The good Father is not very comfortable with my prior vocation."

The lieutenant laughed and stood. "Okay. I can't stay in this oven any longer. I will take you back to the church."

"What will happen to Jane when she is found?"

"Same as before. Whoever gets her will arrange to have her returned to the hospital. Of course, if she resists arrest like she did with my guys, she could get herself hurt."

"Hurt?"

"You saw what happened between her and my deputy. She was lucky. Deputy Nash, the man who tackled her, is a good man. He's a big teddy bear, at least most of the time. He would not have hurt her. He might have hurt you when he thought you were going after him, but he would not have hurt her. The next deputy may not feel the same way. She gets into it with the wrong person, maybe seems to go for a gun, and bang!"

Joe flinched. He thought about Jane on the run and how easy it would be for a cop to misinterpret her behaviors and do her harm. He couldn't let that happen, even if it meant doing something Joe knew Jane would interpret as betrayal.

Jane had told him she needed to return to Opelika to make things right. At first, he'd thought her interest was reclaiming her home, but she'd said things to him during their calls that made him suspect that wasn't the main reason. He now believed she was seeking justice for her mother. The mother she had been accused of killing. She never told him what happened. The only thing she would say about the murder was her mother's last words would clear up everything, and those were on the tape Joe kept for her. He wondered if the tape might have something on it that would indicate where Jane was headed.

Joe sighed. "I don't want her to get hurt, Mel. She's a good person. She's smart and kind. She's just a little confused."

The lieutenant studied him. "You ain't, you know, involved with Ms. Carter, are you?"

Joe raised his hands. "No. Nothing like that. I'm devoted to the Church. That doesn't mean I don't care about her, though."

"Ah. Well, that's why you need to call the police if she turns up here." He wiped a drop of sweat from his face. "Come on. I can't stay in here any longer."

"Wait one," Joe said. He went to his bedroom and retrieved the large ziplock bag from his nightstand drawer that contained Jane's notebooks and the cassette marked with the red tape. He removed the cassette and held it for a moment. Jane would not understand what he was about to do, but if the tape contained something that could help find her and keep her safe, he would risk upsetting her.

He returned to the kitchen and offered the cassette to the lieutenant. "You got anything that will play this?"

The lieutenant took the tape. "I'm sure we have something back at the station. Why?"

"It might be nothing, but Jane told me her mother's last words are on this tape. She said it will clear things up. I suspect she's on her way back to Opelika. Maybe the tape will tell you where to look."

The lieutenant studied the tape for a moment and then tucked it in his front pants pocket. "Okay. I'll listen to it as soon as I get back."

"Will you return it to me once you do? She will be very upset if I lose it."

"Sure. I mean, as long as it's not evidence."

"Evidence?"

"Don't worry about it, Captain. I'm sure there's nothing on it that would prevent me from sending it back to you."

"And your guys won't hurt her if you catch her?"

"No. Of course not."

"I have your word?"

"Cross my heart." The lieutenant made a half-hearted attempt at making a cross sign over his chest with his right hand.

"You did it wrong," Joe said as they left the apartment.

CHAPTER TWENTY-EIGHT

Barry

It was early evening when the coroner took Carl's body away and the last police car departed. Barry had repeated the same story to the EMTs and three separate policemen. Carl had come to the house out of concern for Barry's welfare after not being able to reach him. Barry had inadvertently silenced his phone, missing all of Carl's calls. He and Carl had reviewed a patient's case information in an upstairs bedroom that Barry had been using as an office. After the meeting, Carl had tripped going down the stairs.

Barry told them he had tried to render medical assistance, but as a physician, he knew it was hopeless. Carl had broken his neck during the fall, and the break had been so severe it had resulted in the immediate cessation of all autonomous functions. His poor friend had died instantly. It was one of Barry's best performances. He'd even teared up when telling it.

The police had asked why he was renting the house, and Barry told them he was assisting Carl with a patient, and he was considering setting up a practice in Tuscaloosa. This was all true for the most part. He never mentioned Jane, and no one asked about her, which told him the police had not connected the dots between them. Maybe they never would. It didn't matter. Just as he had many times before, he'd ensure any connection they picked up would lead nowhere.

After the EMTs determined there was nothing they could do, something Barry told them as soon as they arrived, Barry placed a call to Carl's wife, but it went to voice mail. He left her a message saying it was urgent and to call him as soon as she could.

Barry was cleaning up the area where Carl had landed when Jackie arrived. She had been assisting in a surgical procedure when Barry had called, and she came as soon as she could. Now they sat at the kitchen table where Barry went through the whole story again.

She cried when Barry told her how Carl had tumbled down the steps. "He was terrified of those stairs," she said between sobs.

Barry placed his hand on hers. "Yes. He mentioned that right before he fell."

"Oh God," she sobbed.

"Would you like some water?" Barry offered, hoping she wouldn't break down.

"Wine would be better."

He found a bottle and poured them both a glass. They talked for an excruciatingly long hour. She would call a funeral home in the morning and have them get Carl's body from the morgue. Then, she expected she would have some kind of service for him the following week.

Barry imagined Carl's bruised and bloated body lying naked on a steel cart in a refrigerator. The thought might have saddened, revolted, or even horrified another, but not Barry Lieberman. He experienced no more emotion from that thought than had he conjured an image of a discarded piece of equipment. He had used Carl like a tool, and when a tool no longer had a purpose, or in Carl's case, could be dangerous, you got rid of it.

When they finished the wine, Barry walked her to her car. He gave her a hug as he thought it was the thing to do, and she pulled him into her enormous breasts and held him in a way that felt more sexual than consoling. The embrace went on far longer than Barry would have liked. She was both taller and heavier than he and unwrapping her from him felt like wrestling a bear. He got her into her car and watched as its taillights vanished in the deepening twilight.

When he was sure she'd gone, he headed for the cellar. Jane had been down there all day, and now she was going to have a long night.

He lifted one of the two exterior cellar doors and retrieved the headlamp he'd stashed in the corner of the top step. He switched it on and pulled the door closed over his head as he descended.

The headlamp's beam flashed on the bright white sheet covering Jane's body and found her wide-open eyes. He let the beam remain there as he studied her. She squinted and turned her head away from the blinding light. Her restraints rattled. He had not been able to see her eyes long enough to tell, but he was satisfied she was terrified.

He flicked on the light switch illuminating the rest of the room and turned off the headlamp. Her eyes were closed tight.

"I bet that light hurts," he said. "Our bodies are not tuned for the instant transition from total blackness to brilliant white light. The muscles that control your pupil contractions have fallen asleep. It takes a second or two to get them the blood they need to wake up and do their job."

He ran his fingers across her forehead. She turned away to avoid his touch, and he let his finger fall down to her cheek, taking care to avoid her mouth. The itching scar on his neck served as a constant reminder of what that mouth could do. Losing a finger would be hard to explain.

She turned her head back toward him and her eyes fluttered open. "I need a drink of water," she said in a soft, hoarse whisper.

"Of course."

A metal water pitcher sat on a table near the bed. He took it and filled it from a sink in the rear of the cellar. Then he brought it back and poured some of its contents into a plastic cup. He held the cup to her lips while she drank. When she'd had her fill, he set the cup aside and replaced the empty IV bag with a fresh one. Then he took a seat in a chair next to the bed.

"It's been so long. Where shall we begin, Sweet Jane?"

"Why are you doing this to me?"

"I haven't done anything to you." He paused for a moment and added, "Yet."

"Let me go, Barry. Please, let me go. I won't tell anyone. I'll just disappear."

He chuckled. "Oh, how I have missed you, Sweet Jane. Have you missed me?"

"No. I haven't fucking missed you. You destroyed my life."

"That's harsh, Sweet Jane. We had such fascinating talks, and so much... fun together."

She turned from him and murmured something inaudible. He suspected she was hallucinating.

"Are they with you now, Sweet Jane? What did you call them? The Others. Are the Others with you now?"

She turned back to him, those incredible storm-gray eyes shifting between him and something over his shoulder that he knew was not there.

After a moment, she said, "You killed my mother."

"No, Sweet Jane. It was you who killed her."

She laughed, which caught him off guard.

"What's so funny?"

She laughed again, and now her eyes were focused on him, and they had narrowed. They no longer communicated fear, but anger.

"Did the Others say something funny? Let me in on their little joke."

"You had me fooled. You had everybody fooled," she said. "I thought for a long time maybe I did kill her. After all, I'm crazy, right? I see things. But I know the truth now. I didn't kill my mother. You did."

"Ah, Sweet Jane, that's not true. Don't you remember what I said at your competency hearing? You and she had a fight. Remember? She called me. She said you were delusional, claiming all this nonsense about what we did during our talks. Claiming I was raping you. She tried to calm you down, tried to get you to recognize the delusional state you were in, and you became violent. You beat her with a fireplace tool until she died. You crushed her pretty head. Such a tragedy for us all."

Jane continued to glare at him, but she was smiling. Smiling. Her reaction perplexed him.

"Come, Sweet Jane. Tell me what's so funny."

"Stop calling me that."

"What?"

"Sweet Jane. She's not here."

"No? Shall we see if we can coax her out?"

"I won't let you fucking hypnotize me, Barry. Never again. Sweet Jane isn't here. She's gone forever. It's only me now. Jane Carter." She laughed. "And maybe ten of my friends. Can't you see them? They are everywhere. Two of them are right next to you."

He glanced around. "Is that so? Well, let's see if we can get rid of them."

"I won't let you. You can't hypnotize me if I don't let you."

"Who said anything about hypnosis?"

He retrieved a syringe from the surgical cart near her bed and drew a small dose of Propofol, a fast-acting sedative, into it.

She tugged at her restraints. "Don't fucking put that in me."

"Now, now. Relax. You won't feel a thing." He brought the syringe to the IV rig and inserted it into the piggyback port.

"No!" she pleaded.

He smiled at her while mouthing a backward count from ten. She was out by the time he reached six.

Barry was amazed at the thoroughness of Carl's granddaddy's medical instrument collection. It was as if he had planned to use the stuff. Not only had the old orderly swiped an ECT machine, he had taken everything needed to operate it including the head restraint and bite guard.

It took Barry several minutes to get the head restraint straps around Jane's head and neck. Once it was on her, he took a razor and shaved the hair from her temples and applied a dab of conducting gel. He'd bought the gel. Even if Granddaddy had stolen some, it would be over fifty years old and probably not much use. Then he sat and waited for her to regain consciousness.

He didn't have to wait long. The small dose wore off in twenty minutes. When her eyelids began to flutter, he stood and leaned over her. "Welcome back, Sunshine."

She fought against the head restraint, appearing confused at first why she could not move her head. Then her eyes focused on his and a tear escaped from the corner of one eye and disappeared behind her ear lobe.

"What are you doing to me? You fucking monster."

"Hmm. Did you call me a monster?" He laughed. "Why, I always thought of you as my monster."

"You are a fucking psychopath."

He drew the sheet back that was covering her naked body and kissed her breasts as she fought against leather and chain to free herself. He moved his hand over her abdomen and down toward her genitals but stopped before reaching them. Maybe later.

"Technically, I am probably more a sociopath than a psychopath. I am fully aware of what I am doing right now. I am not delusional. My thoughts are clear." He pulled the sheet back over her and grinned. "My affect is not flat. In fact, I am enjoying myself, and I feel no empathy for you, Jane Carter. None at all. At the moment, my only feeling is curiosity." He pulled a thick leather strap tightly across her chest and secured it with a buckle to the bed frame.

"Curiosity?"

"Yes. I want to see if we can reset that super brain of yours."

He moved to the ancient ECT machine. He caught her eyes straining to follow him. He had been dying to try this thing since he'd first seen it. He'd powered it up a couple times in preparation for this moment. All its dials and indicator lights seemed to work fine, and now he would get to see it in action.

"Did you ever have ECT treatment in Hardin, Jane?"

He knew the answer before asking. Carl had shared her files with him. She had never had the procedure.

"What the fuck is that?"

He held up the ancient electrode headset and brought it to where she could see it. "Electroconvulsive Therapy. You may know it as electroshock treatment." He placed the set over the head-restraining straps and made sure the electrodes were contacting her temples. "As a licensed psychiatrist, I am supposed to tell you it's nothing like how it's portrayed in the movies, and for modern equipment, that is true. Unfortunately for you, we won't be using modern equipment."

She tugged against her restraints. "No. Barry. Please."

There was a thick rubber bite guard in the machine case. He held it up for her to see. "This will keep you from breaking your teeth or biting your tongue off." He opened an alcohol wipe packet and cleaned the guard. "Who knows where this has been," he laughed at his own joke.

He tried to push the guard into her mouth, but she locked her jaws.

"Listen to me, Jane. When I flip the switch, you are going to bite down, and if you don't have this in your mouth, you are going to regret it."

Tears were now streaming out of her eyes.

He offered her the bite guard again. This time she opened her mouth, and he pushed it in.

He set the voltage and duration controls at their halfway marks. "What do you say we try 120 volts for 2.5 seconds first, eh?"

His finger pressed the black button labeled TREAT. A light on the control panel turned red, and her body arched against the chest strap. The bed shook and rattled as she convulsed. He was certain she did not think so, but he thought it was over in an instant. The red light turned off, the rattling stopped, and the bite guard dropped from her mouth, along with an ample amount of drool.

"Interesting," he said. "Was it good for you?"

She moaned and stared up at the cellar rafters.

"Any sign of those Others up there, Jane?"

After a moment she quipped in a defiant tone, "You know the electric chair is still a means of execution in Alabama."

"Is that so?" he said.

"Yes. So maybe you will find out what that fucking felt like one day."

"Why would I get the electric chair? All I did was annihilate a few million of your brain cells. With that super brain of yours, you should have more than enough to spare."

"You think you are so smart, don't you, Barry? So sure you thought of everything. So used to getting your way with people."

He moved closer to her face, amused by where she was going. "Yes. I get my way." He placed a hand on her breast and fondled her nipple to emphasize his point.

She grimaced and tried to squirm away from him. "Not this time. You don't know everything, you bastard."

"What don't I know?"

"Mother was dictating notes when you came to the house that day, and she left the recorder on when she answered the door. I have that tape, and do you know what's on it?"

He didn't believe her. There was no tape. If there had been, why hadn't anyone heard it? It had been over eight years since that day.

"Nothing is on that tape because I didn't get there until after you had killed your mother."

She laughed. "I thought you weren't delusional. You sure sound delusional to me. The tape recorder captured you arguing with her in her office. I wasn't even there. I was upstairs. I didn't come down until you'd left. On the tape you can hear her confront you about what you did to me, and you can hear when you hit her with that poker."

"If such a tape exists, why am I not in prison waiting to be strapped into that chair?" He laughed. "It was you they locked up. What was it? Five years in Hardin?" He bit at the nipple he'd been fondling as she tried to arch away. "Did they abuse you in there? You were such a pretty young thing when I helped them lock you away."

"Fuck you, Barry." She laughed a wicked sort of laugh that made him stop and stare at her.

"What's so fucking funny?"

"Your smugness. No tape." She laughed again. "The unbelievable thing is, I had it for years before I listened to it. It was in this box of tapes they let me keep. Just about the only thing they let me keep at Hardin was those tapes. I think some sick fuck like you found irony in letting me listen to my mother's voice when everyone thought I had killed her—even me."

Barry felt his heart rate tick up a beat or two. From the moment he'd heard Jane had been released from Hardin, he'd worried she'd regained enough sanity to pose a risk to him. His initial plan had been simple enough—use his influence over Carl to ensure she was returned to Hardin and kept there for the foreseeable future. The longer she remained institutionalized, the more likely her claims of abuse during their sessions would be attributed to false memories and other symptoms of her illness.

When Carl became less receptive to his suggestions, he developed the plan to use Sandra. At first, he'd intended to use Sandra only as a spy to gain information on Jane's behavior for the purpose of manipulating Carl's assessment and treatment plan. It was only after Sandra and Jane bonded that he came up with the idea for Jane's escape and framing her for Sandra's murder. Holding Jane down here and torturing her was never the plan, but Carl's granddaddy's setup was just too good and Barry's sadistic urges too strong.

The current plan was to play with her tonight, then kill her tomorrow. She would die of an overdose of a mix of her antipsychotic medication and sleeping pills. Her death would not be quick. He would force her to ingest a large quantity of Clozapine and enough Ambien to put a horse to sleep. If she was lucky, the Ambien would knock her out before the Clozapine caused catastrophic seizures. The seizures should cover the tracks of the ECT. He doubted the medical examiner would look much beyond the damage caused by the overdose.

He would drive her to a highway rest area he knew of located halfway between Tuscaloosa and Auburn and leave her body where it would take a few days to find. Beside her, he would place the empty pill vials, both of which would be traced back to Bryce Hospital from where he'd convinced Sandy to steal them.

But now, here was this wrinkle which he still wasn't sure he believed.

"Where is this tape, Jane?"

"Safe."

He wondered if it was in her backpack, the one the police would soon have. "Is it in your backpack?"

"What's the matter, Barry? Worried?"

He stepped over to the ECT machine and turned the voltage up to 150 and the seconds to 3. Then he retrieved the bite guard from where it lay on her chest. A missing tongue would have to be explained. It wouldn't fit the suicide story.

"Where's the tape?"

"Fuck you."

He shoved the bite guard back in her mouth and pressed the TREAT button.

Her eyes rolled up in her head and she shook all over. The bed hopped with her convulsions.

It took her almost a half hour to recover from that one. She still refused to tell him anything more about the tape. He shocked her three more times that night. Each time he upped the voltage and duration until he reached the max 170 volts and six seconds.

She was unable to speak for more than an hour after the last treatment, and when she did, her speech was confused and rambling. It also came out as a low whisper, and the act of speaking seemed to cause her pain.

Barry thought she may have been injured by the chest strap or head restraint during the convulsions. He undid the chest strap and checked her for broken ribs. He found none, but her skin was bruising, and he wondered what the medical examiner would make of it. Next, he unbuckled the head restraint and checked her jaw. It did not appear broken. Nor did it look like she would have facial bruising. He wiped the drool from her chin and neck.

She didn't resist his examinations or try to bite him. Her head rolled about on her neck as if the muscles and tendons that connected it to her body were no longer attached.

"Jane, where is the tape?"

She opened her eyes, but she did not turn her head toward him. She remained motionless with her head facing the cellar wall.

"Jane, where is the tape?"

Without moving she said, "God has it." Then she closed her eyes and appeared to fall asleep.

He turned off the lights and left her like that, wondering if there was much of anything left of Jane Carter.

CHAPTER TWENTY-NINE

Joe

Joe was awakened by the insistent buzzing of his phone on the night table. As he fumbled for it, he read the glowing digits on the clock. It was exactly five-thirty in the morning. The alarm should have gone off an hour ago. Had he slept through it? It took a moment for the brain fog to recede enough for him to realize it was Saturday, the only day he could sleep in.

The name displayed on the phone's screen could only mean something happened with Jane, and the hour suggested it was nothing good.

"Hello, Lieutenant. Is everything okay?"

"Apologies for the earliness of the call."

"Not early at all," he said, suppressing a yawn. The soldier in him didn't want the master sergeant to think he'd gone soft.

"No, Captain." The lieutenant's voice had an edge to it. "I am afraid everything is not okay."

Joe pushed himself up to a sitting position. "What's wrong?"

"The Tuscaloosa City Police found a body yesterday afternoon."

A hollow feeling grew in Joe's chest. He got out of bed, still a little groggy. "Is it Jane?"

"No, but the Tuscaloosa folks think Jane is the killer."

Any lingering sleepiness was shocked away. He was wide awake now. "Why do they think that?"

"The deceased was an acquaintance of Jane's, and there's evidence the person may have aided in her escape."

"Acquaintance? You got any more than that?"

"She was a nurse at the hospital."

The hollowness deepened, and his heart lost its rhythm for a moment. "Sandy."

"You know her?"

"I know of her. Jane talked a lot about Sandy. They were friends. What happened?"

"She was found dead in her car. Strangled."

"Oh God have mercy," Joe said. "Why do the police suspect Jane?"

"She was strangled with the straps of a backpack, Joe. They have the pack. It's a safe bet it will turn out to be the same one you gave to her at the detention center."

Joe moved to the window and peeked through the blinds. The predawn sky was beginning to glow. Jane had mentioned Sandy on many calls. She had been thrilled to have a real girlfriend to talk to. Even at her lowest points during their talks, when she seemed the most troubled and had few kind words for anyone in the hospital, Jane never had bad things to say about Sandy. He could imagine no scenario ending in Jane strangling her friend. None.

"Joe? You still there?"

"Huh? Yeah. Its terrible news, Mel. I will pray for the poor woman," and Jane, he added to himself. "What else can I do?"

"There is a BOLO out for Jane. The police will definitely question you."

"I understand. I will help them any way I can, but nothing has changed since when you asked me yesterday. I don't know where she is."

"I like you, Joe. I respect what you did in the army, I really do, and because of that, I am telling you again you need to be careful. This is very serious. I know you care about this woman, but you can get in a lot of trouble if you protect her. If she contacts you, call the police right away."

"You made that very clear yesterday."

"That was different. Then, she was a sick person on the run from a hospital. Now, she's wanted for murder. Do I have your word as a former army officer you'll contact the police if she contacts you?"

"You have my word as a man of God."

The phone went silent for a moment. "I'm sorry for the bad news, Joe."

"So am I, Mel. So am I."

"I will be in touch when I learn more."

"Wait. Before you go."

"Yeah?"

"What about the tape? It might give you a clue where she is going."

"Got it. I will listen to it today."

Joe offered God's blessings and hung up. Then he dressed and took his breviary out onto the stairwell to say his morning prayers.

It was difficult for him to set aside the news about Jane and focus on the liturgy, and he soon found himself interrogating God instead of glorifying him. Several times he got lost in the reading. Each time, he paused, asked for forgiveness, and started again. It took him three times as long as usual to finish. After he had, he set down his prayer book and called Caleb.

"Joseph." The old man's voice boomed over the phone's tiny speaker.

"Good morning, Father."

"Ah. It's one of those mornings is it?"

"What kind of morning is that?"

"Joseph, I can always tell the nature of your call by the way you address me. When you call me doctor, I know you wish to talk about psychiatry, or science, or maybe even how you are feeling. When you call me Caleb, which you rarely do, I know you want to discuss something personal, or, perhaps, church politics, but when you call me father, that's when I begin to worry a little."

Joe was amused and chuckled. "Worry, Father? Why?"

"Because, my son, you only call me father when your heart is troubled, and that is when it is hardest to be your physician, your friend, and your priest."

The old man's words dismayed Joe. The last thing he wanted to do was to make this man, who had done so much for him, uncomfortable.

"I'm sorry. I don't mean to be a burden."

"Don't be ridiculous. You misunderstand my meaning. I am here as your priest whenever you need me to be, and your physician, and your friend."

"I am forever grateful for all you have done for me, Father," Joe said.

"Bah. Enough of that. Tell me what's on your mind."

"I received some bad news about Jane this morning."

"I'm sorry to hear that. What happened?"

Joe told Caleb what the lieutenant had told him. He confessed to feeling both sad and confused that God would make someone he was sure was both brilliant and kind mentally ill enough to, if the police were right, commit such evil. How, he wondered aloud to the old man, could such a terrible thing be part of God's plan? Caleb reminded Joe of what he already knew, God's plan was just that, God's plan, and the best we could do was trust in His love.

It was the answer he'd expected from his priest. It was one he, himself, had given to others with similar questions, but the answer did not satisfy him, and that worried him.

"What will you do, Joseph, if Jane contacts you?"

"I have to admit, Caleb…" He didn't get the rest of the sentence out.

"Caleb is it?" the old man interrupted. "I guess we are talking as friends now."

Joe laughed. "Yes, sir. If that's okay."

"Yes. Now, tell me, as a friend, what you will do if she contacts you."

"I will tell her to turn herself in, and I will help her any way I can after that."

"I think that is the right answer."

"But I can't just sit here and wait for her to contact me. I'm going to go to Tuscaloosa to look for her."

The old man coughed as if he was choking on something.

"Are you okay?"

"Fine, fine. Coffee went down the wrong pipe. Now, about going to look for her, I think that is an incredibly bad idea. She's wanted for murder, Joseph. The police may not view your assistance favorably. Besides, what makes you think you can find her?"

"I don't believe she killed her friend—not for a minute. Something else is going on, and I am terrified the police will kill her before anyone knows what really happened. Tuscaloosa is only a couple hours away. I am going to go there and look around. With God's help, I may find her hitchhiking. Then I can take her to the police myself and make sure she gets the help she needs."

"Not to challenge the Lord's power, Joseph, but that doesn't sound like much of a plan. What will you do? Just drive around hoping to see her?"

"Not sure what else to do. I'll check the roads around the interstate and the gas stations."

"Gas stations?"

"Father, gas stations, especially ones near interstates, see all kinds of people. One out of every ten of those people will buy an indigent stranger something to eat or drink. One out of every hundred or so, will give that stranger a ride." He thought about Jane helping the homeless man at the gas station near Auburn and how easily she'd connected with him. She may never have known the man's struggles with alcoholism like Joe did, but she'd been in the man's shoes. *Do you know what it's like, Joe? To not know where your next meal will come from?* Yes. He knew, though he didn't tell her. A lump formed in his throat. "That's where I would go, Caleb, if I had no money, and I needed something to eat." In a hoarse whisper he added, "Or drink."

"Don't you think the police will look in those kinds of places?"

"Yes, but she'll be careful and avoid them. She's very smart, Caleb. Very smart. Maybe if she spotted me, she would come to me."

"Now I am going to speak as a psychiatrist, and as a psychiatrist, again, I think this is a really bad idea. If she did what the police say she did, then she must be experiencing severe psychosis. It is likely she is delusional. She may not even know who you are or worse, think of you as a threat."

"A threat?"

"Yes. If she is experiencing a severe psychotic episode, she might interpret your presence as persecution. She might think you are hunting her. She's killed two people who were close to her. I would prefer that you not be the third."

"I don't believe she would hurt me, Caleb. I don't believe she killed her friend or her mother either."

"Well, I've given you my advice as both your friend and your physician."

"What would you tell me as my priest?"

"I'd tell you to trust in the Lord and leave it in His hands."

"I can't do that, Father."

"I know my son. As Carlos is fond of pointing out, that hero still lives inside you."

"I guess so. I'm sorry."

"Don't be sorry. Like us all, you are an instrument of God. We all have a part in His plan, and you must play yours."

CHAPTER THIRTY

Joe

Joe had been wrong. It took him over three hours to reach Tuscaloosa, not two, but he gained an hour when he crossed into the central time zone. It was a little after ten o'clock when he left the interstate and headed into the city.

Tuscaloosa wasn't what he'd expected. He'd imagined something more urban, maybe like a small version of Atlanta, but it wasn't like that at all. It was a sprawling suburban town more like the neighborhoods that surrounded Atlanta than the city itself. Only it was a little more industrial and judging by the run-down condition of many of the businesses and homes he passed, poorer. It reminded him of some of the midwestern towns he'd visited whose mills and manufacturing had gone overseas long ago.

He'd searched the internet for news about Sandra's killing and had found several articles. Most had headlines like "Escaped mental patient suspected of murder in Tuscaloosa." One from a TV news website named the apartment complex where the murder took place. Joe Googled the address and followed the navigation on his phone straight to it.

The apartments were on the northeast side of the city near the river. It appeared to be a new complex. Some of it was still under construction. The builders must be betting on the population spreading out to them because it was kind of in the middle of nowhere, several miles from the university and center of town. From what he saw, it wasn't in walking distance of anything, not even a gas station. The lieutenant said Sandra was found in her car. If Jane killed her, where did she go afterward and how did she get there? Why didn't she take the car? Did she have another ride? Did she jump in the river? Joe prayed not.

Joe drove through the complex's parking lot. A police car was parked near the entrance and another in a parking area by a building that looked to be still under construction. The officer in the car by the entrance did not appear to notice him. Joe found an empty parking spot near what looked to be the leasing office. A sign indicated the spot was reserved for prospective new tenants.

A chime sounded when he opened the door to the office. There were two empty desks along one wall with an open door between them. A video showing what Joe assumed were images of the various apartment configurations was playing on a huge TV mounted on the opposite wall. A glass table with information pamphlets spread about its surface sat in the middle of the room. Beyond it were floor-to-ceiling windows that looked out over a large pool. He stopped in front of the table and stared out the windows.

There were a few children splashing around in the crystal-clear water and a handful of the gleaming white lounge chairs that surrounded it sported sunbathers. It was early, but it was already hot. Alabama was experiencing the same heat wave as Atlanta. Joe imagined the pool would fill up in a couple hours. That is, if the tenants weren't too unnerved by the prospect of a murderous mental patient lurking nearby.

A thin, dark-complexioned woman with long, straight, glossy black hair emerged from the door between the desks. She flashed him a bright white smile which dimmed some when her eyes found his collar.

"Good morning, Father," she said.

"Good morning." He didn't correct her.

"Are you interested in one of our apartments?"

"No. I don't know how to say this, but I am here about what happened yesterday."

Her smile disappeared altogether. "The murder?"

"Yes."

"Oh. Did you know Sandy?"

"Not directly, but I may have known the person the police suspect of killing her."

The woman gasped and took a step back. "The crazy person?"

"Yes. I was counseling her."

"Oh my. You must feel terrible."

Joe nodded. "Yes. That's why I'm here."

"Have they found her? We are all very nervous here as you can imagine."

"I don't think they've found her yet. I've come from Atlanta to look for her and convince her to turn herself in."

"You are working with the police then?" She straightened the already straight stacks of pamphlets.

"Not exactly, but I want the same thing they do."

"What's that?"

"To find Jane and get her where she belongs."

"Prison?"

"If she did what they say, and that's the right place for her, yes."

She stared at him as if she was trying to decide whether to call the police right then or wait until he left.

"How can I help you, Father?"

He shrugged. He did not know how she could help him. "I guess I'm looking for a place to start. Have you heard if anyone saw a strange woman here in the complex or walking on the road?"

"No. My manager might've heard something. Do you want me to call her?"

Joe worried if the woman called her manager, the manager would call the police, and he would spend the rest of the day at their station being asked questions he had no answers to instead of looking for Jane. He shook his head. "No. That won't be necessary."

She studied him, perhaps suspicious by his turning down her offer to call her manager. "You could speak to the police," she offered. "They are still here."

Joe didn't want to lie. He settled on a half-truth. Mel was technically the police. "I've spoken with them already." He looked out the window toward the parking lot. "I came in from the interstate." He pointed in the direction he'd come from. "I didn't pass many stores or gas stations. Are there any close by, maybe in another direction?"

"No. I'm sorry. You passed the close ones."

"It has to be four miles to the last one I saw. Does that sound right?"

"Yeah, it's not exactly a selling point, but our rents are cheaper than comparable properties nearer the city."

"Ah."

"Father?" she said in a mournful tone.

He looked into her large brown eyes and saw they were red-rimmed and wet with tears. "Yes?"

"Sandy was very friendly. She hadn't been here long, but everyone knew and liked her. We talked often. Why would this person you know kill her?"

The woman began to cry, and he moved to console her. She put up her hand to stay him and composed herself.

"I'm sorry," she continued in a soft, trembling voice. "It's just so terrible. Terrible. I talked to her last weekend. Right over there." She pointed out the windows toward the pool. "She was going on and on about this wonderful doctor she was seeing. He was helping her with her diet, and it was working. She was strutting around in this new bikini she'd bought. She must've lost fifteen pounds in the last month. She told me he hypnotized her. Can you believe it?"

Joe steadied himself against the table. "Hypnotized her?"

"Yeah. She was so happy. She was supposed to go to Mexico today. We talked about her trip for weeks. I'm from Mexico. She had so many questions. She wanted to know Spanish words, what to wear, what to eat." Her voice broke, and she began to sob again. "I can't believe she's dead."

Joe put his arm around her. "I'm so sorry. May God bring comfort to you and accept his daughter Sandy into heaven."

"Thank you, Father."

She stepped away. Her eye makeup had run down her cheeks. He noticed a tissue box on the nearest desk and retrieved a tissue for her.

"Do you know the name of the doctor she was seeing?" he asked, handing her the tissue.

She wiped her eyes and nose, then paused for a moment, appearing to search her memory for the name.

"Barry. Doctor Barry. That's all I know. Just Doctor Barry. I think she may have been seeing him, if you know what I mean, Father."

Joe nodded and smiled, but inside he'd gone cold. What were the chances that another Dr. Barry specializing in hypnotherapy in Alabama could be involved with another murder committed by Jane? He didn't have Jane's abilities for instant computation, but he knew the probability was very low.

He thanked the distraught woman and left her still wiping tears from her eyes. Back in his car, he thought some more about Liebermann's connection with the dead woman. It could not be a coincidence. The doctor was part of this. The shepherd in him told him to call the police and tell them about the connection. The soldier wanted to confront the doctor and demand to know what he knew about Jane's whereabouts. The soldier won. He took out his phone and searched his contacts. Carlos had given him Lieberman's number months ago, but he had never stored it. His mentor may still have the number, but Joe could not bring himself to call him. Carlos would side with the shepherd. He went to the internet instead.

Google showed Lieberman's office was still in Auburn. He called the number associated with the listing, but all he got was a recording indicating the office wasn't open on Saturdays and telling him to go to the hospital if he was having an emergency. He disconnected without leaving a message. Then while he had his phone out, he searched the contact list for the lieutenant's entry and placed the call. It went straight to voice mail too, but this time he left a message.

"Mel, it's Joe. Listen, I am in Tuscaloosa. I know, I shouldn't be here, but I am, and I learned something strange about the nurse Jane is supposed to have killed and Jane's former doctor. Call me back."

He spent the next couple hours cruising through gas stations and along random stretches of road. By one in the afternoon, two in Atlanta, he'd covered half the city, and he had seen no sign of Jane. In fact, he hadn't seen any hitchhikers or spotted a single person begging for money near the stores and gas stations he'd driven by. He also hadn't heard back from the lieutenant. The futility of his plan became more obvious by the hour.

He'd made up his mind to call the police, when he turned down another random street and came upon a large, modern-looking church with a sign at its entrance proclaiming it to be Holy Spirit Catholic Church. He'd passed plenty of Baptist, Methodist, Pentecostal, and Protestant churches, but this was the first he'd seen of his denomination, and it was impressive. It appeared to be as grand as Sacred Heart, though its architecture could not have been more different.

Guided by faith, curiosity, and a need to stretch his legs, he turned into the drive and parked in a space next to an old pickup truck and a newer, small SUV. Those were the only cars in the lot, which wasn't surprising for a Saturday afternoon.

He stepped through the entrance doors and took a moment to read a television screen in the foyer that showed the service schedule. Two vigils were listed for later that afternoon—the first in Spanish and the other in English an hour later. Thank God for Latin American immigrants. Without them, there may not be a Catholic Church in the US much longer.

The foyer led into a larger lobby which then led into a cavernous, octagonal-shaped sanctuary. There had to be room for 1000 worshippers. Not even on Easter Sunday could he hope to see so many in attendance at one of his services. The plainness struck him. It was nothing like his beloved Sacred Heart with its gilded dome, ornate niches, and towering stained-glass windows. It felt more Protestant than Catholic, southern influence no doubt, but it was still beautiful.

He paused at a gleaming white marble baptismal font positioned several feet inside the narthex. It was in the perfect location for parishioners to dip their fingers in its holy waters before taking their seats. He touched the water and crossed himself before proceeding down the main aisle toward the tabernacle.

At the end of the aisle, he dropped to one knee and remained down for a long moment while saying a silent prayer for Sandy and Jane. As he straightened, he saw a tall, lean man dressed in a peach-colored polo shirt and dark jeans watching him from behind a partition wall near the altar. The man's skin was tanned a rich bronze and two patches of close-cut white hair blazed in contrast on either side of his high-domed, bald head.

The man nodded and smiled. "Welcome." He stepped out from the wall and stood in front of the altar looking down on Joe. "You're early if you've come for vigil." Then he descended the tabernacle steps and extended his hand for Joe to shake. "My name is Mark Fuller. I'm the pastor here."

Joe took the man's hand and held it as he made eye contact. "Good afternoon, Father. My name is Joe Carroll." He released the pastor's hand and made a sweeping gesture toward the empty pews. "This is some space. How often do you fill it?"

"Not as often as we'd like." The priest appeared to notice Joe's clerical collar for the first time. "Nice to meet you. Father, is it?"

"No. Someday, God willing," Joe said. Then added, "I'm in transition."

"Ah. What parish are you with?"

Joe told him he was with Sacred Heart in Atlanta, and they talked for a while about things going on in the diocese as well as the city. Mark had been to Atlanta many times and knew both Carlos and the archbishop. He was a Braves fan and went on a while about the slump the team was in and what it meant for their playoff chances.

At some point, he got around to asking Joe why he was there, and Joe told him about Jane and his efforts to find her. Mark knew about Sandy's killing. Tuscaloosa had been Alabama's ground zero of mental healthcare for almost two centuries. Though caring for the mentally ill was no longer a large driver of the economy, the hospitals still employed many people, and a mental patient killing a nurse was big news.

After Joe finished his explanation, Mark put a finger to his lips in a thoughtful expression and said, "You know, Bryce Hospital has had a tough couple of days. I was just consoling a young couple about the death of a doctor from Bryce."

Joe raised his eyebrows. "The doctor wasn't murdered, was he?"

"Oh no. He had an accident at his home. He fell down a flight of stairs."

Joe felt a wave of relief spread over him and then felt selfish for the feeling. "That's such a shame. Is the couple related to the doctor?"

"No. They worked for him." Mark leaned in closer. "They are an undocumented couple from El Salvador. They are worried the doctor's death might lead to their deportation. They don't want to talk to the police."

"They didn't have anything to do with his accident, did they?"

"Of course not. They are nervous about their immigration status."

"I don't think they have anything to worry about."

"I told them the same. I told them if the police needed to talk to them about Dr. Walker's death, they wouldn't care about their status."

The hairs on Joe's neck stood, and his skin tingled like he was standing too close to an electrical field. "Excuse me, what did you say the doctor's name was?"

"Walker. Carl Walker. He was a psychiatrist at Bryce Mental Health."

Joe was flabbergasted. "Dr. Walker? Are you sure?"

"Yes. I was just speaking with the couple."

"I can't believe it," Joe said. "I know him. He was Jane's doctor." He searched the empty pews with his eyes. "Is the couple still here?"

"Yes. They are back in the chapel. They wanted to light a candle."

"Can I talk to them?"

"I don't see why not. Follow me."

The pastor led Joe out of the main sanctuary to a small chapel where a man and woman who appeared to be in their early thirties were gazing at a glowing rack of votive candles.

"Excuse us," the pastor said as they neared the couple. "Gina, Mateo, this is Joe Carroll. He's visiting from Atlanta, and he believes he might know Dr. Walker."

The man nodded, and the woman smiled. Both were nervous. Joe thought too nervous for people whose only concern was their immigration status. Joe knew dozens, maybe over a hundred undocumented immigrants, and very few of them had faced any serious threat of deportation.

"I'm so sorry for your grief," Joe said, injecting as much compassion in his voice as he could. "Forgive us for disturbing you. I just now learned of Dr. Walker's death, and I wanted to express my condolences and see if you knew anything about what happened."

"Thank you, Father," Mateo said.

Gina smiled and shrank behind her husband, as if she was hiding. From what, Joe could not guess, but her frightened demeanor made him think of some of the Afghan women who'd stood two steps behind their husbands while Joe and his men searched their homes. Those women's eyes held secrets. So did Gina's.

"Can you tell me anything about what happened?"

Mateo rocked on his feet and dug his hands in his pockets. Then he directed his attention toward the pastor. "Please. We don't want any trouble, Father. We can't go back to El Salvador."

Gina shook her head. Her smile was gone. "No. We no go back. Please, we have babies here. They were born here. They will have a good life."

Joe put his hands together as if he was about to pray. "No one is going to send you anywhere. The doctor's death was an accident." He stared into Mateo's eyes looking for confirmation. "Right?"

Mateo stared at his work boots. "I was not there when Dr. Walker died."

"He wasn't there," Gina blurted.

"Where? At Dr. Walker's home?"

"No. He did not die at his home."

"Where did he die?" Joe asked.

Mateo looked back at Gina for help.

"Abuelo. La casa de su abuelo," she said.

"His grandfather's house?" the pastor asked.

"Si. Yes. He died at his grandfather's house," Mateo answered.

"And you weren't there?" Joe pressed.

"No. Not when he had his accident. When I was there, he was fine. He was good. We talked. I was there for the grass. I cut the grass."

"If you weren't there, Mateo, why are you worried about the police?"

Gina grabbed his arm. "No," she whispered.

Mateo looked at her and patted her hand. "It will be okay."

They were hiding something.

"Mateo," Joe said softly. "What do you know about Dr. Walker's death that has you so worried?"

"I don't know anything about his death, but I found this at the house where he died."

He pulled a hospital bracelet out of his pocket and showed the name printed on the label to them.

Joe knew what the name would be before he read it.

"When did you find it?"

"Yesterday. While I was there with Dr. Walker."

"Was there a woman with him?"

"No. This is her, isn't it?" Mateo murmured. "It's the woman who killed the nurse, the one everyone is talking about."

Joe didn't say anything. He took the bracelet from the nervous man's hand.

Mateo continued. "The doctor wasn't right when I saw him."

"What do you mean?"

"He was worried. I showed him something else I found, and he was worried."

"What else did you find?"

Mateo shrugged. "A sock."

"A sock?"

"Si. It was orange, and it was covered with…" he searched for a word and looked at Gina for help.

She shrugged and said, "Huellas".

"Treads?" the pastor asked.

Mateo nodded. He tapped his palm with the finger of his other hand and said, "Bumps."

"Bumps on the soles of the socks?"

"Yes. White ones, and words. From the hospital, I think."

Joe was familiar with socks like that. He'd spent many weeks pacing the cold linoleum floors of Saint Michael's psychiatric ward in socks with rubber bumps on their soles.

Jane had been at that house. God had led him to this church and now he was leading him to her. He crossed himself. "God's power is limitless," he exclaimed.

The couple crossed themselves, and the pastor, looking somewhat puzzled, said, "Amen."

"Can you give me the address?" Joe asked.

Mateo pulled out his cell phone. "I will text you it now, Father. What is your number?"

Joe gave him his number and rushed from the chapel as his phone buzzed with the incoming message.

When he got in his car, he brought up the lieutenant's number on his phone and tried calling him again. Once again, the call went to voice mail. Joe left another message. This time telling him he was heading to the address Mateo had sent and urging him, once again, to call him back.

CHAPTER THIRTY-ONE

Barry

Barry woke late that morning. His sleep had been untroubled by dreams or remorseful thoughts of what he'd put Jane through the night before. If anything bothered him at all, it was her claim to have a recording of Maggie's murder, but he'd not lost any sleep over it.

Now, as he sat at the kitchen table spreading raspberry jam on his wheat toast, he pondered the existence of such a tape. If it didn't exist, it seemed like an odd thing for her to make up and taunt him with. What could she hope to gain? Maybe she thought she could use it to convince him to let her go, and what the hell did she mean when she said the tape was in God's hands? He knew from their many talks that Jane had nothing but contempt for religion. She, like him, thought the whole concept of a God sitting in judgment over humankind laughable. Maybe it was some new religious delusion she'd developed in the years since he'd last talked to her.

Then it dawned on him. He'd first learned Jane had been released from Hardin when that Georgia Tech professor had called him to tell him a man from the Catholic Church was asking about her. Jane had some kind of relationship with this man. Carl had called him her boyfriend. He searched his memory for the man's name. Joe something. He'd even called the church looking to speak to the man. He munched on more of the toast. Joe Carroll. That was his name.

He finished his breakfast and cleaned up the kitchen. He could not abide mess and made sure everything was in order before he made his way to the cellar.

Jane lay motionless in the same position he'd left her several hours ago. He checked her pulse. Still strong.

"Sweet Jane," he said in a soothing voice. "It's time to wake up."

She did not stir. Perhaps the ECT had done more damage than he'd anticipated.

He shook her shoulders and repeated, "Sweet Jane."

Nothing.

He put his left hand under her chin and turned her face toward him to check her breathing. When he did, she opened her eyes wide and bit his hand with such force that she removed a large portion of the flesh between his thumb and forefinger. She spat the piece at him.

"You don't taste any better than the last time."

The cellar echoed with an animal-like howl that he didn't recognize as his own voice. Blood poured from the gaping wound, and he rushed to the sink and rinsed it off. The water striking the tattered skin and exposed nerve endings made the already excruciating pain unbearable, and he cursed his own stupidity. He knew she'd bite him if he gave her the chance and he had. It was like he'd served himself up on a plate. *Stupid.*

He returned to the bed. She looked like a wild animal after a kill. She was panting, and his blood had run down her chin and neck, and red speckles dotted the sheet. He picked up one of the old scalpels on the surgical cart and considered slitting her throat with it but used it instead to slice a long strip off the sheet to bandage up his maimed hand.

"You're going to regret that."

"Fuck you."

He slapped her hard across the face, causing blood to trickle from her nose and mix with the remnants of his own. It felt good to hit her. So good, he balled up his right fist and struck her hard in her left eye. Let the medical examiner make of those bruises what he would.

She began to scream, long, wailing screams that echoed off the stone walls. Her screams were so loud he wondered if they could be heard above ground. He never knew when that gardener or his wife would show up or, worse, Carl's wife.

He drew more of the Propofol into the syringe and injected it into her IV. This would shut her up. She was out in less than twenty seconds. Then he put the chest strap, head restraint, and electrodes back on her. The pain in his hand reminded him he should never have taken them off to begin with.

While she slept, he returned to the house to clean out his wound and prepare the pills Sandra had taken from the hospital. He used a tenderizing mallet from the kitchen to crush the Clozapine and Ambien into a fine powder. He planned to mix the powder with water and use a funnel to force it down her throat. She would fight him, but he knew he could make her ingest enough to do the job. He would zap her with the ECT a few times to take the fight out of her first.

After he was done, he made himself a sandwich and brewed some tea. Then he sat at the kitchen table watching tiny hummingbirds dart in and out of a feeder the cleaning woman had set out for them. The iridescent blues and greens of their feathers shone like glass in the sun. Beautiful. They looked like flying ornaments. His thoughts turned to the tape and Joe Carroll. Perhaps Jane's suicide would create the right situation to meet this man and maybe determine if such a tape existed.

The beginnings of a plan took form. Mr. Carroll would want to talk to him about Jane. Then it would only be a matter of using a little dark psychology to learn what he knew, and if he had a tape, to convince him to hand it over.

He checked his watch. It had been 45 minutes since he'd put Jane under. She should be coming out of it. He took a few moments to clean up the kitchen—there was always time for neatness and order, then he took the ground-up pills and funnel and headed back down to the cellar.

She was semiconscious, mumbling something incoherent as he approached the bed.

"Rise and shine," he bellowed. The pain in his hand had subsided some. That and the hummingbirds had restored a bit of his good humor.

"I want to talk about Joe Carroll."

Her eyes snapped open.

"Joe?"

"You said he has the tape."

She tried to shake her head, but the restraint held it in place. "I don't know what you are talking about."

"Let's see if we can jar your memory."

He tried shoving the bite guard in her mouth. She fought him, but he got her to take it. Then he set the machine to administer a 150-volt shock for four seconds and watched her writhe against her restraints.

When it was over, the bite guard fell out of her mouth, and she lay motionless. Drool ran down her chin carrying away some of the dried blood.

He bent over her and soothed. "Jane. Can you hear me?"

She did not respond.

"You must be thirsty. Do you want some water?"

She gurgled something that sounded like yes, and he unclipped the straps from her head restraint to allow her head to move from side to side. Drowning her was not part of the plan. Then he placed the funnel in her mouth and poured in a mouthful of water from the pitcher at her bedside. She swallowed and tried to say something, but the funnel prevented it. He added the powdered pills and some more water. Her nose wrinkled and her eyes grew wide in panic as he imagined the medicine taste hit her. Then he poured more water in and removed the funnel.

She coughed and spat some of the mixture on her pillow. "What is that?" she croaked.

He ignored her. "Tell me about Joe and the tape."

She turned her head toward him and whispered something he could not hear. He drew closer to her.

"It's in God's hands."

At that moment, there came a heavy thump from above the doorway and then, two seconds later, another one. Barry recognized the sound right away. Someone had flung open the outside cellar doors. Someone was coming.

He rushed to the lower doorway and flipped the light switch, plunging them into darkness, but it was not total. Light from the open exterior doors seeped through the ill-fitting lower door jams and threshold, forming a bright white outline around the door.

A man's voice called from above, "Hello! Is anyone down there?"

From the bed, Barry heard Jane whisper, "Help me."

He pressed himself into the corner next to the doorway, and his foot struck against something causing it to fall over. Whatever it was, it hit the polished cement floor with a heavy metallic clang. Then something else fell with the same clang. He reached into the corner and put his hand on what felt like a collection of metal crosses leaning against the wall—the grave markers the old orderly had stolen from the Bryce Asylum's machine shop. He took one in his hands and moved toward the outline of the door.

The man's voice called again. This time right outside of the cellar door. "Hello. Is anyone in there?"

Then to Barry's surprise, the man yelled. "Sweet Jane, are you in there? It's Joe."

From the bed, Barry heard Jane scream, "Joe! Joe! Help me!"

The door burst open, and the afternoon sunlight cut through the darkness and lit up Jane's battered and bloodied face.

A tall man with broad shoulders stepped inside and as he moved toward the bed, Barry hit him over the head with the heavy iron grave marker. The man collapsed on the floor, and Jane screamed again.

CHAPTER THIRTY-TWO

Joe

Joe was awakened by a strange rattling and what he thought was someone sobbing nearby. When he opened his eyes, all he saw was a bright light and fuzzy shapes. He was sitting in a metal chair, and his arms were drawn behind him in a painful position with his wrists wound tightly with duct tape. The back of his head hurt like he'd been hit by a baseball bat, and something wet was running down his neck.

The last he remembered, he had found the house Mateo had told him about and got no answer when he'd rung the doorbell. He'd gone around the back of the house calling for Jane, when he thought he'd heard screaming coming from a pair of doors leading into the ground. He'd opened them and followed the steps down to where he was sure he'd heard Jane shouting his name. That was it. He had no recollection of what happened next or how or why he was bound to a chair with an aching head and what felt like blood running down his neck.

His vision began to clear. At first, he thought he was in a hospital room. There was a hospital bed in front of him with someone lying in it, and he was surrounded by medical equipment and furnishings. But as the scene around him cleared, he realized this was no hospital room.

A strange man with a trimmed beard sat in a chair across from him. He had a bandage on his hand. The man looked to be waiting for him to say something. Joe shifted his attention to the bed and was shocked to see Jane with straps around her chest and head watching him as well. A large purple bruise surrounded one of her eyes and blood smeared her cheek and chin.

"Jane, sweet, Sweet Jane, what happened to you?"

The bed shook and rattled, and Joe saw her hands and feet were bound to the bed frame.

"Joe. I knew you would come for me," she sobbed. "The Others told me you'd come. I'm beginning to think they are angels. Maybe all your praying is having an effect."

Somehow, she managed a smile, and that made him smile too.

"I am so glad the Lord led me to you," he said.

The bearded man chuckled, "I am afraid your happiness will be short-lived. Your Lord may have led you to her, but he also led you to me. Now, I will have to change my plans again."

"I'm so sorry, Joe," she sobbed. "He's crazy."

"She's mistaken, Mr. Carroll," the bearded man said. "As I have already explained to her, my mind is quite sound, and with over twenty years as a practicing psychiatrist, I think I am a better judge of my mental state than she is."

"Who are you?" Joe asked, but he already knew. Lieberman. Who else could it be?

"Oh, how rude of me. We've not been introduced. It's not fair that I should know your name, and you not know mine. I am Dr. Barry Lieberman. You'll have to forgive me for not offering you my hand, but of course, you're tied up." He made a mean, sarcastic chuckle.

The bed rattled again, and Joe realized Jane was in the throes of some type of uncontrollable tremor.

"What have you done to her, Dr. Lieberman?"

"Oh. We don't have to be so formal. Please, call me Barry," he said as he stood and moved to Jane's bedside. He ran his finger across her forehead as she struggled to recoil from his touch.

"We've had all kinds of fun down here. Haven't we, Sweet Jane?"

"Stop fucking calling me that," she blurted. Then her body stretched and froze as if an unseen force was pulling her apart. She remained in that tortured position for several seconds before the bed shook again from her convulsions.

Joe called out in a clear loud voice, "Dear Lord, I call upon you now in our time of need to guide us through this and grant us strength."

The prayer seemed to stun Barry for a moment, and then he began to laugh. "Is that a prayer? Really? What now?" He moved from around the bed and stood before Joe with his arms outstretched. "Will your God strike me down?"

He stood there for a moment looking up at the rafters. Then he looked down at Joe and grinned. "Oops, looks like I'm still here. I guess your all-powerful God doesn't care to get involved." He laughed in a wild way, seeming to lose control of himself.

While he was laughing, Joe worked his hands back and forth, loosening the tape.

Barry stopped his insane laughter and glared at him. "I'm sorry," he said. "You praying for help like some savage from the Dark Ages was just too funny."

Joe began again in the same loud voice, "O God, Who knowest us to be set in the midst of such great perils, that by reason of our weakness, we cannot stand upright, grant us the strength that those evils which we suffer for our sins we may overcome with thine assistance. Through Christ our Lord. Amen."

The prayers appeared to infuriate Barry. So much so, he crossed the room and hit Joe with a violent open palm slap across the face.

"Stop your silly barbaric rambling. There is no God. There will be no lightning bolts from heaven to smote me."

Barry pulled his hand back to slap him again when Jane shouted, "The angels are here, Joe. I see them. They've come to save us."

This startled Barry. He turned back toward her. She was shaking violently now. Barry pointed to her and looked at Joe. "Why doesn't your God save her?"

At that moment, a loud voice shouted from the cellar doorway above them. "Joe, are you down there?"

Barry looked up and then back at him. "Who is that?"

Joe recognized the lieutenant's voice. "Maybe it's an angel." Then he shouted "Mel. Help! We're down here. We're being held by a madman!"

Barry grabbed what looked like a metal cross and bounded for the door. The room went black as the door burst open and the lieutenant stepped through with his gun drawn.

Joe yelled, "Watch out! He's got a weapon."

"Where is he?" the lieutenant shouted.

There was a loud grunt and Joe saw Barry bring the metal cross down hard on the lieutenant's head. The gun flew from the lieutenant's hands as he pitched forward and dropped to his knees.

Joe pulled on the tape with all his strength, begging God to grant him more. The tape tore at his skin, and he roared against the pain, against the senselessness of the suffering and against the impotence of his God in the face of such evil. Barry raised the cross to deliver a killing blow and as he did, Joe thought he could see in the doorway light the man's bleached white teeth glistening, like he was smiling some maniacal smile.

The gun had slid across the smooth concrete floor and was lying a few feet away. Joe saw it as the tape around his wrists snapped. He launched himself forward and snatched it up as the cross over Barry's head began its downward arc. The weapon molded to his hands and instincts and habits drilled into him at Fort Benning a lifetime ago when killing was his calling, took over. He assumed a shooters stance, aimed for center mass and with unshaking hands squeezed the trigger three smooth times. The cross flew out of Barry's hands and bounced off the cellar wall. The sound of its impact was lost in the echoes of the deafening report from the 9-millimeter rounds.

Barry's eyes bulged. His expression was more surprised than pained. He tilted his head up to the rafters, perhaps looking for the god he had mocked. Then he collapsed.

Joe moved to the lieutenant who was struggling to stand.

"Mel, are you okay?"

The lieutenant glanced over at the man dying next to him. "Is that Dr. Lieberman?"

"Yes."

A loud rattling came from the bed, and Joe turned to see Jane arching and shaking.

"Oh, dear Lord," he shouted as he went to her.

"She's seizing," the lieutenant shouted as the sound of approaching sirens could be heard above them.

The seizure subsided and Joe unfastened the restraints.

Jane stared up at him and brought her hand up to his cheek.

"Please get me out of here."

The sirens sounded like they were right on top of them now. The lieutenant disappeared up the stairs, and Joe could hear him shouting that they needed an ambulance.

"Joe," Jane murmured, "I want to go up in the sunlight. I am cold, so cold, and so tired."

Joe pulled back her sheet and saw the catheter tube running between her legs. With trembling hands, he pulled it out. Then he wrapped the sheet back around her and lifted her into his arms. She smiled up at him.

"I love you. Even if you are an almost-priest."

"I love you too, Sweet Jane. Even if you are a little crazy," he whispered.

Her eyes rolled back into her head, and she began to seize again. He charged up the steps, clutching her writhing body, then lay her in the grass.

Police officers raced toward them. One of them pushed a rubber tongue suppressor in her mouth while another held her thrashing legs. Joe held tight to her hand and prayed for God's mercy and assistance like he had never prayed before.

After what felt like minutes of violent thrashing, her body went limp. Joe knelt over her, tears filling his eyes.

Her eyes fluttered opened.

"Will you receive Jesus Christ as your savior, Sweet Jane?"

She smiled. "Call me Jane."

"Jane, please let me help you enter the kingdom of our Father," he said through his tears.

She closed her eyes and said, "Don't cry, Joe. We are all just vibrations in the field."

Then she was gone.

CHAPTER THIRTY-THREE

Joe

Joe sat on the floor of a dark motel room with his back propped against the bed. All about him lay the wreckage of a lost battle, one he'd fought for eight years, nine months, and eleven days. The five empty whiskey bottles, the half-empty one in his hand, the wastepaper basket filled with his own vomit, and dozens of pages torn from his once-cherished breviary spoke to the depth of his defeat, but they were merely the outward evidence of the loss. The real casualties were inside and all too familiar. He'd lost them before. Faith, honor, and purpose—all gone again. Maybe for good this time.

The memory of the young deputy sweating under the fierce Alabama sun as he desperately tried to push life back into Jane's pale, bare chest would not leave him no matter how much whiskey he poured into himself. The man had tried. Joe had to give him that. He had performed CPR on Jane for at least a half hour as Joe circled around him telling him it was over, but the deputy would not stop. He'd been trained, probably by the same army that had trained Joe how to kill, to keep going until relieved, and he had done just that. He kept going until the EMTs pulled him off her and took her away in an ambulance.

Joe had never gotten the deputy's name. It had been almost three days since he'd watched the man's heroic but futile efforts, and he could not get the anonymous, boyish face flushed red from exertion and anger out of his head. He should have learned the man's name so he could keep him in his prayers. He picked up one of the pages he'd ripped from the liturgy and croaked a dry laugh. The thought of praying seemed as useless as the man's attempts to save Jane's life. The thought made him angry, and then it made him want another drink.

He lifted the half-empty Jack Daniels bottle to his lips, relishing the sweetness of the liquor's aroma and the anticipation of the spicy bite of its bitter taste. He wrapped his mouth around the opening and poured the amber liquid in, feeling its wonderful heat cascade down his throat and course through his body, warming him all over like the impassioned embrace of a lover who's returned from a long absence. This bottle went down much easier than the first, most of that had ended up in the trash can and on the floor. Drinking as much as Joe had since he'd walked out of the liquor store on the corner carrying half a case of Lynchburg's Old Number 7, was not something you just did after almost a decade of sobriety—not without consequences.

The last of the Jack drained into him, and he let the empty bottle fall from his hand. Then he passed out—at least he thought he did. For how long he did not know, but he was awakened by a faint light that somehow found its way past his sealed eyelids. At first, he assumed daylight was breaking through the drawn curtains, but when he raised his swimming head, he saw no evidence of sunlight invading his darkness. Yet, there was a light, a blue and silver shimmering light coming from a chair in the corner.

However long he'd dozed, it had not been long enough to sober him up, and his eyes fought his attempts to focus on the source of the strange light. After a moment, he could make out a woman's figure sitting in the chair, radiating a pulsing, silverish-blue aura. It was Jane, or what Jane would look like as a hallucination triggered by almost-certain alcohol poisoning.

She looked at him and the surrounding mess and said, "Now this is no way for an almost-priest to behave."

He thought about the people she had told him she saw in her mind, the ones who had tormented her, driving her from Berkeley and robbing her of the doctorate she'd so coveted, just as Joe had coveted the priesthood. She'd called them the Others, because they were, as she said, other versions of herself who visited her from alternate realities in the quantum wave form. In his inebriation, it appeared he had conjured up one of Jane's Others.

"Have you come from another universe, Sweet Jane?" He laughed a giggling, sloppy laugh.

She smiled.

"I don't know, Joe. It looks to me like you are the one in an alternate universe. The Joe from my reality would never give up like this."

Joe sniffled and laughed again, but this time it was a dry, bitter laugh. "Maybe you really didn't know that Joe."

She got up out of the chair and kneeled in front of him. "I think I knew my Joe."

The tears came slowly at first. Just one or two trickling down his cheeks, leaks sprung from a vast well of grief dammed by the force of his will, but that will had been weakened by the whiskey and now this ghost.

She placed her hand on his chest, though he could not feel her touch. "My Joe is a hero."

"No. He's not," Joe almost shouted.

The dam crumbled and rivulets of tears ran down the lines carved into his face by time and sorrow, wetting the three-day stubble that covered his jaw.

"Yes, he is."

She looked at the discarded pages from the liturgy and Psalms. "Why did you tear up your book? You loved that book."

"I could no longer find the answers in it."

She frowned. "Answers to what?"

"Why? Why is all this hurt and suffering necessary? Why?"

"Oh Joe, the answers are everywhere. It's all in the wave, every permutation of every possible state." She looked up and pointed at something he could not see. "Every good, every evil, every love, every hate. It's all here, all happening all the time." She turned back to him. "This is but one version of an incalculable number of alternatives."

"Where is my God in your wave?"

She put her hand back on his chest. "Right in there where he's always been."

He began to sob.

"I don't feel him anymore."

She gave him a knowing look. "You will."

"Why do you say that?"

"Because you need him." She cast a glance toward the empty bottles. "To fill the hole that you can't fill with that."

Joe lowered his gaze, stung and ashamed by her words.

Her hand moved to his chin, and he tilted his head to look into her eyes.

"I need you to do something for me, my almost-priest."

"What?"

"Take me home like you promised you would."

"I can't," he whimpered. "You're dead."

"Yes, you can."

"Where do you want to go? Auburn?"

She stood and looked down on him for a moment before bending and placing a phantom kiss on his lips that he desperately wanted to feel. Time stopped as she lingered so close but not there, then she straightened back up and said, "Take me to where I told you I was happiest. You remember, don't you?" Then she disappeared.

He was awakened by the early morning sun streaming through the gaps in the curtains. His eyes were sore and dry, telling him the memory of uncontrolled sobbing had not been a dream. His head throbbed from a whiskey hangover and the goose egg that remained from the iron grave marker Dr. Lieberman had struck him with.

He stared at the ceiling and thought about the dream until he thought he understood what it meant.

"Take me home."

CHAPTER THIRTY-FOUR

Joe

It had not been a Catholic service. Jane would not have wanted that, though Joe knew she would have expected him to try to get her to embrace God, even after her death. Joe had said a few words. He'd spoken from his heart as Jane's friend, not as a member of the clergy. He hadn't referenced God or salvation once in his eulogy, and he knew the omission may have disappointed some.

Now he stood silent, watching the grave diggers lower the coffin containing Jane's body into the concrete vault where it would remain until the angels blew their trumpets heralding the onset of judgment day.

Besides him, there were few mourners. Jane's parents and grandparents were dead, and Joe had not been able to locate any extended family. A few people from the Brookhaven facility had made the drive from Tuscaloosa as did a nurse from Taylor Hardin. The lieutenant and Charlene had come. Caleb had flown down from New Jersey and he and Carlos had driven together from Atlanta. A man whose relation to Jane he did not know, stood apart from the others. He appeared to be alone, but Joe had seen him talking with the nurse from Taylor Hardin, and it was clear they knew each other.

The Tuscaloosa coroner's office had kept Jane's body for two weeks. Her death was ruled a homicide by intentional poisoning. The cause listed on the death certificate was acute Clozapine toxicity. The monster had killed her using the same drug that had given her back her mind.

With the church's help, Joe was able to claim her body and make the arrangements for her burial.

"Take me home where I was happiest," she'd asked.

Joe had remembered Jane talking about her childhood in Huntsville and how her mother and father both worked for the space program. She'd said rockets were her parents' life, and their time here had been her happiest. He'd learned her mother had been buried next to her father in this small cemetery near the Marshall Space Flight Center. It turned out a family plot had been secured when her father died which included room for Jane. So now she was being lowered into a grave next to theirs. He'd brought her home.

After he'd sobered up from the three-day bender, he wasn't sure he believed what he'd once believed. He knew he had no remorse for killing Barry Lieberman. He'd only wished someone had done it sooner. Soon enough to save Jane's mother, to save Charlie Rossini's daughter, to save Sandra Tally, and to save poor Sweet Jane. Where was his God, Joe wondered, when these women were killed by this monster? Why had his God allowed such senseless evil?

A hand rubbed his back and shook him free of his somber contemplation. The lieutenant had wrapped his arm around him.

"How are you doing, Captain?"

"It's been a difficult couple weeks, but I'm starting to feel better, or maybe it would be more accurate to say less bad." He turned and looked the lieutenant in the eye. "I haven't had a chance to thank you. You saved my life. If you hadn't come when you did, Lieberman would have killed me."

"I think we are even on that count, Captain. If you hadn't shot him, he would have bashed my skull in. It's a damn good thing some sergeant taught you how to shoot straight."

Joe grinned, but he wasn't sure how he felt about the lieutenant making light of the killing.

"I meant to ask you. Did you ever listen to that tape?"

"Yes. That's why I was in Tuscaloosa that day to begin with. I was delivering the tape to the DA to have Lieberman arrested. That's why I couldn't answer my phone. I was stuck in a room with a bunch of lawyers all morning. Then, when I got your last message telling me you were heading to that house, I called the calvary and headed straight there."

"I'm lucky you got the message when you did. By the way, what was on the tape that pointed you to Lieberman?"

"Proof that it had been he who killed Ms. Carter's mother and not her. The whole damn murder was on the tape, including Ms. Carter's mother identifying her killer."

Joe remembered Jane telling him her mother's last words were on the tape. That must have been what she meant. If she'd only played it for him, she would still be alive. He'd never know why she kept it a secret. He guessed after what she'd been through, she found it hard to trust anyone, even him.

"I always knew she didn't kill her mother," he said.

Charlene was standing close by and said, "So did I."

"Lieberman did some other terrible things, Mel. I think he may have caused the death of a woman named Elizabeth Rossini."

"Charlie's daughter?"

"Yes."

"Lord have mercy," Charlene exclaimed.

"I'll look into that when I get back home. I'll have a talk with the DA and see about reviewing the deaths of all his former patients."

"What about Sandra Tally?"

"Don't worry. The Tuscaloosa police are all over it. They found some hairs in the back of the nurse's car. It's a good bet they will get a DNA match with Lieberman. No one believes Ms. Carter committed that murder."

"That's good, but listen, you need to look into more than his dead patients. He was raping Elizabeth and Jane. No telling how many of his patients he abused."

Charlene gasped, and the lieutenant promised again to bring all of Lieberman's past crimes to light.

The three of them shared a hug, then the lieutenant and Charlene said goodbye and picked their way through the headstones to their car.

The rest of the mourners were departing as well. Joe looked for the strange man and noticed he had moved closer to the grave. Joe went to him and introduced himself.

The stranger shook his hand. "Oh yes. Mr. Carroll. I heard about you. My name is Tom Reynolds. Jane was my patient." His voice cracked, and he used a handkerchief to wipe his eyes. "I treated her for several years."

"It's really good to meet you, Doctor," Joe said. "Jane talked about you often. She said you had fixed her."

Dr. Reynolds smiled, but it was a sad smile. "Did she? She was a special girl. Very smart." He sobbed, and Joe put his arms around him.

"I should have helped her more. I shouldn't have left her. She tried to tell me Lieberman had abused her, but I wouldn't listen. I didn't believe her." He blew his nose into his handkerchief. "I thought it was a persecution complex. So many people with her disease get them. They believe all kinds of things—horrible things about their own loved ones and caregivers. They can't help it. But she was right, and I abandoned her."

"I don't think she felt abandoned by you. You gave her back her math, and she was profoundly thankful for that."

The doctor held onto him for several moments before regaining his composure. Joe watched as he stopped to drop a flower into the open grave before walking away.

Joe was still staring after him when Carlos and Caleb came to him. Carlos put his hand on his shoulder and told him he wished him peace and reminded him Jane was in the Lord's care.

"Even though she was a nonbeliever, Father?"

Carlos studied him, but there was only compassion in his appraisal. "Dear Joseph, you know limbo is no longer considered an absolute. God has mercy on all his children. Jane will find her place in heaven."

Carlos turned to Caleb. "I will wait for you at the car." Then he turned back to Joe. "See you at Mass soon?"

Joe smiled. "As soon as my heart leads me back."

Carlos nodded. "I would expect nothing else."

After Carlos walked away, Caleb took Joe's arm. "Let's walk a little, my son."

Joe led Caleb to a path that wound its way all the way around the cemetery and back to the parking lot. It was less convenient than cutting through the headstones as the other mourners had done, but it would give them time to talk.

"How are you, Joseph?"

"Well, it's been sixteen days since I had my last drink." He glanced at his watch. "And, ten hours."

"That's good. Very good, but how are you here?" the old man touched his temple, "And here?" he placed his hand on his heart.

"I don't know, Father."

"Caleb. Let's stick with Caleb. I want to talk as your friend, not your priest, not your doctor."

Joe smiled and patted the old man's arm. "I had no problem shooting that man, and I have had no nightmares about it. What do you think that says of me?"

"It says you did what you had to do. Just as you did in wartime. Taking a life should never be easy, but there are times when a man must act to save himself or others. God does not require us to lie down in the face of evil and to give our lives over to it without a fight. No. He demands the exact opposite. Had you not acted, you and that police officer would be dead, and that monster might be free. You did the right thing, Joseph."

Joe nodded toward Carlos still making his way to his car. "Do you think Father Santiago believes that? Do you think the bishop does?"

"As your friend, I say who gives a damn."

Joe laughed.

"What if I asked you as my priest?"

"I'd still say who gives a damn."

This time they both laughed.

"What will you do now, Joseph? Will you go back to the church?"

"To tell you the truth, I am not sure. My heart is troubled. My faith is shaken. I can see God's hand in everything, even the way he guided and aided me through that day, but I can't get past why it was necessary. Why is such evil necessary? Why must the answer remain hidden to us?"

Caleb said nothing, and they made their way all the way around. When they neared the parking lot, Caleb finally spoke.

"You could come back to New Jersey. Maybe stay with me for a while. We could work on it together. Maybe your calling is not the priesthood. Maybe it's something else."

"I have only ever been a soldier and a man of God. If I am no longer a man of God, where does that leave me?"

"Come stay with me. We'll work on it."

Joe shook the old man's hand and drew him in for a long embrace. "Thank you, but I think I need to find my own way for a while."

"Will you stay in touch?"

"I promise I will call often."

"When you need a doctor or a priest?"

"When I need a friend."

THE END

EPILOGUE

It was a clear mid-October morning. A perfect day for a long run.

The route he'd chosen took him past the marina, and he chanced glances of the rows of boats bobbing in the East Bay as he ran hard along the waterfront. A red backpack was drawn tightly against his body to prevent it from bouncing too much with his strides. He was comfortable running with the pack. It felt familiar. He'd logged many miles in his youth, shouldering far larger and heavier ones than the one he ran with now.

It was warm, and the fog that he'd watch creep across the bay at sunrise had already begun to burn off. He ran without a shirt, and his lean body glistened with sweat. He'd lost a lot of weight since the summer. He didn't know how many pounds, but gone was the layer of fat that had accumulated over many sedentary years. In its place, muscle had started to reemerge, built with each heavy box he loaded onto a trailer at the warehouse where he worked.

Beneath the straps of his pack were elaborate tattoos he'd had worked into his skin when loss and hatred consumed him, and then later, when he'd been redeemed. Images in once vibrant red, black, green, and blue ink told of loss, suffering, and renewal. They were chapters in his story.

The ink had faded with time, and the images, like the memories they represented, had become part of him. No longer as vivid, but always there. He'd kept the tattoos hidden for so long, just as he'd kept the memories buried, but he had learned hiding the past, like hiding a tattoo, does not make it go away. One day, when he was ready, he would add another chapter to the story, and she would be part of it.

He made the left on University Boulevard and ran up the steady incline through the crowded streets of downtown Berkeley. He was breathing hard when he reached the university. Making the turn on University Drive, he picked up his pace and was out of breath when he reached the base of the soaring bell tower everyone referred to as the Campanile for its resemblance to the tower in Venice.

He removed his backpack and retrieved a water bottle and a black T-shirt from one of its compartments. He took several gulps from the bottle and stretched. The campus was becoming more familiar to him. He was enrolled in a class on interpreting quantum wave theory and was auditing a few math classes. It had been many years since he'd studied math, but he had always been a good student, so he was keeping up despite the advanced material.

His watch said it was ten minutes before nine, and ten minutes before his appointment. He'd cut it close. He pulled on the T-shirt and made the short walk to the tall building that housed the Mathematical and Physical Sciences Department.

He rode the elevator to the top floor. His reflection in the polished steel doors told him he needed a haircut and a shave. His red hair had grown several inches since he'd last seen a barber and it now hung in long, sweat-soaked strands upon his brow and around his ears, and he had a full beard—something he had not had since they shaved him in the hospital at Landstuhl over twelve years ago.

The doors slid open, and he stepped out into a maze of hallways and offices. He wandered around the floor for a few moments before he encountered an older woman with spiked silver hair.

"I have an appointment with Dr. Martin," he said.

She studied him for a moment. "Are you an instructor here?"

He laughed. "No. I'm actually a student. We are meeting to discuss some work a friend of mine had done."

"I'll take you to his office."

She led him to the department head's door. It was open and his office empty.

"I'm sure he will be right back," she said, as she left him admiring the view through the office window of the campus and the bay beyond.

Dr. Philip Martin arrived moments after she'd left. He was a stocky man with a square face, thinning salt-and-pepper hair, and enormous hands. He looked more like a wrestler than the dean of one of the most prestigious math and science programs in the world.

"Good morning," he announced as he came through the door. He stepped behind his desk and tapped a few keys on his computer keyboard then peered into his monitor. "Ah, you must be Joe Carroll." He straightened and extended one of his massive hands. "Nice to meet you."

Joe gave up his hand to the dean's grasp where it disappeared like a small child's in the hand of an adult. "Thank you for seeing me this morning."

"No problem at all." He motioned to the visitor chairs in front of his desk. "Please, have a seat," he said as he dropped into his own chair.

Joe took off his backpack and placed it in one chair and sat in the other.

"You know, you are a bit of a celebrity around here," the dean said.

"Is that so? Why is that?"

"I believe you are taking Dr. Nandi's Quantum Interpretations class."

Joe nodded.

"She tells me you ask some very profound and difficult questions about God and the quantum world. She said you challenge her by your knowledge of the links between the Vedic texts and Schrodinger and Everett's theories."

"Ahh. I hope I am not being too disruptive."

"No, I don't think so. Dr. Nandi says she enjoys the probing. She thinks you may have some theology training."

"Some," Joe admitted.

"I see. Well, you should know, your spiritual questions have led to some of the graduate assistants calling you Father Joe."

Joe laughed as he considered the irony of the once-coveted title being bestowed on him as a nickname, probably a derogatory one at that. "I'll keep that in mind. Perhaps dial it down a bit."

The dean shrugged. "That's up to you. So, what's this work you would like to discuss??"

Joe opened his backpack and withdrew a large plastic ziplock bag containing Jane's notebooks. He held them for a moment as he recalled the memory of her scribbling intensely in one during their drive from Atlanta to Auburn. Then he placed them on the dean's desk. "I've brought you these."

The dean looked at him with a puzzled expression as he opened the bag and removed one of the books. He flipped through it for a moment before returning his attention to Joe. "Did you do this?"

"No. No way. Those were done by a genius. I believe you knew her. Jane Carter."

The dean fell back in his chair as if hearing Jane's name was like receiving a physical blow. "Jane Carter. I haven't heard that name in a very long time." He picked through the book some more. "This is her work?"

"Yes."

"Then she's doing better?"

"She was."

"Oh. How is she doing now?"

"She passed away, Doctor. She asked me to see that you got these. She said you would know what to do with them."

"I'm so sorry to hear she passed."

"I am too, believe me, but I know if she could hear us, she'd laugh and tell us there are plenty of other versions of her alive and well somewhere in the wave."

He gave a knowing smile. "Yes. That does sound like something she'd say."

The dean picked up another of the notebooks and flipped through it. "These look very promising. The proofs will keep us busy for a couple weeks, but if this is what it appears to be, I'd say another of the seven has been solved."

Joe stood and put on his backpack.

The dean rose with him. "What should we do about the prize? It's Jane's work. What would she want done with it?"

Joe had no idea what Jane would want done with the money. He shrugged. "She said you'd know what to do with the books. I guess that means the prize money too." Out the window the sun glinted off the bell tower. "I'm sure she would be happy if the school found a use for it."

The dean followed his gaze and nodded. "I'll see it gets put to good use."

Joe turned to leave, but paused, "Say the gift is from Margaret and Jane Carter. I think she would like that."

The dean smiled and his eyes settled on Joe's chest. "What does your T-shirt say?"

Joe spread his arms to give the dean a better look at the white lettering.

We are all just vibrations in the field.

ABOUT THE AUTHOR

Daniel Burke lives outside Atlanta, Georgia where he devotes time to writing, travel, and grandchildren. When not pecking away on a writing project, his favorite place to be is on the back of his Triumph motorcycle winding through the North Georgia mountains. He has had a lifelong addiction to great fiction and hopes his stories touch others with the same need.

NOTE FROM THE AUTHOR

Word-of-mouth is crucial for any author to succeed. If you enjoyed *Vibrations in the Field*, please leave a review online—anywhere you are able. Even if it's just a sentence or two. It would make all the difference and would be very much appreciated.

Thanks!
Daniel Burke

We hope you enjoyed reading this title from:

www.blackrosewriting.com

Subscribe to our mailing list – *The Rosevine* – and receive **FREE** books, daily deals, and stay current with news about upcoming releases and our hottest authors.
Scan the QR code below to sign up.

Already a subscriber? Please accept a sincere thank you for being a fan of Black Rose Writing authors.

View other Black Rose Writing titles at www.blackrosewriting.com/books and use promo code **PRINT** to receive a **20% discount** when purchasing.

Made in the USA
Coppell, TX
10 May 2023